JALA'S MASK

MIKE AND RACHEL GRINTI

JALA'S MASK

an imprint of Prometheus Books
Amherst, NY

Published 2014 by Pyr®, an imprint of Prometheus Books

Cover image © Marc Simonetti
Cover design by Jacqueline Nasso Cooke

Inquiries should be addressed to
Pyr
59 John Glenn Drive
Amherst, New York 14228
VOICE: 716–691–0133
FAX: 716–691–0137
WWW.PYRSF.COM

18 17 16 15 14   5 4 3 2 1

Library of Congress Cataloging-in-Publication Data

Grinti, Mike, author.
    Jala's mask / by Mike and Rachel Grinti.
        pages cm
    ISBN 978-1-61614-978-9 (paperback) — ISBN 978-1-61614-979-6 (ebook)
    1. Fantasy fiction. I. Grinti, Rachel, author. II. Title.

PS3607.R5684J35 2014
813'.6—dc23

2014023873

Printed in the United States of America

For Jenn K.
Slash away!

CHAPTER 1

T he king's grayships spread out down the length of the coast-
line, their red-streaked sails visible between the palm trees. Jala
watched their approach from the roof of her family's manor. It was a calm
day, and the sails hung slack.

Nearby, Jala's father swore. "How are we supposed to feed them all?
We'll be eating palm leaves and grass by the time they're gone."

"But there'll be dancing," Jala said. She'd been practicing for
months now. What would it be like to dance with the king? With any
man, for that matter. She'd only been allowed to dance with other girls
until now. It wasn't fair, really. Jala's cousins danced with anyone they
liked, and no one thought twice about girls and boys from the village
dancing together.

"You don't need a feast for dancing. Just a drummer," her father
muttered. "I'll tell your mother you're getting ready." He started down
the steps but paused for a moment to say, "I'll miss you. You know that.
But I'll be proud, too. Prouder than I've ever been. You know what this
could mean for our family?"

Jala smiled at him. "I know." She'd heard this same speech a hundred
times, but her father was never one to let her forget how much pressure
she was under.

The king's ship landed. Six men disembarked and formed a line on
the beach. The king came ashore next. He wore fine silks taken from the
Autumn Lands, gold-spun wool from Renata, and necklaces inlaid with
stones that glittered red and blue in the sun.

My future husband, Jala thought. *Maybe.*

Only the earring in his left ear didn't shine. It was half the heart of
a shipwood reef, white and gnarled. The King's Earring. Its other half
would be worn by the queen.

Jala heard someone coming up the stairs and turned to see Marjani,
her closest friend. "You missed the fleet coming in."

Marjani shrugged, peering over the edge. "Well, he's not short, or scrawny. But that earring looks heavy, doesn't it? I wonder if it'll stretch out your ear."

"If it does, I'll just wear one on the other ear that weighs the same."

Marjani stepped closer and hugged her. "You're scared, aren't you?"

Jala nodded. "Maybe I wasn't until everyone started asking me." She rested her head on Marjani's shoulder and took several slow breaths to calm herself. "You know this is his last stop? He's had girls like me thrown at him for weeks."

"It's all right if he doesn't pick you."

"You know it's not," Jala said.

"Well, it's all right to me. I'd rather you stayed anyway," Marjani said. "Since you're set on it, I made this for you." She held out a comb made from carved and polished palm wood.

Jala ran her fingers over it, then slid it into the rows of thin braids gathered at the crown of her head. Marjani straightened it for her and smiled.

They'd been friends since they were five years old. Twelve years of seeing each other nearly every day. *And if everything goes right, I might not see her again for months.*

"You can visit me," Jala said. "As often as you want, and I'll send you messenger birds every day."

"Hah! Like you'll have time for that. You'll probably forget all about me."

"You're right, I will," Jala said. "I'm forgetting already. Everything's fading . . . it's like the last ten years of my life never existed." She squinted at Marjani and imitated her grandmother's quavery voice. "Excuse me, little girl, have we met?"

"Very convincing," Marjani said. "I wish I could hide up here until it's over. It's not that I want you to face it alone, of course. But I don't want to marry the king, so I don't know why I have to pretend I'm interested."

"My mother's a bully, that's why." Jala was only half joking this time. She didn't think her mother had relaxed for more than a few moments since they heard the king would be visiting. And if Zuri couldn't relax, no one could.

"She told me not to worry so much and that he won't want me anyway. I *think* she meant it in a nice way."

"That sounds like something she'd say. She probably did think she was helping." They watched the king approach the manor, escorted by his guards. The white sand of the beach was blinding, but when Jala peered over the edge, she could just see him pass through the main gate. "Come on, looks like it's time. We'll never hear the end of it if we're late."

Marjani nodded and allowed Jala to pull her away from the edge of the roof to the steep staircase leading down to the halls below. The king was probably already being greeted by Jala's parents. Then they would present the older members of the family. Finally, they would introduce him to the eligible daughters in the Bardo family. Jala would be introduced last.

Jala heard a drum reverberating through the brick walls. A slow beat, at least ten heartbeats apart, played on a lighter drum. That meant it was an occasion for moving slowly, for considering, but not a solemn day. She let the steady rhythm calm her.

"Stand up straight," Jala whispered to herself. "Don't play with your hair. Look him in the eyes when he addresses you and smile, but don't stare or you'll scare him off." They took another set of steps down, turned left into a smaller hall, and stopped outside a door with two of Jala's cousins.

From beyond the doorway Jala heard a man's deep voice declare, "Presenting Azi, of the Kayet family, king of the Five-and-One Islands. Where are the heads of this island and its family?"

Jala's father said, "I am Mosi of the Bardo. Welcome, my king. The ships of the Second Isle greet you with raised oars and lowered sails."

"I am Zuri of the Bardo," said Jala's mother. "Welcome, my king. Our family greets you as a guest, with slow drums and swords unsharpened."

"I accept your hospitality, and I wish your fleet good hunting," a new voice said. Jala leaned closer to the door to listen. *It must be the king.*

Then Jala's aunts and uncles introduced themselves, followed by the members of the Kayet family that had come with the king on his bride hunt. Traditionally they came to support the king, but in reality they would spend most of their time telling him who they thought he should marry.

Remember, Jala's mother had said, *the king will love you for your looks and charm. But his family will approve of you because you will seem quiet and easy to control.* Her mother had gone on about everything Jala would do for her family once she was queen, but Jala hadn't really listened. Her father had been teaching her how to be queen for two years now. She knew everything they had to say.

Jala ran her hands down the folds of her dress, smoothing it in case her skirts had ballooned out on her way back. The skin of a rainbow serpent around her shoulder added whirls of color. Her braids spiraled in elaborate patterns and just brushed her shoulders.

"Here," one of her cousins said, handing Jala a vial of palm oil. Jala pulled out the stopper, poured a little into her hands, then rubbed it into her cheeks and forehead and down her arms. She passed the vial to Marjani and pushed the bracelets on Marjani's thin wrists farther up her arms so they wouldn't jangle.

The drum stopped. Jala's heart stopped for a second. The traditional part of the meeting was over. It was time.

"My king, would you like to meet the daughters of the Bardo?"

"I would, Lord Mosi." Something about the way he said it made Jala think that what he really meant was *Let's get this over with.*

"My king." It was her mother's voice. "Please let me introduce my sister's daughter, Nia."

Nia arched her back slightly, opened the door, and walked out slowly. "I am most pleased and privileged to meet you, my king."

"She's a fine girl," Jala's mother said, "with a good head to help you lead the islands and good hips to bear both our families' children."

"How old is she?" asked the man who'd introduced the king. There was some haggling between the two families, with Jala's mother making a case for her niece and the king's family criticizing. Soon the other girl was called, and Marjani after that.

"Why does this one look so sullen?" Jala heard the same man say. "Is this the best that the blood of the Bardo can present to the king of the Five-and-One Islands?"

"Surely there is more to a queen than looks," Jala's mother said, but there was an edge to her voice, and Jala hoped Marjani wouldn't get lectured later. She scowled to hear them talking about Marjani like that, even if exaggerated criticism was expected. Jala's mother made her case for Marjani for another minute, then moved on. "But if she is not to the king's liking, then may I present my own daughter, Jala."

Jala took a breath and then walked out into the manor's greeting hall. Her aunts and uncles stood along both sides of the wall on one end of the hall, the king's guards on the other. Her parents waited with the king at the center. All eyes were on Jala. Her palms were sweaty. She hoped he wouldn't notice if he took her hand.

Soon she was by her mother's side, standing in front of the king. He looked different than she had expected. Beneath the layers of finery was a boy only a year older than herself. A wicked scar cut across his shaved head, stopping just above his left eye. It was a raised, ugly, pinkish thing that stood out from his black skin. Yet the effect it had on him wasn't ugliness. Instead, it made him look dangerous, fierce. He stood still and silent, almost rigid, as he watched her approach. Jala tried to keep her breathing even.

This was not quite the king she had imagined. Jala had met his brother, Jin, the boy who had been in line for the throne. Jin had smiled easily and liked to flirt. He put everyone at ease. But Jin had died, and this younger brother had taken his place.

"My king," Jala said. She realized she was staring and bowed her head.

"Hello," the king said. He said nothing for a moment, still watching her.

Jala's cheeks warmed under his gaze. She felt stupid staring at his feet, but she was suddenly nervous about meeting those dark eyes again. Nothing ventured . . .

She let her eyes wander over his lean arms, then higher. Her gaze lingered on his lips, and she was suddenly thinking about how soft they looked.

Her mother was talking again, but Jala wasn't listening. She needed to say something, to break through this monotonous ceremony. Something clever or funny, maybe? But her mind was busy wondering what it would be like to kiss the king. How could she be speechless? She and

Marjani had spent the last week thinking of little else. She knew they'd come up with a thousand things for Jala to say when she met him.

Jala met his eyes and saw he was already distracted, his gaze darting to the man standing beside him, the one who'd insulted Marjani. Thinking of Marjani's reluctance, she realized just how many times he must have seen this exact scene played before him. If she was nervous, might he be nervous, too? Or was he just bored? One thing was clear, his mind was already moving on, probably wondering what her family was serving for dessert.

"We're having spice cake," she said.

The king blinked and looked back at her, as though he was seeing her for the first time. "Sorry, what did you say?"

"I said we're having spice cake for dessert tonight. You looked like you'd rather be eating right now, and honestly so would I. I thought I'd let you know, in case you don't like spice cake."

"Jala!" her mother said. But she didn't seem to know what to do. She couldn't yell in front of the king and his family, not without making Jala's rudeness worse. Jala wasn't sure if she was being rude or flirting. Possibly a little of both. But she had his attention now.

"I do, in fact, like spice cake," he said, and there was a hint of a smile on his face now. "So, Jala. What are your feelings on spice cake? Or if that's too personal, your thoughts on dessert in general."

It was completely ridiculous to be talking about cake right now, but of course it wasn't about cake. It was about saying anything to keep the moment from ending. She wanted to talk to him again, even as part of her wanted to run and hide. This wasn't at all the way her mother said she was supposed to behave, but it didn't matter. She was talking to the king, and she wanted him to keep looking at her the way he was now. That look that was halfway between amused and arrested. Neither of them looked away.

"I like cake well enough," she said. "But I like dancing more. Well, actually it depends on the cake . . . and on the dancing partner. There's a dance tonight, of course, and we have the best drummers you've ever heard. If you think you can keep up, you should ask me to dance."

The king smiled widely now. "I think I will."

The king was led away to his quarters, with his family trailing behind. Then the Bardo family's calm order dissolved, and everyone rushed to prepare for the dance. Jala stood in the center of it all, taking in sweet, slow breaths. In the middle of the floor, several large circles were being drawn. A little girl laughed as she helped to throw chalk onto the floor. It hung in the air and made Jala cough.

The commotion was like the distant wind, the chatter and cries of her family like the surf. She heard it one moment and forgot about it the next. Yes, it was true, the king always chose one daughter from each island to dance with. But he wanted to dance with her. She had seen it in his smile, in his voice, in those brown eyes that had watched her so intently.

"Come *on*." Marjani pulled her out of the hall and up to their rooms. "We have to get you into something you can dance in. I can't believe you did that. What did your mother say?"

"She hasn't said anything yet. I'm sure it's going to depend on whether I fall on my face during the dance."

Marjani helped Jala into a simpler dress, a strip of silk pulled low around her chest and a skirt decorated with bright flowers from the Bluesun Peninsula. She slipped a hoop of gold through Jala's left ear; the other Jala kept free.

Jala's mother arrived, looked her over, and nodded her approval. She leaned in close to Jala's ear. "Your little game has worked for now, but don't be a fool and think you've won. He clearly finds you charming, but the uncle, Lord Inas, is not happy the boy asked you to dance. He'll be watching you closely. If the king asks you to walk alone with him, be sure to hesitate before accepting. If he kisses you, you must push him away, but not too hard. Otherwise he'll think you don't find him attractive. You must leave him wanting more."

"I know. I practiced with Marjani." Jala wasn't sure she wanted to do any such thing. She didn't like the thought of being that way herself. And why should she hide what she thought or what she wanted? He might be a king, but Jala wanted to be a queen. It was a good thing her mother couldn't watch her too closely tonight. There were other guests to look after.

Her mother whisked her out of the room and back to the main hall, with Marjani trailing after. Jala could hear the murmur of the guests waiting for the dance to begin. A few stray beats reverberated through the brick walls as the drummers warmed up.

She sat down at the head table, while her parents and Marjani took their places on the other side of the table. King Azi was seated next to Jala, and his sleeve brushed against her arm as he sat. Like her father, the king was now dressed in a simple robe that hung loosely over his body. He wore golden rings around his wrists and ankles.

From across the table, Marjani batted her eyes at Jala and puckered her lips like a fish. Jala choked on a laugh and kicked her friend under the table. At least, she *hoped* that was Marjani's leg. She faced the king, but she still saw Marjani making faces from the corner of her eye. Deep breaths. Giggling uncontrollably was not going to make a good impression. Marjani was going to pay for this later.

"Will you be competing in the wind-dance, my king?" Jala asked.

The king nodded, his smile widening. "I've heard your father is a tough man to beat. I'm looking forward to it. Though to be honest, it may not be much of a show. I haven't had a chance to wind-dance since Jin . . . since I was called off ship."

Jala winced. *Nice work. I'm sure you're the first girl that tried to charm him by reminding him of his dead brother.*

The king looked over at Jala's father. "I hope you won't embarrass me too much, Lord Mosi."

Jala's father grinned. "There's nothing embarrassing about losing to a master."

Servants set pitchers of palm wine on the tables, along with more exotic drinks: grape wine in two colors, beer made from barley and ginger, and liquor made from peppers that one of the ships had stumbled onto in the Autumn Lands.

"Be careful with it, my lord," Jala's father told the king's uncle, Lord Inas, pointing at the green-hued pepper liquor. "It's like drinking the fire mountain's piss. It burns your throat, then your belly, then your brain.

You feel like a god and walk like a fish." He stood. "Bardo and Kayet, welcome. Today we celebrate the rise of a new king and, I hope, the rise of our two families as one. By the king's will, together our two families will lead the Five-and-One ahead to days of even greater splendor. And now, my friends, let's eat and dance!"

It was just like her father to start with something so presumptuous. The Bardo cheered and began to eat, but she saw Lord Inas scowl. The king offered Jala half of an orange, and she took it, glad to have something to keep her hands busy. Just the smell of the pepper liquor made Jala's eyes water, so she stuck to white wine.

The center of the floor had been cleared for dancing once everyone had eaten, but for now a storyteller took to the center. She bowed first to the king, then to Jala's parents. But when she spoke, she smiled broadly and turned in place, including all the guests. "What story shall we hear? The wedding of Ipo of the Bardo and the hurricane Inok that would have washed away all the islands if not for their love?"

"Ipo was Kayet, not Bardo," one of the Kayet guests called out good-naturedly.

"Then everyone has heard the story wrong," the storyteller said with a slight bow. "But if that doesn't please you, what about the meeting of Baya and Kai, who would later sail across the Great Ocean in the first grayship? Perhaps I could tell of one of the Three Nights of King Badru and the sailor Jamil?"

This last caused a few laughs and giggles. The Three Nights were bittersweet and erotic, and would have been more appropriate at a wedding or repeated between friends or lovers. She'd heard two of three nights told by her older cousins, and had thought about them more than once lying awake at night. She snuck a glance at the king and was glad there was no way for him to see how hot her face felt. Maybe the wine wasn't a good idea. Maybe sitting so close to him wasn't a good idea. That story was definitely not a good idea.

People shouted out their favorite from the options the teller had given, and others she hadn't mentioned. But Lord Inas's voice silenced them. "Tell us of the Lone Isle and the Fire Mountain, and the family whose name no teller can tell."

Heads turned, and more than one whisper could be heard over the drum. The stories of the Three Nights might be a little risqué, but after all, the king was supposed to be picking a wife, so it was only a little presumptuous. The story Lord Inas had asked for was old and dark and bloody, and had no place at a feast like this.

But the teller showed no surprise or hesitation. Lord Inas and the Kayet were guests, and the choice was theirs if they insisted on it. "Very well, my lord," she said, and began to speak of a time before the families had united the Five-and-One Islands under a king and queen. A time when there were six families instead of five, and they warred amongst themselves.

"The fire mountain was known then as the Green Mountain, for it was lush with trees, and on these trees grew every fruit from every land in all the world. Every fruit but the fruit of life that makes a man immortal, for that can no longer be found in the living world.

"Though no reef grew around the Lone Isle even then, and the Sixth Family had no ships with which to raid the mainland or make war on the other families, they were left alone in peace. Because there was one more fruit that grew on the mountain: the fruit of secrets, a fruit sweet as wine and bitter as roots, and when they ate from it they heard the whispers of fire and wind and water and learned the ways of sorcery and magic. They called down storms and raised great waves. They saw far-off places and heard the songs of whales beneath the Great Ocean. It's even said they gave the birds of the Five-and-One the tongues of men and women so they could repeat our words.

"But while all the other fruit sated their hunger, the fruit of secrets only made them hunger for more. One by one they cut down the trees of the Green Mountain to plant more secret trees, until the mountain became angry. Smoke rose from the top, fire spilled down over the mountain like water, and the secret trees, and the Sixth Family, burned."

"Not the usual choice for a feast, as far as tales go," Jala's father said casually. "But I did always enjoy this story."

"Really?" Lord Inas said. "And do you enjoy the lessons it teaches us?"

He was threatening her father, Jala realized. Or warning him, at least. But her father seemed unconcerned.

"That power leads to foolishness? That one too many schemes can undo even the most feared family?" He smiled his most friendly smile. "I think that's always been my favorite part."

The king rubbed at his temple. "Well told," he called out. "A reminder to all of us that too many whispers and secrets aren't healthy. But let's have something less serious next. Tell us of Baya and Kai. It's been a while since I've heard that story."

The storyteller did as the king asked, though the king hardly seemed to pay attention, instead staring down at his own plate in disinterest. Jala ate everything on her plate but tasted little of it, and she spent most of her time sneaking glances at the king. Her father, meanwhile, drank some of every wine and tasted some of every dish. Jala's mother savored her favorites. Lord Inas nursed his liquor.

Finally most of the guests seemed to have had enough of food and stories, and the drums took on a faster beat. People began to bang on tables, clap their hands, slap their legs. The storyteller sat to eat her own meal. The dance floor was open.

Jala's father stood and said, "Well, King Azi, I would be honored to have the first dance."

"The honor is mine, Lord Mosi."

They went to the circle in the center of the floor. Both of them took off their robes, handing them to family members assigned to the task. It left both of them naked except for a tightly wrapped loincloth.

"If you're going to stare," her mother said under her breath, "at least try to be subtle about it."

Jala quickly looked down, embarrassed. But she couldn't help glancing at them again a moment later. They had stepped into the ring, and Jala's father was signaling the drummers. A low beat started to play. Outside, more drums took up the beat. Around the hall people clapped their hands and banged on tables. Jala felt lifted by the sound, as though her blood flowed quicker to match.

"Dance well, my lords," one of the drummers shouted.

"Like the wind," Jala's father called back.

The king and her father danced. They started with the basic form of the dance, circling one another, switching places as they lunged, kicked, twisted. Then their moves became fancier: handstand-kicks and throws that became graceful cartwheels. Their golden rings flashed in the firelight. The dance was violent and energetic, full of implied brutality coupled with stunning grace. Any one of the blows could have brought them to their knees, yet none ever quite connected. Always the kick was caught, the force redirected to keep the wind-dance moving through its circular path. Sweat glistened on the king's skin, and Jala found herself staring. What would it be like to touch the wiry muscles of his arms and chest?

It was clear that Jala's father had taken the lead and would not give it up. The king had to work just to keep up. The drummers egged the dancers on, playfully mocking and complimenting in turn. Other men entered the dance rings together, blocking Jala's view of her father and the king. The hall seemed to swim with the movements of the wind-dance.

"He's gonna knock that boy flat on his back, and then where will we be?" Jala's mother muttered into Jala's ear, "For all his whining about the cost, you'd think he'd be a little more careful." She turned and smiled at the king's uncle. "Your nephew dances very well."

Lord Inas snorted. "He was always the better dancer." Inas was a stocky, balding man with a crown of dark hair and a full moustache, both going gray. His forehead was lined with wrinkles as he scowled at Jala. "Did you know Jin? I'm sure you two must have met."

Jala nodded. "We did. He was charming."

"He always was to girls like you." Inas poured himself a bowl full of the pepper liquor and drank heavily, then coughed for a long time. The drink was so strong it made his eyes turn bloodshot and water. Jala's mother deftly moved the liquor out of his reach in the guise of making space for more food and drink.

The king returned to the table with Jala's father. He drank some of the palm wine and held out his hand to Jala. "I haven't forgotten. Will you join me?"

Jala took his hand, and he pulled her between the dancers and into the circle that had been set aside for them. He took the center first, for when the king was looking for a queen the traditional order was reversed. She danced around him, following the outline of the circle, swaying and spinning, showing off her body and her grace. At least she hoped that's what she was showing off. She tried to lose herself in the movement of the dance, to forget how nervous and excited she felt, but the thoughts kept running through her head. *I'm dancing with the king.*

The king did not dance the male part of the courtship dance. Instead, he took her hands and pulled her close. They spun in the circle together. The air was hazy with smoke and chalk. His hands were strong, his fingers rough and calloused. Her heart beat too fast and too loud, distracting her from the rhythm of the drums.

The king leaned in close and whispered, "It's too noisy, and I'm tired of dancing. Is there somewhere quiet where we can talk?" His lips brushed against the tip of her ear.

Jala didn't hesitate. "Of course."

She took his hand and led him out of the circle. They slipped out down a side hall, away from the guards who tried to follow and into the open air. Bonfires burned up and down the beach, and drummers played fast, lively music. One of the sailors was juggling knives. Another drank deeply from a cup, then held up a lit brand and spat. The ball of flame rose ten feet into the air, shaking the leaves on the palm tree overhead.

They headed away from the fires and the crowds. The wind from the ocean was cool and salty. Jala took them past crowds of dancing villagers and along the walls of the manor. They stopped near a group of trees.

"It's quiet enough here," Jala said. Her voice was shaking. The king still held her hand. Her whole body ached when he smiled at her, his teeth almost glowing in the moonlight. It was a good thing this corner was well lit.

"I'm glad it was only the four of you," the king said. "Sometimes these things take forever. They parade girls in front of me for an hour, every second or third cousin they can pull out of a village and claim some semblance of royalty. Not that they really expect me to notice them, but they think it makes the *right* girl that much more enticing to me. With you, they only brought out two cousins, and of course that girl who scowled at me to try to make you look prettier. They shouldn't have bothered. With any of it."

Jala realized he meant Marjani and felt suddenly protective. "And what's wrong with scowling at you? Not everyone wants to marry you, you know, and they don't much like being paraded either."

"There's nothing wrong with her," the king said quickly. "I just meant that nobody there really expected me to look twice at her, not even you."

"Well, maybe you should have looked at her twice, then. Or three times. Or however many times before you saw how amazing she was. Wouldn't that have been a surprise for all of them?"

He laughed. "I don't usually surprise anyone. It's not really something anyone wants in a king. But if you're right and she's not interested in me, it's all worked out for the best, hasn't it?" The king shook his head. "You know . . . most girls try to talk themselves up, not defend their supposed competition. I think I've been trying to compliment you."

Jala felt her cheeks warm. "Her name's Marjani. She's my friend, not my competition. We've been friends forever."

"I'm sure most of the girls have had friends like that. None bothered mentioning them when they were alone with me, though." He walked in silence for a while, then stopped. "This isn't easy, you know. It's not fun for me, ignoring girls I'd gladly kiss because their families aren't worth considering, charming others because their families have as many ships as yours and I'm not supposed to offend them. It's driving me crazy, and what's any of it for? In the end my uncle will tell me who to pick, who he's made the best alliance with. My family doesn't even trust me to pick my bride for myself."

So, her family's plans were for nothing after all. He already knew who he'd marry, and this whole trip was just for show. But how could he be so easily swayed by his uncle? "I don't think I understand. You're the king," Jala said. "You can marry whoever you want. Your brother would have."

"I wish he could," the king said. "Then I really could do what I want and go out there." He waved at the beach and the Great Ocean beyond. "I want to sail home with ships full of silk and dyes and wine. I want to drink with my friends on the beach and visit Ko—" He stopped himself and shook his head. "If I had what I wanted, Jin would still be here. Dead sails," he cursed, leaning back against the wall and staring out over the water. "I'm sorry. I didn't mean to make things so sad and serious. I just thought we could talk some, and maybe I'd steal a kiss before we went inside again. It's been a long month."

"You don't want to be king?" Jala asked. She'd wanted to be queen all her life. Ever since the first time her mother had said, *You might be queen someday*, in a voice tinged with hope and fear and expectation, she had wanted it.

"I did when I was younger," the king said, "but I always knew what the cost would have to be. Anyway, younger brothers in line for the throne aren't encouraged to want it too much."

Jala wasn't sure she should press him, but she did anyway. If they parted ways after tonight, she might never be alone with a king's full attention again. "Do you miss him?"

The king shrugged. "I guess. I missed him long before he died. I was on a ship while he was off with my father, learning how to be a good king. Sometimes I think maybe I should have been the one that died. I almost did, when some merchant's wife gave me this scar for trying to take her rings. Meanwhile he scratches himself with a rusted sword, and I'm the one that lives?" He sighed. "It doesn't matter now. Things are the way they are."

None of this was going the way it was supposed to. Jala could almost hear her mother's voice: *Get him to talk about your looks. Tell him he'll make a great king.* She squeezed his hand. "I'm sorry about your brother," she said softly. "But I'm glad you didn't die."

He leaned forward, hesitated, then kissed her on the mouth. His lips tasted salty, just like the air, but they were soft and hot. Jala let herself relax into his hold. It was so easy to kiss him, somehow. She found it hard to remember that there was any reason to stop. She could feel his heart beating quickly, as fast as her own. The wind felt cold over her bare shoulders.

In just a minute, I'll tell him to stop.

"Here they are," someone shouted, and suddenly they were surrounded by voices. Azi pulled away from her. People stared at her: the guards who were supposed to keep an eye on her, her mother and her cousins, men and women from the village.

"So this was your plan?" It was the king's uncle, standing next to Jala's mother and speaking loud enough for everyone to hear. "To have your daughter seduce the king so that he felt obligated to choose her? I wonder how many others she's kissed back here. Now I see the kind of queen the Bardo offer."

The king reached for her hand, but Jala pulled away in the guise of straightening her hair. A braid had come undone, so she tied it back once more. If she could do nothing else, at least she could try to maintain some dignity.

"I have to go," Jala said.

Azi stepped between Jala and the others. "I'm sorry, I shouldn't have done that. I'll talk to my uncle, you've done nothing wrong."

"Let me pass," Jala said, then added, "My king."

He looked like he was about to say something, but instead he stepped aside. "Of course. Go to your family, and we'll sort this out tomorrow. Good night, Jala."

"Good night, my king."

She walked through the crowd with her head high. Her mother tried to pull Jala to her side, but she ignored her. Her heart was still pounding, and her stomach was twisted up into a knot. She wasn't sure why she bothered pretending. Dignity was important for a queen, and she had no chance of that now.

CHAPTER 2

Azi sat in the Bardo guest room and stared at the wall. How had everything gone so wrong, so fast? His head pounded and his muscles ached from trying to keep up with Lord Mosi. The old man moved so fast, and Azi has been glad to escape and dance with Jala. *What were you doing, kissing her like that? You made a promise. You swore.* Even as he berated himself, a part of him knew he would have kept on kissing Jala if he could. Even now the thought made the blood pound in his ears. That definitely wasn't helping his premature hangover.

Will you still love me now that you'll be king? The words had been with him as he visited each of the four families, running through his head each time he danced with another would-be queen. Before, it hadn't even been a question, but now . . .

What was he thinking? That he could love this Bardo girl? It was ridiculous. He'd only just met her. He couldn't really feel . . . whatever it was he thought he felt. *Why did I kiss her like that?* He shouldn't have. He shouldn't have told her all those things about being king, about Jin. He'd even almost told her about Kona. He was tired of this whole thing. He just wanted to be home again.

He tried not to think about Jala. About the way her hips moved when she danced with him. About the way she smiled. The way her chest and stomach pressed into him when they kissed. The way she said surprising things that made him laugh or stop to think.

A banging on the door startled him. "Azi, open up," his uncle shouted.

"All right, all right, keep it down," Azi said as he stood and unbarred the door.

Lord Inas shut the door behind him, then took hold of Azi's shoulders and laughed. "You did your uncle proud today, boy. You should have seen Mosi's face when he heard about his daughter. Can't say anything when we turn him down, now, can he? I don't know when you got it into your head to try a scheme like this, but I'm glad you did."

Azi pulled away from his uncle and turned to face the window. A few fires still burned, and some of the drummers kept on playing even though the celebration was supposed to be over.

"It wasn't on purpose," Azi said. "I didn't mean to get her in trouble with her family. What does it matter anyway, when you planned for me to marry that Rafa girl even before we started this trip?"

"Well, whether you meant it or not, it's happened," Lord Inas said with drunken cheerfulness.

"What will happen to her?" Azi asked. *Why do I care what happens to her?* There was just something about the way she'd kept arguing with him, the way she'd kept forgetting to act subdued in front of him. She wasn't even the most beautiful girl he'd seen traveling, but she couldn't hide the fire in her eyes.

"Oh, she'll probably marry some rich lord as soon as we're gone. Nothing we need to worry about, eh?"

"What if I want to worry about it?" Azi said. "What if I don't want everyone saying I tricked her?" *What if I don't want to marry a quiet girl who'll do whatever I say? Or is that whatever* you *say, Uncle?* "What if I want to marry Jala? What would you say to that?"

Lord Inas laughed again. "I'd say you're a fool."

Azi clenched his fists. "I'm king, aren't I?" he whispered. "If I want to marry Jala, then I'll marry her. It's my decision, and hers. Your hatred for Lord Mosi isn't mine, and I won't ignore Jala because of it." He thought of the look on her mother's face when Jala had called him out on being bored. Even now it made him want to smile.

Lord Inas scowled at Azi. "You're letting your mast steer the ship, boy. She may be nice to look at, but she's Bardo. Mosi only cares about his own family and his own power. You know why you have to marry that wretched Rafa girl! Dry hells, boy, I've had too much wine to lecture you. Do your uncle a favor and forget her. It shouldn't be hard, you'll never have to see her again once we've left in the morning."

Never see her again. The words rang in his head. "Fine," Azi said. "But I want her to hear it from me. I want everyone to hear that I never meant to trick her."

"There's no reason to make a spectacle out of it."

"I am king, aren't I, Uncle? Do this one thing for me."

His uncle smiled crookedly. "Of course, you are king. I'll have her brought to you first thing tomorrow morning."

CHAPTER 3

Jala didn't sleep much that night. When she woke the next morning, her mother hovered over her bed offering leftover spice cake for breakfast. "How are you feeling?"

Jala's father came in a moment later. "Is she up?"

"What's going on?" she asked, pushing away the cake.

Her mother perched on the edge of the bed and patted Jala's arm. "We just wanted to make sure you weren't blaming yourself for any of this. We know it's not your fault. The boy clearly fell for you."

"It's that damn traitorous Lord Inas," her father agreed. "He's scared of us, wanted to refuse this marriage before he ever arrived. This is just an excuse, meant to embarrass our family. I wouldn't be surprised if he put the boy up to it."

He wouldn't, Jala told herself, though she had no proof. *That kiss was real. It had to be.* What would she do now? All her life she'd hoped to be queen one day, then in a single night it was all gone. She'd failed. Her parents said they didn't blame her, but why else were they barging in on her before she'd even had breakfast?

Marjani came to her after they left, dutifully reporting everything the servants were saying. Word had already spread that Jala would not be queen. Some said that she had seduced the king, like Lord Inas claimed, while others said the king had lured her outside with false promises.

"They sound so smug," Jala said. "Are they glad to see me look like an idiot? You'd think they'd want me to be queen."

Marjani put her arm around Jala's shoulders. "They don't really mean it. You know how people like to gossip. Some of them are mad at the Kayet and have been telling horrible stories about the king's uncle."

"It was just a kiss," Jala whispered, leaning her face against her friend's shoulder. "Just one long, stupid kiss. I would've stopped it soon enough."

They sat in silence. After a time, Marjani asked, "So . . . how was it?"

"Not worth losing a throne for," Jala said.

"You're a terrible liar sometimes."

"I'm not lying," Jala protested, but her cheeks felt too warm. It wasn't just the kiss, or the throne. Had she only imagined the way he'd watched her? Did he talk to everyone the way he talked to her? Maybe telling her about his family had just been his way of getting her defenses down.

She should have nodded politely, said kind things to him, told him she was sure he'd make a perfect, handsome king, the way her mother wanted her to. Why was it so hard to pretend around him? Why did he make her want to say what she really thought even when it could ruin everything?

Someone knocked on the door. "My lady, the king requests your presence."

Jala looked at Marjani, but her friend held up her hands as if to say, *I haven't heard anything.* Jala opened the door. One of her maids stood uneasily outside the door.

"What's wrong now?" Jala said.

"The king and his uncle have requested your presence. Your parents are waiting for you in the greeting hall." The girl hesitated, and Jala could tell she didn't want to say more.

"Well?" Jala asked. "How did the king look?"

"I didn't see the king, but Lord Inas looks very pleased with himself," she said softly. "I'm sorry, my lady."

Jala sighed and looked down at herself. "I'm not dressed to see the king, but I don't suppose that matters now."

"I'll come with you," Marjani said.

Jala helped her friend up, then hugged her quickly before leading the way to the king's rooms. *What can he possibly want with me now?*

She met her parents in the main hall. It was empty now except for the king's uncle, their assorted guards, and a few Kayet hangers-on. She was almost glad Lord Inas was here. She could tell her mother and father wanted to lecture her, and she wasn't in the mood.

"The king wishes to speak to you once more before we depart," Lord Inas said.

Jala's heart sank. It was what she'd expected, but somehow she'd hoped. *That he changed his mind? That he'd disobey his uncle?* The best she could hope for was that he'd sail away without pouring salt into the wound, but it looked like even that wasn't going to happen.

"You must apologize to him," her father hissed as they made their way to the king's guest room. "Or Inas will have him hold this over us for years to come. Dry hells, girl, it would have been better if you'd just stayed in your room."

Lord Inas knocked on the door, and a minute later the king strode out. He'd dressed in his finest robes of white and purple and spun gold. He looked magnificent. Was he *trying* to make her feel worse than she already did?

Marjani flashed Jala a reassuring smile. Jala stepped forward and gritted her teeth, ready to apologize. But why should she apologize? The thought came unbidden to her, and just as quickly she realized her apology wouldn't make any difference anyway. If the king had already let his uncle talk him out of marrying her, assuming he'd ever seriously considered her at all, then nothing she said now would make a difference.

She took a deep breath and looked up, meeting Azi's eyes. For a moment she found herself distracted by them. They were so dark that from far away they seemed black, but up close, in the firelight, they were a deep, melancholy brown.

"I'm not sorry you kissed me," she said. She ignored the whispering from those who had gathered to watch. "I'm not sorry I kissed you back. And I won't be made to feel like I did something wrong, because I didn't. If that means you no longer care about me, that's your choice."

She retreated to stand beside Marjani without letting go of his gaze. "I do think you'll make a good king, once you accept that it's what you are."

The whispers were louder now. Jala knew that soon she'd feel embarrassed for everything she said, soon her mother would be sympathetic and condescending, soon her father would rage against Lord Inas and the Kayet. Soon this moment would be over, and she would want to cry.

She meant to leave before that happened. Without waiting for the king to respond, she turned to go. But before she could take a step, he was beside her. He put a hand on her arm, gently, so gently she couldn't have broken free with all her strength.

"I do care about you," he whispered, his voice hoarse. "I want to marry you. Before I leave the Second Isle. Right now, if that's what you want."

Marjani gasped. Jala could only stare, unable to believe she'd heard right.

"Azi!" the king's uncle hissed.

The king spoke louder, loud enough for everyone to hear. "Jala of the Bardo. I would marry you and make you queen. Will you have me?" He turned his back on his uncle and stared straight at her.

Lord Inas swore loudly and turned to Jala. "You were never meant to be queen. You'll have no friends among the Kayet, no allies among the other families. He'll learn to despise you soon enough. You'll be alone, surrounded by enemies."

But Jala wasn't worried about what the other families thought. She was thinking about being queen and about the way Azi's lips had tasted when he kissed her.

"I will," she said. "I accept you. I'll marry you. I'll be your queen."

The room seemed to be spinning. People crowded around her and the king. Somewhere nearby her father laughed.

The king took her hand and squeezed it briefly. He looked around at Marjani and Jala's parents and the guards and his uncle. "I present to you your queen. Queen Jala of the Five-and-One Islands."

Everything fell silent. Then Jala's mother shrieked with happiness and threw her arms around her. Her bony fingers dug into Jala's back. "You did it," her father hissed in her ear. "You actually did it. My little queen!"

And suddenly everyone seemed to be saying it. "My queen."

Finally her father's laughter broke through the chaos. "The look Lord Inas gave me was hot enough to burn the fire mountain herself. If he had a sand-grain's weight of sorcery in him I'd have died on the spot, but luckily the only thing in him is last night's drink. I'm almost content just seeing it happen once." He grinned at Jala. "Almost, but not quite."

Jala smiled back because they were celebrating, but her father's laughing words felt heavy in her chest. Her father wasn't the one who was going to be living with Lord Inas. She didn't want to think about it, didn't want to listen to her father's gloating right now.

"I have to change," Jala said a little desperately. "A queen can't be seen looking like this."

"Not even queen for a day and already vain," her father teased, laughing. But then he leaned forward and whispered to her. "You've always looked like a queen to me. Don't forget that."

She held on tightly to Marjani's hand as they led her back to her room, then pulled her friend inside the room before shutting the door. Her father's words had already faded to the back of her mind, replaced by the thousand other thoughts screaming for attention, only to be pushed aside a moment later.

"So is the new queen going to give me my hand back?" Marjani said, tugging at the hand Jala still clutched tightly.

"No, the new queen is not," Jala said in her best imperious tone. It still took her two tries to get the words out. She pressed her head against Marjani's arm and laughed. "It's like I've forgotten how to breathe."

"You're breathing right now," Marjani whispered.

"What if I'm dreaming right now? What if in a moment I'll wake and it'll be this morning all over again?"

"And he'll still pick you, and you'll still be queen. Do you want me to pinch you?"

"No. If it's a dream, it better stay around for a while. At least long enough for me to kiss Azi again. In fact, it can just skip right to that part."

Marjani laughed weakly, but she looked away. "Are you scared?" she asked.

"Terrified," Jala admitted.

"Well, you won't be for long. That's how you are, you'll have it all figured out," Marjani said. She hesitated, as if she was going to say something else but was cut off by a sharp knock on the door.

Jala's mother entered the room without waiting for an answer. Her smile was bright and determined. "Marjani, I'd like to speak with our new queen, please."

Marjani nodded. "You really do need to let me have my hand back now," she said. "I promise it's not going anywhere."

"Sorry," Jala said, though what she really meant was thank you. She let Marjani go.

"You won't be able to stay in here forever," her mother said once

Marjani had left. "Your father's already planning a feast tonight. We want all of our cousins to see you. Let the villages speak of how much like a queen you look." As she talked, her mother began to go through Jala's clothes, pulling out outfits she thought might suit a queen. It was almost a reflex, Jala thought.

"Wasn't Father complaining about the cost of all the feasts just a day ago?" Jala said.

"And he'll complain about these to me as well," her mother said. "We have a lot of planning ahead of us. Here. I think this will do well enough for the day. Not too bold, not too humble. Good enough for your king and your father both, I think."

Jala's mother stopped fiddling with clothes and turned to look at Jala. She smiled a little sadly. "There was a little part of me that was glad you wouldn't be leaving quite so soon. Did you know about this the whole time? I thought you took things too far trying to convince that boy to pick you, but you showed me, didn't you?"

"I didn't know," Jala said. "And I wasn't trying to convince him of anything. I just . . . wanted to kiss him."

"Well, you'll have time for that once you're married. Get dressed. They all expect to see a queen."

Then her mother left, too, and Jala was alone. She dressed, ignoring the clothes her mother had laid out for her and instead chose bright, bold clothing and an elaborate hairpiece of lacquered mainland wood and feathers from local birds. She looked at her reflection in the full-length looking glass her father had given her as a present on her sixteenth birthday.

It was a gift worthy of a queen. Unlike cloth and precious stones, glass, especially a pane so large, was almost impossible to take unbroken on a raid. Instead, it had to be traded for in the Constant City, the great bazaar-city of the mainland. She'd probably have to leave it behind when she left. She'd have to leave a lot of things behind.

She adjusted the hairpiece and took several deep breaths until her expression was calm and her excitement and fear no longer showed. Looking back at her from the looking glass wasn't Jala, but a queen. She wasn't just a normal girl anymore.

For the first time, she thought to wonder what Azi was thinking at this moment. Did he feel the way she did? Was he glad that he'd gone against his uncle's wishes? He won't hate being king if he has someone to help him, she told herself. With my help, he'll be a better king than his brother could have ever been. Better than his father, too. She would tell him that the next time she had a chance . . . whenever that would be. They weren't going to let them be alone together, not now that everything was settled.

"It won't be that long," she whispered to the queen looking back at her, thinking again about that kiss. Then she turned away and went to face the Bardo, and the Kayet, and all of the Second Isle.

She was wrong, though. It was a long time. Azi had said he'd marry her that day, but that had been more of a threat aimed at his uncle than any real intention. There would be a proper royal wedding. They would both be shown off to the five families. It wasn't about them getting married, not really. It was about a king marrying a queen. So the unbearably long hours stretched into unbearably long days, and somehow those turned into weeks. According to tradition, the king couldn't be alone with her until the day of the wedding. Jala could only manage a few words to Azi, always in the company of both families, always too formal for her to say anything meaningful. There was no more midnight kissing.

As the days went on, Jala became more and more aware of how little she knew about Azi. She knew next to nothing about him as a king or as a man. She'd thought about being queen, and she'd imagined many times what it might be like to be with a man, but she hadn't thought much about being married.

The feasts and dances were a welcome distraction, but even that was frustrating. The king wasn't allowed to dance with her, so she was back to dancing with Marjani, like a child. The rest of the time she had nothing to do but wait while everyone made preparations for her wedding. The nearest family, the Gana, arrived the next day, and the rest trickled in over time.

Servants packed Jala's clothes only to unpack them every time she needed a new dress. Her hair was redone each night in increasingly elaborate styles. Beads and shells clattered when she danced, until she thought the chattering sound would drive her mad.

"It's all so unreal," Jala said to Marjani. It was almost time for another dinner with one of the families, and Marjani had been busy with Jala's hair for hours. "I never thought it would feel so . . . oh, I don't know. Sometimes I feel like I'm flying above a storm, and other times I want to crawl into a hut on the other side of the island and hide there until this is all over."

"Did you at least remember how to breathe?" Marjani asked.

"I think so. But maybe you could remind me sometimes, just in case I forget again."

Marjani laughed at this, but weakly and without looking at Jala. "Do you think you really could? Run off, I mean?"

"There are only five islands to hide on. Mother would find me," Jala said. "Besides, I'm going to marry Azi. I'm going to be queen! Those parts are fine; it's this endless wedding that I can't take anymore."

"You never hear stories about the queens," Marjani said. "They probably thought they were going to be great too."

Jala jerked her hair out of Marjani's hands. Beads clattered to the floor. Her scalp ached where her hair had gotten pulled, but it didn't hurt as much as Marjani's words had. "I never said I was going to be great. But I'm going to try. What's wrong with that?"

"Nothing. Forget about it," Marjani said. She bent down and started to collect the beads.

"You've been acting strangely for days now. This isn't all about me. It's about our whole family. So why aren't you happy?"

Marjani was quiet for several moments. When she spoke, her voice was soft. "Because you're leaving and you don't even care. Everything's about being the queen or about Azi. When's the last time you asked about me? Or about anything happening here not related to your wedding?"

"Of course I care that I'm leaving," Jala said. "But there's nothing I can do about it, is there? It's hard enough having to leave home without you throwing it in my face."

"If I'm making things so hard for you, you can do your own damn hair." Marjani let the beads she was holding fall to the floor and went to the door.

"Wait," Jala said, half standing. "Don't go. I'm sorry, I didn't mean it. I know everything's been about me. And I have to act happy all the time, even if I'm scared, too. I have to start acting like the queen, and I don't know how. I wish you could come with me. You know I do."

"I know," Marjani said softly without turning around.

Jala walked over and took Marjani's hand with both of hers. "I think you're the only one who cares more about me leaving than about me becoming queen. Why don't we sneak out to go swimming tonight? On the other side of the island, away from everyone. I only have to act like a queen where someone might see me."

"We haven't done that since we were little," Marjani said, the hint of a smile on her face. "But your mother won't like it if she finds out."

"Well, I am the queen, as she's often reminding me," Jala said. "We'll go tonight."

CHAPTER 4

J ala chose a simple dress for her midnight swim, one she could ruin without her mother noticing. She locked her door and sent away the servants who came to help her dress for the night's festivities. But there was still her mother to deal with. Lady Zuri arrived shortly after Jala had dismissed the third servant.

"Jala?" Her mother tried the door. "Are you even dressed yet?"

"I don't feel well," Jala called back. "I'm not going tonight."

"Queens don't allow a little headache to keep them in bed," her mother said. "You'll get up now and make yourself presentable."

"It's not a headache," Jala said, letting her voice waver a little. "I can't dance tonight. I don't think queens get sick all over their dress in front of everyone."

"Well, if she did, she'd pretend it didn't happen, and so would everyone else." Her mother sighed loudly. "But we don't want you keeling over in the first dance. You're excused for tonight."

Jala held her breath until she heard her mother's footsteps retreating down the hall. Then she threw a scarf over her head to hide her face from a casual glance and slipped down the hall in the opposite direction.

A few minutes later, Marjani met her outside with a rolled-up blanket and two towels, and they walked along the beach to the north side of the island. They kept to the edges of the bonfires until they were well away from the manor. Except for the occasional offer of a drink or a dance, nobody paid them much mind.

It took nearly an hour to reach the north side of the island. The beach was deserted. Everyone had gone off to celebrate Jala's upcoming marriage and drink Lord Mosi's wine.

The moon was bright, and the water in the bay was cool and calm. For a while they splashed and laughed the way they had when they were children, then when they were tired of that they floated side by side and stared up at the stars.

"Don't fall asleep," Marjani said. "The Kayet will blame me if you drown."

Jala snorted. "Lord Inas would probably thank you."

Somewhere out past the sandbar that kept all but the high tide at bay, she could hear the splash and whistle of dolphins playing. Sometimes they would jump the sandbar and spend a while teasing anyone in the bay, but tonight Jala and Marjani had it all to themselves.

"I should probably get back, before I get any more wrinkled," Jala said.

"Maybe your king would like you with wrinkles," Marjani said. "You'll get them eventually, anyway."

They swam back to the shore and dried themselves. But Jala made no move to actually start walking again. Neither did Marjani.

"If you didn't have to marry him . . . if you could stay here. Would you still want to go?" Marjani asked.

Jala nodded. "I always wanted to be queen, and not just so I can help our family." She grinned. "And I like the way it sounds. Is that terrible of me? 'Queen Jala of the Bardo.'"

"Is that the only reason?" Marjani pressed. She seemed to want something, though Jala couldn't tell what. "What about Azi? If you weren't going to be queen, would you want to marry him still?"

Jala had to think about this for a little longer. Her parents had always told her she might be queen one day, that she might marry Jin. He was held up as her ideal husband, but she'd hardly known him. But being around Azi was different. He was real, not just *the boy who will be king*.

"I don't know if I'd marry him," she said slowly. "Not right away. But I'd want to be with him, I think." Her grin widened, and her face was warm despite the cool air. "I'd definitely like to try kissing him again. And then some. He's good at kissing."

"What about that scar on his head?"

Jala shrugged. "He's a sailor, and sailors have scars. Don't tell me you never watched any of the younger sailors while they worked. Remember that time we sneaked over to the men's side of the shore to watch them bathing?"

"I remember," Marjani said. She looked away from Jala and stared out over the water. "Has he tried to sneak into your room since you were betrothed?"

Jala sighed. "No! Not even for a quick kiss. Or a long kiss. Or *anything*."

"I remember we used to practice kissing sometimes," Marjani said.

"Ha, I remember that too." She poked Marjani's arm. "You weren't so bad at it yourself." She almost wished they could go back to those days, when everything was simpler and she didn't have to worry about whether she was good at kissing or not. "You'll be able to find someone to be with now, without me making things difficult. I know it wasn't easy the way my parents kept an eye on me."

"No, I won't," Marjani said. She took a deep breath, as if preparing herself for something she was afraid of. "Because . . . I did find someone. It just wouldn't have worked. Because for her, kissing me was only practice. Because she's getting married. Because she's going to be queen, and I won't see her again, and it doesn't matter if she never wants to speak to me again after I say this."

Jala fell silent, not sure how to respond. She felt slower than a sea turtle on land. She and Marjani were together nearly every day and had been for years. How could she not have noticed anything? Was she that selfish? Only a terrible friend wouldn't notice her friend's feelings for her. Unless. . . . "How long have you felt this way?"

Marjani shrugged and looked away. "A few years, maybe."

So much for hoping it was a recent development. No, Jala was just completely oblivious to things that were right in front of her.

Marjani kept talking, still not meeting Jala's eyes. "I didn't want it to change anything between us, so I never said. But then I thought about it, and I didn't want to have any secrets between us before you left. There's already going to be an ocean separating us. And I know you don't feel the same about me, and that's all right. I knew that, too, and I didn't think it would help anything to bring it up."

She was speaking quickly, and Jala could tell she was going to keep talking until she'd convinced herself the world was falling apart around them.

"Marjani. Look at me. Can you even remember a time when we haven't been friends? I can't. Why would I ever stop speaking to you? So, as your queen, I order you to stop worrying."

"I'm sharing my deepest secrets with you and you're making jokes," Marjani said, not quite succeeding in sounding indignant. "And you can't order me to stop worrying."

"I think I just did."

"Well, then I'll rebel against you. I'll run away to the Lone Isle and become a sorceress and worry all I want," Marjani said. "You'll be all the way on the First Isle anyway, how will you know?" Some of the sadness had crept back into Marjani's voice.

"I'll be back to visit," Jala whispered. "And you'll come visit me, too, as soon as you can. I wish you could come with me now."

"I wish I could, too," Marjani said, her voice breaking only a little. "I'm going to miss you."

Jala didn't respond but held Marjani's hand tightly. For the first time, it really hit her that she was leaving Marjani. She'd always thought home was the manor, the island, her family . . . but it was Marjani, too. Maybe it was Marjani most of all.

Could she ever be as close with Azi? Maybe not in the same way, but perhaps just as strongly. *You want too much*, she tried to tell herself. But she wanted it anyway, and she wanted Marjani to stay with her. She wanted to leave for the First Isle, but she wanted to stay, too.

Everything was going to change, and right now, under the stars alone with Marjani, she let herself feel scared.

To Jala's surprise, the next day her mother made no further comment about her absence from the night's entertainment or the sorry state of her hair. She just hugged Jala briefly and said, "It's all right to be nervous. Just don't make it a habit. Now let's get you something to eat."

Jala's stomach rumbled and she let her mother lead her out to the beach, where breakfast was already waiting for them. After she was finished, Jala sat back and tried to stifle a yawn. She'd been up most of the night, and the food only made her bed seem that much more inviting. "I'm going back to my room to pick out my clothes for tonight," she said.

Her mother's eyes narrowed. "If you're going to sleep, at least do it sitting up so Marjani can fix your hair."

Jala smiled innocently. "I'll be down for lunch, I promise."

She went to her room feeling better than she had in days. She wasn't going to wake Marjani just yet. It seemed like only a moment after she closed her eyes that a knock came at her door.

Jala sat up and pinched herself to wake up quickly, but her eyelids still drooped. "Who's there?"

"We need to talk," her father said.

Jala tried not to seem too disappointed. She'd been dreaming about Azi, and when the knock on the door came, his face was still in her mind. Well, she hadn't *really* expected Azi to risk more trouble for them by visiting her private rooms.

"Give me five minutes," she said. There was a bowl of water by her bed, and she splashed her face with it and tried to wash the sand out of her eyes. Then she dressed quickly and opened the door.

Her father smiled at her. "You look more like a queen every day."

"I'd feel more like one if I could have gotten my sleep," she complained, but she was smiling too.

"I know you're losing sleep over the wedding and what will happen once you're on the First Isle," he said with a wink. Then his voice took on a more serious tone. His lecturing voice, Jala thought. "It will get easier, one day, I promise. But not soon. Not for a few years, at least. You have a lot of hard days ahead of you. I've tried to raise you to be strong in case this day came, but even the strongest-looking ship is untested until it's sailed the ocean."

"Was that supposed to be inspiring? Maybe it's all this sand in my ears, but I don't feel very inspired."

"It was supposed to be a warning," her father said. "Up until now, your cousin Akali has been my ambassador to the Kayet. He speaks with my voice at the Sectioning. He knows the other families. They respect him, and that's no easy achievement for a man who turns green as soon as he steps foot aboard a grayship. But now that you're queen you will be expected to speak for us instead."

"I haven't forgotten," Jala said. "I've been paying attention."

"The other families will try to take everything they can from us. From you, really. Not just because they think they can, but to prove to each other and to themselves that you're weak."

"Then I won't let them." Did her father think she knew nothing about the world? She'd been at his side for two years watching and listening.

Her father shook his head. "Not letting them isn't enough. We won't even let them try. We'll show them what kind of queen I intend you to be from the very beginning. The kind of queen people fear. The kind of queen people obey."

"How?" Jala asked, a little afraid to find out, and a little excited as well.

"Only the Rafa are allowed to raid the lands around the city of Two Bones. It's been that way since the first king and queen. There're more riches there than they could ever hope to take. Riches that we deserve. Riches we're finally strong enough to take." Her father smiled again, but this time his lips were pulled into something almost like a snarl. "You're going to take it from them. And I'm going to tell you how."

CHAPTER 5

Two days later, the day of the wedding had finally come.

Jala's mother burst into her room well before dawn. "Up, up, up!" she sang as she lit the lamp beside Jala's bed. "So much to do before the wedding. You need to eat as much as you can now, there won't be any time for food later."

Jala shaded her eyes with her hand and squinted up at her mother. "Are you sure I need to be awake so early? Do you want me to sleep through my own wedding?" She rubbed her eyes.

Her mother clicked her tongue impatiently and pushed Jala's hands away from her face. "Stop that, you'll make your eyes all puffy. Into the bath with you."

Jala nearly dozed off in the warm water, but too soon her mother was calling her out of the bath and over to a table piled high with food. She focused on eating, blocking out her mother's constant stream of instructions and chatter. Her mother acted as though the whole wedding would fall apart if the flowers were the wrong color or if her cousins wore the wrong jewelry. Who would remember the color of the flowers after it was over? She hoped she'd have much more interesting things to remember.

Marjani was awakened to help Jala and keep her company. Cousins were roused from their beds and sent off on last-minute errands. "You're lucky to be a part of this," her mother would scold if one of her cousins complained or wondered when the wedding would be over already. "You won't live to see another Bardo queen marry."

"Your mother might not live to see this one, either," Marjani whispered. "Someone's going to kill her if she doesn't manage to do herself in first."

Jala laughed, a loud laugh that had as much to do with her own nerves as anything else. "What do you think Azi's doing right now? Do you think he had to get up this early?"

"Considering how much wine they had on the Kayet ships last

41

night? Probably not that early," Marjani said. "Lord Inas has gone out of his way to leave all of the planning and preparation to us, your mother says. Though they probably wouldn't do much anyway. Probably why they have the wedding on the queen's island instead of their own."

"I don't mind," Jala said. "Well, not too much anyway. I could do with less shouting and more sleeping." She closed her eyes and tried to ignore the way Marjani had to tug on her hair to secure her braids into the complicated twists her mother had decided would fit best with her dress. She closed her eyes for just a moment. Then a moment more.

Then suddenly Marjani stopped, her hands still holding on to a section of hair. Everything seemed to have gone quiet.

"Just leave it for now," Jala's mother said from the doorway. "Jala, try this on, in case we need to adjust it."

Jala opened her eyes. Her mother stood before her with the best dressmakers and seamstresses on the Second Isle, each of them holding a piece of her wedding costume. A headdress of feathers, each one a different color so that it seemed they must have one from every bird on the Five-and-One Islands. For her neck, a necklace of polished bronze. For her ears, small shells hanging on fine silver chains. Around her arms, wooden hoops covered in natural whirls of red and brown.

And there was the dress itself. Based on the whispers starting up around the room, the dress was a surprise to anyone who hadn't seen it yet. Everyone had expected the dressmakers to try to combine as many styles from the mainland as possible to show off how widely the Bardo raided. They'd tried, and the result had been a gaudy, uncomfortable thing. Jala's mother had made it clear to the dressmakers that a Bardo queen would wear something better.

"There's a difference between trying to convince them of our strength, and wearing it with confidence," she'd said.

The dress they'd finally come up didn't use styles from the mainland at all, just the silks and dyes and cotton the Bardo often took from merchants who traveled between cities there. Jala let them dress her, first in a simple gown the color of white sand, cinched at her waist by a length of red and brown silk that was folded tight at one end and hung down her leg at the other. Over her shoulders they placed a blue tunic with white checks, and then over that loose shawls of green and red. All this they folded and twisted carefully to create the right effect.

It was, she had to admit, still uncomfortable to wear, and she didn't look forward to wearing it under the midday sun. But the effect was worth it. She was the Second Isle as seen from a distant ship: the white sand and tree line shining brightly in the day, then as she spun, the setting sun, the midnight sky, the moon reflecting in the water.

"Do you think he'll like it?" Jala whispered as Marjani tucked in a fold of the shawl.

"He's an idiot if he doesn't," she whispered back. "You look amazing."

The sun had only risen a few hours before when everything was finally ready, and Jala's family led her out onto the beach. In spite of Marjani's words, the Kayet were awake. The nobles and captains stood in solemn rows along one side of the beach, the Bardo nobles and captains along the other. Everyone else, the sailors and villagers, surrounded them in a great circle. A few of the nearest trees bowed with children brave enough to climb to the top in order to get a better view.

They all stared at Jala, and she knew the dress was worth it.

Then she saw Azi, standing at the other end of the line of people. But he wasn't looking at her dress. His eyes met hers, and she held his gaze, forgetting about everyone else.

But though later she would remember the day as just that one bright, burning moment looking into Azi's eyes, there was still a lot of wedding left before they could be together. There were stories first, about isles before the secrets of the shipwood reefs were learned, when each isle made war on the others. There were stories of the first king and queen and their great deeds, stories of the Thoughtless Boy and his disastrous marriages.

Then there were speeches. Jala's cousin Zalika had been married, and there'd been only two speeches, but now it seemed that every cousin and captain had something to say; neither family wanted the other to have the last word.

Finally, Jala and Azi stood on the beach together, surrounded by both families. The water sparkled from the bright noon sun, and the glare from the beach's white sand made Jala's eyes water. The sand had been pleasantly warm when they started, but it had become hot in the noonday sun. Her dress clung to her, and she could feel one of the shawls slipping, but she was afraid to make it worse by trying to fix it.

They were all saying the same thing. Jala was getting tired of being congratulated and flattered and congratulated again.

She snuck a glance at Azi. How was he not bored by this? If anything, he looked attentive. He stood perfectly still, and he met each speaker's gaze. He was a sailor before he was a king. Maybe he was just used to long, boring hours spent staring at the water. She watched him a while longer, until she caught him yawning through his nostrils during a particularly long speech. That made her feel better.

Finally, the wedding bird was brought out by one of the Bardo bird trainers. The bird was one of the prettiest Jala had ever seen, a male with a large yellow crest and bright orange-tipped wings. It cawed in a loud, clear voice.

The trainer held the bird carefully so it wouldn't struggle as he brought it to Azi. He nodded slightly, and Azi said, "I am Azi of the Kayet, king of the Five-and-One Islands. Jala of the Bardo will be my queen until I die."

Then the bird was brought in front of Jala, and she said, "I am Jala of the Bardo, queen of the Five-and-One Islands. Azi of the Kayet will be my king until I die."

"King Azi of the Kayet," the trainer repeated. "Queen Jala of the Bardo. May their rule bring good wind and many riches."

The bird repeated their names. The trainer released it into the air, and it flew out over the water, off to tell the Great Ocean and the winds that a new king and queen had been united.

Lord Inas handed Azi the Queen's Earring with a scowl, not even pretending to be happy for them. Jala affected not to notice. She tilted her head, and the king gently put the earring on her ear. The earring *was* a bit heavy, as Marjani had predicted, but it was a reassuring weight. It reminded her that she really was the queen. She wasn't going to wake up tomorrow and find out it was all a dream or that she was an imposter.

Everyone was looking at her, but she didn't think they were seeing her. They saw the Queen's Earring. They saw their queen. It was a facade she could hide behind, and she smiled confidently at them.

After the ceremony, Jala's mother and father came to her and hugged her tightly. Jala let herself cling to them like she had when she was a child.

"You make me so proud, my little queen," her father whispered in her ear. "I look at you, and I think, how can they help but bow to you? We'll give that old whale Inas something to fear, yes?" Then he kissed her once on each cheek, and she didn't know if the wetness on her face were his tears or her own.

With the wedding over, Jala and Azi boarded a Bardo grayship. From a distance it looked narrow and sleek, as if it was made of wood like a common fishing boat. But up close you could see that the hull was gnarled and potted. Grayships weren't lashed together; they were grown from the coral surrounding the five islands. Jala had to be careful as she was helped aboard, for the coral was sharp and burned fiercely if it pierced your skin.

With the Kayet on one side of the ship and the Bardo on the other, they were pushed out into the water. A great Kayet barge waited for them, a grayship grown to show off their own power more than for any practical purpose. Even the term "grayship" didn't fit, for while most raiding ships were specially treated by the shipgrowers to turn them gray and make them hard to see, the barge's hull was all bright reds and pinks against the cool blue water.

The Kayet reefs were the largest of any of the islands. They could afford to flaunt their coral and the skill of their shipgrowers. And while even raiding ships had wooden planks over the coral hull, this one had a deck large enough for dancing and cabins where the king and queen could sleep in privacy and comfort.

Where she and Azi could sleep. Or not sleep. The thought made her heart beat faster and her mouth feel dry. A ship large enough for dancing and feasting, with food from the Kayet's own rich stores, and somehow Jala didn't think she was going to notice any of it.

Deep down, Jala knew she would cry for home later, when she was alone and it had all sunk in. But now excitement for what was to come rose in her, filling her up and leaving room for nothing else.

As the Second Isle receded, Jala could still hear her family cheering for her.

CHAPTER 6

T he start of their journey to the First Isle was a blur of songs and stories and drums. The deck of the barge trembled under Jala's feet. Unlike wooden ships, grayships were alive and could sense their reef even hundreds of leagues away. They were the only way to cross the Great Ocean that separated the islands from the mainland. Other ships got lost as soon as they were out of sight of land. Jala had felt a little lost herself ever since her family's island was nothing more than a speck on the horizon.

She tried to distract herself by watching the sailors. This Kayet barge was even large enough for a few of the sailors to attempt the winddance, though the motion of the ship on the water made it that much harder. The wine didn't help, either. There was plenty of laughter and a few bruises, too.

They're not celebrating me, Jala reminded herself sternly. She couldn't let herself forget that the Kayet were not her friends. That was what her father had told her. Or was it simply that, unlike Lord Inas who pointedly looked away from her, the sailors didn't much care what island their new queen came from? Maybe the Kayet weren't her friends, but they didn't all have to be enemies, either.

And maybe one of them would be something more fun than either option.

She'd been seated at one end of the expansive ship while Azi sat at the opposite end. He wasn't really watching the celebration but was instead casting her long glances every chance he got. Jala couldn't stop glancing at him, either. The wind blew, and his loose tunic opened, showing off his chest. She wished he'd wind-dance again. She wanted to see his muscles tense, see the way he moved with ferocity and grace. But he'd turned the offers down.

Maybe he was nervous. She was nervous after all. It wasn't as if she didn't know what a woman could do with a man. She'd seen men naked from afar, listened to the stories her mother had told her to teach her of such things, listened in when her cousins told stories that weren't meant for her to hear at all. But it was different now, with him, with the Queen's Earring pulling at her ear. This wasn't a dream, wasn't a kiss stolen on the beach beneath a palm tree.

It wasn't as if she had to do this. She could feign tiredness, or illness, or something. The illness was only a partial lie anyway—her stomach felt all queasy with nerves and too little sleep and too much wedding. The tiredness wasn't a lie at all.

But she did want to be with him. She was just . . . nervous. Maybe it was always like this the first time between men and women? *I wonder if it'll be any different for Marjani*, she thought. *Not so many new bits and pieces to worry about.* She didn't really think that was the problem, though. She was sure she'd like all his bits well enough. She liked the rest of him well enough.

Then she thought to worry if he would like *her* the same. Well, he had to, right? He'd chosen to marry her, hadn't he? And men were supposed to like breasts. She had enough of those, so let them do something useful for once. She shifted a little in her seat, tugging surreptitiously at her dress until it slid down her front just the slightest bit.

He watched her, and she watched him, and she watched him watching her.

The sun set with agonizing slowness. Stars filled the sky from horizon to horizon. No one danced, but the stories and laughter and wine flowed unabated, and the drums never slowed. They would beat all night, whether she was tired of them or not.

But they stopped for Lord Inas as he stood and clapped his hands for silence. "My friends, I think the time has come to put our king and queen to bed."

The Kayet cheered and laughed, and then a Kayet woman gently touched Jala's shoulder. "I can take you to your cabin, my queen."

Even the Kayet's oversized barge had only a few cabins, but the largest of these were the king's and queen's cabins at the rear of the ship, above deck. She followed the woman through a single door that led to a short hallway, hardly long enough to take three strides. The king's cabin was on the port side. Hers was directly across the hall.

The woman closed the door behind her as Jala entered her cabin. There was little more than a bed and a glass porthole, but both were unheard of on ships. Beds wasted precious space, and glass had to be brought back from the mainland. She wondered if Azi's bed was bigger than hers. The queen was meant to visit the king's bed so that she could leave and go back to her own cabin if she wanted. It would make sense to give the king's cabin a bed that could easily fit two.

Jala sat and waited, her heart beating quickly in time with the muffled drums beyond the cabin's wooden walls. There was a faint click as the outer door opened, then a slightly louder one as Azi opened and closed the door opposite her own.

Should she have gone to his room right away and surprised him? Did he expect her to be waiting for him already? Well, it was too late now. She sat on her bed and waited, giving him time. Or just putting it off, she wasn't sure which.

I wanted this, she told herself. *I want this.* And she did. And she didn't. Her head and heart were filled with contradictions. Certain other parts weren't exactly quiet about making their opinion known, either.

Then she took a deep breath and stood, opened her door, and took the single step to Azi's door. She opened it. Azi froze, seemingly in the middle of pacing back and forth. He smiled hesitantly. His eyes were wide. "You looked beautiful today. With the dress and . . . everything."

Jala smiled, too. "I'm sure my mother will be glad to hear it. I hope you don't expect me to look like that every day."

He laughed at that, and for a moment his smile looked more like the one she'd seen on the beach weeks before. Was this his real smile? Azi the sailor's smile, perhaps? And if that was true, was Azi the sailor the real Azi?

"I didn't know if you would come," he said. "But I hoped you would."

"I hoped I would, too," she said. There was a moment of awkward silence before Jala realized the silence didn't have to be awkward if she didn't want it to be. She kissed him. His mouth was warm, and her lips parted against his. Azi's hands ran down her side, and his fingers brushed lightly over her back. Why did that make her shiver? She wanted to touch him, to run her hands over his chest. So she did. But the feeling of his skin and muscles beneath her fingers just made her want to touch him more. His hands tightened around her waist, as if he would pull her closer.

But instead he pushed her back and then turned away from her. "I'm sorry, I can't," he said, breathing heavily.

"What do you mean, you can't?" Jala said, not quite able to keep the annoyance out of her voice. "Did you have too much wine? Are you tired?" In spite of the possible reasons, she still reached for him again, but he backed away, keeping her at arm's length.

"No, it's not that. I just . . . I can't."

Jala shook her head. "You don't mean you can't," she said. "You mean you don't want to."

"I do! I've wanted to since the night we met, and every other night since then, but . . ."

"But what? Have you changed your mind about having me as your queen? You're a day late if that's the case."

"I don't want another queen," he said, his voice so emphatic she almost forgave him. But when he reached out to take her hand, it was her turn to pull away from his touch.

"Then what is it?"

"I don't know. It's everything. We've hardly been able to talk the last few weeks, and I haven't been home in twice that time. They're going to expect me to be a king for real now. There's going to be the Sectioning, and I'll have to sit in judgment and . . . and I'm scared. Of all of it."

"It's no different for me," Jala said. "I'm no less scared. And at least you'll be home, with your family and friends around you. You haven't had to give up everyone you know."

Azi's mouth twisted down. "What do you know about who or what I've had to give up? You only know Azi the King, ruler of the Five-and-One. If you'd met Azi the sailor you'd have hardly even looked at him. Your family wouldn't deign to let me dance with you, much less marry you."

Why was he bringing her family into this? The last thing she wanted to talk about right now was her parents. "Is that so different from the way your uncle looks at me still?" Jala demanded. "You don't know me any better than I know you, either one of you. There are only two, aren't there? Or is there some other Azi I don't know about?"

He flinched, as though she'd hit on some nerve. "The only thing my family hasn't chosen for me is you. We're the king and queen now. Why shouldn't we take our time? If we were both commoners we wouldn't be bound by anyone else's schedule. We could do what we wanted when we wanted, marry or not marry, wait as long or as little as we needed to . . . to know who we were. And that we were right for each other. As Azi and Jala, not just as King and Queen."

If they weren't right for each other, they'd both made a pretty big mistake, hadn't they? But she thought she understood. They hadn't had much time for just talking. They were talking now, and everything felt more awkward than before. She wanted to be back on the beach stealing kisses and hiding from everyone and their expectations.

Azi sighed and sat on the bed. "I don't think I'm ready for this. For any of this. Do you?"

"Yes," Jala said. "No. Did you feel ready the first time you crossed the ocean? Or the first time you drew your sword?"

"This isn't the same thing," Azi said, and she wasn't sure if he was talking about being the king or being with her.

She wasn't even sure she disagreed with him. She hated that, hated feeling confused and hurt and lost. Better to just jump in and hope everything worked out. Well, maybe not always better. But easier.

"Maybe you're right," she said, turning away from him and opening the door. "Maybe you're not ready."

She opened the door and stepped across the small hall into her room. It was dark, with only the slightest sliver of light from the stars and the lamps on the deck making its way into the room, but there wasn't much to see. She took off her crumpled dress and climbed into bed.

Jala lay awake for a long time, thinking of her family and the First Isle . . . and Azi. In spite of herself, she couldn't help thinking of him and remembering the moment—so brief, and yet it had felt so long— before he'd turned away from her.

I should have told him I was scared too, she thought, floating in the darkness between the waking world and dreams. But it was too late, and soon sleep took her.

CHAPTER 7

ala slept late the next day, but eventually she knew she'd have to go out and face Azi. They were seated beside one another now, but they said almost as little as they had when they'd sat at either end of the ship. This, Jala noted, in spite of everything he'd said about learning more about each other.

What made the whole long journey even more frustrating was that despite being annoyed by him, she still couldn't help wanting to be near him. But just sitting next to him all day made her want to throw something—or someone—overboard.

She lay in bed that night, again unable to sleep, waiting for the sound of footsteps just outside her door. She wasn't going to go to him again, but he would come to her, she was sure of it.

He didn't come. Not that night, and not the next, and then there were no more nights left between them and the First Isle.

A hot, humid rain fell that morning, and they sat together. Her dress was damp and clung to her skin, and she pulled at it in irritation.

"I'm sorry the journey wasn't more exciting," Azi said. "It wasn't what I wanted for us."

"You could have changed it easily enough. You've hardly spoken to me this whole time," Jala said, not bothering to mask her frustration. "I'm sure your uncle's pleased."

"My uncle . . . isn't speaking much to me either. He's been taking mournroot again, I think. I'm sorry I've been like this. It will be better soon, I promise. I'll make sure of it. All that's left is the gifting ceremony, and then you'll get to see your new home. My home. I hope you like it."

Jala wanted to say something to show him that she hadn't forgiven him, but then he reached out and took her hand, and for a moment she held her breath. "I hope I like it too," she said, her voice quiet and uncertain. He squeezed her hand, and even though she knew something so small shouldn't erase the boring days and lonely nights . . . it made her feel better.

In spite of the rain and the wet clothes, she smiled. They were both new to this. Things would be all right.

"There it is," he said, pointing needlessly at the island that appeared out of the rain and mist. "The First Isle."

"Sails at half," the captain called. Two sailors were already by the mast, clearly anticipating the order. The sails slackened, and the already slow ship moved more slowly as the island grew closer and more distinct. Soon Jala could see the beach where they would land and where the gifting ceremony would be performed.

"Sails slack. Oars down," the captain ordered. Oars were lowered into the water, and they were rowed ashore. Azi took her hand again to help her down off the ship. Jala didn't need the help, but she took the hand anyway.

The other three families, the Gana, Rafa, and Nongo, had sailed ahead to land on the First Isle and make preparations for the gifting, and now they waited for Jala and Azi on the beach. Two wooden thrones had been set out for them, with palm fronds overhead to keep the rain off. They sat, and each of the ambassadors gave Jala gifts to welcome her and pledge their loyalty. There were fine dresses, combs and hairclips, rings and earrings.

The Rafa gave her a bird with a magnificent silver plume as fine as a spider's web. "It speaks better than any bird found on our islands," the Rafa ambassador said, "and sings songs from far-off lands that it never forgets." The Gana gave her a bottle of rare and very beautiful purple dye that had the misfortune to smell like rotten fish. They also gave her a jar filled with a thick cream made from the liver of some fearsome mainland beast. "They say it will make your skin stay smooth and beautiful, like the sky on the night of a full moon. Though now I see that our queen is so beautiful she may never need it."

The Nongo brought her many trinkets of gold and copper, and one final gift: a large, brittle tome filled with gilded markings. "You see?" the ambassador said, laughing. "On the mainland, their minds are so dull that they cannot remember their own tales. But the illustrations are very beautiful."

Jala had heard of the mainlander art called writing, but she'd never seen it before. It seemed so ridiculous, like catching fish with your feet instead of throwing a net with your hands. Careful to keep the rain off of the paper, she opened the book. The pictures were beautiful, just as the man had said. One caught her eyes as she continued to turn the pages: a man and a woman, fighting. Each of them wore a different mask over their faces. The man stood on a mountain, and on his mask was drawn a mountain. He held stones in his hands and threw them at the woman. She stood atop a wave or winding river, and her mask was a serpentine river. The stones did not hit her, and her river broke against the mountain.

Jala realized she was holding her breath, losing herself in the picture the way she might lose herself in the words of the very best storyteller.

"Thank you," she said. "A truly unique gift. Perhaps I will hold a contest to see which island's storyteller can find meaning in these pictures."

The ambassador smiled widely. "I have no doubt the Nongo would win such a contest, but the tales themselves would be a gift to all the islands. Wondrous new tales for a wondrous new queen. A promising start, yes?"

"Did your raiders find you a golden tongue, too, my lord?" Jala asked with a laugh. She dismissed him with a wave of her hands. The Nongo ambassador bowed and walked away, still smiling with self-satisfaction.

Jala looked down at the book again, flipping to another page. Someone had drawn thick, dark lines through the writing here and obscured the drawing with streaks of dark ink. She thought it might be flames, but it could just as easily be another mountain.

A promising start . . . not if her father had his way. But what could she do? No more than the river could, beating itself against the mountain.

Her family's presents waited for her in her room. By tradition, they gave her old, familiar things to help her feel more at home when she arrived: drapes from her old room, a pair of her mother's earrings, one of Marjani's dresses. Jala decided she wouldn't have it resized. She set the birdcage on a windowsill, and after a few minutes the bird repeated several dirty jokes. She wondered what she was supposed to do now that she was queen.

Of course, her parents already had their plans laid out.

The Bardo are royalty now, her father had said. *Why should we scuttle after scraps when others eat from the table? The Rafa were great once, I don't deny it, but now they're old and weak. They don't have the ships to raid all the lands they lay claim to. It's time for us to get our share.*

"I just have to figure out how to make it happen," Jala told the bird.

Her father was right; the Rafa were too weak to raid all of their towns and caravans. But the Rafa were proud, and they'd blame her. When she brought it up, her father had just laughed and said, "Rafa anger is like the mountain's fart. It's harmless, and the stink will pass soon enough once the winds blow."

She needed to speak with Azi. But when she opened her door, a maidservant was there, standing in her way like a very polite boulder.

"I want to see the king," Jala said. "Please take me to him. I haven't learned my way around yet."

"Wouldn't my queen prefer to rest after her journey?" the woman asked, not making any move to let her pass. "I can bring you fruit and wine if you're hungry. The hot springs are close by. If you don't mind the rain, it's very restful."

"I've been resting for three days," Jala said with a sigh. "I'm sorry, I should have asked you your name."

The woman smiled. "Iliana, my queen."

"Hello, Iliana." As impatient as she felt, Jala decided she probably should eat, or she'd be hungry *and* irritable. And she shouldn't take her frustration out on a stranger. "The food does sound good, and the wine. I'll take both. When I'm finished, will you tell the king I want to see him?"

Azi came to Jala's room two hours later. He leaned against the wall near the door. "Are you glad the ceremonies are behind us? There'll still be a feast tonight for the other families. They'll all drink to your health until they can't walk straight, but it should be low on speeches. They'll be saving that for tomorrow."

"For the Sectioning?"

Azi nodded. "I've never had to preside over it before. But you won't have to worry about it. Just don't drink too much, or all the shouting will make your head hurt. But I don't want to think about that right now. How do you like the First Isle so far? You haven't seen much of it yet, but you will as soon as things slow down a little. Just wait until there's a cold wind blowing and you sit in the hot springs. You'll never want to leave, I promise."

"Iliana already told me about them. They do sound nice."

Azi's face fell a little. Did he really think she was dependent on him to learn everything about her new home? "Oh. Well, there are other things I can show you. How about food? We have so many different things. There's food in the cellars that no one's even tried yet, from all over the coast and far into the mainland where there's no river to carry our ships."

"Hmm, I don't think I want to be the first to try something no one knows how to cook."

"I want you to like it here," Azi said. "What can I do to make your stay here better? I haven't given you a wedding present yet. I'm king now, might as well do something worthwhile with it all. Tell me what you want and it's yours."

"Oh," Jala said. "Thank you." She fell silent. What did she want? The question had caught her off guard. Before, she would have said, *I want to be queen*, but she had that now.

I want him to love me.

Where had that thought even come from? She wasn't supposed to want his love, not like this. Not if it meant she might love him, too. She'd been taught from a young age that love was something you felt for your family, and with that love came duty. While her cousins could hope to build love out of their marriages, and the villagers and sailors could marry whoever they wanted, her father always said romantic love would only blind her.

She didn't feel blinded. She felt free for the first time, giddy to be feeling something that wasn't supposed to be for her. But love wasn't something you could just ask for.

"Well?" Azi said, smiling expectantly. "There must be something you've always dreamed of having."

She wanted him to love her, but she couldn't ask for that. If he could give that, he'd give it freely. And if not . . . she tried not to think about that and instead concentrated on something else. Jewels, clothes, she had all that. She had an exotic bird, even if it did sing the worst songs. Maybe a storyteller to recite all the Forty Tales of Love for them. She'd heard most of them already from her cousins, laughing with Marjani the whole time, but she'd always tried to imagine what it would be like to hear them in some sailor's arms.

But no. They could have that too easily enough, if he wanted it, and asking now would only be a frustrating tease if there wasn't anything they could actually do.

A kiss? Simple and heartfelt, something she could have at any time but worth the price of a precious jewel. It would be a nice gesture, at least. A better start than they'd had so far. Just a kiss, nothing more, and it would be enough for now. Maybe it would help them start over.

But even as she opened her mouth to say it another thought came to her, souring her fantasies like a bad smell. Jala's excitement vanished. Her parents would never forgive her if she wasted such a perfect opportunity. She knew what she had to ask for. What she was supposed to want. "I want you to give my family the city of Two Bones at the Sectioning tomorrow."

Azi laughed. "What? I can't just take the Rafa's city from them."

"You can, if you make it a present. Tomorrow, at the Sectioning."

Azi's smile was gone now. "You've only been here a day. Don't you want to . . . can't you wait for your clothes to be unpacked and your bed to be slept in before you start making enemies?"

Jala shrugged. "My father says we're all enemies, we just haven't fought in two hundred years."

"Well, my uncle says the Bardo are like sharks only without the good manners, but I don't always listen to him."

"You asked what I wanted," Jala said. "And I told you. You can't keep throwing the fact that you disobeyed your uncle to marry me back in my face."

"Yes, and I thought I married you, not your father." Azi stopped speaking and took a deep breath. "I don't know how we managed to turn this into an argument. That can't be what you want, not really. It's what your family wants. I want to give something to you, not for Jala of the Bardo or Jala the queen of the Five-and-One."

Jala was silent for a moment. "I'm all of those things. I never pretended not to be. This matters to me. My family matters to me."

"I thought you were different," Azi said. "Not just a tool for your family."

Jala flinched but didn't let her gaze waver. *I am different!* she wanted to say, though a part of her wondered about even that. She made herself respond. "You mean you thought I'd just sleep through all the parts where we actually rule. If that's it, I don't know who you were walking with on that beach when we met. But it wasn't me."

"That's not what I meant—"

Jala shook her head. "You asked what I wanted, not what you wanted to give me. If you want to take back your gift, just say so."

"No, you're right. I offered you anything you wanted, but I expected . . . it doesn't matter. Are you sure this is what you want?"

No, Jala thought. "Yes," she said.

"As you wish, my queen. If you'll excuse me, I'm tired from the journey, and I haven't seen my mother in weeks."

Then he was gone.

Jala shut the door behind him and sat down on the bed. *Queens don't cry*, her mother had told her. "Well?" she said to the bird the Rafa had given her. "Sing me something, one of those beautiful foreign songs you're supposed to know. Or are you just a joke they decided to play on me?" The bird sang, in a language she didn't understand. It was beautiful, just as they said. But it sounded like a love song. Everything the bird sang sounded like a love song.

She finally had to throw a shoe at the bird to make it stop.

CHAPTER 8

*T*hat evening, dinner went as Azi had predicted. The wine flowed freely, though Jala noticed that Azi, like her, drank little. They danced together, but Azi held her stiffly and his speech was distant and formal. Jala excused herself from any further dancing and sulked at the table. *He can't stay mad forever. You did what you had to, and he knows it. He would have done the same thing for his family, and everyone would expect as much because he's a man.*

Once everyone tired of dancing, they ate the main course. Tonight it was salted meats from the mainland and freshly caught fish, followed by sweet cakes made from coconut milk.

After that everyone settled down to drinking and boasting. A Nongo captain told Jala about how his ship had found the book of tales given to her as a present.

"The winds were weak, and we found ourselves in some kind of strange undertow, pulling us off course. We had no idea at all where we'd landed and were afraid we'd be going home with nothing more than the laundry off some fisherman's lines. Not that we saw any fishermen, even. It was all rocks and mountains.

"But then old Adisa saw something up on the cliff. You'd never see it if you weren't looking at it from the right angle, and if you didn't have Adisa's hawk-eyes. Lucky for us, it turned out. We spent two days trying to find a way up, and when we'd almost given up, there it was, a hidden path with a small spring bubbling nearby.

"We snuck in, and we found old men, books, and gold. More old men than gold, as our luck would have it, but there was enough to fill the holds and bring back something special for my queen. They flung themselves on the book, those old men, trying to keep us from it. We made sure not to get any blood on it, though. You know what they say: blood on the gift makes bad blood between you. And that goes double for queens, I'm sure."

Jala'd heard the saying before but hadn't really thought about it much. She pictured the old men huddling with their books, imagined Nongo sailors using clubs and sword hilts instead of blades to keep the pages clean. They wouldn't have killed them all, Jala reminded herself. Just the ones who tried to stop them. That was another saying. *Whatever you can take belongs to you, but leave a little for next time.* It was just the way things were. Even before the first king and queen the ships of the Five had raided along the mainland's shores and down its rivers. The shark didn't spend too much time wondering if it was wrong to eat the fish.

The other families' captains all had similar stories, of raiding towns and catching caravans unawares. Even the ambassadors spent much of their time reliving old raids, and the more they drank the more they tried to outdo each other. After a while all of the stories started to sound the same.

When she'd sat through enough of the stories to satisfy politeness, Jala excused herself and retreated to her rooms.

She laid in bed and flipped through the Nongo's book by the light of the moon shining through a window. It seemed so foolish to write stories down like that. Stories were alive. They had to change depending on what someone needed at the time of the telling, and they couldn't do that pinned to a sheet of paper.

She liked the illustrations, though. As she examined each intricately painted page, she tried to imagine what stories might be told about them. After a while, she fell asleep.

During the Sectioning of the mainland the next day the ambassadors and captains sat slumped in their seats. One even rested his forehead against the table.

Jala leaned over to Azi, who seemed much less hungover than the rest. "Are you sure they're alive?" she whispered.

Azi shrugged. "My uncle says if you let them come fresh and awake, they'll argue until the next morning. This way they just want to get back to bed." He banged his fist on the table to get their attention. Several of them flinched at the sound. "The sooner we begin, the sooner it's over, my lords. Shall we start with the Autumn Lands?"

The Gana ambassador said, "Keen-lay has had a drought. Wan-lay to the south fares better, but they spend their riches on ships to patrol their coasts."

Somehow, everyone's territories were having a hard time. There were bad crops, wars, plague, and natural disasters. Jala thought it was a wonder that anyone came back with silk and gold at all. It would be a greater wonder still when the storm season was over, and trade fleets set sail for the Constant City loaded down with the very goods that—to hear the ambassadors tell it—had become as hard to find as a dry fish in the Great Ocean.

Of course, when the Bardo's territory came up, she told them about the great flood that had covered the Orange Road in mud, blocking any caravans from getting through. Everyone knew it was an act, but that was how the Sectioning went, and all she could do was play her role.

"What about Two Bones?" Azi asked. He talked differently at the Sectioning, Jala noticed. Slower and more forceful, so that each word carried clearly through the entire room. *More like a king.* It didn't quite sound like *him*, though.

The Rafa ambassador shrugged. "A poor city, long fallen from its former glory. But it has always belonged to the Rafa, and we value our traditions more than gold."

"Truly, my lord? I hear they still make a beautiful red dye there that my wife adores. Since the city is poor, it should be no great loss to the Rafa if I make Two Bones a gift to my queen."

The other ambassadors sat up straighter, suddenly paying very close attention.

"But, my king, Two Bones has been ours for two hundred years."

"Long enough, I think. You may find that new gold is an adequate substitute for old traditions."

"Are we being challenged?" The Rafa ambassador sat rigid in his chair.

Any family could challenge for a territory: the family that had the most ships to commit to the territory won that territory. It was the Kayet's task to keep a tally of all the ships grown and lost in the past year, counted and memorized by the teller-of-lists. He stood now, along the wall, waiting patiently. It was rare that he actually had to speak. Challenges left too much bad blood. Any family might find themselves short a few ships because of bad luck at the next Sectioning. Mostly the families preferred to bicker and argue and make deals.

"Of course not," Azi said. "Nobody's challenged the Rafa in years. In exchange for Two Bones, the Rafa will get the city of Shek. We've already heard from my queen how the city has grown in recent years."

"The Rafa don't give away their lands. Not since the first Sectioning have we been challenged, and only through challenge can our lands be taken from us." He pointed at Jala. "The Rafa unified the Five Islands while the Bardo were still growing their own food, not a single grayship among them, yet now you want to give our lands to them?"

Jala felt a flash of anger. "We had no ships because the Rafa burned them all. Only a few weeks before the first king and queen married. Or, by some accounts, a few weeks after."

"You see, my king?" the Rafa ambassador said. "See how already they try to undermine everything our families have worked for? They're liars, upstart thieves!"

"Sit down," Azi commanded. "That's your queen you just insulted."

But the Rafa ambassador went on as though he hadn't heard, speaking to the other ambassadors. "Will you stand there and let them do this? The Bardo know they don't have the strength to match the Rafa, so they come at us from behind, stealing what they can't take by right of strength."

Jala stood, her hands balled into fists. How dare he say such things about her family? She'd given him a way out, and he'd spat in her face. Fine. She'd do this her father's way. "Is that what you want? Then the Bardo challenge. Read out the lists."

The Rafa ambassador nodded, and the teller-of-lists opened his mouth to speak.

"The real count, my friend," Jala said. "Not the count the Rafa pay you to recite."

The teller-of-lists glanced at Lord Inas and whispered, "My lord?"

Azi sighed. "The real count, as your queen said."

The teller recited the numbers. The Rafa had too few ships, fewer than any other family. The Rafa ambassador looked back and forth between the teller-of-lists and the other ambassadors. "They're lying. The Rafa are strong. She's the one who paid him to lie."

The desperation in his voice made Jala queasy, but she pushed the feeling aside. She repeated the words her father had told her. "You've lost nearly half your fleet to the ocean's temper. Your shipgrowers won't be able to replace what you've lost for years." She took a breath to steel herself. "But if you still insist I'm lying, my family's ships will meet yours on the open water." *You have to threaten war*, her father had said. *It's the way of things. Show no fear, my little queen. It is only another wind-dance.*

"That won't be necessary," Azi said quickly. "Two Bones has already been gifted to the Bardo, therefore the Bardo can't challenge for it. Isn't that right?"

The ambassadors seated around the table refused to meet the Rafa's gaze. There was no help coming. His jaw clenched, but he nodded to Azi.

"Good. We're all agreed, then, that this was a fair trade."

The other ambassadors muttered their assent. Azi tried to go on as if nothing had happened, but a few minutes later the Gana ambassador challenged the Rafa for one of their smaller territories and won. Other ambassadors did likewise, until an hour later the Rafa had lost all but a few of their best territories. Then the ambassadors challenged each other all over again for the territories they had just taken, and the Rafa lands changed hands a few more times.

As she listened, Jala felt more and more miserable. This wasn't what she'd intended. Even her father hadn't intended the Rafa to be stripped of all they had. At least, he hadn't said so. *But he must have known. He just didn't care.*

When the last of the challenges had passed, the Rafa ambassador stood, bowed stiffly to Azi, and walked out. The other ambassadors followed, whispering among themselves.

"I wish you hadn't done that," Azi said, rubbing his face.

"I warned you about the Bardo," Lord Inas said from behind him. "If you don't stand up to her, she'll have them all up in arms."

"This was going to happen sooner or later even without me," Jala said defensively.

"And better for us all if it had happened later," Lord Inas said. "If the challenge had been started by one of the other families. But no, I can smell your father's schemes in this. You wouldn't have thought to do something like this on your own. He had to prove that the Bardo had *power*. Well, he's proven it and frightened everyone else. The Rafa may have fewer ships, but their voice still carries weight."

"They wouldn't dare do anything against my family while I'm the queen," Jala said.

"Maybe not while you're queen, no. But you won't be queen forever. At the rate you're going, maybe not even for very long."

Azi leapt up from his seat. "Uncle!"

"You're right. I won't be queen forever," Jala said hotly. "But on that day the Bardo will still have Two Bones."

Lord Inas shook his head. "You see what you've married, my king? The perfect little puppet."

"I didn't mean for this to happen, but he shouldn't have forced her to challenge. It was stupid. So stupid." Azi rubbed his eyes. "What should I do, Uncle?"

Lord Inas looked at Jala. "Leave us. We have a lot to talk about if we're going to clean up the mess you made."

Azi wouldn't meet her eyes. Suddenly, she wanted nothing more than to be gone from there. It wasn't until she'd made it to her rooms and locked the door behind her that Jala realized she couldn't stop shaking.

Jala watched a flock of messenger birds fly from the manor and disappear in the distance.

The messenger bird she'd requested had fallen asleep waiting for her to speak. She should feel satisfied. She'd done what her father had wanted. Instead she just felt angry. Angry at Lord Inas, at her parents, at the Rafa ambassador for being so stupid and proud. At Azi for not stopping it before it got out of hand. And most of all, angry at herself for feeling like this. *Never regret what you do*, her mother had told her. *You're the queen. What you do is right.* Easy for her mother to say, all the way back on the Second Isle.

"Wake up," she said, poking the bird in the chest. It squawked and tried to bite her finger. She put her hand on the bird's wing and waited for it to settle down, then began her message. "Listen. For Marjani of the Bardo."

"*Marjani of the Bardo*," the bird repeated, mimicking her voice and inflection.

Jala paused. There was too much to say. "I hope you miss me as much as I miss you, because it wouldn't be fair otherwise. I hope you're happy. I imagine you walking the beach looking for shells. It's the right time of year for it, all wind and waves. Try not to get washed away." She toyed with the comb Marjani had given her, picking out some of the hairs caught in its teeth. "Things here aren't exactly the way I thought they'd be."

A knock sounded at her door.

"Damn it," Jala said, taking her hand off the bird.

"*Damn it*," squawked the bird. Jala swore again. She'd have to start the message over now.

"I've brought your dinner, my queen," Iliana called from behind the door.

Jala let her in. She tried to smile, but it felt awkward. "No feast tonight for our honored guests?"

Iliana hesitated. "There is, but the king said that you have a headache and preferred to have dinner in your room tonight. He made your apologies to the other families."

"Am I being punished?"

"I couldn't say, my queen."

Jala snorted. "You mean you won't say." She sat down again and stared out the window. Iliana set the food on the windowsill in front of her. Down on the shore, a circle formed, and someone tucked a small hand-drum under their arm. She watched the wind-dance and wished she could think of what to say to Marjani.

"The wine will grow warm if you wait too long," Iliana said.

Jala looked away from the window. "You're right. I should eat instead of sulk." She poked at the crab meat on her plate. It smelled delicious, but for some reason she had no appetite for it. "Is he very angry with me?"

"It's hard to say. Lord Inas is furious, he makes no secret of that. The king . . ." Iliana hesitated. "He's been different since Prince Jin died. He may be angry, or sad, and yet he looks and acts the same. The day he returned from the Second Isle with you was the first time he looked happy in a long time."

"Well," Jala said. She took a bite of food and made herself chew it. "I suppose today I have a headache."

"Is there anything I can get you?" Iliana asked her. "Mournroot to help you sleep?"

Jala was about to refuse, but the mournroot had given her an idea. "No, thank you. The queen . . . the old queen, I mean. Azi's mother. She's still in the manor, isn't she?"

"She is, until her days of First Mourning are over."

Jala nodded. With her oldest son and husband dead, the old queen's grieving had lasted many months already. "I'd like to join her for dinner. If she's feeling well."

"I'll tell her," Iliana said. She took Jala's plates and left.

Jala waited, watching the sailors and soldiers dancing on the shore. She woke the bird again and touched its wing, and repeated what she'd said before, then added, "I miss you. Fill this bird's head with anything trivial. Tell me what you find on the beach. Tell me how you felt this morning and which of our cousins you're not speaking to." Jala blinked the tears out of her eyes. It was almost too hard to send the message, but she'd promised, and she was already several messages overdue.

"Thank you for the comb. It really is lovely." She snapped her fingers. The bird gave her a tired look, then hopped up on her arm, gripping painfully with its talons. She stuck her arm out the window and jerked it up. "Go!"

The bird took off in a blur of orange and blue. Soon it was nothing more than a speck flying toward the Second Isle.

CHAPTER 9

All anyone could talk about at dinner was what happened at the Sectioning, and Azi was sick of hearing it. He was sure the ambassadors were giving him sideways glances, though they always seemed to be busy eating when he turned to look. And he missed Jala. He'd already gotten used to having her by his side at all of the feasts and dances and speeches, even if they hadn't spoken as much lately.

This is her fault. If she wasn't so . . . so. . . . The words *bold* and *beautiful* kept coming up, which wasn't at all what he meant. She hadn't even waited a day before trying to seize power. *I thought you were different.* His words kept repeating in his head, taking on a mocking tone. Who did he think she was going to be?

He needed to get out of there. "If you'll excuse me, my lords, the food doesn't agree with me tonight." As he made his way past the ambassadors, his uncle smirked at him as if he knew exactly where Azi meant to go. That only made Azi angrier.

Once he was out of the dining hall, Azi removed the King's Earring and stuck it in his pocket. It weighed on him constantly, itching and irritating his ear the way no other earring ever had. But it was more than that. It was the way people looked at him now, as if they only saw what he was and not who he was. People who hadn't given him a second glance, or who'd seen only a second son, a sailor or a shipmate or a friend now saw the king of the Five-and-One Islands. Even without the earring dragging on his earlobe he still felt it there, like a mask he couldn't take off.

He'd thought Jala could see through it, but he'd been deluding himself. When she put on the Queen's Earring, she put on a different mask than he did. It was her father's mask. Maybe his uncle had been right.

He took the servants' entrance out of the manor. The beach was again a long, sprawling party. The drums pounded in his chest, and the bonfires blazed tall and bright, throwing burning ash up into the sky.

There was one person he thought might still remember the old Azi and not this king he'd only just met and barely knew. But she wouldn't be out there on the beach; he was sure of it. She'd be at her mother's cottage, waiting for him.

He stuck to the shadows, though the light from the fire made it impossible to see what was underfoot. He tripped on fallen branches, stones, and a few people who'd decided to sleep off their drink somewhere dark and quiet. The village was only a short walk from the manor, one of many that dotted the coast of the First Isle. Small huts sat almost on the water, fishing boats nearby, while larger cottages sat farther back on a low hill.

More fires lit the way for him, but he didn't need them. He would have been able to walk this path with his eyes closed. His heart was racing by the time he reached the cottage's door and raised a hand to knock. It swung open before him, and she stood in the doorway, her smile bright from the distant firelight.

"Azi," she said, throwing her arms around him. "I waited for you."

"Kona," he said, the name he'd whispered to himself so often in the weeks before he'd met Jala.

"Why haven't I seen you at all since you got back?" Kona looked at him reproachfully. "I stayed up all night yesterday waiting for you, but you never came."

"I'm sorry," Azi said. "There's just so much to do. I couldn't miss the first feast, and there was the Sectioning."

Kona pulled away from him. "And you have a wife now. Some say that the Bardo girl has hooked you, and you'll go whichever way she pulls, but I didn't believe them. I thought it must be some plan of your uncle's. I mean, you're here, aren't you?" Kona smiled.

Azi had never lied to her about anything that mattered before. It was easy not to lie when your life was simple, though. He wanted to lie now. "It wasn't my uncle's idea. He wanted me to marry a Rafa girl. He threatened to leave my side entirely. I told him he couldn't. I ordered him to stay."

You can't stop being my uncle just because you don't want to be, he'd said. *Not unless I say so.* The words had sounded so cold, far colder than he felt. Uncle Inas was his only family except for his mother, and she was leaving him for her Gana family in just a few weeks.

Kona spoke softly. "So it's true. You picked this girl against his will. You *wanted* to marry her."

"I don't know. It wasn't that simple." It had seemed simple enough on the beach with Jala, though, hadn't it? At least, it had until that night with Jala on the barge, when he couldn't stop seeing Kona's face.

"You said you didn't care who your uncle picked for you."

I won't love her, he'd said. *She won't mean anything to me.* So maybe he'd lied after all. Who knew that promises could turn into lies so easily? The truth seemed to change depending who he talked to, slippery as an eel.

"I can't let my uncle be king for me," Azi said. "I have to make my own decisions."

"What's wrong with letting your uncle help you? Even your brother needed his help, and Jin was born to be a king. You were meant to be a sailor, and that's all I ever needed from you."

"You're right," Azi whispered. He didn't push her away. "I love you." He was in his brother's place, where he didn't belong. Not like Jala. Jala was raised to be a queen. *Why are you still thinking about her when you have Kona right in front of you?*

"I love you," he repeated, trying to make it sound real again. It didn't.

He closed his eyes and tried to shut out all the thoughts, the promises, the feelings he couldn't put into words. All the things that were trying to steal this moment from him.

She pulled away, as though she could sense the direction of his thoughts. "Do you love her?" she whispered.

"Yes," Azi whispered back. "I hardly know her, but . . . I think I do. Even when she sounds like her father."

"I see." Kona was quiet for a long time. "Will you still come to see me? We can just talk."

"I will," Azi promised. But neither one of them was sure whether to believe it.

Azi didn't know how long they stood together. Only when the drummers on the beach faltered and stopped did Azi turn to go. Someone was shouting, he realized, and it was more than a drunken argument. A breeze blew in from the manor, carrying with it a strange, sulfurous smell that hung heavy in the air.

"Something's wrong," he said. "What's that smell? I could almost believe the fire mountain was paying us a visit." He stepped away from her. "I should find out what's going on."

"It's probably nothing," Kona said. She touched his arm. "You don't have to go yet."

Azi gently took her hand and squeezed it. "I have to. I'm the king."

CHAPTER 10

J ala heard the drums out on the beach as Iliana led her down the hall and past its many windows. Azi's mother had accepted her dinner invitation. Jala could almost hear her mother saying, *A Bardo queen doesn't attend on others, she doesn't knock on doors and wait to be let in. Everyone is the queen's guest, never the other way around.*

But Jala didn't want a guest, she wanted a friend. It was a lot easier to win arguments when it was only her mother's memory she had to contend with. Jala knew her mother wouldn't have thought twice about the Sectioning. She'd acted the part of a queen her entire life. *So why can't I be like that?* Jala wondered. *What's wrong with me?*

"The queen is here, Lady Chahaya," Iliana said.

"Let her in." The old queen's voice was hoarse, though Jala thought it must have been strong once. "Sit down, my queen. Heh, it feels strange to be addressing someone else like that."

Azi's mother sat at a square table in the center of the room. She was a large woman, but the flesh on her face sagged as though she hadn't eaten well in weeks. Only the half-grin on her face gave her any semblance of life.

"I was wondering if you'd come," Azi's mother said. "I know how lonely it can be to find yourself among the Kayet without friends or family, but I thought you might be too proud to admit it. I was when I first arrived." She laughed. "And now I find myself too proud to want to leave, even though I long to be with family. Remember, Queen Jala of the Bardo, a king is king for life. But there may come a time when you're no longer queen, and you'll need your family again."

"Lord Inas said the same thing," Jala said. "Though I think it was more of a threat." She looked down at her food. "I'm sorry, you're still grieving. I shouldn't have intruded on you with my problems. Things are probably hard enough for you without them."

Azi's mother snorted. "I'm alone on an island filled with Kayet who no longer give a whale's ass about me, and because I'm in mourning I'm not supposed to go anywhere or do anything. Any break from routine is welcome. And I'm curious to meet my replacement, especially after the trouble you caused at the Sectioning."

Jala's face grew warm. "I did what I had to do."

"You never have to do anything, my queen." Azi's mother emphasized the title, as though they both shared some joke together. "If you let them, they'll be more than happy to keep you safe and sound through all the dinners and dances and meetings. Your presence isn't even required at the Sectioning, you know. You'd never have to say or do anything except what's most polite and pleasing."

"I'm not just a pretty decoration for the throne room."

The woman shook her head knowingly. "Of course you don't think you'll be anything of the sort. But what about a year from now? Five years? What about when you're tired, tired of fighting, tired of making mistakes? And you will make them, I promise. Then, oh, then you'll be tempted to close your eyes and let the Kayet do your talking for you."

"Is that what you did?" Jala asked.

Azi's mother chuckled. "Eat your food, little queen. A full stomach doesn't sour, not even when talking to a bitter old woman."

Jala ate, glad for an excuse not to talk. Lady Chahaya, too, was silent for a while. Outside, the distant drums beat slow and steady. Eventually Jala said, "Tell me about Azi."

Azi's mother set down her fork, the meat still on it. "I can't tell you anything you won't find out soon enough. Nothing that would help you understand him. Some days I think I hardly know him myself. He spent so much time at sea." She looked up. The sardonic smile had vanished from her face. Without it, Jala could see how old and tired she really was. A woman who'd recently lost a son, a husband, and a throne.

"One piece of advice. The most important I can give you. The most useless. Don't have a son. A daughter is useless to the Kayet. A daughter carries your name. But any son you bear is Kayet first and foremost." Her voice had fallen to a whisper. She wasn't looking at Jala anymore but past her. "I tried the herbs and the secret dances to make sure I never had a boy . . . well, you see where that got me? I've heard such magic exists on the mainland, but magic is a lot harder to steal than gold and swords and silk. Besides, what man wants to steal such a thing? No matter that they are ruled by their mothers and their queen, that there are women fighting beside them, they all still hope for sons. Pompous, self-obsessed fools."

"You're right," Jala said. "That is pretty worthless advice."

"I think you really might be as dangerous as Lord Inas says," Lady Chahaya said after a while. "But not for the same reason."

Jala was trying to figure out if that was supposed to be an insult or a compliment when the drums outside stopped. The silence hung heavy in the air, only to be broken by shouts a moment later. She went to the window to see what was happening. A heavy fog lay on the water. It seemed to glow with its own light, and strange shadows moved slowly inside it.

"Put out the candles," Jala whispered. Behind her the candles were snuffed out one by one, then Chahaya came to stand next to Jala.

"Those aren't shadows," Jala said, squinting. "They're ships."

Ships made out of brown wood instead of gnarled gray reef, ships without mast or sail. They were flat-bottomed, like barges, completely unsuited to face the waves of the Great Ocean . . . but the ships didn't touch the water at all. It was the fog itself they traveled over, quiet and steady. There was no one on the decks that she could see, but the ships were tall and wide, with plenty of room below deck for . . . who? The fog rolled out over the beach.

Azi's mother sniffed the air. "Can you smell that? It's sorcery," she said.

The lead ship didn't slow, and Jala heard more shouting as the ship beached itself. A shiver ran up Jala's spine. "I think it's an invasion."

CHAPTER 11

J ala smelled the magic now, an acrid smell that burned the back of her throat. How else could anyone have reached their islands without grayships?

Her dinner sat heavy in her belly. She touched the Queen's Earring, running her fingers over the rough surface. Its weight wasn't reassuring now. It was a reminder. It was responsibility. *I have to do something. It's my job now.*

"I have to find the king," Jala said. "Excuse me."

Chahaya nodded, glancing outside again. "All this time I tried to convince myself death wouldn't be a relief, and now it looks like I might die anyway. Ha! Might as well go with a full stomach." She sat down again and continued her dinner.

In the hallways, servants and nobles all ran through the halls, crowding to see out the nearest windows.

"What is it?" a woman asked.

"The Rafa are attacking. Who else could it be?"

"Those aren't Rafa ships. They're hardly ships at all. Wouldn't last an hour on open water."

People still shouted in the manor, but near the windows the talk grew quiet as they waited to see what would happen next. Jala stopped to ask, "Where's the king? Do the captains know of this?"

They stared at her. An older noble with a trim beard raised himself up. "Word has spread. Surely the king has heard."

"But you're not certain. We have to be certain." Jala pointed to three younger nobles. She hoped they couldn't see her hand shake in the dim light. "You three. Go to all of the captains, send boats out to the barges. Make sure they know what's happened, or before long they'll be too drunk to fight." They stared at her, each of them taller than her by at least half a head. She wondered if they were as scared as she was.

They glanced at the older man. He nodded. "She's right. Do as your queen commands."

They ran.

Jala found a maid and pulled her aside. "Where is the king?"

The maid hesitated. "He's in his chambers, my queen. His stomach troubled him."

"Take me to him. Quickly," Jala said. The Kayet manor was massive, three times the size of the manor she'd grown up in. She still wasn't sure of the way to Azi's rooms, and this was no time to get herself lost.

"My queen, he asked not to be disturbed. I couldn't intrude on him."

"Look outside if you haven't already. Whoever those ships belong to, they're not going to wait for his stomach to settle."

The maid looked frightened, but she led Jala down the hall. They turned a few corners, walking past rich tapestries and cloths, swords and tall mirrors. They stopped at a door of dark-red wood from the mainland. Azi's bedroom. This wasn't exactly how she'd imagined first seeing it.

Jala banged on the door. "Azi, are you awake?" When no one answered she pulled open the doors. Azi's rooms weren't quite as lavish as the hallway implied they would be, meant more for actual living instead of showing off. The furniture was made of palm wood, familiar and simple. The empty bed hadn't been slept in.

"Where is he?" Jala asked, turning to the maid.

"Maybe his stomachache passed, my queen. He might have gone down to the ships to drink with the sailors or decided to sleep out on the beach. He says he prefers sand to fine linen. If that's where he went, he must know about these ships already."

Jala banged on the door in frustration. Even as she did she heard her mother's voice in her head. *You're acting like a child, not a queen.*

"My queen?" the maid said. "It's the storm season. Do you really think this could be an invasion?"

"I don't know what this is," Jala said, trying to keep the panic from her voice. "I wish I did. What about Lord Inas? Is he down on the beach somewhere as well?"

"No need to go looking," a voice said from behind her. Azi's uncle held himself up against the wall. His eyes were bloodshot, but an old, notched raider's sword hung from his belt. "Go back to your rooms. You'll be safe there. For a little while, anyway."

Jala stared at him in dismay. "You're drunk."

Inas pushed himself off the wall. "I am not drunk, little queen. I'm in mourning."

Next to her the maid whispered, "Lord Inas does not sleep well at night. He often takes mournroot with his dinner."

"If you're too sick to lead, let someone else do it," Jala said. "Too drunk or too sick, it's all the same right now."

"What do you know of sickness? Of leading? Go and hide. Take the girl with you. There will be fighting in the manor soon." The maid glanced nervously from Inas to Jala.

"You think it's hopeless," Jala said.

"You can't think a human foe would be capable of this. Sorcery enough to move a fleet of ships . . . it would kill a man. A hundred men, a thousand. Who would pay such a price? We won't find men inside those ships, I promise you."

"You can't scare me with stories of sea monsters and demons," Jala said. "I'm not a little girl." But her heart pounded hard in her chest just the same.

Inas leaned down to stare at her face to face. "I think you are a little girl. I think you haven't seen the things I've seen, sailing out of sight of land. You know nothing of the world, though you aspire to rule it."

Jala stepped back but forced herself to meet his eyes. "Azi is out there somewhere. I need you to take command. I'll come with you. My father says sailors should see their lord before braving the Great Ocean, so let them see me now, since the king's misplaced himself."

There was a moment of tense silence. Through the walls, Jala heard the war drums starting. She made herself breathe.

Finally Inas whispered, "Fine. Come along if you insist." He turned away and strode down the hall, only a little unsteadily.

Jala glanced back at the maid. "You're free to go. Find somewhere you feel safe." Then she ran down the hall after Lord Inas. The drums continued, playing over each other with different rhythms, alerting the villages. She wasn't sure how much good it would do. There hadn't been a real war among the islands since the first king and queen, and the mainlanders had no way to reach the islands. Or so they'd thought. Nobody expected anything like this. They weren't ready.

Men gathered in the great hall of the manor. Nobles carried swords that hadn't been drawn in years. No one spoke. Everyone looked tired and grim. Some of the servants and noblewomen helped barricade the windows and doors, others brought lamps and torches. Iliana was arming all of the women with spare swords and kitchen knives.

A man ran up to them and bowed hurriedly. "Lord Inas." He looked at Jala, realized who she was, and bowed again. "My queen. No one's come off the ships. They're just sitting there. Our lookouts on the roof haven't seen anyone on deck."

"You've sent men to our ships?" Lord Inas asked.

"Yes, my lord. A few were already awake. The Nongo planned to attack without waiting for us to combine our forces. Their captain is stupid with bravery. Some of the Gana captains plan to run. They've already raised sail."

"We should burn these ships," Jala said. "Stop them before they can disembark and put an end to it now."

The man shook his head. "We tried, but the fire won't catch. My lord, we can defend ourselves better inside the manor. We can wait, and if no one comes out we'll push them back into the water with the tide. Let the ocean decide what to do with them."

Lord Inas shook his head. "What makes you think they'd attack us here first? There are too many villages along the beach. No, if we're going to face them, we have to move now, combine our strength with the Nongo and board the ships before they're ready."

The closest sailors looked at one another, then nodded. They were Kayet, and the villages around the manor were filled with their family and friends. Jala felt a pang of fear, for a moment regretting her decision to follow Lord Inas. But she couldn't take back what she had said now, not if Lord Inas was ever going to treat her as queen.

"At least then we'll know what these invaders are," Lord Inas said. He pointed to a thin girl who looked barely old enough to be on the crew of a ship. "Namu. Send birds to the other families. If things go badly for us, maybe we can hold out long enough for help to arrive. Help or scavengers."

The girl nodded and ran off.

"The rest of you, we're moving out," Lord Inas called out.

"You're not our captain or our king," one man said stubbornly. "Why should we risk our lives for you?"

Lord Inas drew his sword. "I'm the head of this family in the absence of the king. You'll do as I say."

"I'm not Kayet, and I have my own head, thanks," the man said. Jala looked closer and realized he was a Gana captain.

"We should get to our ship," a Gana woman added. "With good wind we can be home by noon to help our own family."

Lord Inas opened his mouth to speak, but Jala cut him off. "You won't have your head for long, if any of us live through this. I'm here, and I speak with the king's voice. Do as Lord Inas commands. Once the First Isle is safe, you can all go home. The Kayet will send ships to aid whichever family needs them."

Jala held her breath as she waited for him to respond. She didn't know if she had it in her to order a man's death. But luckily the captain kept his mouth shut, though he glared at Jala.

"We'll face them now," Lord Inas said. "We'll give them no time to rest and catch their bearings. We'll keep them trapped on the beach where their feet are uncertain." He pointed to two of the servants. "Open the doors."

They cleared away the makeshift barricade and did as he commanded.

It was pitch-dark outside. "Put out those lamps, damn it," Lord Inas hissed. "We need to see."

The lamps were blown out, the torches taken away. They all followed Lord Inas out into the dark. *If we lose, it won't be any less dangerous inside anyway*, Jala told herself. It didn't help.

The stars above them dimmed as they entered the fog that surrounded the ships. The air became thick and hard to breathe, and the smell made Jala's head swim. As they neared the ships, she realized that the nobleman at the window had been right. These "ships" were little more than wooden boxes, flat-bottomed like the barges the mainlanders used to travel on lakes and rivers.

She wondered if there were more ships coming. How many soldiers could each ship hold? Even more reason to find out what was inside.

Someone called out to Lord Inas. Jala tensed, wondering if this was it, if the fight was starting. But no, Lord Inas called back in greeting. Moments later, more men and women joined them, arriving from the nearest village. They were armed with knives and fishing spears. Jala spotted Azi among them.

She walked toward him as quickly as she could without running. The villagers parted to let her pass. It was embarrassing how relieved she felt to see him.

"Jala," Azi said. "You should be inside where you'll be safe."

"No," Jala said. "I shouldn't. We've gathered nobles from the manor and some of the sailors that were on the beach. But they're tired and drunk, and some are badly armed. A few of the Gana ships have already sailed, and I was afraid others would follow. I couldn't find you, but I thought at least one of us should be here. To help keep the families together."

"I came as soon as I heard," Azi said. "How many in each ship?"

Jala shook her head. "We don't know. Nobody's seen them."

He looked past her. "Damn it, what're they waiting for? They didn't come here just to listen to our drummers."

"Your uncle thinks we need to see who or what's inside, even if they won't come out on their own. He thinks there'll be monsters inside, but he's sick with wine and mournroot."

Azi winced. "Well. My uncle may be a drunk sometimes, but he was my father's right hand. I trust his judgment."

Jala started to respond but was interrupted as Lord Inas reached them and greeted Azi. Azi let go of her hand to take his uncle's.

"My king," Lord Inas said. "The men are ready to board the ships."

Azi nodded. "We can't wait out here all night. Fetch some ladders."

One of the nobles bowed, motioned to two other men, and ran with them back to the manor. When the ladders came, Azi chose one of the outlying ships to try first, saying, "I don't want us to be surrounded." They leaned two ladders against the ship's side. Four sailors held them steady while others climbed up onto the deck.

So close to the ship it was impossible to see what was going on. Jala waited for the clash of metal, for the screams. She hated waiting. Hated not being able to do anything, hated not being wanted. Next to her Azi passed his sword from one hand to the other. "What's taking so long?" he muttered.

A woman's face appeared over the edge. "They're all dead, my king."

"This is no time for jokes, sailor," Lord Inas said.

The woman shook her head. "I wouldn't joke about this, my lord. It's just bodies up here and they're ages dead, it looks like. We checked the hold and it's all skeletons and dust."

Lord Inas scowled. "Dead men don't sail ships. You missed something. They're hiding."

"I'm going up to look," Azi said. "Uncle, send some men to check another ship."

Jala couldn't take it anymore. If she didn't do something, anything, she'd explode. She bunched up her skirts in one fist and started to climb after Azi.

Someone grabbed her ankle. "My queen, wait!" Jala kicked the hand away and climbed on. By the time she reached the top, she was out of breath and her face was hot.

A breeze blew from the ocean, and the scent of sorcery grew stronger. It smelled like something burning, like spices that seemed vaguely familiar but that Jala couldn't name. The smell clung to the back of her mouth and made her nose tingle and her throat burn.

Some of the sailors were gathered around an open hatch, and a few had lit their lamps once more to venture below. The smell was nearly overpowering there, and Jala had to hold her sleeve against her nose to keep from retching. She leaned forward to look inside.

The ship was filled with decaying bodies.

Then Jala blinked and looked again. *They aren't decaying at all. They're . . . dried out.* No maggots, no flies. Just dry, brittle faces and long strands of thin white hair falling over armor that still looked clean and new, faces partly covered by tall helmets with painted eyes, hands holding swords and spears as if they intended to attack at any moment. She watched as a dead man's jaw cracked and fell, shattering on the ground. Dust rose into the air.

Jala looked away. "What are they? Floating tombs?"

One of the men who had taken ladders to the other ship came up behind her. "They're dead on the next ship, too." He peered past her. "Don't look quite so old as these, though."

Jala heard Inas calling out orders as the remaining ships were searched. Suddenly the strength that had kept her going, ready for a bloody fight, left her. She felt giddy and light-headed, and she swayed. She sat down on the deck. Azi emerged from the hold and sat down next to her. "There were enough men here to kill us all twice over. If they'd lived. I wonder what happened to them?"

Jala's head throbbed. Azi's uncle climbed aboard the ship, and she fought a desperate urge to laugh. "It looks like you were wrong, Lord Inas. We've yet to find a single demon on board."

"We'll see," Inas replied. "Azi, they found some still alive."

"What?" Azi jumped to his feet. "How many?"

"Three of them, still breathing. Hurry!"

Azi slid down the ladder, and Jala followed, climbing down as quickly as she could. By the time she'd boarded the last ship they'd already dragged the three invaders up on deck. They were old and withered. One of them stared with huge eyes that darted back and forth. Another, a man who was completely hairless, squinted at everyone through eyes white with cataracts. Their limbs were thin and their backs bent; they didn't have enough strength to hold themselves up in the heavy armor they wore. Azi's uncle ordered them stripped, and they stood naked, each held by two Kayet soldiers.

"Do you recognize the markings on their armor, Uncle?" Azi asked.

Lord Inas shook his head, then turned to the old men. "Who are you? Where did you come from? Speak before we cut out your tongues."

One of the men screamed something in a language Jala couldn't understand. His voice was cracked and raw. Jala's throat hurt just listening to him.

"Can you understand me?" Azi asked.

The man screamed again. The blind man giggled, while the third clutched at the hands that held him.

Azi sighed. He looked as exhausted as she felt. "We'll have to find some of the old traders, see if any of them can speak his language. I don't think it's anything I've ever heard, but it's hard to tell. It all sounds the same when they're screaming at you. Uncle?"

"First let's make sure that they're human." He pointed toward the third man. "That one won't last the night anyway. Let him go." The sailors holding him obeyed and stepped back. The man fell to his knees and started to crawl.

Lord Inas drew his sword and with one quick strike cut off the man's head. There wasn't even time to look away. Blood spurted over the deck, and in the silence that followed Jala could still hear the crack of his spine.

"They bleed," Inas whispered. "That's good." He handed the sword to one of the sailors to clean and ordered the body tossed into the water. Then he pointed at the last two invaders. The wide-eyed man was still rambling in his broken voice, staring at the body. "Take them to the manor and leave them in the basement. Make sure you tie them up tight and don't drop them on the way down. They don't have many falls left in them."

Each of the invaders was picked up by a sailor and hauled over their shoulders like a bunch of twigs. They couldn't have weighed much. Azi's uncle went after them. As he went past, she thought he looked a little smug. "Sleep well, my queen."

Azi took her hand and helped her step onto the ladder. After that, everything seemed to happen in a sort of dream. She walked with him back to the manor. At the top of the stairs Azi took her hand again, for just a moment, before letting her go. The stairs seemed longer now. It took forever for her to get to the top, and she felt as though she would fall asleep as soon as she lay down. But instead she sat staring at the wall, trying to ignore the smell of magic that invaded her rooms with each breath of wind.

CHAPTER 12

B y the next day, only charred lumps marred the sand where the invading ships had been. Someone—many someones—must have been busy all night.

Jala was already awake when Iliana knocked softly at her door.

"Good morning, my queen," Iliana said. There were bags under her eyes, and her hair was wrapped haphazardly around two combs. She carried a wide wooden bowl, a cup, and two towels.

"You look like you didn't sleep well either," Jala said.

Iliana tried to smile. "It was a long night. For once I felt grateful that my room doesn't face the water. I think it'll be a while before the sound of the ocean can lull me to sleep like it once did." She set the water down on the table next to Jala's bed, then opened Jala's chests and closets and held out dresses, shirts, tunics, and pants for Jala to choose from. "You were there, weren't you, my queen? You saw the old men in the demon boats?"

Jala leaned over the bowl and splashed the cold water over her face. "I saw them. Is Azi awake? I'd like to have breakfast with him. If he wants." She didn't want to be alone. But she couldn't tell Iliana that. She had to look strong, even if she didn't feel strong, or she didn't know if she could make herself leave her rooms.

"I'll find out for you." Iliana held up a dark-purple dress. "Perhaps this one?"

"Maybe . . . maybe something brighter," Jala said. "I want to set the mood for the day, not the other way around."

The clothes she finally chose were cheerful shades of yellow and blue. The dress had been cut and sewn with another one to show off the different styles, and the top flowed down her arms on one side and opened up on the other. Washed and dressed, Jala felt a little more like herself.

Jala thanked Iliana, and the woman left, taking the bowl and towels with her.

With nothing to do but wait, Jala picked up the book the Nongo had given her, hoping the pictures would distract her. The stories became clearer as she studied the illustrations. There was one about a young boy who made some toy people out of clay, only to have them come to life when he breathed on them. His toys began to fight among themselves, and he left them in the sun only to have them dry and crack. He reminded Jala of the Thoughtless Boy who was the hero of so many island stories.

Soon Iliana returned. "The king is awake and would be happy to have you join him."

Jala followed her down the stairs and to the Kayet nobles' wing of the manor. As they walked, Jala said, "Last night, I went to Azi's rooms when the invaders came, but he wasn't there. What was he doing in the village last night?"

Iliana hesitated just a moment too long. "I wouldn't presume to know the king's business, my queen."

She's lying, Jala thought. Most likely every servant in the manor knew every noble's business. But though she might only be a servant, Iliana had been born on the First Isle, and that made her a cousin of the Kayet. They were still family to her, and Jala couldn't expect her to gossip about her family—her king—to a stranger. Jala decided to let it go for now.

The door to Azi's room was open. Azi rose from the table to greet her. "You look beautiful for someone who hasn't had any sleep."

Jala tried to smile at him as she sat at the table, but she didn't think it was very convincing. "Did you manage to find someone to talk to the two men who were still alive?" She tried to avoid staring at the scar running down Azi's head. It had seemed dangerous and exciting before, but now it just reminded her how close Azi had come to being killed, then and now. How easily they all could have been killed.

Azi shrugged. "One of the old men came and tried, but he says they don't speak any language he's ever heard of. They don't even seem to understand the traders' cant. He thinks they've gone mad. They don't look at you if you talk to them, just keep repeating their nonsense. I think we should let them die, but my uncle wants to keep them around."

"They weren't old when they sailed, were they? Their weapons and armor were still good. And I saw their spears and swords. They weren't just ornaments."

He nodded. "It was madness to try and use sorcery to cross the Great Ocean. They'd have been better off swimming." Azi gestured for her to sit down. When he'd joined her, he swept a hand to encompass their surroundings. "These were my father's rooms, you know. I hate eating here alone. It still feels like I'm intruding. Jin was the one who spent all his time here, learning from our father. I wish they were here now." His eyes met hers, and she saw past the king to Azi, lost and unsure. "We aren't prepared for this. We aren't prepared at all."

"Does that mean you think more will come?"

"I think they already have. Birds from the Nongo arrived an hour ago. Two ships landed on the Fourth Isle. The Nongo say the things they found inside one of the ships weren't human anymore, but the men on the second were alive and well. The nobles barricaded themselves inside their manor and prepared a counterattack while their villages were burned."

Jala forced herself to speak. "And the Second Isle? My family?"

Azi shook his head. "I've sent birds to all of the islands, but it'll be at least a day before we hear anything."

Jala thought of the Bardo manor, of her home. Two guards at the gates, a few more inside, just to keep someone from running off with her father's best mainlander wine. She thought of Marjani walking on the beach in the quiet hours.

She imagined the bird reciting her message to corpses. Jala stood, knocking her chair back. "I have to go. I'm sorry."

Azi took hold of her arm. "There's nothing you can do right now. Eat with me. We'll both need our strength." He looked like he wanted to say more, but instead he stood and picked up her chair.

Trembling, Jala let him guide her back to her seat. When she looked down at her food, Jala found she was hungrier than she knew and finished her breakfast quickly while Azi picked at his food. After a few minutes of silence, she decided this wasn't the time to ask if she could have what he didn't eat.

"What do you know of sorcery?" Jala asked.

"What everyone knows, I guess. It's dangerous and unpredictable, and the price for whatever you want is usually too high."

"But dangerous means powerful, too," Jala said. "Maybe we should try to learn more about it. We might use it to protect ourselves somehow. Everyone says there are sorcerers living on the Lone Isle. Maybe they can tell us something about these invaders and their magic."

"All you'll find on the Lone Isle are madmen who listen to voices on the wind."

Jala sighed. Azi was probably right. If there were sorcerers on the Lone Isle, they must not have much power. She'd never heard of them using it, anyway. "Well, you said these invaders were mad. Maybe madmen can tell us about them. We have to do something. We can't just wait until they're burning my home and killing my family."

"We don't know that they came to the Second Isle," Azi said gently.

"They came here. This is my home too," Jala said. "We have to send ships to the other islands in case they need help. Not just the Second, all the others. I can go to the Lone Isle while you take care of things here."

"Jala, what are you talking about? I can't let you go to the Lone Isle. It's dangerous. And we don't have enough ships to reach every family. Once we know which family needs help most, we can start sending ships."

"By then it might be too late."

Azi grimaced, his hand clenched around his fork. "I know. Damn it, I know, but we can't just send the ships off at random. Once we know how many invading ships there were, where they landed, what they're *doing* here . . ."

He stopped, but Jala seized on the opening. "So we have to know more about the attacks and the invaders. And if not me, who? You'll need Lord Inas here. None of the nobles will go. I can't do anything to help you here."

"But I want you here with me," Azi said. "And what if something happened to you on the Lone Isle?"

"I'll have a ship full of sailors with me. What can happen?" She tried not to think about all the answers that suddenly popped into her head. *At least he cares enough about me to be worried.*

They sat in silence for a minute, then Jala said, "Will you at least send ships to the Second Isle? Please. I'm worried about my family. You know what it's like to lose someone you love."

"I don't know if I ever loved my father," Azi said. "But yes, I know what it's like."

"Then send the ships," Jala said. "And let me go to the Lone Isle. I feel so helpless just sitting here."

It took Azi a long time to respond. "All right. I'll send them. And you don't need my permission to go to the Lone Isle, you know that. Just . . . promise me you'll come back safely. I don't want to do this without you."

CHAPTER 13

"Have you ever been to the fire mountain?" Jala asked Captain Natari as the crew dragged his grayship into the water. This wasn't like the Kayet barge she and Azi had sailed in but a raiding ship, long and thin and sleek. The coral that made up the hull was still sharp in many places, and the sailors had to place their hands carefully to keep from cutting themselves on it.

"Once," the captain said. He was a short, powerfully built man, with a serious face and a deliberate, thoughtful way of speaking. "There was sorcery in my sister. She dreamed of the Lone Isle, heard it whispering to her. She begged my parents to take her. She threatened to run away and swim there herself. By then my parents were scared of her. I went with them when we left her on the beach. I didn't see much of it. I just remember the smoke overhead from the mountain."

Jala tried to imagine what it would be like to be abandoned on the Lone Isle, watching your family sail away without you, but it was too much.

"Do you think she's still alive?"

"If she is, I hope she doesn't remember me. She was barely five then, and I avoided her. I suppose I was a little afraid of her, too. She'd be about fifteen, now." The captain was silent for a moment, then added, "I've never heard whispers or dreamed of the Lone Isle, if you're worried about that."

"I wasn't," Jala said. "And is the island truly full of sorcerers?"

"There were people there," Natari said. "But I don't know if they were all sorcerers or not. Some of them must have families, and some of those children must be born as normal as either of us." He sniffed the air. "There's a storm coming. It may pass us by, but we'll have steady wind, and in the right direction. Should take us half a day to get there, but it won't be comfortable."

"I've traveled on raiding ships before, Captain," Jala said. "My father made sure I knew my way around a ship."

Natari only smiled at her. "Raiding ships, perhaps. But you've never been on *my* ship."

Iliana emerged from the manor carrying a large basket on each shoulder, followed by two other women who brought small casks of wine. Iliana set the baskets on the ground near Jala. "Food enough for several people. Where are we going?"

"The Lone Isle," Jala said.

Iliana's easy smile disappeared. "My queen, perhaps I might stay here? The mountain's been angry lately."

"You're needed, I'm afraid," Jala said. "Whatever we learn there, you can tell the Kayet and they'll believe you."

Iliana looked around to the women who'd come with her, as if they could get her out of this somehow, but neither of them met her eyes.

"I don't look forward to being there either," Jala said. "We won't stay long."

Iliana took one last look behind her at the Kayet manor, as if she wanted nothing more than to flee. But then she lifted up the baskets of food again, and jerked her head over to the ship, signaling the women with the wine to follow. They sloshed through the water while Jala took off her sandals. The sailors took the supplies from them, then lifted Iliana aboard.

Jala hiked up her dress until it hung about her knees, then walked across the sand, shivering as the cold waves slapped against her legs. A wind blew from the ocean, spraying water into her face, so that by the time she reached the boat her dress was wet and her lips tasted of salt. Captain Natari helped her onto the ship.

"Thank you," Jala said as she straightened her dress. She looked around at the crew. "I've brought food and wine from the king's personal store. The sooner we get to the fire mountain, the sooner we can open it, my friends."

Captain Natari called for the ship to be pushed out. Oars were dropped into the water, and the ship jerked forward. Once away from the shore, they raised the sail. The wind, which had felt pleasant on the island, battered the sails, and the First Isle receded quickly. The ship rocked as it broke over a wave and landed hard in the water, and the shipwood trembled under her feet.

Natari grinned widely. "How do you like the *Burst Hull*, my queen? Is she fast enough for you? It may be a rough trip back if we get caught by the storm."

"As long as we make it back in one piece," Jala said. "And by then someone should know what's happened on the Second Isle."

"I hope so. I wish I was heading back myself." Natari shook his head. "I hope you find some answers."

Behind them, two of the sailors began arguing loudly.

"I told you they found men made of gold in there, but the damn Kayet don't want to tell anyone so they can keep it all for themselves."

"What about those two old mud-sailors they brought out? Didn't look gold to me."

"I didn't say that was all they found, did I?"

"It's demons they found in there. I heard one of the Kayet talking about them."

"Demons and invaders, it's all to keep anyone from getting on those ships and taking the treasure."

Jala wished the ships had contained treasure. If they had, would anyone have told her? Azi would have, she knew that much. Jala turned her attention away from the sailors' conversation and saw a thin column of smoke rising from the top of the fire mountain. "Looks like she's awake today, Captain."

Natari nodded. "Let's hope she isn't angry, as well."

One of the sailors brought out a small hand-drum and started a quick, bouncing rhythm. "What tale should we tell on this long trip?" he asked, and the other sailors took turns calling out stories to the beat. The drummer rejected each, usually insulting whoever had suggested it in the process: "Too long for you, you'll be retired before it's through" or "We've heard it too many times, but then, our brains don't leak like yours."

"The Thoughtless Boy and the Fire Mountain," Jala called out on the beat.

"Ah," the sailor said, nodding his head to her, "as every storyteller who still has a head knows, it pays to oblige a queen." As always, the story started out "There was a boy who couldn't remember his own family's name, who thought little and then only of himself." But from there the storyteller did what he wanted. This time the Thoughtless Boy was captain of a rowboat, and he traveled the islands trying to remember what his favorite foods were and finding adventure instead. One day he found the Lone Isle, and he climbed to the top of the fire mountain where a piece of cork had been set into the mouth. A tree grew from the cork, and on that tree was the fattest, juiciest mango the Thoughtless Boy had ever seen. It was, in fact, one of the fruits that could make a man immortal if he ate it, and it had taken root in the cork when one of the Four Winds spat out a seed on his way to the mainland.

The Thoughtless Boy tried to take one of the mangoes, but the fruit wouldn't come off, so he pulled and pulled even though the tree begged him not to. Until, finally, he pulled out the cork, and the fire mountain exploded with a thousand years of pent-up fire, creating more islands in the process. The Thoughtless Boy was burned all over, and he would have died, except that in his greed he'd eaten the whole fruit before he even realized he was on fire. The liquid fire of the mountain burned away his immortality, but he survived. The fruit of immortality, he decided afterward, was his third-favorite food in the world.

"Luckily our queen has brought us food from the king's own table," the storyteller said, bowing again, "so we shouldn't have that kind of problem."

Jala clapped with the others and waited for more. In this way the time passed, if not quickly, then at least steadily. When she remembered to look back at the Lone Isle, she found the fire mountain looming ahead of them, the smoke that had seemed a thin wisp before now a great black cloud above them. By the time they actually reached the island, her body was stiff and aching from standing for so long, and the first storyteller had long since stepped down and been replaced by a drummer, and then by another storyteller.

The captain called out, interrupting their diversion. "Landing, sails at half." One of the sailors let the sail go slack. The rest got out the oars. "We'll come in slow and row down to that village." Natari pointed, and Jala could just make out a cluster of grass huts and some fishing boats. Large turtles sunned themselves on the beach's black sand.

As they neared the shore, a small crowd gathered to watch their approach. "Don't draw your weapons unless you have to," Natari said.

Then he and his men jumped over the side, splashing into the shallow water at the shore. They helped Iliana down, then Jala.

Jala walked slowly through the water. From the First and Second Islands, the fire mountain had always been something of a comfort to her. Mysterious and awe-inspiring but also familiar and safely distant. Standing beneath it was different. The mountain's shadow lay dark and oppressive over thick jungle, and the heavy black smoke pouring out from its mouth was stark even against the storm-gray sky. How could anyone stand to live under that presence? But then, the people living here had no choice, did they? It wasn't as though her own family was offering them a home among the Bardo.

Men and women armed with spears and clubs stood in a semicircle on the beach ahead of them. From the way people talked about the fire-islanders back home, Jala had almost expected to find everyone running around half naked, chanting and casting spells. She might have been walking into a Bardo fishing village, if you didn't count the weapons. And of course she wouldn't have needed an armed guard to visit a fishing village.

An old man led the group of fire-islanders. He walked with a bent back, and his face and arms were covered in burns, angry patches of pink bright against his dark skin. "And who are you, girl, that you come armed to our village?" he asked. "Or have you been brought here? The daughter of some lord who's afraid of the voices that speak to you?"

Jala cleared her throat and tried to sound, if not like a queen, then at least like her mother. "I am Jala, queen of the Five-and-One islands. I've heard that the people who live on the Lone Isle are sorcerers. I need knowledge that only sorcery can give me."

"Hello to you, Jala who calls herself queen. My name is Kade. As for sorcerers, well, maybe some of us are. Maybe I am. But sorcery has a price. You won't get any easy answers this way."

Jala felt her put-on queen's voice slipping. "I wouldn't have come if we'd any other choice."

The old man scratched the rough hairs on his chin. "Well, I admit I'm curious, so perhaps I'll hear you out. I don't promise anything more, though. Come, we can sit inside and talk. Bring a guard if you must, but more than one won't fit in my cottage."

The old man turned and walked away from the beach.

Natari touched Jala's shoulder. "I'll come with you."

"No," Jala said. "It has to be Iliana."

Natari started to speak, but Jala said, "If they want to harm me they will, whether you're there or not." She felt more at ease commanding her father's men. Her father's will backed up whatever she said, so they were inclined to listen. Jala wondered who they would obey if her father contradicted one of her commands.

"I would feel better by your side," Natari said. "I'll stay close with the rest of the men."

Jala nodded thanks, then hooked her arm around Iliana's and followed the old man. Once past their armed reception, Jala saw that huts and cottages lined the end of the beach and back into the thick jungle that ran up the skirts of the fire mountain.

"My father told me you can sometimes feel the mountain breathing," Jala said. "That the whole island shakes."

"It's true," the old man said. "She hasn't breathed for months, but I remember when she breathed many times a day." He stopped and pointed. "You see, there? Where all the trees are missing? Fire rolled down the hill, burning everything it touched. Luckily it rained, or we'd have all been burned. It's happened before. Likely it'll happen again."

Jala shivered. "I hope I won't need to wait that long for answers."

The old man snorted, then gestured at a small cottage. "This is my home, come inside and sit. It's not like the grand halls you're used to, and I'm sure our food won't be to your taste, but we live simply here."

He was right. The cottage was cramped. Clay jars stoppered with leaves filled the shelves that lined its walls. A table and two chairs took up the middle of the room, and against one wall was a fire pit lined with clay bricks. A bed of dried grass filled the far corner.

"Your girl is welcome to sit on the bed, if she likes. I don't think it has any bugs, but I don't have much use for it these days."

Iliana glanced at the straw and quickly shook her head. "I'll stand."

Jala sat down at the table. "You said these were your people?"

"They listen to me, sometimes, so right now I speak for them." The old man lowered himself into the chair. "Tell me what you want, little queen."

"There was an invasion," Jala said. "Or an attempt, anyway. Their ships sailed on fog, above the water. It could only be sorcery. The men inside the ships that reached the First Isle looked like they'd been dead for years, but some of the other ships had live men or things that were no longer men at all. We don't know who they are or if they'll come again or how many there might be."

"Hmm. Perhaps I can help you answer these questions," Kade said. "But to bring ships and men across the Great Ocean without shipwood to guide them . . . such power is never free. It would have cost many lives, and it's clear they still couldn't control all that power they called forth. The dead men on those ships were probably young and strong when they set out, till the magic sucked the life right out of them."

Jala shivered. "We'd guessed as much."

The old man's gaze wandered out to the beach. "Have you brought anything of theirs?"

With a sinking feeling, Jala shook her head. "I didn't know I had to."

"My queen." Iliana stepped forward. "I have something. It isn't much." She reached inside a fold in her dress and pulled out a clump of white hair. She set it down on the table. "It's from one of the prisoners. Some of the sailors have been selling it, and my mother asked for some."

The old man picked up a strand of hair and inspected it. He smiled, and Jala was surprised to see that he still had all his teeth. "Yes, very good. This will do nicely."

"Thank you, Iliana," Jala said with relief. She didn't ask what Iliana's mother had wanted the hair for. She decided she probably didn't want to know. "So do you think you'll be able to tell us anything? We should hurry."

"You can hurry if you like, but it'll take me time to prepare. And before I do that, we still need to talk about the price. Not the price the magic takes from me, but my price for helping you."

Jala nodded. "Tell me what you want. If your requests are fair, the king will pay."

Kade smiled. "I want spices from the mainland. Fish and birds and roots get old even faster than I do. And wine, too, anything not made from grass or coconut. Something new to wake an old tongue."

So little? She nodded again. "Of course. We'll bring you casks of our best wines and enough spices for everyone living here, if you plan to share."

"Then we have a deal." He grabbed a clay jar and poured a heap of finely ground meal on a wide leaf. "Stone root," he explained. "You can find it near the top of the mountain if you know where to look. It doesn't burn, you see. Not easily. Nasty, bitter-tasting stuff, though you get used to the taste eventually."

"Why eat it at all, then?" Jala asked.

He grinned. "It coats your tongue and throat. An unpleasant feeling, to be sure, but the potions I make can burn away a man's voice and tongue. Because I like to talk, I put up with the taste."

They said nothing for a while. Jala tried not to think of her throat being burned away. Suddenly the silence was broken by shouts, and then a scream. With surprising speed the old man was out of the cottage. Jala followed. Nearby, a woman held down a stick-thin man with a patchy beard on his face and leaves and grass in his hair. His skin was blotchy with scars and old burns. He struggled in vain against the woman's grip.

"I found him skulking in your garden, Kade," the woman said.

The thin man stopped struggling. He smiled up at the old man, revealing cracked teeth. "I helped plant that garden. I have as much right to it as you, and I need supplies for my work."

"Piss on your work, Askel," Kade said. "You were spying."

"Who is he?" Jala asked.

"No one. A petty thief."

Askel snorted, then looked at Jala. His pupils were too wide, and she found his stare uncomfortable. "He lies, my queen. I can help you. He's frightened of the fire mountain, frightened of my power, of what I could do if I didn't have to spend my days in hiding."

"Shut him up," Kade said.

The woman pounded her fist against Askel's head. He grunted and then hung limp, his eyes glazed.

"Good." The old man waved a hand dismissively. "Hang him over the mountain."

The woman nodded and dragged Askel away. But before she'd

gotten far, Askel twisted and slipped down through her arms. He kicked her in the stomach then ran. A few fire-islanders gave chase, but the thin man was faster than he seemed and disappeared into the jungle before any of them were even close.

Kade cursed loudly and ran to the woman to make sure she was all right. When he and the woman had yelled and cursed long enough, he returned to Jala.

"Just a thief, was he?" Jala said. "Nothing else?"

"Our island isn't your concern. Don't you have more important questions? Come."

Jala and Iliana followed the old man back into the cottage. Kade took four jars down from the shelves along the wall and brought them to the table. Using a smooth stone and a wooden bowl, he ground the ingredients together with more stone root. He built a small fire in the brick hearth and set the bowl above it. The flames licked at the wood, the bowl smoked, and the ingredients hissed. The cottage started to reek, and Jala was grateful for the wind that blew through the uncovered doorway and windows.

Kade added the invader's hair last, then poured a dark liquid over it. It foamed, spilling over the lip of the bowl. He picked up the concoction and drank.

"Now we wait," he said in a hoarse voice. "It shouldn't be long. The recent past is usually the easiest to see." He coughed, then gasped and doubled over, clutching his sides. Jala dropped to her knees beside him and slid an arm around his back to hold him up. She could feel him struggling to force air into his lungs. Her mind raced. Had something gone wrong? She'd have to make him throw up. She'd seen it done before, just stick a leaf or a finger down his throat.

"Iliana, help me."

The old man tried to push her away. "Be silent . . . I need to concentrate, or I'll forget everything I see." He held out a shaking hand. "Take me to my bed, then leave me be."

For what felt like a long time, Jala and Iliana sat at the table, with only the sound of his shallow breathing and the patter of rain outside for company. Captain Natari came to see if Jala was all right, and she told him she was. The old man still looked like he was dying. His skin had turned a sickly gray, and his face was sweaty and tense. Eventually he fell asleep.

"Should I wake him?" Iliana whispered.

Jala shook her head. "Let him sleep. Natari will want to wait for this storm to end anyway." They sat together at the table. The drumming of the rain made Jala sleepy, and she found herself nodding.

A soft rustling near the door made her sit up with a start. The wind whistled as it blew through the cottage, and the sky was dark, though Jala didn't think it was night yet. Rain lashed against the walls of the cottage and sprayed in through the door and windows. The old man was still asleep. Iliana dozed as well, leaning against a wall with her knees pulled up to her chest.

A shadow crouched in the doorway. "My queen," it hissed.

Trying to stay calm, Jala peered at it through the gloom. It was the man she'd seen them drag away, the thief the old man had called Askel. Water ran in heavy rivulets down his face and arms.

No one'll hear if I cry for help, Jala realized. She stood slowly, feeling behind her with one hand to try to get a grip on the stool. "What do you want?" she said.

Askel lowered his head to the ground. "Please, my queen. Please help me. They hunt me day and night. I eat bugs when I can't steal anything better." He looked up. "I have work I should be doing, great work. Take me with you. I'm a greater sorcerer than he can ever be. I'm not afraid of power the way he is. I can help you."

Jala made herself take a deep breath, trying to gather her thoughts. "Even if I wanted to, how could I? I have only a few men with me. I can't risk their lives for you."

"My life is worth a hundred of theirs, my queen. I promise you."

"They're family," Jala said. "No outsider is worth more than family."

"Perhaps you need a demonstration," Askel said. "Something to make you believe how dangerous I can be." He grinned, and his eyes rolled to the back of his head. He moaned. Then he straightened, and in the dark he suddenly looked less withered than he had before. The way the shadows fell across him made his arms and chest seem to be knotted with muscles that hadn't been there, and the raindrops turned to steam when they touched him.

Next to her Iliana stood, too. "My queen, we should call for the captain."

Then Kade stirred, and Askel ran, vanishing into the storm.

Jala let him go without protest. She'd come here for information, not to step in the middle of a sorcerer and his rival. She went to Kade. "What did you see?"

The old man took a shaking breath and blinked several times as though he couldn't focus. She thought she could see new lines on his old, weathered face.

Finally, the old man spoke. "An ocean, not of water but of sand, along a great river. There is a city there, and seven people in masks, with brown skin instead of black. I heard them in my dreams, and they called themselves the Hashon. I followed the river for many hundreds of miles, until it split off and became a brook, and then a mountain stream. And in the mountain was a hidden city overlooking a sea. The Hashon kept a book there that told of the world's beginning, but the book was gone, the city in ruins." The old man shut his eyes and breathed deeply. "You stole it, didn't you? The book is sacred to them, as sacred as the shipwood is to you. They won't stop. Hundreds died to bring these ships here, and they died willingly. More ships will come."

"Can you use your magic to stop them?" Jala asked.

"Can you stop a wave by throwing rocks at it? You think because you manage to steal some scraps from the mainland that your people matter, but you're nothing more than flies to them. Or you were. Now you've bitten them and they mean to swat you for it."

Iliana bristled. "How dare you insult us like that? Our grayships are feared up and down the mainland coasts. There is nothing these mainlanders don't have that we couldn't take."

"Shut up and listen, both of you," Kade said. "Understand, for once, how small you are. Among their empire, your entire race could disappear. Even if I sacrificed whole islands, I would be powerless against them."

"Then what do we do?" Jala asked.

"Don't you understand? Do nothing, for all I care. It'll all be the same in the end."

It can't be that bad, Jala told herself. *He's trying to scare you.* Well, it had worked. She couldn't help imagining more ships heading toward them even now, filled with living warriors instead of the dead and dying. Living warriors, or worse. *But they're not demons, not the way Lord Inas thought. They're people. Or at least they were before they sailed.* She had to remember that, no matter how much they scared her. People could be bargained with. She just had to reach them before they sailed, that was all. There had to be a way.

The old man shut his eyes, and Jala thought he was going to fall asleep again, but then he grabbed her arm. "Help me up, island queen."

Jala pulled him up carefully. He stared out into the darkness for a minute, then sighed. "I suppose you and your people can stay until the storm passes. But after that, you'll take your ships and leave. I wish you luck, though I have no love for you, little queen. I need to be alone now. I will take you to Yambi's home. She'll stay awake and make sure that the thief doesn't bother you again."

Without waiting for a reply, he walked out into the rain. Jala hesitated a moment, then followed him. She stumbled immediately, buffeted by the wind. One hand trying to keep her dress under control, Jala held out the other for Iliana. The woman took it, and together they followed the old man. He swayed back and forth slowly as he walked but otherwise didn't seem to feel the wind at all.

They were soaked by the time they reached the nearest hut. Yambi turned out to be the woman Askel had kicked, and she stood as they entered. She exchanged hushed words with Kade, gave them a sour look, then took up the spear resting on one wall.

"You may sleep," she said. "I will watch over you."

Satisfied, Kade left, and the woman said nothing more. Jala and Iliana sat down on the floor together, wet and miserable.

"I don't know how he expects us to sleep after what he told us," Iliana whispered.

"We had to learn this sooner or later, though. If we even believe him."

"I believe him," Iliana said.

Jala sighed. "Me too." She made no move to try to fall asleep, though she knew she must have drifted off eventually because she didn't remember night falling, nor the storm easing into steady rainfall. The next time she woke, it was to a sunbeam in her eyes. The storm had passed, and the new day was rising brilliant and orange out of the Great Ocean. Natari came to her and told her that they were ready to sail again.

The storm had been severe enough that they'd been forced to beach the ship and take cover on land. Now the sailors pushed it out into the water with Jala and Iliana on board. One by one they climbed into the ship, then set sail.

A cold, steady wind blew across the water. It would have made for quick sailing had they sailed with it, but it happened to blow from the First Isle, and so they zigzagged into the wind in order to keep moving. The journey back took longer than the journey there had, and the wet night had left everyone tired, but the sailors seemed more at ease now that they were putting the fire mountain behind them.

"Did you find out what you needed to, my queen?" Natari asked Jala after a while.

"I learned a lot," Jala said. "But I don't know what good it'll do us." She hoped Azi would know what to do.

She went to see him as soon as they landed on the First Isle, not even bothering to change her clothes. By now there must have been news from her family. She knocked on the door of his room.

"Come," he said, his voice faint.

She opened the door and saw him pacing up and down the length of his room, his face twisted up in obvious worry. He looked up at her and stopped.

"Jala. You're back."

Something was wrong. Something had happened while she was gone. Her throat felt tight, and she could hardly get the words out. "My family. Has something happened to them?"

Azi shook his head. "No, no, they're fine. You even have a message from your friend. What was her name again? Marjani? The bird is waiting in your room. Did you find out anything useful from the people on the Lone Isle?"

They were safe. Marjani, her mother, her father. They were all safe. But Azi's smile looked forced. "What's wrong?" she asked.

Azi looked away, toward the window that looked out on the coast. "It's the Gana, my mother's family. We've had no word from them. I'm sending a ship to find out what's happened. Maybe it's the storms. Sometimes birds do get lost or just slowed down. It could be anything."

"It could," Jala agreed. The last thing she wanted was for him to leave her behind, but she'd be useless if there was fighting. And just like she'd had to go to the Lone Isle, he had to do this. Even if she'd only just gotten back. Even if all she wanted was to ask him to hold her and make all of this go away. But she didn't ask.

"Go, then," she said. "Call back the ships you sent to my family, but don't wait for them. Take all the Kayet ships, take Captain Natari's ship, and go. And hope it isn't too late."

CHAPTER 14

"Land," the lookout cried from the front of the ship. Then, "Fire!" Azi followed the lookout's gaze, but it took him a several moments before he could clearly make out the thick column of dark gray smoke rising high into the air.

"Maybe the lightning set something on fire," Azi said.

"Hmm," Captain Paka said, standing beside him. He was a tall, broad man who seldom used his deep voice when he didn't need to.

"Even if these invaders, these Hashon, landed on the Fifth Isle, we don't know how things went," Azi said. "They might be burning the bodies. The ships too."

"Too much smoke," Paka said. He fingered the hilt of his sword.

Soon Azi could make out a sliver of beach beneath the smoke, the white sand turned gray from the ash. He resisted the urge to ask the captain how much longer before they landed. He'd sailed on ships all his life; he knew how far away they were. The beach and the smoke seemed to draw closer impossibly fast.

Once you pass the reef, they'll look to you. On the water, a ship's captain was king, but inside the reefs he was their king. At least they were all Kayet soldiers. They trusted him and would probably obey. In a way, though, that only made it worse. Their lives would be in his hands. *And if the mainlanders really did land on the Fifth Isle, you might not be able to hold on to them all.*

He wanted to curse Jala for making him send away half his fleet to protect her family. True, the Bardo were closer to the Gana, but it would take time for the bird to find them. How long before they arrived to help? A day? Two days? They had no way of knowing. *What would you have done, if it was your family?* He wanted to curse her, but he couldn't. *She was there with you on the beach, ready to fight if she had to. Ready to lead.*

The single plume of smoke soon became many. Off to their left, some fishing huts lay burnt and smoldering. Bonfires raged in a few spots on the beach, and smoke rose from the trees farther back. Some kind of debris lay all over the beach.

"The rain should have put the fires out," Paka said. "They're setting new ones."

There were figures on the beach. They flailed about, swinging their long arms at the ground. Azi saw flashes of metal. "Can you tell who they're fighting?"

"Ghosts?" Paka said.

Azi couldn't tell if the captain was joking. "I've never seen anyone fight with a sword in each hand before. What are they doing?"

The lookout made a choking sound. "Bodies. Those're bodies all over the place, and they're . . . they're attacking them. Why would they attack them if they're already dead?"

The island was coming fast now, and Azi could see it for himself, though he didn't understand any more than the lookout. They were hacking at the bodies with their swords. Quick, steady overhand chops. He scanned the beach until he spotted the Gana manor, situated farther back from the water. He squinted, and a movement caught his eye. One of the invaders was pacing on the roof.

Azi pointed. "They've taken the manor."

Paka nodded. "We're passing the reef now, my king. Do we anchor and wait for the other ships to arrive?"

Azi turned to look at the man, but his face was unreadable. Was this a test of his courage, or was the stone-faced captain truly unsure, maybe even afraid? *I know I am.*

"No. We won't wait while they do such things, while they crawl like vermin through our cousins' homes. We stop them now."

Captain Paka nodded. "Yes, my king." Then in his booming voice he cried out, "Swords ready! Landing, full wind." All around them sailors and soldiers loosened their swords and grabbed hold of the bulwark to brace for the impact. Azi did the same. *Full wind.* They weren't dropping sail but beaching the ships at full speed. The maneuver always made Azi sick. Judging by some of the ashen faces around him, he wasn't the only one. A sailor on each end started signaling the other ships, but the nearest had heard Paka's voice clearly and passed the message along.

The beach grew larger and larger. Azi had a dizzying view of bodies and blood-caked sand and debris, of the invaders turning to look at them, pointing, running. One of them was ankle deep in the water, directly in front of their ship. The man shouted something, brandished his swords. Azi could see his lips moving but never heard the words. He saw only a final glimpse of the man's face, a zigzagging pattern burned into the cheeks and forehead. Then the man was impaled on the grayship's razor-sharp hull.

The ship smashed up onto the beach, sending sand and bits of coral flying in all directions. The impact jerked Azi hard against the bulwark. The ship and the beach all seemed to shake, as if the fire mountain were right under their feet instead of miles away, and he clung to the bulwark to keep from being thrown overboard.

The screams of the invaders hit him even as his head was still reeling from the impact. He pushed himself up, swayed a moment, then drew his sword. "Blood!" he shouted, jumping off the side of the ship. "High tide!"

Other sailors took up his cry, landing all around him, but it was drowned out by the invaders. The invaders screamed wordlessly at them, their faces contorted with what looked like . . . joy. Blissful joy. The same zigzagging pattern was drawn or burned onto their faces. The burns were still raw and red, as if they'd been burned since they landed. *Flames. The patterns look like flames.* None of the other invaders he'd seen had anything like that on their faces, but he only had a moment to wonder what this meant before the invaders were on them.

Azi brought his sword up moments before a wide, reckless swing could dismember him. The clang of metal cut through the screams of men, and the battle was joined.

With the ship at their back, Azi pressed forward with the other Kayet soldiers on either side of him. The first few invaders fell quickly beneath their blades. But they were only the first. More arrived, and soon Azi was stepping back, barely avoiding the wild attacks.

Some of Azi's sailors yelled threats meant to intimidate merchants and local militias and guards. But this wasn't a raid, and these invaders showed no fear. Next to him one of the Kayet sailors screamed and fell to the ground. More screams, again and again. Each time, he wondered: *Was that Kayet or invader?*

Azi jabbed forward with his sword, catching his opponent in the side, but another blade came down on his arm as he pulled away. His blood ran down his hand and spilled on the ground. He stared at it stupidly. The pain hit a moment later, so cold and sharp it numbed his brain and dimmed his vision. He kicked out wildly, connected with something, then stumbled backward. Captain Paka stepped in front of him, cutting down Azi's opponent with a quick slice.

Azi took the moment of respite to look around. The invaders were dying, but so were his men and women. They'd barely made it twenty steps toward the manor.

He looked down at his slashed arm. Greater men had died of lesser wounds than this. It occurred to him briefly that if he called the retreat now he might seem like a coward, running because of his injury. Well, so what if they did think that, and so what if he was? If they stayed here much longer they'd have no chance at all.

"Retreat," he cried, as loud as he could, again and again. "Push the ships back to the water, before it's too late. Retreat!"

For a moment it seemed that the battle was too loud or his voice too weak. No one moved to obey. But then a few sailors broke off and ran to the ship. The rest tried to follow. Ignoring the pain in his arm, Azi stuck his sword back in the sash around his waist, found a spot and pushed. Sweat streamed down his face. He put his shoulders into it and shut his eyes. *Any moment now I'll feel a sword in my back, and then I'll fall, and it'll be over.*

Water sloshed around his feet. A hand grabbed his shoulder. He jerked away, but it held him fast. "My king," Captain Paka yelled. "Get up now!"

Azi wiped the sweat from his eyes and shook his head. "We're not far enough out yet. The wind will blow us back onto the beach."

There was a deafening roar, and a rush of hot air engulfed him. He spared a moment to look back. One of the grayships hadn't made it off the beach, and the torch boy had lit the keg of oil and alcohol. The fireball hung in the air for half a moment before dissolving. The ship burned bright and hot, adding its own smoke to the distant fires.

Grayships were never to fall into mainlander hands, but it had been seasons since any Kayet ship had gone up in flames. *Damn it. Damn it, damn it all . . .*

The fighting was up against the ship now. Kayet sailors climbed up the side of the ship using the pitted coral as hand and footholds where it had been sanded down, choosing the right ones without thought after years of practice. The coral was less forgiving of the invaders, cutting and tearing their hands when they tried to follow. Screaming, they fell back, only to be cut down by the Kayet men still on the beach.

The water was up to Azi's knees, his thighs. *Far enough*, he thought. "Everyone on board," someone yelled. "Now, my king!"

Azi put his hands up to climb, afraid his arm wouldn't hold him, but then strong hands grabbed him and pulled him up. He fell to the deck, dizzy with loss of blood. He hardly felt it when someone took his arm and bound it tightly to stop the bleeding.

The ship rocked violently as the sail turned and caught the wind, and then they were away, the last of the invaders falling away screaming. For a while there was no sound in the ship except for a few moans from the wounded. Azi sat up, nodded thanks to his saviors, and counted heads. Seventeen lost on this ship, the entire crew of another, and who knew how many on the other ships. *This is my fault. Why didn't I just wait?*

More invaders swarmed over the beach. How many were there? One hundred? Two hundred? If he could find the large, unwieldy ships these monsters used, he might have some idea of their numbers. They sailed along the coast a short distance, and Azi had his answer. The burned wreckage of a large, lumbering invader ship smoldered on the sand. He could see several more farther down the beach. He thought he saw grayships among the wreckage.

"The Gana must have burned the invaders' ships when they set their grayships on fire," he said. At least the Gana had managed to do that, though it would cost them greatly.

"We'll be safe until the other ships arrive," someone said. Azi looked up to see a thin, gray-haired woman, her face and shoulders crisscrossed with scars, standing by him. Her expression was grim. "I'm Captain Darri. Paka didn't make it back."

"He saved my life," Azi said. He fell silent for a moment, but there wasn't time to honor dead heroes now. "How many birds do we have left, Captain?"

Darri shook her head. "Just one. The other we sent already, and the rest were on the *Shark's Fin*."

Azi rubbed his eyes, then forced himself to look up again. "All right. I'll send it to the Bardo and tell Lord Mosi to send his fleet, too. I think we're going to need the help."

A murmur spread through the crew. The Kayet were the strongest of the Five-and-One Islands. They weren't used to asking for help. "Might be right, my king," Darri said. "You think he'll come?"

"I did marry his daughter," Azi said, trying to smile. They were all staring at him, waiting for him to say something. He fingered his sword nervously. He'd have felt more comfortable with his own notched blade. The one he held now was bright and sharp, well taken care of but rarely used. The pommel had been decorated with small white and blue shells to create the shape of a fish.

It was the sword his father had given Jin for his fourteenth birthday. A sword meant for a king.

Azi stood and drew in a deep breath. "It'll be safe here, you're right. But those are villages they're burning. They'll work their way down the island. Maybe we're no good head on, but we can be fast and quiet. We'll hit them at night. We'll hit them when they're alone. We'll hit them hard, hurt them, then disappear again. We'll make them bleed for every man and woman who died on this beach, and when the rest of the fleet arrives, we'll make them all dead."

"As you say, my king," Captain Darri said. "Everyone hear that? Steer it around the west side, and the rest of you get any sleep you can. We land again at midnight."

CHAPTER 15

$\mathcal{J}$ ala stared at the book, flipping the pages gently. She understood the stories were sacred to the invaders. But they didn't *feel* sacred. Why these stories? Why this book? Couldn't they just remember the stories that were so important to them? Couldn't they make another book?

The bird on Jala's windowsill fluttered his bright orange-and-green wings and started to peck at one of his feathers. "Speak," Jala told it.

The bird captured just enough of Marjani's intonation.

Dear Jala,

I suppose you'll want me to call you *my queen* now. I think I won't. You need me to keep you humble. Don't worry, I'll be good when anyone else is around. Probably.

We got news of the invasion a few hours ago. Everyone's acting like the fire mountain just birthed another island, but we didn't see or hear anything. Everything's the same. Well, I say that, but of course it's not really. You're not here. It's like . . . all the color's drained out of everything. The sunlight doesn't seem so bright, the stars in the sky are dull, the birds sing, but it's like I'm hearing them from under a pile of sand.

Ugh, listen to me, I sound like some lovesick little girl. I am, I guess. Lovesick. A little. Maybe this'll be good for me. It's not like I hadn't tried to stop thinking of you before, but how could I when hardly a day went by that we didn't see each other?

I was being dramatic before. The birds are still way too loud, for one thing. And not everything's lost its shine. I made a new friend. Her name's Nara. Not that I'm trying to replace you. But I can't not talk to anyone, right? You've probably made all sorts of friends on the First Isle.

Anyway. Nara. She's Gana, but her sister married a Bardo sailor and she was visiting while the husband was off raiding. She's nice. Very pretty, too, not that there's time for anything to happen. She's going home as soon as all this storm of invasion talk passes by. But I can dream, right? I'm good at dreaming.

Your mother still wants to make a match for me with one of the noble families. Some third or fourth cousin who doesn't need to have children. Or a widow who's already had children, I suppose. It doesn't matter. I'm not a noble, so she can't make me marry anyone, no matter how much she tries to bully me into it. And I'm going to keep ignoring my mother's mournful hints about grand-children, too.

I've talked too long. The bird will probably forget half of the message by the time it gets to you. If it's remembered everything so far. . . . I miss you. I wish you were here, no matter what I said before. You promised me a bird every day, and you're way behind already. Queens are supposed to keep their promises, you know.

The bird stopped speaking. Jala poured some water into a small bowl, and it drank greedily. When Marjani had sent the bird she still hadn't heard the latest news. Six days had passed since Azi had taken what was left of the fleet and sailed for the Fifth Isle. Six days, and there'd been no word. At least, no word that had gotten through to Jala. If Lord Inas knew anything, he wasn't telling her.

Jala tapped the bird on its beak. "Listen," she ordered, then she sat there not knowing what to say. "Thanks for sending the bird. I needed to hear a friendly voice. I should have sent a bird myself, but. . . . You've probably heard the news by now. The Fifth Isle, the Gana. I hope your new friend's family is safe.

Maybe by the time you get this we'll know what's going on. Dry hells, you're closer to them than we are, so you might have heard already. It'll turn out there was a sudden storm and they were blown off course, or they're too busy drinking Gana wine to send news.

I know, my excuses sound ridiculous even to me. I keep telling myself that I'll hear *something* soon, but then I'm afraid of what that will be. I wish Azi were here instead of out there. I know why he had to go, but that makes waiting for him that much worse. Why is it the queen who always waits on the king? I hate waiting. I hate not knowing.

We hardly even had a chance to be married before this happened. And no, we haven't had sex yet. We've hardly even kissed. I thought it was the argument we had after we arrived. I'm sure that was part of it, but he was distant on the way here, too.

I wish I had something to laugh about. I wish you were here with me. Tell my mother I want you to come and visit. Tell her there are lots of nice Kayet girls for you to meet. She'll probably tell you there's no such thing as a nice Kayet, but some of them are. At least to my face.

I'm serious. You have to come and visit. After this storm has passed, like you said.

After we know that everything will be all right again.

Jala sat quietly for a while, but there seemed to be nothing else to say. She waved the bird away. "Go, to Marjani of the Bardo on the Second Isle."

With a resentful squawk the bird flew off, and Jala was alone again. A knock came at her door. "My queen?" Iliana said.

"Come in," Jala said. "Is it time already? How do I look?"

"You look worried, my queen. But so does everyone else. The dress does suit you." She craned her neck to look at the book still lying open on Jala's bed. "Is that it? The book the sorcerer told us about?"

Jala nodded. "I keep thinking about it. I know it's crazy, but maybe if we can find some way to return it they'll leave us alone."

"But we took it," Iliana said. "If we can take it, then it should be ours. That's the oldest story in the world, told even before there were words to tell it with. Besides, the Nongo won't like it, and neither will any of the other families. It was a gift to you on your wedding."

"I know all that," Jala said. "Never mind for now." She shut the book with a thump. "Might as well get this over with. Lead the way." She followed the maid out of her room and through the Kayet manor. "How's Lord Sourbelly today?"

Iliana coughed. "He's sober, and I don't think he's happy about it. He's angry with you, but that's nothing new."

"Wonderful." Jala sighed. They'd reached the side door into the main hall, the one meant for the king and queen to use. It was open, and she could see that Lord Inas was already inside, sitting on a stool beside the two wooden thrones. She rubbed her face, trying to wipe away the worry and frustration. Then she walked inside and took her seat.

Only then did she let her eyes focus on all the Kayet nobles and captains who were seated on either side of the hall and the first few petitioners who had been allowed into the hall. Normally most of the nobles wouldn't have bothered showing up unless they needed something, but everyone was curious to see their new queen in action. *Especially after the Sectioning, and with Azi gone*, Jala thought. Only Lord Inas kept his gaze straight ahead.

The teller-of-lists stood. He spoke loudly and clearly. "Our king is gone. Who has the wisdom to preside over this day's procession? Who has the right to judge the people of the First Isle?"

"As your queen, I claim the right," Jala said, trying to make her voice equally commanding. "I speak with his wisdom and dole out his justice. I am your queen."

The man nodded. "We will hear you."

"Then call the first petitioner," Jala said, and sat down to wait.

"Don't get too comfortable," Lord Inas said quietly. "You might not be married for long."

"How can you say that about Azi?" Jala whispered back. "Don't you care about him at all? Or is it that you don't want him to come back? Maybe you'd rather see me gone than have your nephew home again."

Lord Inas looked like he was about to respond, loudly, when the teller-of-lists cleared his throat. They both turned to look back at the main hall. A young couple, both near Jala's age, stood nervously before her. "Presenting Bayo and Alita, from the village of Morntide. They're to be married today and have come to ask for the king's blessing."

Jala made herself smile at them. "You have it, of course. Please let me give each of you a gift. Tell me your heart's desire."

The girl stepped forward. "My heart's desire is to marry Bayo. But if I could have any other thing, it would be a new sword so that I can provide for our family and our future children."

"You'll have it," Jala said. A new sword was the expected request for a sailor about to be married.

The boy stepped forward. It took him a moment before he could speak. "My heart's desire is to marry Alita. But if I could have any other thing it would be a ruby earring, so that I can look good for my wife on our wedding day."

"You'll have it," Jala said, nodding with approval. It was another practical gift; most likely he'd sell the earring to a trader once they were married, and that was expected, too.

Smiling at each other, the couple was escorted out. Jala watched them go and thought of Azi's face when she'd asked for Two Bones as her wedding gift. This couple had asked for practical gifts, but their intent was very different. Where she'd thought of family duty, they thought only of each other. It was no surprise Azi had been so disappointed.

As they waited for the next group to be brought forward, Lord Inas spoke, though he didn't bother turning around. "You have no idea what you're saying. No idea how much I've sacrificed for him and for Jin. I have two sons of my own. Two sons I never had time to teach because I was busy showing my brother's sons how to be men. My brother never taught Azi how to be a king. No, when Jin died he simply gave up and died as well. I taught Azi, I helped him, and in the end he spat in my face. I don't wish him dead. But wishing never stopped people from dying. We'll hear soon enough."

Jala had no reply, and there was no time anyway. A group of seven boys and three girls had been brought forward, all of them no more than twelve and all of them beaming with pride.

"Here are boys and girls from the villages of Morntide and Little Waves who have come of age since the last storm season."

Jala made a show of looking them over. "They seem strong and willing. Are there any captains who will take them on to train as sailors and soldiers?"

A few of the captains stood, asked some questions, then made their choices. They were all expected to return the next morning to begin their training. But for now, each was allowed to take as much food from the manor's stores as they could carry. Their families had probably had them lifting rocks to build up their arms for months now.

When she was finished with the new recruits, Jala lowered her voice again and spoke to Lord Inas. "I'm sorry about your sons. And I'm sorry about your brother and Jin. But you can't rule for Azi, and you shouldn't want to. He needs to be a strong king on his own, now especially."

Lord Inas snorted. "I don't need your pity or your condolences. He was my brother. I did what I had to do."

His words hurt. They shouldn't have, but they did anyway. "If you're so devoted to your duty, then you know why I did what I had to at the Sectioning."

"Of course I do," he said, almost sympathetic. "That's why you can never be trusted. You're your father's daughter."

More people were waiting for her. An argument over broken pottery that involved a village elder, another marriage, a ship's captain accused of cutting shares. She dealt with them all, and more were let in to line up at the end of the hall. All the while, she tried to keep from worrying about Azi and what was happening on the Fifth Isle. *Everything's the same*, she thought, thinking back to Marjani's message. Almost like nothing had happened. Almost.

Lord Inas, who was supposedly there to give her advice, added nothing. Only after the cheating captain had gone did he speak again. "He doesn't love you. He can't love you, not truly. Where do you think he was the night the mainlanders came? In the village, meeting with the girl he'd found before he was king. She's just a village girl, of course, not someone he can marry. But he can be with her. Every night, if he chooses to. The whole island will know, and the storytellers of the other families will tell stories of their forbidden love and the cold, ruthless queen he stays with only out of duty."

"Shut up," Jala hissed. "You're lying."

Lord Inas glanced back at her, and his mouth twitched up into a nasty smile. "Her name is Kona. A pretty name, don't you think?"

Jala stared, unable to speak. *He's lying. It has to be a lie. He wants to see you break down in front of all the Kayet, he wants you to go searching for this girl who probably doesn't exist.*

He wants to ruin you. He wants you to ruin everything with Azi.

Unless he was telling the truth. Unless there was nothing to ruin, because Azi did not, would not ever love her. *I never asked for love*, she told herself. But she wanted it now.

Damn you. Damn you to every one of the dry hells. I'm the queen. I'll find some way to hurt you. Some way that Azi never has to know about. She made the vow, but it didn't feel real. Nothing felt real except the tears she couldn't cry.

Not now. Not yet. Not until she was alone. She wouldn't let him see her cry.

CHAPTER 16

A zi sat high in one of the island's trees, covered in leaves. Nine other men and women were hidden in the trees around him.

Nearby a bird cooed loudly. *That's the signal. They're coming.* Azi's muscles tensed, his right hand holding a vine that had been tied to the tree, his left hand gripping his sword. The arm still ached, but the mournroot had dulled it enough for him to hunt. The first few mainlanders appeared beneath them, jogging recklessly through the forest, heading toward the fire some of the Gana had set to lure them out.

There were too many warriors for ten of his people to take on, of course. There were always too many. But they were hunting, not fighting, for now.

The spotter cooed again, signaling that no more were coming. Azi counted to five under his breath. Stones fell from the trees opposite Azi. Some of the invaders stopped, clutching their skulls and looking around in confusion as their friends pressed on ahead.

Now. Azi kicked off from the tree and slid down the vine. As soon as he hit the ground he tossed his sword to his right hand and slashed at the nearest mainlander just as the man began to turn around. In only a moment, seven invaders lay dead at their feet.

Someone shouted in a foreign tongue. Men were turning back. Azi grabbed a sword off his victim, then turned and ran. The other Kayet did the same, each running in a different direction.

More screams tore the air as some of the invaders who tried to give chase were cut down.

If your enemy is afraid, the battle is already won, the saying went. But these men seemed to know no fear. For two days Azi and his crews had crept about the island, hunting individuals and smaller bands, laying traps and ambushes. The invaders' bloodthirst made them reckless and easy to catch unawares, but it also made them deadly.

A bird squawked nearby. Two cries, one long, one short. It wasn't even a very good imitation, but these mainlanders didn't know what island birds sounded like. *Come see, not in danger*, the signal meant. Azi followed the sound.

One of the other sailors found him first. "My king, there are survivors," she said.

He followed her to a cluster of trees almost swallowed in vines, and there, hidden among them, were several Gana villagers. They were crawling out with the help of the Kayet sailors, soaked through and mud-spattered. Four women, three men.

"I am Azi of the Kayet, king of the Five-and-One," he said, not too loudly. "Is your village nearby? Are there others hiding here? We have a little bit of food and plenty of water."

One of the men stepped forward. Seeing him standing tall, Azi thought there was something familiar about him. And his clothes, torn and dirty as they were, had been fine once.

"We've met, my king, though I don't blame you for not recognizing me," the man said. "I am Lord Orad, head of the Gana family. I admit, I didn't expect you to come. We didn't think anyone would come."

"We tried to take back the manor," Azi said, "but there were too many of them. I've sent word to the Bardo. Lord Mosi will send ships. We've been trying to hurt them where we can in the meantime." He hesitated. "Lord Orad, what about your grayships? I haven't seen them on the beach."

"Burned," Lord Orad said. "All burned."

"I'm sorry," Azi said. But he felt more relief than sympathy. If the invaders had somehow stolen grayships, they could use them to lead another fleet to the Five-and-One, this time without the added danger of sorcery. All they'd have to do is follow the grayship home.

"Where are the rest of your people?" Azi asked.

"Burned as well, more than likely," Orad said grimly. "We've seen nothing of them."

But that turned out to be wrong. After taking Orad and his family back to the ships, they resumed their search and soon found other survivors. Whole villages had taken to the jungle to find food, hide from the invaders, and even kill them where they could. Many of the sailors had died, so it was up to fishermen and merchants and children to do what they could with nets and fishing spears and whatever weapons they could find.

At first Azi gave them weapons when they found any, food if they had any to spare, whatever water they had. They stole any fishing boats they could find and set the fishermen fishing night and day, trying to feed the survivors. But they were running out of food, of sleep, and especially of hope.

But how could Azi sleep? Every hour he did nothing was another village burned, another Gana murdered somewhere on the island.

If only we could take the manor. They'd have no food themselves, they'd have nowhere to hide. The thought ran through Azi's mind as he made his way between trees, listening carefully in case anyone was following him. He'd lost count of how many times he'd landed a force on the island, but each time he wondered if this was the time that would kill him.

But no, again he was lucky. The trees ended ahead of him, and he'd managed not to get himself lost. There was a cove here, nearly hidden in the side of an overhanging cliff. One of the Gana doctors had shown them the place, and they'd taken to using it as a convenient place to land when a better location wasn't available. He climbed down a ladder someone had hastily woven out of vines and hoped that both his injured arm and the ladder held until he reached the bottom.

As he stepped out onto a narrow ledge and prepared to duck into the cove, something caught Azi's eye: another grayship sat out on the water, and it wasn't one of his. Every family had their own distinct way of growing grayships, so you could always tell one family's ship from another if you knew what to look for.

It was a Bardo ship. Help had finally arrived.

Azi found Lord Mosi speaking quietly with Lord Orad and a few of the surviving Gana captains.

Mosi rose and smiled when Azi entered. "Ah, my king. I'm glad you're safe."

He held out his arm, and Azi clasped it firmly. "Thank you for coming, my lord, though we could have used you sooner."

"We weren't ready to sail, I'm afraid, and when we did the storms hit us hard. But we're here now and ready to do whatever we can. Lord Orad has already filled me in on your fight here."

Orad nodded. "Mosi's brought the entire Bardo fleet, and he says there are barges on the way with food and fishing nets and more men to help my people rebuild."

Azi hadn't thought to ask for food and supplies. His focus had been on how to get rid of the invaders, apparently at the expense of everything else. That was fine for his captains, but as the king, he shouldn't have let himself be blinded by battle. His lack of experience could have cost more lives if they'd all starved. Azi was grateful for Lord Mosi's foresight.

"Most of the mainlanders are hiding in the manor," Azi said. "They have enough food to last them for months. But with your fleet we should be able to drive them out and finish this."

"The manor is old," Orad said. "It's built to be defended."

Lord Mosi grinned. "I don't think my king intends to retake the manor. Do you?"

"No," Azi said. "We burn it."

It took several hours for everything to be ready. While the Bardo waited for nightfall, Azi waited for his own people to return. Then, since only one grayship could fit inside the cove, the Kayet soldiers had to be ferried back to their own ships. Azi made sure everyone ate and slept while they waited, though he himself ignored the advice until Doctor Abeo threatened him.

"You need rest, and your arm needs to heal," the Gana doctor said. "You shouldn't be fighting at all. You'd think you'd remember the way your brother died. But if you insist on swinging a sword, you must at least try to sleep. And no mournroot. You need real sleep, though I'll drug you if I have to."

The ship ferried Azi to Lord Mosi's ship, where he slept fitfully, distracted by the pain in his arm and the knot of fear in his belly.

When Azi woke, the sky was dark. Only a thin sliver of moon shone weakly through the clouds. *Let's just hope it doesn't rain.*

Lord Mosi stood nearby, stretching his arms and back. Somehow he managed to make the simple motions look graceful and strong. Azi remembered the wind-dance on the Second Isle. He hoped the man was as good with a blade.

Mosi glanced back at Azi and saw that he was awake. He flashed a smile. "It seems that the older I get, the more warning my body needs before I can dance. Remember that when you're older, eh? It's almost time now. You're sure you want to go with us? There's still time to take you to one of your ships."

Even with food and a short rest, the Kayet were tired, many of them wounded. They would attack as a second wave after the Bardo, all of them except Azi. He shook his head. "You know I can't do that. I need to be up front, not hiding on the water while braver men die." He smiled. "Jala knows that. She was there on the beach when the dead ships landed on the First Isle."

Mosi cocked an eyebrow at him but said nothing more. The grayships floated gently, out of sight of the manor. The wind was good today. With full sails they could land in front of the manor in minutes. They just waited for the signal. Two Gana fishermen took two barrels of oil in an old rowboat. Once they landed on the beach, they were to roll it up to the manor walls, set them ablaze, and run.

A plume of orange and red flame suddenly rose up into the sky, shaking the trees, and then it was gone. A moment later Azi heard a roar like distant waves and felt a wash of warm air rush over his face. Thick gray smoke billowed up into the sky, and he could just make out the flicker of firelight between the trees. The Gana manor was on fire.

Immediately the sails were raised, and with a jerk the grayship sped toward the beach. Wind whipped at Azi's face. The island was a shadow among shadows, and as they sped closer the fire only made it harder to see anything else. This time, at least, they let the sails go slack and dropped ores to slow the ship before beaching it. But even then the impact came as a shock.

Azi followed Lord Mosi off the ship, his sword ready, visions of their first landing flashing in his head. But this time there was no one else there. The beach was empty. They walked slowly toward the manor. The exploding barrels had splashed the walls with oil. The fire had spread all the way to the roof now, and the wet wood smoked horribly. Anyone inside would be just as likely to die from smoke as from the fire.

"Where are they?" Azi asked. "Why aren't they coming out?" Maybe it was empty and he'd burned it down for nothing. Could the invaders have known somehow and fled into the forest? But then he saw someone moving in one of the windows. He tightened his grip on his sword.

Men suddenly rushed through the front door, running through the flames with their swords held high. Their skin glistened with oil. They were soaked in it, and when the fire touched them they burst into flame. They screamed. And they kept on coming.

The flames rising from their faces looked like grinning masks as they ran through the Bardo and the Kayet, slashing with their red-hot swords, flicking burning oil from their arms as they swung. Screaming, always screaming, they threw themselves bodily on Bardo swords only to grab hold of their killers with burning hands.

The air reeked of oil, and burning hair, and burnt meat.

Azi fought just to stay out of their reach. Everyone was running, shoving, trying to get away from the madness around them. Azi stumbled and fell to one knee. Something hit him from behind, and he was knocked face-first into the sand. He pushed himself up just as another burning man ran past him.

The man stopped. Azi stayed still, afraid to move. The sounds around him had grown muffled, and his heartbeat was too loud in his ears, urging him to run, run, run. The man opened his mouth wide and then collapsed on the ground, writhing in pain. Azi watched in horror as the man rolled on the sand, his skin charring off his face, his fat and muscles melting.

Azi pushed himself up. All around, the invaders were falling, burning away on the sand until only the flames still moved, dancing in the wind. The air was filled with smoke. *We've won*, Azi thought, coughing. But he wasn't sure what they'd won. His head spun, and he couldn't seem to focus his eyes. He sat down on the sand again, just for a minute, and then he passed out.

He woke to bright sunlight in his eyes and a splitting headache. Somewhere nearby people were talking, sometimes shouting. Someone put a wet cloth on his head. The water felt so cool he couldn't help sighing. Azi closed his eyes for a moment, then forced them open again.

"Good morning, my king," Doctor Abeo said. "You were hit on the head during the fight. Good thing it was only the flat of the sword, eh? Can you walk?"

"I can try," Azi said. He fell twice but managed to stay upright on the third attempt. He looked around. A grayship bobbed on the waves nearby, its load so heavy that it rode low on the water. Two more grayships waited farther out while sailors pulled the first ship ashore.

The bodies had been cleared from the beach, he was glad to see. A team of Bardo sailors dug through the burned ruins of the manor, searching for anything useful that might have survived the fire.

The burned grayships were being removed too, he noticed. The one he'd lost was there, but also the hulks of many Gana ships. All of them, Lord Orad had said. Azi couldn't imagine what it had taken to order all the ships destroyed. Without them, the Gana were no longer a real family.

"Lord Mosi is here," Doctor Abeo said from behind Azi. "He's been quite anxious for your recovery."

Azi looked up to see Mosi standing behind the doctor. "I wouldn't think those barges could travel so quickly with such a heavy load, my lord."

"They came as quickly as they could, my king," Lord Mosi said. "But not that quickly. You've been asleep for a day. Doctor Abeo told us to let you rest."

Azi started. "It feels like only a moment ago." He rubbed the back of his head and flinched. "Have you sent any birds to Jala or Inas? They should know what's happened here."

Lord Mosi nodded. "Of course. But I think that as soon as you're ready, you should go back to your island and rule, my king. I believe Lord Orad is going with you. Difficult decisions will have to be made soon. I'll stay and help our cousins rebuild. I'm sure we'll see each other soon."

What're you planning? Azi thought as they took hold of each other's arms and said good-bye. He sighed. *Mountain's piss, I'm starting to sound like my uncle.* It bothered him that so many Bardo had come to help rebuild, though he couldn't quite put a finger on why.

"If my king is feeling better, I will go tend to my other patients," Doctor Abeo said.

Azi nodded. "Please tell someone to find Captain Darri for me. We're going home."

CHAPTER 17

J ala walked down to the beach as she had done the last few days. She kicked off her shoes, waded ankle-deep into the cool water, and dug her toes into the sand. She let herself relax, her eyes wandering over the water. A bird had come from her father to let her know that the Kayet fleet was returning, with Azi safely aboard.

Her father had said more news would follow, hinting that something important was going to happen. *Well, you'll find out soon, and then you'll probably wish you didn't know.*

She was just grateful Azi was alive, though he was taking his time getting back. She spent too much time here, watching and waiting for him, but she couldn't bring herself to stay away. When he came back, she'd be here waiting for him.

There'd been rumors of fire rising from the Fifth Isle, but nobody knew what that meant. She wondered if he'd stood on the beach waiting for her to return from the Lone Isle. Or if he'd just gone off to spend time with Kona, whoever she was. If she was real. If he still cared about her.

She wanted to spend all day here, but she had responsibilities she couldn't put off forever. It was time to go. Jala started to turn around, but something on the horizon caught her eye. She put a hand on her forehead to block out the sun. Gray sails against a strip of blue sky.

Azi's fleet. It had to be.

Jala stayed on the beach, watching and waiting until she could make out the red streaks on the ships' sails. By then, a small crowd had gathered around her. Boys and retired sailors loitered about in case the crews needed help pulling the ships ashore. A woman holding an armful of medical supplies barked orders, preparing to treat any injuries.

Finally the first ship's bow hit sand. Sailors jumped over the side and pushed the ship onto the beach. Jala scanned the deck looking for Azi. She finally spotted him standing next to a tall man she didn't recognize.

As soon as he disembarked, she ran to him and wrapped her arms around him. Even though she'd been expecting him any day, the suddenness of seeing him alive and well made her heart race.

"You're not dead," she whispered, and she pressed her face against his bare shoulder. He was damp from spray and smelled of smoke and sweat. She didn't mind. If he smelled, he was alive. Not knowing what else to say, she kissed him. His kiss was hungry, almost desperate, and they held each other close until she was almost out of breath.

Definitely still alive.

Azi broke off the kiss with a reluctant smile. Jala almost objected, but then she remembered they had an audience. A rather large audience, in fact. Her face flushed with heat as she realized a crowd of people watched them with a mixture of raised eyebrows and amusement.

"Jala. My queen." Azi's voice was heavy with weariness. His left arm was bandaged, and he looked like he hadn't slept in days. Azi gestured to the man beside him. "This is Lord Orad of the Gana. He's the head of the Gana family."

Orad was older than Azi by at least ten years, with angry red burns on his face and chest. When he saw her he straightened his hunched shoulders and bowed stiffly. When he spoke, it was obvious that it took effort just to keep his voice steady. "My queen. Thank you for allowing me and my family . . . what's left of my family . . . to reside here."

"Your family is welcome, of course," she said, glancing at Azi. Her father's message hadn't mentioned this. She wondered what else had been left out.

"The Gana are no more," Azi said. Orad winced. "The invaders' ships landed on the Fifth Isle with all the men inside still alive. They took the manor and killed most of the family."

"We barely had time to burn our ships," Orad said softly.

Then they really were a dead family. It was one of her biggest fears, and he was living it. "The worst storms are often followed by the clearest skies," she said, hoping the words didn't sound as empty to him as they did to her. "You did what you had to do, and all of the other families will honor you for it."

Orad lowered his eyes, and she looked away as well, leaving him to his grief.

By now most of the other grayships had landed and were in the process of being pushed ashore. The wounded were helped or carried off the boats. As the sailors were greeted by friends and family, a murmur grew among those gathered on the beach.

A small knot of men and women now stood behind Orad. Jala nodded toward them. "Your family, my lord?"

"My brother's family," Orad said. "And some of my cousins. My wife . . ." He shook his head. "Please, forgive me. We're all very tired."

Jala wasn't interested in how tired Orad felt just then. She wanted to know what had happened. But right now Azi needed her to play the royal hostess. "I understand. If you and your family will come with me to the manor, you'll be well cared for."

Orad waved his family over, and they followed her into the house. Once inside, Azi whispered, "We'll talk soon," then pulled away from the group, heading for the Kayet wing.

Jala led the Gana to the guest wing. "We have no other noble guests right now, so you may each have rooms to yourself, if you like. I'll send someone to see to your needs."

One of the women stepped forward. "Would you please have someone tell Lady Chahaya that we've arrived?"

But Azi's mother was already waiting for them. "I'm sorry I didn't come out to meet you. It's so good to see you again, Panya." Chahaya walked up to one of the women and embraced her, holding her tight for several seconds before hugging the others just as fiercely. Her eyes were red, and Jala wondered if she'd been crying. "Is it true, then? We're all that's left of our family?"

"Yes," Orad said. "It's true."

"I didn't want to believe it. I had planned on going home soon."

Orad's voice turned hard. "We're only as dead as we let ourselves become. We're still here, no matter what the Kayet say." He glanced at Jala. "My apologies. My family and I have much to talk about, and I'm sure you have worries of your own. Thank you for your hospitality."

"I'll show them to their rooms," Azi's mother said, trying to regain control of her voice. "I've been here a lot longer than you have, and I know which rooms don't stink of fish when the morning catch is brought in."

Jala nodded. "I hope you'll join me tomorrow. Maybe lunch on the beach, if the weather permits it." As she left the guest wing, she heard

Orad whispering behind her but couldn't make out any of the words. She wondered what would happen to the remaining Gana now. How long would the Kayet allow them to live here? How long before they were no longer recognized as nobility?

Azi's mother is Gana. Surely he'll let them stay for as long as they need, for her sake, if nothing else.

Jala went back to her rooms, where she washed and changed into a new dress. Outside, people had already begun to celebrate the fleet's safe return. Bonfires again dotted the beach. Drummers started to play, and jugs of palm wine and grass beer were being passed around. *They're celebrating as if the Gana don't matter at all.* But then, maybe they didn't. Not to the Kayet. *Maybe it's just better to celebrate the good. The fleet's back, Azi's back. Doesn't that make you want to dance?*

But there was another thought, too. A thought that went, *Are you sure he's happy to see you? Are you sure he doesn't wish he was with his village girl right now?* She tried to push the thought away. It was only Lord Inas trying to hurt her. She'd go to see him now and prove it was nothing but mean-spirited gossip.

Jala swept through the Kayet wing of the manor and knocked on Azi's door. Before she could knock again the door opened and Azi stood in the doorway. He'd taken off his bloody clothes, washed, and had his bandage changed. Now he wore a plain silk shirt, buttoned low at his navel. His sword still hung at his waist, partially obscured by his flowing pant leg.

He looked like a king. He looked . . . like something out of a romantic tale, like the Nameless Wanderer or Ekundayo the Dolphin, who swam through wave and storm to reach his love.

"Hi," she said.

He pulled her to him without saying a word and then held her tight for a long time. *He needs you*, Jala thought as he held her. *And you need him.*

After a while he pulled away, though he kept his hands on her shoulders. "Hi," he said, smiling at her.

Behind him, Jala saw a pitcher of wine on the floor, the cup beside it empty and unused. "Did you want to join your people?" she asked. "We could dance, if you're not ready to talk yet. Or just walk along the beach."

"I'd meant to," he said. He waved a hand at his clothes. "I let them dress me up as if I was some kind of king." His smile wavered. "But I don't think I'm in the mood to celebrate. I'll leave that to my sailors. They need to. The whole island does."

"I think you do too," Jala said. She laid a hand gently on his uninjured arm. She could feel the wiry muscles beneath the light silk. "Celebrate with me, at least, if you don't want to join your family." She hesitated, knowing where this could lead. But she wanted to be with him, and from the way he kept trying to sneak glances at her, he wanted to be with her, too. "Why don't we go to those hot springs you kept going on about? We can talk there. Or not."

She had to admit, she was particularly interested in the potential within that simple *or not*.

Azi took in a deep breath, never taking his eyes off her. "That . . . would be nice, yes. And I'll tell you everything, if you still want to hear it. The sooner I get it over with, the better. Just promise you'll pull me out of the water if I fall asleep."

Jala pretended to be offended. "If you fall asleep with me there to occupy you, you deserve to drown."

Azi stepped into a pair of sandals and slid the King's Earring through his earlobe. Then he took a small brass lantern from a shelf. "A souvenir from my first trip across the Great Ocean," he told her as he closed the door behind them.

They walked through the Kayet manor, and as they walked, Azi told her about his life there, about what it was like to grow up as the king's second son. "I got away with a lot more. People weren't so concerned about me, as long as I was out of the way, so it was easy to get into trouble." He pointed to a door. "Through there are the kitchens and the way down into the cellars where we keep the mainlander food. I was always sneaking in and tasting things, usually leaving them behind with little Azi-sized bites out of them."

They avoided the main hall and exited the manor through a smaller side door. The sun had already sunk low, with only the top of its head peeking out above the trees. They stopped for a moment while Azi lit his lantern. Then he led Jala down a well-trodden path away from the beach.

Insects flitted around in front of the lamp, bumping noisily against the glass in an effort to get closer. Their footsteps settled into a slow, easy rhythm.

"There's a different cellar where we keep dyes and perfumes and the like. Anything that isn't food but still smells. Jin pushed me in once and held the door closed until my eyes watered and I started to cry."

"We have a cellar like that," Jala said. "When we were little Marjani and I would steal perfume."

"To wear?"

"To spray on our cousins," Jala said with a grin. "Even the few that smelled nice were awful if you used more than the tiniest bit."

Azi laughed. He had a good laugh, Jala thought. It made her want to laugh, too, whenever she heard it. "One time I stole some green dye from that cellar," he said. "I wanted to color the well water and scare everyone, but all it did was make the water smell funny for a day. Which was lucky for everyone, really. I might have taken the yellow dye, which is poisonous. They say one of the queens even died from wearing too much of it."

"My father always says . . ." Jala deepened her voice, mimicking him. "The only thing you can trust from the mainland is their metal, and even that'll cut you if you're not careful."

Azi snorted. "My uncle says something like that too. Do you think there's some special storyteller that only old men know about? The one who teaches them this stuff?"

They both laughed at that.

But maybe they're right, Jala thought, thinking about the book the Nongo had taken. Such an innocent-looking gift to be the cause of so much death. Azi led them up an uneven hill, and they reached the springs a few minutes later. Five pools, the smallest big enough for three grown men, the largest for twenty, lay before them. Wisps of steam curled over the surface of the water.

Azi set the lantern beside the smallest pool. He picked up a large, smooth stick leaning against a tree. He grinned at her. "Don't worry. They don't usually bite."

Jala frowned and was about to ask what he was talking about when he started to poke at the water with the stick.

"Come on, out you get!" he called. "Find another spring, this one's taken." Then in the light of the lamp she saw snakes on the surface of the water, heading for the sides of the pool. One slithered over her foot, and she squealed and jumped back, which made Azi grin at her.

"You could have said there were snakes. You just wanted to scare me!"

"Nonsense. Why would I want to do that?" he said, still grinning. "It should be fine now, I just didn't want you stepping on one." He started to take off his shirt.

Feeling suddenly shy, Jala turned around while he stripped off his clothes. But she couldn't help glancing back at him briefly before he jumped into the dark water with a splash. He followed her lead and covered his eyes with both hands while she undressed, but she wondered if he was peeking, too. Her skin tingled at the thought.

She lowered herself into the pool and sighed as the hot water covered her body. Her muscles relaxed. She slid closer until their legs were touching and leaned her head against his arm, breathing in the warm air. *No kissing or anything else right now, though*, she told herself sternly. No matter how much she wanted to just forget the horrible things that were happening and lose herself in his arms. Now was not the time. Well, not unless *he* started it.

Azi reached over and poured some wine for them. "We say that some of the fire mountain's blood flows underground. That's where these springs come from, and the red earth."

"Are you sure it's not just that the First Isle has terrible gas? Though I guess that doesn't explain the clay."

"Whatever causes them, they're nice to have."

They were both avoiding what they'd come to talk about. "Tell me what happened to the Gana," Jala said.

Azi sighed and looked up at the sky. Night had fallen quickly, and the stars shone brightly above them. Then he started to speak, his voice low and flat. He told her about being driven back on the beach, about the days of hit-and-run attacks, about that last, horrible battle when the manor burned. Then he stopped.

Jala waited to see if he would say more, then asked the question he'd carefully avoided answering. "How many died?"

"Maybe two hundred between our families. Twice that many Gana. Two of our ships were burned as well."

Feeling suddenly suffocated in the hot water, Jala pulled herself out of the pool, her back to Azi. She got dressed—talking about massacres was definitely not going to lead to anything more fun. "They'll come again, until we're dead or they have their book. There has to be a way to return it to them."

Azi nodded. "My uncle thinks they've lost too many men to try again. But he didn't see the men on the Fifth Isle. He didn't see what they'd become. There's something happening here we don't understand, something more than the book or revenge or . . . I don't know. Damn it, we just don't know. We don't know who they are or where they come from, and we don't know if they'll come back or not."

"We know they're called the Hashon. And we have the prisoners. Maybe they'll talk if I show them the book."

"I don't think you'll have much luck, but you're welcome to try. I'll have Boka the Trader help you. He tried to speak to them before and knows more of the mainland languages than most."

"Thank you," Jala said. She sat down next to Azi, dangling her feet in the water.

He looked up at her, his face serious. "You know that whoever you send . . . well, they'll probably never make it back."

"I'll send one of my family's ships when the time comes," Jala said. Captain Natari would go if she asked him. The thought made her feel queasy. She had never imagined herself sending someone to their death.

Azi stood with his back to her and stretched, then got out of the pool and wrapped his robes around his waist. "I forgot how much I love this place. I used to come here all the time before Jin died."

Of course he's been here before, Jala couldn't help thinking. The words came out of her mouth before she could stop them. "Did you bring Kona here, too?" She hugged her knees to her chest as though they could shield her from his reply.

"What?" Azi stammered. "Who told you about her?"

"Were you with her that night when the ships came?"

"No!" he said quickly. Then, just as quickly, "Well, yes, but it's not what you're thinking. Or what you've been told."

"You don't know what I've been told," she pointed out.

"I know it's nothing good. I was. . . . I met Kona back when I was just Azi the sailor. We never thought I'd become the king. I did go to see her that night, but I told her—I didn't know what to tell her. But things between us are over."

"Did you love her?" She couldn't bring herself to ask, *Do you still love her?*

Azi let out his breath in a long sigh and leaned back. "I loved her for a long time. Or I thought I did. Before Jin died, before everything changed. I thought we could get married, if I could just make my uncle and father understand."

"You'd have been the king's brother. You'd never have been able to marry a village girl."

"I never lied to her. I just hoped. We both did. Anyway, it was enough for her that we were together."

Jala's chest ached, and her heart was pounding. She had to force herself to draw in her next breath, and even then she could hardly speak. "And now?"

"I still miss her," Azi said. "But she's not you."

She's not you. Jala turned toward him. The corner of his mouth twitched up in a small smile, and the look in his eyes made her stomach flutter. Of course he'd cared for others before her. He'd had a life before he met her. She had, too. But he was choosing her here, now. He knew her, and he wanted to be with her. And she wanted the same. They needed each other. She reached out and took his hand.

"I miss people, too. But you can't see her again for a while, even if it's just . . . to see her. It's not fair to me, or to her. If she loves you, I don't think she'll be satisfied with just a piece of you. No more than I would."

"Do you?" Azi whispered. "Love me, I mean."

"You know I do." Had she ever said it out loud? She wasn't sure. She'd thought it, but it was different to say it. To hear it. "Or anyway, you know it now."

"I love you too," he said. "So we both know it now."

CHAPTER 18

zi's words repeated in her head as Jala stood on one side of a cellar beneath the manor, facing the two prisoners from the mainland. She tried to focus on the task at hand, but she wished she could be back in the hot springs now instead of staring down at two naked, dirty prisoners. The whole cellar smelled like human waste. Grime coated the prisoners' skin, and most of their hair was gone, sold off by the guards.

"I tried every language I know when they were first brought in," Boka the Trader said. "I've been trying for two days. They don't respond. I don't even know if they can hear me."

"Then we'll have to try again," Jala said.

"Even if they do know a language I can speak, their brains are mush." As if to prove his point, one of the prisoners giggled. Boka pointed. "That one always laughs. The other just stares. What do you expect me to do with this?"

"I don't want to be here any more than you do, but we have to know where they came from," Jala said. "I brought the book with me this time. Show it to them, but don't let them touch it until they've been washed." She handed the book to Boka.

"I hope you don't expect me to wash them as well," he muttered as he took the book. He dangled the book in front of the prisoners, speaking to them in different languages. They stared past him. One of them started to drool. Boka turned back to Jala. "There, you see? I've seen dead fish look more lively."

Maybe they were too far gone after all. Jala brushed past Boka and shoved the nearest prisoner. "Are you Hashon? Is that a place, your home? Do you want to go there? Where do you come from?"

"Hashon," he whispered.

Jala barely heard him, for the other had started screaming. "Get him out of here and shut him up," she snapped. Boka called for a guard, and the prisoner was dragged away, still screaming.

"Hashon," the first prisoner replied. His tongue was thick and swollen, and his voice cracked.

Jala's head spun with the thick, foul air, and she tried to breathe through her sleeve. "Show him the book again. Open it and let him see it more closely. Something's going on inside his head."

Grumbling, Boka did as she asked and opened to a random page then turned it to face the man. The prisoner hunched forward awkwardly and squinted at it. Then he thrust it away and covered his eyes with his hands. He fell to his knees and spoke so softly that Boka had to kneel down on the floor to hear.

"Well, that's something," Jala said. "Can you understand any of that?"

Boka's brow furrowed, and he leaned closer to the man, turning his head. "A moment, my queen. I think . . ." He stopped and listened. "I think he's speaking some form of Lowsun." Boka turned to the man and made a slow-down motion with his hands. "Slower."

The man took a ragged breath and spoke again. Slower, and with a clearer voice. Boka listened. "He keeps slurring the words, and his accent's all over the place. It's hard to follow."

"But you've gotten something out of him, yes?" Jala asked impatiently. "Tell me."

"He wants you to pick up the book. He can't hold it, or he's scared to hold it? No, he's not allowed to hold it. By throwing it on the floor he's . . . offended it? That doesn't make sense." Boka glanced back at Jala. "To be honest, I'm not sure he wants to see it at all. He's terrified of the damn thing, keeps saying that he can't look at it because his face is uncovered. Whatever that means."

Jala picked up the book and brushed it off. She stared at it in her hands. "It's full of pictures. I don't know if they're supposed to be gods or what, but they're always masked. Look." She found a page and showed it to Boka. The Hashon man pressed himself into the corner, turning his face away, covering his eyes with his hands. "I wonder if that's what he means when he says his face is uncovered. Something about masks."

Boka shrugged. "It could be, my queen. Or he could be raving. There's no way to know, I suppose."

Jala closed the book again. "This is what they came for," she said. She looked up at Boka. "So you're wrong. There's a very simple way to know. Tell him he will have a ship and a crew to take him to the mainland, and from there he will take us to his lands and his people. They can have the book if they want it so much. It means nothing to us. We'll return it to its rightful place. Make him understand."

Boka spoke for a long time. Finally, the prisoner nodded, his eyes on Jala.

"Good," Jala said. "Now you just have to teach him how to talk."

The next day, Jala took Azi to her room. "I want to show you something. This won't take long, I promise."

"That's good," Azi said. "You know how much I would hate to miss even a moment of politics with my uncle." He smiled, but he still looked tired. He'd only had a day of rest, and since then he'd been busy preparing for another gathering of the five families. Until the Gana could grow new ships, their raiding routes were up for grabs. It was almost like a second Sectioning. *Only there's no way I can make things worse this time.*

"I was brokenhearted when I heard he didn't want me to be part of your talks," Jala said.

Azi snorted, then took her hand and leaned in close to her ear. "Was this just a ruse to get me up here?"

"No," she said reluctantly. "I do actually have something to show you." Jala let him go and led him to her table. She opened a small wooden box and took out some dried seeds. She shook them in her palm so they rattled softly. "Here, stupid bird."

With a squawk and a flutter of wings the mainland bird the Rafa had gifted her flew in through the window and landed on the table. It tried to peck at Jala's hands until she dropped the seeds onto the table, where it ate them greedily.

When it was done, Jala tapped it on the head. "Sing me a song of the Hashon."

The bird cocked its head to the side for a moment, then stretched out its neck and opened its mouth. Voices filled the room. Jala couldn't make out any words, and the singers never stopped for breath. The sounds rose and fell, creating harmony at one moment and discord the next.

The bird broke off abruptly and switched to one of its favorite dirty songs. Jala rolled her eyes and shooed it away.

"I think it's ugly," Azi said after a moment. "Ugly and . . . strange. There's something about it. You keep waiting for the voices to come back together, like you're waiting for the tide. But how can they dance to that? The beat is something you'd play for a baby!"

"Maybe they don't dance," Jala said. "I don't care whether they dance or not, as long as they leave us alone."

"Everybody dances." He leaned closer and touched two fingers to her heart. "Because only the dead don't have a drum."

She thought he was about to kiss her, but a knock interrupted them.

"My queen, a ship has come," Iliana said through the door. "A Bardo ship. They're saying it's your father."

"My father? Why would he come in person?" But she answered her own question a moment later. *Because birds can be intercepted and made to talk.* The spark of joy she'd felt at the news was suddenly replaced by a queasy feeling in her gut. This was about the meeting. She looked back at Azi with regret. "I have to go see him." She started toward the door.

"Jala, wait," Azi said. "When you talk with him . . . try to make him understand. We need the families together. Whatever his plans were before, this isn't the time."

"I will," Jala said. "I promise I'll still be me when I come back, not Lord Mosi of the Bardo in a dress."

That made him smile again, and he followed her down to meet their guests. Lord Inas was already waiting. He nodded at Azi but didn't bother to acknowledge Jala's presence. Her father entered the hall moments later, his ship's captain and a few soldiers behind him.

And, walking next to him, was Marjani.

"Marjani!" Jala ran to Marjani and hugged her tight. "I missed you, and I was so worried, and you have to stay for at least the season," Jala said.

"Not if you're going to choke me like this," Marjani managed, but she was smiling, and when Jala let her go they both laughed. Marjani looked her up and down, then smirked at Jala. "You don't look any different, you know. Same girl I grew up with. Are you sure you're really the queen?"

"I can't help that I've always looked like a queen," Jala said, tilting her head up in mock pride. They laughed again.

Her father spoke by her side. "It's true, you have," he said. "My little queen." Jala turned to look at him. His smile was wide, and the wrinkles around his eyes made him look so kind. "And have you missed me, too?"

She hugged him, holding him as tightly as she'd held Marjani a moment before. "Of course I missed you," she said.

"Just as I've missed you," he whispered, hugging her back. "There's so much to do. These are exciting times, and I know it's frightening, but you should be excited, too. Great things are in store for us. For you."

Jala pulled away from him, a feeling of unease burrowing its way into her stomach. "What are you talking about?"

Her father waved a hand. "Later, my little queen. For now you should be with your friend. Grayships are no way for an old man to travel. I need strong wine and a soft bed and several hours before I'll feel much like talking."

He'd been talking about how old he was getting since Jala was eight, and anyone who'd seen him dance couldn't believe it, but she was glad for the excuse. "Let me show you around," she told Marjani.

"Don't I get to meet your husband?" Marjani said innocently, looking over her shoulder to where Azi was greeting the Bardo captains.

"You met him the same day I did. Come on already." She dragged Marjani out of the hall and back up to her rooms. As soon as the door was closed Jala hugged Marjani tight again. "Why didn't you tell me you were coming?" she asked. "You could have sent a bird to give me something to look forward to. I've missed you so much."

Marjani grinned. "You already said that. You'd think the queen would have more to occupy her time than missing me."

"No," Jala said. "With everything that's happened, I missed you more than ever."

Marjani's smile faded, and for a moment she looked older. Tired. Marjani took her hand. "I missed you, too. But I'm here now. Oh, your mother sends her love. I don't think she knows what to do with herself now that you're gone. She's spent so long preparing you for this, and suddenly she has so little to do. Everyone thinks she's going to go crazy.

If your father would let her start marrying off some Bardo nieces and nephews, maybe she'd calm down, but he wants her to wait."

"Wait until what?" Jala asked with a laugh.

Marjani shrugged. "You know how your father is. He has plans. I'm sure he'll talk you to death about them soon."

Jala sighed. "The last time he had plans, I don't think it went that well. Not for me, anyway. How long are you here? It had better be a while. I demand it."

"Oh, you demand it? Then I have no choice but to do whatever my queen commands." Marjani made an elaborate bow. "But you owe me news. Is it true that you went to the Lone Isle? What was it like?"

"Not as exciting as it sounds," Jala said, but she told the story anyway. Marjani oohed appreciatively at the descriptions of the people there and shuddered in sympathy as Jala described the potion Kade brewed and her strange meeting with the sorcerer-thief Askel.

Jala finished her tale, and Marjani was quiet for a while. "Do you have the book here?" she finally asked. "Can I see it?"

Jala pointed to a chest pushed against the wall. "It's on top. I didn't want the bird trying to eat it. Be careful with it. I plan to give it back to them, if I can."

Marjani flipped through the pages carefully. "It doesn't really seem worth it."

"No. It doesn't," Jala said. "I'm really glad you're all right. That none of them landed on the Second Isle. I was so worried, I had Azi send part of the Kayet fleet, just in case."

"I know," Marjani said. "And thank you for that. I just wish you could have sent them all to the Fifth Isle instead. I know there was no way you could have known. I don't blame you. No one does. We didn't even know about the Gana until that bird came from the king, even though we could see the smoke in the distance, just a faint black line. It didn't seem like much until you got closer, when you could see how much had been burned down, and could see the . . . the bodies in the water." She drew in a shivering breath.

Jala started. "Wait, you were on the Fifth Isle? When?"

"I went with Nara, the friend I told you about. She didn't know if her family was all right. I got her a spot on one of the first barges your father sent. I thought she might need a friend."

"And did she?"

Marjani nodded. "Her father was killed, and one of her brothers was badly hurt. Her mother and sister survived, though. They were lucky."

Jala pulled Marjani close and held her. "I'm sorry," Marjani whispered. "We should talk of something happier."

"At least my father sent help. And I mean to keep this from happening again. If we return the book . . ." The words sounded hollow, now. Whatever she did wouldn't lessen what Marjani's friend went through, wouldn't help any of the Kayet or Bardo who had died fighting on the Fifth Isle. Wouldn't let Azi and Marjani forget the destruction they'd seen. Or maybe it was that the whole plan felt so hopeless. *Am I really only sending someone off to die?*

Marjani wiped her eyes on Jala's bedsheets. "It's all right, I'll be fine. Maybe I just need some wine, like your father. I don't like ships much, and the memories are still fresh." She leaned back against the wall and looked around. "I like your old rooms back home better, but these aren't too bad. And I bet the food's good, with all sorts of exotic treats from the mainland. Why don't you have some brought up?"

Jala nodded. "I'll do that. But I should—"

"—probably go talk to your father, I know. You go do that while I pull myself together. And Jala . . ." For a moment her voice turned serious again. "Listen to him. He sent those ships to help the Gana, and he saved the rest of Nara's family, but there's more to it. He has a plan."

That's what I'm afraid of, Jala thought. But all she said was, "It'll be all right in the end. We'll make it right, Azi and I will. I'm sure of it."

Marjani looked up her. "You've never said 'Azi and I' like that before. You love him, don't you?"

Jala nodded. "If this isn't love, then the real thing would kill me," she said softly.

"Ah, my little queen," Jala's father said. "You've done so well, as well as I ever could have hoped."

Jala smiled up at him. Even after everything that had happened, even though she wasn't a little girl anymore, his praise still meant so much to her.

He put his arm around her shoulders and steered her out of the manor. "Let's talk outside. Too many unfriendly ears in this place, as I'm sure you've found."

What could he have to say that he didn't want to get back to Azi? Maybe he was worried about Lord Inas, though. Once they were out of the manor, she pointed. "If we walk this way, I can show you where the invaders landed."

They walked along the shore with the setting sun at their backs. The ocean was quiet tonight, and the waves lapped gently over the white sand. Several seabirds circled overhead, sometimes letting out high-pitched cries. Long-legged insects buzzed past Jala's face, and she waved them away. When they were far enough from any listening ears, she spoke.

"Azi told me about all the help you sent to the Gana," Jala said. "It's hard to imagine a whole island of people are nearly gone. I'm glad our family could help."

Her father nodded. "How could we do less? There's hardly a Bardo without at least a distant cousin on the Fifth Isle. Orad might have been able to run away, but the rest of our Gana cousins must live with the destruction. So, we do what Orad can't."

"I'm sure Lord Orad is grateful for our help," Jala said. "He couldn't have prepared for that kind of attack. What Marjani and Azi saw there . . . that can't happen again."

"Maybe he is grateful," her father said. "We'll find out soon enough." He stopped walking and faced her. His eyes were serious. "I know that none of this is quite how you imagined it, and I know it's been hard for you. It'll get harder. But you're strong, stronger than any of these Kayet fools, stronger than you know. But *I* know, as I've always known. You will lead the Bardo to greatness, and sooner than I dared dream."

His words were familiar; he'd said nearly the same things to her many times before. She'd always felt proud of his belief in her, but today she wasn't just his daughter. She wasn't just a Bardo anymore. "Our family's greatness doesn't really matter right now, does it? With the invaders and the Gana and everything else. We should all be working together to help them rebuild. And we need to work together if we're going to keep all five islands safe."

"Yes, exactly," her father said. "This meeting your boy king has called isn't just about raiding. It'll determine the future of the Fifth Isle. I'd bet Inas has already tried to convince the Gana to marry into the Kayet, and the rest of the families will do the same."

Was he even listening to her? Jala thought she saw where this was going, and she narrowed her eyes. "You want me to convince him to choose the Bardo, instead."

He just smiled. "I don't think you'll have to convince him. He has no choice. Either the Gana marry into the Bardo, or they lose the Fifth Isle to us anyway. Our soldiers are already on the island. The Gana have no fleet, and what sailors they have left are working with our own to rebuild. Orad's people have already made the practical choice. You just need to make sure he understands."

"I understand that you aren't listening to me," Jala said. Had he only sent help because he was hoping to profit? "Father, we can't just land some ships on the Fifth Isle and say it's ours."

"We can, and we have. And soon we'll have more." He made a sweeping gesture with his arm that seemed to encompass the whole ocean. "Just imagine, in a few years the Bardo will have more ships and more sailors than even the Kayet. When you have a son, he won't be just a king, he'll be a Bardo king!"

Jala's mouth was dry. "And where does Azi fit into this plan? Or is this island ours now, too, since you've landed me here?" She didn't know why she was surprised. This had always been his dream; he'd made no secret of it. But it was different imagining what it might be like to be queen someday and to hear stories of how she might unite the islands for her family. And of course back then he'd never told Jala those plans included destroying families and putting countless lives in danger. Years later, she was finally getting the rest of the story.

Her father shrugged. "The boy will be fine, don't worry. I saw the way he looked at you. He loves you, as well he should. After this meeting is over and the Fifth Isle is ours, you can talk to him and soothe him, convince him it's for the best. Lord Inas is a problem, but obviously his hold over the boy isn't as strong as he might have hoped."

"He's not just a boy," Jala said. "He's your king, too. And I'm his queen. Do you really think I can look him in the eyes and tell him this plan will benefit anyone other than the Bardo?" She went on before he had a chance to reply. "And what if Lord Orad refuses you? What about the other families? They won't just let this pass, not after what you had me do at the Sectioning."

"So many questions! You never doubted yourself before, my little queen. Don't start now. When the winds of fate blow, you can only raise your sails and see where they take you."

If she were still ten years old, her father's words might have made her feel better. But she was beginning to see that he'd never really meant his compliments. She was strong and powerful and smart, but only when she did exactly as he said. And that was no compliment at all.

But he was still her father, and he loved her. He was doing what he thought was best for their family. It just wasn't what was best for her anymore. She tried again to make him hear her. "I'm not doubting myself," she said slowly. "I'm doubting you. How can you look around at everything that's happened and still talk about stabbing the other families in the back? Everyone on the Fifth Isle might be dead now if Azi hadn't gone to help."

"You speak as though any of them are trustworthy. I promise you they're all plotting against us, especially now that you've shown them the kind of queen you are." He put his hand on her head like she was a child. "I taught you better than this. You can't trust any of them."

Jala pulled away. "If we can't trust each other, there might not be much left when more of those ships land. You keep calling me a queen, but you're still treating me like a little girl."

"You're still my little Jala," he said. "But I'll try to remember you're grown and married now, if you'll indulge an old man's forgetfulness now and then."

"You're not that old," Jala said, but she smiled. Things might be different between them now, but maybe he was trying. They walked for a while in silence, and her father examined the beach where the invading ships had landed. Much of the wreckage had been cleared away, but the tide had been leaving bits and pieces on the shore. A scrap of armor, a bit of ship, and, occasionally, a waterlogged body that must have fallen from the ships as they reached the island.

"What's really troubling you about the Gana?" her father asked, prodding a rusted and broken sword with his foot. "Are you worried about what your boy king will think of you? Neither of you believe the families will fall in line because of some mainlander magic. We've always fought amongst ourselves."

"I can't do this," Jala said. "I won't." She stared down at the rusted blade. Once it had been a tool used to bring death, and now it was nothing more than a bit of scrap even the ocean didn't care to keep. She was afraid her people—all of her people—would end up forgotten, lost in the ocean. The sorcerer on the Lone Isle had said the islands were small, insignificant next to the enemy they faced. If the Five-and-One were destroyed, who would know there were ever islands here? What would Bardo or Gana or Rafa mean if none of the families lived through the year?

"Don't be petulant," he admonished. "You're a queen, not a child, as you so recently reminded me. I'll speak to Orad myself then, but you'll support me when it's brought up. You'll see the right choice is the one that's best for our family."

"Best for our family or just for you?" Jala asked.

"No, not for me," he said, and his face softened. "For you. For your children. I'd hoped seeing your friend again would help you make the right decision, but I see it's only confused you."

"You only brought her to manipulate me into doing what you want?" Jala dug her nails into her palms to keep from shouting at him. "You're acting like Lord Inas, all schemes and nothing else. When was the last time we talked of anything but what I'm to do next to help our family? Would you have visited just to see me, or am I out of your thoughts until you want to use me in some new plot?" His moment of silence was answer enough. "No . . . you wouldn't have." She turned her back on him and ran for the manor.

He called something after her, but his words were nothing but wind howling over the water. By the time she reached the manor, she was breathing heavily, but she didn't stop. She didn't run, not wanting to draw attention to herself and be forced to speak to anyone, but she walked as quickly as she could.

She headed toward her room and to Marjani, but halfway there she changed her mind and went to find Azi instead. He was eating dinner alone in his room.

"Jala? I thought you'd be eating dinner with your friend and Lord Mosi tonight. But of course you can stay if you want," he added quickly. "I admit I was a little jealous that your family would be stealing you away from me, even if it's only for a few days."

"No, that's all right," Jala said. "I don't think I can eat just yet."

Azi put down his knife. "What's wrong?"

Jala sank into a chair and took several deep breaths to calm herself. "Nothing. I'm just tired. There's so much going on." She looked away. Her father would want her to keep Azi quiet until it was too late to change anything, not ask Azi's advice on how to prevent it. But exposing her father's plans still felt like a betrayal. *Did I really mean it when I said Azi and I would make things right? I can't keep quiet, not even to protect my own father.*

"No, there is something wrong. It's my father," she said. "I spoke with him, and he plans to take the Fifth Isle for the Bardo. With most of the fleet already there, and more arriving, he doesn't think there's anything the Gana—or you—can do to stop him."

Azi looked down at his plate. "I can't say I'm very surprised. When I saw his ships there, full of food and nets and willing hands, I wondered. Your father's never been known for his generosity."

"You knew? Then why didn't you say something?"

"I didn't know. I hoped for the best, hoped that maybe I'd just been listening to my uncle too much. Anyway, if I told you, would you have believed me?"

Jala sighed. "I don't know. Probably not. I think I had to realize it for myself, and I almost wish I still didn't know any of this. But you could have tried to stop him, couldn't you?"

"I don't know that I want to stop him," Azi said. "Not while he's helping the Fifth Isle as much as he is. Maybe he really can convince Lord Orad to marry into the Bardo. If he does, I won't try to stop him."

"But—"

"I know what it might mean for my family. But it will take years, and Lord Mosi won't always be head of the Bardo. By then you'll be a great queen, and we'll figure it out together."

He won't always be head of the Bardo. . . . The words echoed in Jala's mind. She couldn't imagine home without her father storming around. But it wasn't really home anymore, and he'd made it clear she was more *useful* to him here. She pulled her chair closer to Azi. "I don't know what to do," she whispered. "I hate this. I hate it."

"We'll think of something," Azi said. Tentatively, he reached out and put an arm around her, and the gesture made Jala feel a little better. She wasn't alone, even if neither of them had any idea what they were doing. After a moment, Jala closed her eyes and leaned into him, resting her head on his shoulder.

"We'll have to think about it soon," Azi said. "But we don't have to think about it now." Even more tentatively, he turned her face toward him and kissed her.

Jala kissed him back. It was a long, slow kiss, and it left her breathless. "You're just trying to distract me," she teased, her voice quavering.

Azi grinned. It made his mouth look even more kissable. "Maybe. Is it working?"

"A little bit," Jala admitted. For a minute or two she forgot everything except the feeling of his skin and the beating of her heart and his lips on hers. But it ended too soon, and the world rushed back in along with her breath.

She sighed and laid her head on his shoulder again. "It's no use. Tell me a story instead. A funny one that doesn't involve kings and queens and nobles."

Azi wrapped his arms around her, holding her close. "I think I can manage that. My time as a sailor turns out to be useful after all, it seems."

CHAPTER 19

Despite Azi's attempts to distract her, Jala couldn't stop thinking about her father's plans. She took her seat beside Azi as people filed into the meeting hall. Her father smiled at her as he strode confidently to his chair. Clearly *he* wasn't concerned about the way things would play out today.

Jala fidgeted with her rings, the metal bands clinking against each other softly. Azi glanced at her and put his hand over hers. He didn't say anything, but he didn't have to. She wasn't facing this alone. Whether he agreed with her or not, her father would have to listen to her now, in front of everyone. Or he'd have to listen to Azi, if not to her.

Azi stood, and the room fell silent.

"The Gana have no ships. Their island is burned. If not for the Bardo, their people would be starving. We're here to decide who will use their raiding routes until they have new ships."

Azi paused for a moment, as though collecting his thoughts. Jala's gaze wandered over to the Kayet guards standing at attention in the each corner of the room. Was Azi expecting trouble?

Lord Orad spoke up during the pause. "Why should we lose our routes? The Nongo caused this invasion. They are responsible for the death of my family. Let them give us ships and sailors to rebuild."

The Nongo ambassador sneered. "Maybe if Gana soldiers weren't so drunk they couldn't lift their swords, your family would still be alive, Lord Orad. We faced these invaders too. Nothing but old men whose bones rattled in their armor."

Azi raised his hands, palms up. "Peace, my lords. We don't blame the Nongo. But Lord Orad has a point. If we all lend the Gana ships and sailors to sail them, they can rebuild, and every family can share the burden."

"Nongo ships belong to the Nongo. They will burn before any strangers touch them."

The Rafa ambassador shook his head. "Your plan is a good one, my king, wise and generous. Sadly, the Rafa have no ships to spare, as was shown quite clearly at the Sectioning."

Azi turned to Jala's father. "Lord Mosi, you've shown your generosity and were the first to bring food and supplies to the Gana. Do you also disapprove of this plan?"

Jala kicked Azi's ankle under the table. He ignored it and waited for Lord Mosi's reply.

Jala's father stood slowly. "It doesn't seem that the Gana's plan will work, my king, unless you plan to take grayships for them by force. But there's a simpler solution. As you say, the Bardo have already helped the Gana far beyond any expectations. Let Lord Orad marry one of my nieces and take the name of Bardo. We will see to it that the Fifth Isle rises from the ashes stronger than ever before."

Orad stared at Jala's father, his face tense. He opened his mouth to speak but hesitated a moment.

"My lord," Jala's father said, "you have no choice. You know that."

"I have the choice of honoring my people's wishes," Lord Orad said. "We're grateful for your help, but we weren't told it came with such heavy strings attached. There may be no choice, but I'm not ready to give up everything yet."

"Not everything," Lord Mosi said. "Think of it as gaining a new family, not losing an old one. Or do you think your people will thank you for your blind stubbornness?"

The Rafa ambassador laughed. "You'd have us believe you do this for their good, Mosi? You care as much for them as a fish for fire. The Rafa were the first to feel the greedy hands of the Bardo around our necks. Now the Gana feel them too. Of course Lord Orad has no choice, when Mosi has no intention of giving up the Fifth Isle now that his men have overrun it. And who will stop him? Not our king. Not while this Bardo queen, chosen against the wishes of wise Lord Inas, rules alongside him. Rules, I say, but we see who rules her."

"No," Jala said. "If Lord Orad won't take the Bardo name, then the Bardo will leave the island. Though I hope we can stay long enough to help those in need."

Jala's father froze, but he managed to keep the smile on his face and in his voice, though it didn't find its way to his eyes. "Of course my daughter speaks for the Bardo. But I believe Lord Orad will see the wisdom in our plan."

Out of the corner of one eye, Jala saw Lord Inas's mouth twitch into a smirk. She tried to ignore it. "We're not going to bully Lord Orad into a hasty decision. If there's wisdom to be found, it will be there next week or next month as well."

The Nongo ambassador laughed. "Maybe Lord Mosi's little bird isn't as well-trained as he might have thought. Looks like she's already forgotten all the pretty words you taught her, my lord."

"You're making a fool of yourself," her father hissed. This time even the Rafa ambassador grinned. Azi glanced from her to her father and opened his mouth to speak. But he didn't seem to know what to say or how to wrest back some semblance of control over this mess.

Her father's expression was determined, and Jala knew he was going to make things worse any moment. She stood quickly. "Lord Mosi, you will not address your queen this way," she said, hiding behind the formal tone. "I will speak for the Bardo at this gathering. If you cannot keep silent, you may leave." She forced herself to meet his gaze. He had to see now that she wouldn't let him do this. Not without causing a scene and making himself look weak.

Her father laughed in surprise, a short, sharp sound. "You think to tell me how I should speak to my own daughter? I taught you better, didn't I? Well, I'll teach you now."

Jala's hands shook. She balled them into fists, so tightly her rings cut into her skin. He didn't care at all, did he? They already thought he was controlling her, which made everything that much harder for her, but now he was trying to prove it. "You may leave," she said again. "Or stay, I don't care. But if you stay, you'll hear what I have to say whether you want to or not."

Beside her, Azi found his voice and added it to hers. "Sit, everyone. We're here to talk, not war with each other."

Jala turned to the Rafa and Nongo ambassadors. "If I guarantee that the Bardo will offer ships to the Gana without threat, will you do the same? We're the Five-and-One. We should be uniting against our common enemy, not tearing each other apart."

The Rafa ambassador shook his head. "How can you guarantee us anything with Lord Mosi leading the Bardo, my queen? We've seen how little he respects your position. Once your back is turned, the Fifth Isle is as good as his."

"If your daughter was sitting up there now, you'd do the same," Jala's father said. "You're just angry because I got there first."

Jala willed him to look at her, to see what he was doing, but her father's gaze was locked on the Rafa lord's face. She knew her father had never cared what she thought of the king he wanted her to marry. He didn't care about Azi at all, but she'd thought he cared about her. She was starting to see her father through the eyes of Azi, of Lord Inas, of even the Rafa lord. Greedy, grasping Lord Mosi. Once he'd gained control of the Fifth Isle, did anyone really think he'd be content to stop there? She was a stepping stone, one that could be set aside when it was of no more use.

The islands had to be united, but not under his reign. She looked at Lord Orad. The man's whole body was tense as he waited to hear the fate of his family. The Nongo lord was looking back and forth between her father and Azi. Azi's eyes met hers, questioning. What could they do? The Rafa lord was right. As soon as her father was out of sight, he'd take the Fifth Isle, regardless of the decision made today. He'd told her as much the day before. He thought he was invincible now, that because she was queen, he was nearly a king himself. And he wasn't going to back down.

The Rafa lord's words echoed in her mind. *How can you guarantee us anything with Lord Mosi leading the Bardo?* She couldn't. And so there was only one thing left to do, only one route her father had left open to her. Her father and the ambassadors were still arguing. It was as though they'd forgotten she and Azi were there.

Jala reached for Azi's hand. His fingers wrapped around hers, warm and reassuring. He still trusted her, and he needed her help.

She leaned close to him and pitched her voice low, for his ears alone. "The Rafa are right. As long as my father leads my family, we can't have peace. But that's one thing I can change."

Azi's grip on her hand tightened. "Jala, no. Your father is still alive. You can't know what it's like to lose your father, not yet. You know I'd never ask you to do that."

"I know." That's exactly what her father had counted on. "But I have to."

"You're sure?"

She nodded. Her mouth was dry. One more chance. She could give him that much.

She slammed her fist down on the table. The sound wasn't as loud as she'd hoped, but it got their attention for long enough. "Lord Mosi," she said. "Will you agree to leave the Fifth Isle in peace?"

He pointed a finger at the Rafa ambassador. "So that he can take it as soon as I'm gone?" He swept his hand around, taking in the room. "Any one of them would take the island, especially your king. But I'm the one who took it, and I saved his life and many others in the process." He saw Jala flinch at that reminder of what had happened on the Fifth Isle, and a smile tugged at his lips. He thought he'd won. He looked past her at Azi. "Will you go to war with the Bardo, my king, and undo all the good we, together, have done? And will the rest of you go against your king?"

"Lord Mosi," Jala said. He hardly looked at her. Maybe he thought she wasn't important anymore. Maybe he was too fixated on his own victory, premature though it was.

It's for the best, she told herself. *It has to be done.* All the things people say when they're about to do something they know they'll regret, something that will haunt them for years to come. Even if the words were true. Especially if the words were true.

"Lord Mosi, I remove you as head of the Bardo family."

Now he did look at her, and for just a moment there was a look of surprise and hurt there that made her want to cry. All of the talking and whispering and shuffling in the room had suddenly stopped. There was only silence.

"I take away your name. You can have no family. You can captain no ships. Your wife will be a widow, and your children fatherless. From this day, until the day the ocean dries."

His face twisted, the pain sinking deep beneath the surface and leaving only rage. "Who do you think you are?" he hissed at her. "I raised you. I taught you. I made you into a queen, and this is how you thank me?"

There was no going back now, she knew that. She had to finish what she'd started. She squeezed Azi's hand so tightly she was afraid she'd break his fingers. She fought back her tears. There'd be time for tears later, when the other families couldn't see. "Guards," Jala called. "Take Mosi No-Name. Put him in a cellar. Bring him something to sleep on."

Her father stared at her, then at Azi and their linked hands. He exploded. "You. You did this. You turned my own daughter against me. But it won't mean a damn." He jerked forward toward Azi, but the guards were on him now. One grabbed his shoulder, and he kicked out at the man's kneecap. There was a sickening pop and a scream as the man toppled over. But then a guard punched her father in the kidneys, and as he turned, another guard tripped him and struck him in the face. Her father kicked out again, but his foot caught the guard in the gut instead of the throat. They held him down while another guard kicked him.

"Stop it," Jala said. And to her surprise they stopped. They stopped and looked at her. "Don't hurt him any more than you have to. Even a No-Name deserves that much."

Her father struggled limply as they raised him up by his arms. But though his face was bloody and swelling, his voice was strong enough to carry in the silence. "Orad! *Lord* Orad you call yourself, but you can't hide your family's disgrace. You let them take your grayships, *Lord* Orad. You didn't burn them when you should have." He was looking at Jala now. "Lord Orad watched his ships sail away while his villages, his people, burned. Will your boy king help the Gana now? Will his precious Rafa marry them, do you think?"

Everyone stared at her father, then at Orad.

"Is this true?" Azi said, his voice barely audible.

"He lies. All of our ships burned," Orad said. But his voice sounded dull and lifeless. He was lying and everyone there saw it.

The Nongo ambassador spoke first. "They won't make it to the mainland, not during the storm season. And even if they did, they have no navigators to feel which way the ships want to go."

"They might learn," Azi said. "Or their sorcery might help them. And once they learn how to navigate the Great Ocean, they can do so any time they wish and lead a thousand ships to our beaches."

The ambassadors said nothing as they took in his words.

While Azi spoke, Jala's father was dragged out of the room. She wanted to go to him. She wanted to run and hide and never see him again, to never *be* seen again. To disappear somewhere where no one knew what she had done . . . not the other families, not Azi, not even herself.

"They have magic," Jala said. She spoke softly, but they all stopped to listen. "Strong magic. Even if they didn't take any sailors with them, they'll figure it out. If they reach the mainland, I don't know if it'll matter what we do with the Gana."

Then she stalked out of the hall and stopped the first Kayet she could get her hands on. "Bring me Boka the Trader," she commanded. "And while he's with me, gather whatever clothes and things he might need for a long journey."

"Tell me about your people," Jala said to the prisoner. Some of the fever in his eyes had dimmed. They focused steadily on her as she talked, jumping only to look at Boka the Trader as he translated. "What kinds of promises do your people hold sacred? In the Constant City a guest is safe once invited. Is this a custom of your people as well?" The man spoke, halting several times as he searched for the right words. Boka translated. "We honor the guestrite as made law in the Anka. That's their name for the book. Let's see . . . for three days a guest must be treated with the dignity afforded by his station and within the means of the house."

"And treaties? How do you honor those?"

The man spoke. Boka glanced at Jala, then shrugged. "He says they don't make promises to thieves and murderers."

"We stole. You killed. Perhaps thieves and murderers can deal together."

The man listened to Boka, then spoke two words. "Not murder. Justice," Boka said.

"There will be a treaty, or the book will be destroyed. I'll personally throw it into the fire."

Boka and the prisoner went back and forth a few times. "He says that their promises are held sacred when they are bound in marriage. He was trying to explain the concept to me. Apparently he thought we wouldn't know anything about marriage."

"Right," Jala said. "So I just need to find someone willing to marry one of these." She waved a hand at the prisoner.

The prisoner spoke again. "No man would marry the . . . no father would sacrifice a daughter to be . . ." Boka hesitated. "My queen, he insults you. Perhaps you'd like someone to beat him? He'll sulk for a while, but he's much more cooperative after, I promise."

"I wonder whose sons and daughters they're willing to sacrifice to send ships across the Great Ocean," Jala said. "No, don't translate that. I have what I came for. If we can reach the Hashon, I'll have three days to convince them to make peace. Tell him that we sail tomorrow."

Boka laughed nervously. "My queen, you can't be serious. The storm season!"

"I know about the damned storms," Jala snapped. "We don't have any choice. If we wait until they're past, we'll sail right into a Hashon armada."

"I understand, my queen," Boka said. "But when you say 'we,' of course you don't mean me?"

"I'm sorry, my friend," Jala said. "But there's no time, and I need you to translate. We'll be going to the Lone Isle first. Maybe we'll get some good news there."

The thought of visiting the Lone Isle didn't seem to cheer Boka any. *At least I'm not marrying you off to one of them*, Jala thought. *Be grateful for that.*

Azi met her as she was climbing back up the stairs. "I was looking for you."

Jala brushed past him and kept walking. "I'm going back to the Lone Isle," she said over her shoulder so she didn't have to look at him when he realized she was leaving again. "Don't try to stop me, either. You know I have to go."

"Wait, Jala, slow down," Azi said. He caught up to her and took her hand. "What do you mean you're going back there? When?"

"Tomorrow. If it turns out that the ships have reached the mainland, I'll sail for the mainland from there. I have to go. I don't know who else

I can trust, and if I'm going to risk sending others there, then the least I can do is risk my own life alongside them." She met his eyes so he'd know she was determined to go.

"I wish you wouldn't," Azi said. "But I knew since you first went to the Lone Isle on your own that this is how things would be. That I'd never quite know what you would do, and that I have to trust you. But I need you here."

"You want me here," Jala corrected. "And I want to be here, too. But I can't."

He reached out and wiped the tears from her eyes, then he nodded. She hadn't even realized she was crying until then. She'd lost her father, and now she was going to lose Azi, too.

CHAPTER 20

ala sailed early the next day, aboard Captain Natari's *Burst Hull*. The ship was filled with food and loot to trade at the Constant City. Traveling with her was a sullen Boka the Trader as well as the Hashon prisoner. And Marjani. That was one person she hadn't lost. Yet.

"I don't know how you convinced me to let you come," Jala said to her friend as they watched the Lone Isle grow larger. "I don't know if . . . I don't know when we'll be back."

"You were pretty tired when you agreed," Marjani said. "But I could tell you wanted me to come."

"I'm pretty sure I said you should take the first ship back home and make sure my mother is all right. And that I was not going to drag you across the ocean just so I'm not lonely."

"Oh, well, you *said*. I didn't listen to what you *said*. I knew you'd be miserable without me, and I'd be miserable thinking of you out here alone. It's too late now, so stop moaning about it." Marjani's tone was light, but she was watching Jala's face carefully. She'd been acting like this ever since Jala had told her about what had happened with her father.

Marjani was right. Jala had wanted her to come. She'd also said no, rather firmly. Jala sighed. "You'll have to stay with the ships once we arrive."

"You know I won't," Marjani said. "I want to see the mainland too. If it makes you feel any better, I wouldn't have been any safer if I'd stayed behind, would I? I saw what those people did. If they have ships, then I want to do whatever I can to help. Even if all I can do is keep you company."

"Fine," Jala said. Then, much quieter, she added, "Thank you. It'll be nice to have a friend with me. I just don't want to drag you into something awful. I don't want you to get hurt because of me."

"I know. I'm scared too," Marjani said. She squeezed Jala's hand. "But at least I won't have to sit around and wait with nothing to do but hope I don't wake up to another invasion."

Kade was waiting for them on the beach by the time they disembarked. His face seemed even more lined than it had the last time Jala had seen him.

Before Jala could speak, he called to them in his scratchy voice. "If you seek answers again, look elsewhere. I can't help you this time."

"I only want the same help you gave me before," Jala said. "A small bit of information, and this time in exchange for more than gratitude. I've brought cloth and fine foods for you."

"What you ask is too dangerous. Last time I looked, their sorcerers felt my eyes on them. Since then they've haunted my dreams." He gestured to the villagers around him. "If I help you again, my people won't be spared when they come to destroy you, island queen."

"Do you really think they won't kill you anyway?" Jala said.

"I don't doubt they'll kill me. But as long as there's some hope that they'll spare others, I have no choice. Be gone."

"I'm going to return the book to the Hashon. If they have it back, they won't have a reason to return. Help me make peace. Then when I return, we can talk about whether the Lone Isle needs to remain alone any longer. There's so much we can do for each other. Please. We need your help."

"If I actually thought you had a chance, I'd think about it." He turned away and walked slowly back toward the village.

"It's a better chance than your people will get from the Hashon," Jala said. "I'll wait until tomorrow morning so you have a chance to change your mind."

They returned to the ship, and one of the sailors pulled her and Marjani aboard.

"Well, that didn't go very well, did it?" Marjani said. "Do you really think he'll change his mind?"

Jala sighed. "No, not really. I just wanted to buy some time. I suppose I could threaten him, but I don't think that would work very well."

Boka cleared his throat. "My queen, it seems foolish to risk our lives sailing through storms when we don't even know if the ships ever reached the mainland. Nobody can deny your courage for trying."

"I say we sail on regardless," Captain Natari said, glancing at Boka with disdain. "If the ships ever made it to shore, word will have spread. Someone in the Constant City will know."

"I'd feel better if we were sure," Jala said. *And if we had an army instead of one ship.* She'd even thought she might try to convince Kade to go with her. Having some of their own magic seemed like a good idea right now. But then, he wasn't the only sorcerer on the Lone Isle, was he? There was that other one, the one who'd scared her. Hadn't he sworn loyalty to her? Right before threatening her, of course, but maybe he'd be loyal enough if they offered him a way off the island. At least, she hoped so.

"Captain Natari," Jala said. Both the captain and Boka stopped in the middle of the argument they'd been having. "There's another sorcerer somewhere on the island, a fugitive. If he's not captive, then he's hunted. I think he'll come willingly, if we can find him. I want you to send a party ashore to search for him once it's dark."

"The island is large, my queen. How long should we spend on this search?"

"Just this night, no more. But he should be near the village. He needs to eat, after all, and I think he'll be interested in us. He called himself Askel. Just try your best to find him."

Natari nodded. "We'll be ready by nightfall."

Jala tried to rest, but sleeping on the ship was awkward. Her arms were stiff from cushioning her head, and she couldn't move because Marjani was using her legs as a pillow. She listened to the sailors decide who would search for the sorcerer and who would stay behind. After that, the only sounds were Marjani's quiet snores and the lap of water against the ship.

An hour later, the search party returned. Jala shook Marjani. "They're here." Marjani didn't stir. She gently reclaimed her legs and went to meet the sailors. "Did you find him?"

Natari stepped aside and held up a lantern so she could see the figure shivering on the bench behind him. It was Askel, and he looked worse than she remembered. His limbs were nothing but bone, and his stomach was distended, but somehow he managed to look smug.

"Greetings, great queen." His voice was so hoarse she could barely hear. "I'm glad that her majesty remembered Askel." He coughed. "Her loyal servant."

"They found him hanging in a cage above the mouth of the fire mountain," Natari said.

Askel smiled crookedly. "A warning bell, in case the mountain became angry. If the mountain bubbles and burns me Kade can feel it and get his people to safety. Not me, of course. He doesn't think of me as people anymore. Not like you, my queen."

"If you're as loyal as you claim," Jala said, "then help me now. The invaders, the Hashon, have taken grayships and sailed them into the storm. I need you to tell me what happened to them. Do you have that kind of power? Or do you, too, fear their magic?"

"After living in that cage, fear is an old friend to me," Askel whispered. "I'll help you . . . though I'm weak. Weak, but not stupid. I knew what you would want. Even from my cage I heard much." He tried to laugh but instead coughed for a long time. Jala glanced up at the smoke rising from the fire mountain and took a deep breath of fresh air.

Askel held out his hand, gesturing wordlessly toward one of the sailors. The man handed Askel something wrapped in palm leaves and seemed relieved to have it out of his hands. Askel unwrapped the leaves. Inside was a rock the size of two fists held together. It glowed a dull red and gave off a dry, unpleasant heat.

"It's still liquid inside. The fire mountain's blood. Real power, with none of Kade's damned herbs. You have to know how to fish it out. Delicate work, requires concentration. That's when Kade found me." Askel spat, then looked back at the rock, his eyes wide and his mouth open in a wide grin. "Find me something soft, oh queen, something for me to lie on while I grind the stone root."

The sorcerer used a small, sharp rock to cut the stone root, then to beat it until it was soft enough to put into his mouth. He sucked and chewed on one piece while he worked on the next.

When he was ready, Askel sat down on a borrowed bedroll and unwrapped the fire rock once more. He struck it hard with the point of his stone, and the exterior broke like a bird's egg. Inside, Jala saw the molten fire, the blood of the fire mountain.

"This might kill me, oh queen," Askel whispered to Jala.

"I'll risk it," Jala said.

The sorcerer laughed, then put the mountain's blood to his lips and drank. The smell of burning flesh filled the air. He swallowed the last drop, and the shell fell from his twitching fingers. His eyes rolled back into his head and he fell onto the deck. Black smoke rose from his mouth and ears and nose. Thin tendrils curled out from behind his eyes. Jala held her breath, certain that he had killed himself. But Askel still breathed.

"Mountain's piss," Natari swore softly under his breath.

Jala shuddered. "I think maybe we've been a little too free with that curse."

Askel's breathing was shallow, and his eyes darted back and forth behind his eyelids as if he was having a nightmare. Jala wondered if Natari was picturing his sister practicing sorcery like this.

"Do you think the invaders have magic like this too?" Marjani asked after a while.

"No," Askel rasped. His eyes flickered open. "Not like this." He coughed. "I've seen them, my queen. Your ships. They have your ships."

"Send a bird to Azi and let him know," Jala said. Natari nodded grimly. Minutes later, the *Burst Hull* set sail for the mainland.

CHAPTER 21

None of the men who returned from the raids ever spoke much of the journey there and back, and now Jala knew why. There was nothing to say. Less than nothing. Most of the time she couldn't tell one day from another. There was just the Great Ocean, stretching out in all directions, and the sky broken only by the ever-present storm clouds that gathered and flashed and broke apart.

When there was calm, Jala wished for a storm just so something would happen. When the storms hit, she prayed to gods she never bothered to name. She and Marjani curled up together, holding on to each other and to anything strapped down. The wind howled, water sloshed over the bulwark, and hail bruised their skin. Lightning flashed all around.

Only the prisoner seemed unmoved by the storms. He simply sat at the back of the ship, his hands tied to a hook on the bulwark. Jala could feel his eyes on her and on the chest of clothes where she'd stowed the book.

"Can't you do something about the storms?" she asked Askel once after hours of darkness and rain and thunder so loud that it still echoed in Jala's ears.

"If I had such power over the winds, do you think I would have let myself be hung over the fire mountain?" Askel said in reply.

At night, the stars filled the sky above them. But unlike the islands, where the stars moved slowly with the seasons, above the Great Ocean the stars seemed to change every night. There were old, old stories of sailors using the stars to reach one island from another. But the skies above the Great Ocean offered no such possibility.

The sailors sang and told stories to pass the time, but a few days in, it felt as though they'd sung every song and told every tale a hundred times over. Her back ached, and everything tasted of saltwater. *How can Azi like this?* Besides the boredom and the storms, the worst part was having to hang your ass over the side to piss. The sailors were used to it, but she and Marjani took turns holding a sheet for the other for some semblance of privacy.

Sometimes, high above, Jala caught sight of enormous birds soaring on great wings. Captain Natari told her how the birds would sometimes swoop down and try to grab a sailor from the ship. But from that, at least, they were safe. During the storm season the birds flew high above the clouds and rarely descended. Beneath them, too, were creatures Jala had never seen before, but these were hard to see in the dark waters. Sometimes a whale would surface, spraying water into the air. Once, a school of dolphins followed them, and the sailors struck the water with their oars to drive them away.

When she asked why, Natari explained. "Out here, they can't be trusted. They sometimes tip over ships. It's said there's a city under the water, built by those who fall in when they're near. They're as smart as we are, but they need hands to build with." The stories didn't say how the people below the water survived. Captain Natari thought they might be drowned. Who knew what sorcery lay beneath the waves?

They saw none of the demons Lord Inas had hinted at so many weeks ago. But when she asked the captain about them, he shrugged. "Many things live above and below the Great Ocean, and no man has seen more than the smallest part of it. There are as many stories about strange things on the waves as there are sailors, but it's bad luck to tell them when on the water. The creatures of the depths are drawn to stories about themselves."

Captain Natari's mood was odd. He was pleased with the speed they were making, but more than once Jala heard him whispering with their navigator about the strange undertows they kept encountering.

"It's almost like something wants us to reach the mainland ahead of the worst storms," the navigator said at one point.

"If that's so, best to keep silent about it," Captain Natari said. "Bad enough to be noticed by something that could bargain with the Great Ocean, but to let on that we've noticed it too? Can there be a more unlucky thing? I fear this trip will end badly, and by then we might wish for a death as right and natural as drowning."

Jala wondered at his ominous words, but by now she knew better about Captain Natari's superstitions than to bring it up while they were still out on the Great Ocean.

Askel watched the water and the dolphins with an almost desperate intensity. He watched the sailors as they went about taking care of the ship. He listened to the stories and ate their food as if he'd never done any of those things before.

"Were you born on the Lone Isle?" Jala asked him once.

Askel shook his head. "Kade told me I was abandoned when I was just a baby, but I don't remember it. I've been there my whole life." He looked at her and gave her a crooked smile. "How old do you think I am?"

Jala shrugged. "Old. Sixty years, maybe?"

Askel snorted. "Only twenty. Not much older than your king, I suspect." He turned away from her. "At first, when Kade warned me about the cost of my sorcery, I didn't believe him. When I learned he was right, I looked for a way to have others pay the price instead. That was when he banished me."

"That sounds horrible," Jala said. "I'd have banished you, too."

"Horrible to you, perhaps," he said. "Not to the fire mountain. Not to the Great Ocean. All these things have power, all of them demand the same price, and none of them care about any of our quick, small, little lives. When you make deals with gods, you have to put such things behind you."

Jala shivered at his words and let the subject die.

So the time passed until one day the sky ahead of them was clear of storms, and Jala realized the horizon was no longer flat.

"That's the Great Lighthouse of the Constant City," Captain Natari said, pointing to an impossibly tall, thin stone tower. "Long ago one of their kings decided to build a lighthouse so great and tall that no matter where a man stood he would be able to see its light. He died, of course, and it wasn't finished. If such a thing could ever be finished." Natari turned to her as they passed under the shadow of the lighthouse. "We have no friends here, my queen. Remember that. They'll tolerate us, but we're in danger as long as we're on the mainland."

Jala and Marjani waited at the dock while Boka took a few sailors into the city to trade for transportation and a guide. From the water, the city looked like a piece of gaudy jewelry, with domed towers of bronze and gold, flags of all colors fluttering in the wind. Up close, standing on the dock, everything looked dirty and gray. The buildings pressed in so close in places the sun hardly touched the ground. And it smelled, of fish and rotting food and human waste.

When Boka returned, Jala and Marjani and all but six of the sailors prepared to leave. The sailors left behind would stay on the ship as long as they had food and drink. At least one of them would need to be awake day and night, ready to light the drum of oil and set the ship on fire if anyone tried to take it.

Surrounded by thirty sailors, Captain Natari, Boka, and Marjani, Jala watched the *Burst Hull* sail out into the water and wondered if any of them would see the ship again.

"Don't worry," Captain Natari said. "We'll make it back. We both have husbands waiting for us back home, and I plan to make sure they aren't waiting longer than they have to."

"I didn't know you were married," Jala said. "I never asked you anything about your family, did I? I've been too wrapped up in my own problems."

"And the fate of our people," Natari said with a wink. "I'd say you're excused, my queen."

It didn't make her feel much better. It would be all too easy to get caught up in the big picture and forget to see the people standing right in front of her. The people risking their lives for her mad plan.

"Well, come on," Boka interrupted, waving them all forward.

"Tell me about your family now," Jala said, falling into step beside Natari. "While we walk. What's your husband's name?"

"Onan," he said, and then he told her about how they met and the life they'd made together.

The sounds of the city washed over Jala as they walked the streets. There were people everywhere, talking and arguing and laughing. Jala had expected them all to look like the Hashon, with light-brown skin and the straight hair Azi had described, but most of the people here had the same black skin that Jala did, and she kept seeing snatches of home as they walked past: a silk dress from the Bluesun Peninsula in a style her mother had liked, intricate bronze earrings from Shek or the silver-smiths of Iz, a shirt dyed the same rich purple that had been a gift to Jala on her wedding.

She knew the clothes, but none of the people. They had bronze rings in their noses or eyebrows or tongues. Some of the men wore their hair long, in styles Jala had never seen, and some of the women had no hair at all. And it felt lonely to be surrounded by all these people and have no idea what they were saying.

Jala's group wore scratchy brown robes, the kind they'd normally only use for making sacks or pouches, but Boka had thought it best to go unnoticed as they traveled. The Queen's Earring still dangled from her ear, but it was a symbol only recognizable to the islanders.

"I never thought there could be so many people in one place," Jala said, as much to hear a familiar sound as anything else. "And the smell's getting worse. I wish there was some wind at least, so I could breathe."

"Maybe you should have brought more ships," Marjani said. "It feels like we're being swallowed up. How long before we reach the other end?"

Boka laughed miserably. "If you brought the entire Kayet fleet the Constant City would still swallow it up. We won't see the end of the city until the sun has set, I think, but my queen won't have to walk the whole way. There are the horses now."

He pointed at four huge creatures lashed to wooden carts. As Jala approached, the beasts stared at her with their large eyes and stamped their hoofed feet on the ground. One of them snapped at her with its yellowed teeth, and Jala jumped back with a cry. The man sitting atop the cart laughed at her and said something Jala couldn't understand.

"Are they safe?" Jala asked Boka quietly.

"Nothing here is safe," Boka said. "Stay away from the horses, stay away from our guides, and don't ask me to translate what they say, because you won't like it. Unless you'd rather return to the ship and wait for my trade ships to arrive so they can take us home."

"No. We're here now, so we go on," Jala said. She waved at the drivers. "Will they take us to the Hashon?"

"Not all the way. They say that there's a river that runs to that land, though, so they'll take us that far."

The sailors, too, gave the beasts a wide berth as they loaded one of the carts with chests and crates and barrels. The cart was soon piled high with food and wine for their journey, as well as two small chests of coins.

The cart bounced hard on the dirt and brick streets while Jala and Marjani watched the city slowly pass them by. They passed through a bazaar, and for a while the smells of the city were drowned out by the smell of cooking food. Jala almost told Boka to stop and buy her something. It felt like forever since she'd tasted food without salt. But they'd just eaten on the ship, and stopping now for food was probably too frivolous. Too soon, they left the bazaar behind them.

The carts turned down one street and then another, seemingly at random, and soon Jala had no idea which way would lead her back to the ship or even the ocean. She hadn't been able to hear the waves for hours. The only noise was the noise of the city.

"It doesn't seem like it'll ever end," she said. "Like you could spend lifetimes here and never see it all."

Marjani shuddered. "Why would you want to spend a lifetime here? This place is awful."

They passed through an old, crumbling stone wall, and Jala thought they must have reached the city's end, but beyond the wall were more houses and more people. It wasn't until they passed through a second wall, taller but just as ruined, that the houses stopped. The plain outside the city was crowded with caravans and carts and pack animals of all different shapes. Even out here people bartered for goods while they waited to be let into the city itself.

"We'll travel at night for a while," Boka said. "Try to put some distance between us and the city, and lose anyone who might try to follow us."

"Why would they follow us?" Marjani asked.

Askel answered instead. "To take your metal and your clothes and maybe your lives. Or did you think you were the only thieves on the mainland?"

"We're not thieves," Jala snapped.

"As you say, my queen." Askel bowed his head, but there was a note of sarcasm in his voice. "No doubt being from the Lone Isle it's just harder for me to see the difference."

Jala ignored him and feigned interested in the scenery. Not that it was very interesting. The land around them was full of hills but few trees. Most of it was grass and dirt and sun-bleached stone. Everywhere she looked she saw another road splitting off and disappearing behind a hill or down into a valley somewhere. Hundreds of roads, all leading to the Constant City.

"How long has this city been here?" she asked Boka.

"A long time," he said. "Maybe before the fire mountain birthed the Five-and-One. The Nongo have a story that they used to live here, until a great flood came and washed them up on the Fourth Isle. The way they tell it, they populated all the other islands, and all the families are really Nongo children."

"I've never heard that one," Jala said. "Sounds more like something the Rafa would tell."

"I don't think it's meant for other families to hear. A Nongo story, meant for the Nongo."

The sun set, and they rode on, their way lit by bright moonlight. Against the starry sky, Jala watched thin plumes of smoke rise from nearby campfires. Other travelers, other caravans, perhaps a village somewhere nearby. The cart rocked and rattled and creaked while the horses breathed loudly and the driver whistled to himself. After a while, Jala fell into an uneasy sleep. It was still night when Boka woke her to tell her they'd stopped. She barely remembered eating before she curled up on a sleeping mat.

So it went for several days, as they passed fields of gold-brown plants that Boka called grain, or fields covered in vines. Sometimes they stopped at smaller farms and traded for melons or fresh bread. Every day the sun seemed to grow brighter, and the grass thinner, until one day Jala looked out of the cart and almost thought she was home again. Palm trees grew along the shores of a river. And beyond the river, beyond the grass and palm trees, was an ocean of sand.

There was a cry from the guards. The prisoner struggled against the ropes, crying out in his own tongue. "*Hashana! Hashana!*" He stared at the river, his eyes wide. The Bardo sailors fought to hold on to him as he thrashed about.

"Take him down to the water," Jala said.

The sailors glanced at her, then shrugged and did as she commanded. The prisoner stopped struggling as they walked him down, but then he wrenched forward, tearing the rope out of their hands. He fell to his knees at the water's edge and lowered his head until his forehead touched the muddy riverbank. He whispered prayers under his breath.

When they pulled him up again, he seemed to stand straighter, and though his eyes shone with tears, they were bright as they took in everything around him. He called for Boka as they brought him back to the carts.

Boka went out to meet him, and they spoke briefly.

"He says this river will take us to his people," Boka said afterward. "Captain Natari thinks we'll be safer if we travel by water. We'll trade for a boat as soon as we can." He waved a hand at the horses. "It'll be nice to be away from these stinking beasts, too."

"They do stink," Marjani said, "and I'll be glad to be on a ship again, but I think I'll miss them anyway. I won't miss him, though." Her eyes flicked to the prisoner. "I don't like the way he stares at you. What if he tries to hurt you now that he might actually be able to make it home?"

"I know," Jala said. "But what else can we do but trust him?"

Boka smirked. "He asked to talk to you but wouldn't tell me why. Should I tell him yes, since you trust him so much?"

Jala glared at Boka. "All right. I'll hear him out."

"As you say, my queen," he said, and called for the prisoner to be brought closer.

Marjani leaned in to whisper, "Are you sure that's a good idea?"

"If thirty sailors can't keep me safe from him, then I don't see what difference it makes," Jala said. She stepped off the cart to meet the prisoner.

"Thank you," the man said. He struggled with the words, but it was clearly Jala's own tongue that he spoke. She glanced at Boka sharply, but the trader just shook his head as if to say, *I didn't know.* "You are . . . great criminal . . . but thank you." He gestured at the river. "*Hashana.* Once more see *Hashana.*"

"Hashana. Is that the name of the river?" Jala asked, unsure what else to say.

"*Hashana* is river. *Hashana* is home. *Hashana* is people. *Hashana* is . . . life." The prisoner nodded to her, then turned away to stare once more at the water.

Captain Natari came to stand next to Jala. "My queen, we should move soon, before the sun is too high and hot."

"No. There's something we need to do before we go any further in Hashon land. We'll rest here for a while. If the river really is life the way our friend seems to think, then I think we can all take this opportunity to wash, as well."

"I'm sorry if our smell offends you," Captain Natari said with a hint of a smile. "We've smelled worse. But a rest won't be unappreciated."

They all did as Jala had suggested, washing and sleeping through the hottest part of the day.

"Your pet Hashon is right," Askel whispered as they sat listening to the river. "This water is alive. It travels a long way, listening as it brings life and death. Did you know that all water is one, oh queen? I think somewhere this river must reach the Great Ocean, and from there the Five-and-One. Maybe that's how they found us without a grayship to guide them. There's power in this land. Not so much as in the fire mountain, perhaps, but it's an old power, and it does not sleep the way the fire mountain does."

Later that day, they passed through a small village, but the people there eyed them suspiciously and wouldn't part with any of their fishing boats. It was two more days before they found a larger town where they could trade for two large boats to carry all of them upriver.

Captain Natari scowled as he walked the length of one of the boats. "The wood's rotten, and I've seen better craftsmanship from the boats my son makes out of sticks. I wouldn't trust this to float in a puddle of piss."

"If you'd rather swim, be my guest," Boka growled under his breath. "They don't trust us, so this is all we're going to get from them, and we're lucky we still have anything left to trade."

Natari glanced around then leaned in to whisper in Jala's ear. "My queen, we have thirty sailors. Let's simply take the boats we need tonight."

Jala hesitated. It made sense, but she didn't like it. They had no grayship to escape on, and more was at stake than their own lives. "We don't need them to cross the Great Ocean, just sail down a river. They'll be fine. And we don't need to draw any more attention to ourselves than we have to."

"Drawing attention won't be a problem when we're all drowned," he muttered. "I won't be captain on one of these. It's a disgrace."

"I'll be your captain then," Jala hissed. "We take these boats, and we leave."

Natari gritted his teeth. "Yes, my queen."

For a while it felt good to be back on water again, and Jala liked having the familiar palm trees around them. But that feeling only lasted a little while. During the day, the sun shone down mercilessly on them, so hot it made the deck painful to walk on. At night, the air turned cold, and they huddled together for warmth.

Often, Jala sat and watched the people around them as they paddled or poled their small boats loaded with goods, or fished along the riverbanks. It had been impossible to tell the color of the prisoner's skin, for it had gone ashen with his premature aging, but now she saw that many of his people were lighter than she was, with brown skin and shiny black hair that lay flat and straight. They wore it plain, either cut short or in long tails that could be easily bound back with a piece of thread. Jala felt a childish urge to style it for them.

The river grew wider and more heavily trafficked as the day went on. Inquiries into their business came more often. They had little left to trade, so they couldn't be merchants. They didn't speak the language, and so far from the Constant City even the trade speech was becoming useless. Boka had to rely on what he'd managed to learn of the Hashon language. How would they ever reach the rulers of this land when they could barely speak with the people?

Their prisoner took pleasure in hearing the cries of the other boaters to each other, but it made Natari nervous, and he kept the prisoner back under the canopy that covered two-thirds of the boat. More than once, Jala saw the prisoner's eyes linger on the chest where she kept the Hashon book.

She pulled Askel aside. "We have to hide that book somehow. If something happens and they take it from me, then there's no reason for them to deal with us. There must be some sorcery that can help us. Can you make it invisible? Or change it into a rock? Things like that used to happen in the old stories."

"If such magic ever existed, it's beyond me," Askel said. He considered her for a moment. "But maybe there's another magic that can help you. Tell the captain to stop when night falls." A few hours later they beached the two boats on an empty bank on the same side as the ocean of sand. "Come," Askel told her and he led Jala and Natari out across the dunes.

"Where are you taking us?" Natari asked.

"Nowhere," Askel said, smiling in the moonlight. "A place no one could ever find again. Bury the book here and it will be safely hidden." He gave Jala a shrewd look. "There is a price for what I'm about to do. One that I must pay, and one that you must pay, oh queen."

"What price?" Jala said.

Askel's voice was hungry. "The Lone Isle. The fire mountain. I want them. No more skulking around for stone root and food, no more Kade. Give me the Lone Isle, and you will have magics unimaginable at your command. That I swear, oh queen."

"And what will you do with the people there?" Jala asked.

"Learn from them," Askel whispered.

He was lying. He'd go back to using them up to fuel his own power. "No. There must be another way," Jala said. "I rescued you from death, and I'll keep you alive if we ever make it back. You will have a place to live, comfortable and undisturbed. We'll bring you whatever materials you want from the Lone Isle, or take you there with guards to keep you safe from Kade. But you won't be allowed to hurt anyone else."

Askel scowled as if he'd swallowed something bitter. "Who will pay the other price, then? The only way you'll find the book again is to link someone to this place. All he has to do is leave a piece of himself here. A finger will do." Askel turned to Captain Natari and grinned. "Give me your blade, my friend. I promise the cut will be quick."

Captain Natari looked at Jala, and even in the dark she could see the determination on his face. "My queen?"

He'd do this for me if I commanded him, Jala thought. "Not him. He needs his hands to hold a sword."

"Then who?" Askel asked. "Your friend Marjani, perhaps? Or that merchant, Boka? They don't need their hands. Or you could agree to give me the Lone Isle. Then I would gladly do this for you, my queen."

"I'll do it," Jala said. "I won't ask anyone to do this for me. A queen doesn't need all her fingers to rule." *And the Hashon are less likely to kill me right away. I hope.* She tried not to worry about what Azi would think if she came back with a maimed hand and told him she'd cut it off for sorcery. He had scars from his own journeys, of course, but this wasn't quite the same thing. Still, she had no choice, and if a missing finger was the least of her worries by the time this was over, she'd count herself luckier than the Thoughtless Boy in all his stories.

She held out her left hand and curled all but the smallest finger into a tight fist. She tried to sound calm. "Make it quick, Captain, just like our friend said."

"My queen, this feels wrong," Captain Natari said. "There must be some other way."

"I'm listening," Jala said softly.

Captain Natari met her gaze, but he had no answer for her. He drew his sword. "It would be better if I had a knife. I could slip and cut your hand, or worse."

"I trust you," Jala said simply. "You won't slip."

He didn't look happy, but he held out his sword. "Kneel down and put your finger against the blade."

The metal was sharp and cold against her skin. The skin of her arm tingled with goose bumps. Captain Natari took her finger in his free hand and squeezed it tight.

"You're sure about this?" he whispered.

"It has to be done," she said.

He pulled down on her finger, sliding it across the blade, and at the same time he yanked the sword up with his other hand. Blood welled out of the stump before she felt the pain. Her severed finger fell to the sand. She wanted to scream, but she looked away and bit down on her lip hard. Captain Natari pressed a cloth to her hand.

"Not too tightly, now, my friend," Askel said as he gingerly picked her finger up and brushed off the sand. "We mustn't stop the bleeding altogether. Give me your hand, my queen."

Jala pulled her hand out of Captain Natari's grasp. Gritting her teeth, she pulled off the strip of cloth and held it out for Askel. Warm blood ran down the stump of her finger and down over her palm. She thought she was going to be sick, but she made herself watch anyway.

Askel took her hand and shut his eyes. He whispered something under his breath, then he touched her severed finger to the stump.

She felt a strange burning in her finger. The feeling grew until it was a fire, until it was worse than the cut had been, and as the smell of sorcery filled her nose she cried out. But the desert and the night swallowed her voice. Captain Natari was on his feet in half a heartbeat, the edge of his sword at Askel's throat.

"Hurt her again and I'll kill you," Captain Natari spat.

Askel released her and she fell back, clutching her hand to her chest. Slowly the burning ebbed, leaving a painful throbbing in its place. The stump still bled, but slowly.

"It's already finished," Askel said. "So long as her hand bleeds, the finger will remain alive. As long as the finger lives, we'll be able to find it again. The piece always seeks the whole from which it came. Just like a grayship and its reef, yes?"

"No," Captain Natari spat. "This is nothing like that. This is . . . wrong. Evil. Like the invaders' ships. I'm sorry, my queen. I should have stopped you."

"Give me the book," Askel said. "We will tie them together."

Jala reached into her robe and pulled out the Anka. Carefully side-stepping Captain Natari's sword, Askel took the book from her. He took a thin strip of cloth and tied it around the finger and then bound the finger to the book. He dug a hole in the sand and left the book there. It was covered moments later, like they'd never been there at all.

Captain Natari helped Jala stand. She felt weak at first, but as she walked, she felt a little better. Her hand still throbbed terribly, and worse, she could still feel her missing finger itching, only there was no way to scratch it. It was maddening. She clutched the bloody cloth to her hand, but it didn't help, and it made Askel frown at her until she loosened her grip.

"How long do we have before we can't find it again?" Jala asked after a while.

"Perhaps a week," Askel said. "Maybe a few days more. I've made sure the blood will flow slowly and the wound will take a long time to close, but still, we don't have much time."

"Then I hope we find them soon," Jala said. "And I hope this wasn't all for nothing."

They reached the boat, and the sailors stared at her and whispered among themselves.

"What happened to your hand?" Marjani asked.

But Jala was too tired to explain. "Sorcery," she said. "Ask the captain, but tell no one else."

Captain Natari called out orders, and they set off again.

"How much longer?" she asked the prisoner when the boats were underway again.

"Soon," he said. "Very soon."

His words echoing in her ears, Jala went to sleep and dreamed of dark blood falling on the sand. The sand clumped where the blood touched it, as if the desert was drinking it in. Suddenly the sand was rising all around her, smothering her, drinking her up like it had Askel's blood. She couldn't breathe.

Jala woke to feel a hand over her mouth and bony fingers digging into her neck, choking her. She tried to scream but couldn't. A dark shadow blocked the thin moon. Bony knees pinned down her arms. It was the Hashon prisoner. Had he killed the others? Was Marjani lying facedown in the water even now? *I don't want to die. I can't die, not now!* Her heart was pumping fast now, and the terror was replaced with a rush, a sudden burst of strength. She bit into the man's fingers and wrenched her arms free.

He was lighter than she'd expected, and he fell over with a muffled grunt. Jala threw herself on top of him. Using her weight to hold him down she lifted her right hand and slammed the base of her palm down on his nose. She felt something give and heard a sound like twigs breaking. She stopped for a moment, queasy. Hot blood spurted out from her attacker's broken nose and onto her hand.

Then pain exploded in the side of her head, and she toppled over. Her vision swam, and she heard herself moan. She tried to move but found she couldn't. Everything was losing focus.

She heard her attacker cursing in the tongue of the Hashon as he rummaged through her chest, throwing traveling clothes and dresses onto the deck.

I need those for when I meet the Hashon rulers, she tried to say, but her mouth wouldn't move. It didn't seem to matter that the shadowy figure had tried to kill her. Only that she needed her dresses so that she could look like a queen.

The man returned, looming over her. "Where?" he hissed at her. He shook her, and her head bounced against the wood.

Then his hands wrapped around her throat again.

"He's escaped," someone shouted. "There, grab him before he gets away!" She felt the fingers around her throat relax, and then her attacker was gone. She felt the thud of feet running over the deck of the ship, and then she heard a splash.

"Go in after him, damn you. Bring him back." More splashes.

And then Natari was bending over her. "My queen? Are you hurt?"

I'm fine, Jala tried to say, right before she passed out.

A splash of cold river-water revived her, and she woke to find Marjani and Captain Natari kneeling beside her.

"What happened?" she asked. She could speak, though her tongue felt slow in her mouth.

"The prisoner's escaped," Captain Natari said. "Looks like he managed to fray the ropes holding him. He got away, my queen. I'm sorry."

"No, my head," Jala said. "Why does it hurt so badly?"

"We think he hit you with a stool," Marjani said. "It, uh . . . broke. On your head."

Jala stared at her friend for a moment, and then she laughed. Marjani snickered too. They laughed until Jala felt dizzy again, and then Captain Natari and one of the other sailors helped her back to her bed.

The next day she still had a headache, and the sun made her feel queasy, but by the evening she felt better.

That was when the chariots came. She saw them first as dust clouds on either side of the river growing steadily bigger, and then she saw the horses pulling strange two-wheeled carts filled with armed men in bright bronze armor. They caught up to the boat and yelled at them while nearby boats sped up and slowed down to get out of the way.

When Jala's men didn't respond, the men on the right side of the river took out hooks tied to long ropes, twirled them in the air, then threw them at their boat. The hooks caught on the bulwark and the mast, tore through sails. The horses turned, and the ropes pulled tight. The ship listed to the side as they were drawn toward the riverbank. Natari's sailors slashed at the ropes with their swords, but they were thick, braided strands that frayed only slightly at the assault. They tried to throw the hooks back in the water instead, but there were too many of them all over the ship, and the men on the shore just threw the hooks again.

Captain Natari's face was grim as he tested the weight of his sword. "We're lucky they didn't simply kill us from the shore with rocks or arrows. We may still have a chance of fighting our way through them, but you and your friend must stay close to me."

"I told you this would happen," Boka hissed. "You've gotten us all killed on this idiot's quest."

Jala reached out and took Marjani's hand. "Put your weapons down," she said.

The sailors glanced at each other, then at Captain Natari.

"Put your weapons down," Jala commanded. She looked at Captain Natari. "These are the very people we're supposed to be making peace with. Killing them won't help our mission. Besides, we're outnumbered and lost in a foreign land. What if I'm killed and there's no one to bargain with them? Without me, we can't find the book. What if Boka is killed and I have no one to help me speak with them? Put your weapons down, and let our friends here take us where we want to go. I was tired of this boat anyway."

Captain Natari stared at her for a long moment, and then he nodded. He and his crew sheathed their swords.

Hashon soldiers shouted as they boarded the boat. They surrounded Jala's people and led her former prisoner past them. He scowled at her while the Hashon ransacked the boat, ripping up the boards, emptying chests, and shredding the clothing inside.

They were looking for the book. But of course they wouldn't find it.

"I am Jala, queen of the Five-and-One Islands." She spoke loudly, both to be heard above the noise they made searching and to try to mask her fear. "I would speak with your king and queen."

CHAPTER 22

Azi sighed inwardly when he saw Inas waiting for him at the door to his room. "What is it, Uncle? I'm tired."

"We have to talk about the Gana," his uncle said. "In private, my king."

Behind his uncle stood a woman dressed in loose robes. Her face and shoulders were covered in the ritual tattoos of a shipgrower, each one symbolizing mastery of another aspect of the mysterious craft. Azi recognized a few of them: the dolphin represented the ability to hold your breath underwater for minutes at a time, the seed represented the knowledge to cultivate a new reef. Others, like the snake on the woman's forehead, had meanings known only to the growers themselves.

In her hands she held a clay jar, sealed tight with grass and twine made of tree bark.

"It's important, my king," the shipgrower said softly.

Even a king could not refuse one of the reef masters. But what did a shipgrower have to do with the Gana? "All right, come in. I'll have some food brought for us."

They walked into his rooms. The shipgrower set her jar down on the table where Azi sometimes ate his meals but didn't sit down herself. Neither did his uncle, who chose to pace instead.

Azi closed the door then sat. "Well?"

His uncle stopped pacing and cleared his throat. "I know you don't want to hear this, but your queen is most likely gone. Even if she makes it back, it'll only be because her mission failed."

Azi's temper flared. "Do you think I haven't thought of this? If you don't have anything new to add, then get out."

"Be quiet and listen," his uncle said. "You know she has little chance of succeeding. But she did do one thing right. We now know these mainlanders have grayships. What will you do when the storm season ends?"

"I don't know," Azi said through clenched teeth. "We'll post watches, have our ships patrol the waters around the islands. What else can we do? Jala must succeed. That's the plan."

"No. It isn't," his uncle said. "Not if you're brave enough to truly be king. Grower Ellin. Please educate my nephew."

The shipgrower bowed, then carefully opened the jar on the desk. Curious in spite of himself, Azi peered over the jar's rim. Inside was a thick red-brown liquid. It looked like mud.

"Do not touch it, my king," Ellin said. "It can have damaging effects on people even in small amounts. Those of us who learn the art of brewing it spend many years around it so that we may do so without going mad."

Azi glanced at his uncle, then back to the shipgrower. Wherever this was going, he had a feeling he wouldn't like it. "What is it? Some kind of poison?"

"It is called clay wine. And it is a poison, yes, but not one meant for people. The clay wine is deadly to shipwood. If it touches a reef's heart, the reef will die, and its grayships will become lost and unable to return home."

Azi looked into the jar again. "I've never heard of this before."

"It's made from the red clay found only on our island. On its own, of course, the clay is harmless, but we have certain ways to extract the essence needed to brew the wine. Its very existence is a secret known only to a few, my king, and the secret of its making is kept only by three master growers of the Kayet. It has been passed down among us for two hundred years."

He met his uncle's gaze. "You want to kill the Gana reef so that their grayships can't make it back. Is that it?"

"It's a better plan than your queen's," Inas said. "At least it will work. I didn't say it was a nice plan, just a necessary one."

"Jala might still succeed," Azi said. "I'm not going to just give up on her."

"How long will you wait?" his uncle said. "Until the end of the storm season? Or later still? How much time will you give them to destroy us? You're the king. You have to make this choice."

Azi stood. "What choice? There's no choice here, there's just murder!"

Ellin raised both hands in a calming gesture. "It need not be done at once, my king. To destroy the entire reef we will need more of the wine than we currently have, and the process takes time."

"Fine. Do it," Azi said, looking away. "But we won't use it until we're sure. Not until we know there's really no other choice."

The shipgrower bowed. "There is one concern. My king knows better than me that the currents can be fickle. It's not impossible for the clay wine to spread to other islands."

"You mean the Second Isle," Azi said softly.

"The Second Isle, yes, but others as well. Even our own reef may be harmed. Not enough to kill the whole reef, you understand, but there will be a price, of that I'm certain."

A price you'd be more than happy to see the Bardo pay, Azi thought. His uncle put a hand on his shoulder, then walked out of the room. Ellin followed close behind, taking the clay wine with her. When they were gone, Azi put his head into his hands. *You have to come back*, he thought. *I don't know if I can do this without you. I don't think I'd want to.*

Jala would know what to do. Or if she didn't, she'd go do something mad like visit the fire mountain or take a ship across the Great Ocean. She'd try anything because anything was better than nothing. He missed that about her. He missed everything about her.

CHAPTER 23

"They won't dare harm us until they know where the book is," Jala reassured Marjani. Then one of the Hashon soldiers rammed his fist into Jala's stomach, and she doubled over, fighting to breathe. Through a fog of pain she heard Captain Natari swear as he tried to break free of the soldiers on either side of him. He knocked them to the ground and tried to reach her, but two other soldiers caught him. One of them drove his fist into Natari's side, then the second into his back. They took turns hitting him until he, too, was on the ground.

Jala was afraid they would keep hitting him until he was dead. But once he fell, they let him lie there. No one else moved. Jala forced herself to stand in spite of the pain. *I'm still a queen*, she told herself. *They can't beat that out of me.* She hoped they wouldn't try.

The soldiers bound their hands. Then they were tied together in groups of four, and each group was tied to a cart. One of the soldiers tied a green flag to a long spear and raised it above his head, waving it back and forth. Across the river the other group of soldiers did the same, then they got back into their two-wheeled carts and rode away.

Then they stood, waiting. Watching. The sun rose steadily, reflecting off of helms and their mail armor. All of them wore helmets that partially covered their faces and sloped up several inches above their foreheads. Each one had a different pair of eyes painted on the metal surface, and they seemed to look down on her with scorn.

When any of Jala's people moved more than an inch, they were hit, once, hard and fast. The same if they made any noise. After a while, the soldiers picked up Captain Natari, bound his hands, and tied him to a cart as well.

What are they waiting for? The sun rose, beating down on them. Two more soldiers were hit, and Marjani as well, for nearly passing out in the hot sun.

Jala cursed them for that and earned herself another blow.

Only when the sun was past its zenith, only when their throats were dry and their skin felt burned and the islanders had learned that they were not in control did one of the soldiers shout a command.

They snapped the reins, and the horses began to walk, the carts began to roll, and the ropes grew taut. Jala stumbled and almost fell, but she caught herself in time. Painfully, stiffly, Jala and her people walked.

Throughout the day and into the night the soldiers had shown no emotion. They talked little, laughed never. Finally they stopped, well past midnight, and the soldiers made camp and took off their helmets. Then they began to talk and laugh and drink and curse.

Jala was tired, hungry, and still thirsty after the little bit of water she'd been given. Her feet were blistered and burned from walking on hot stones and sand.

"We'll be all right," she whispered to Marjani as they lay on the hard ground.

"I don't believe you," Marjani said. Jala didn't argue. She didn't believe herself either.

The Hashon soldiers had lost interest in their prisoners for the moment, and Jala was able to speak quietly with nearby sailors, passing messages to Boka and Captain Natari.

A few moments later, Marjani nudged her elbow, and Jala turned to see one of the soldiers creeping toward them, the blade of a knife glinting in his hands. His helmet was off, but there was something strange about his face, like it was covered by something. It looked like he was wearing a mask of some kind.

"Help us," she cried, though she knew they couldn't understand her. "Help us or your book is lost!"

The man with the knife stood and leaped on the nearest sailor, slashing down with his knife. But luckily her cries had roused her own people enough, and the sailor brought his hands up in time to catch the knife. The others tied to him tried to help as much as they could with their hands bound together. There was blood on the knife and on the ground around them.

A desperate part of her wondered if they might take their attacker's knife and cut the ropes that bound them, escape down the Hashana, and forget this mad plan of hers.

But then the Hashon soldiers came with long knives of their own. They dragged the attacker off and took the knife. The man screamed and cursed, and the whole time his eyes were on Jala. They tore the mask off his face and threw it in the river, then slit his throat. They checked the sailor's ropes. They buried the body.

The next day, Jala could see the sailor who had been attacked more plainly. He had ugly gashes on his hands and chest that bled as he tried to walk, and his eyes had become distant and feverish. When they stopped midday, he collapsed on the ground and couldn't be goaded into getting up.

The soldiers cut his throat, too, and dragged his body away from the river.

There were no more strange masked men, but Jala and her people learned quickly that night was more dangerous than the day. During the day, when the soldiers were on duty and wearing those strange helmets, the islanders were safe enough if they stayed quiet. But at night when the soldiers took off their helmets, they threw stones at the islanders, spat at them, tried to kick them if the soldiers still on duty weren't watching. At night, they were unpredictable.

The whole thing felt like a nightmare that wouldn't end. But then, on the third day, the city of the Hashon rose up ahead of them in a burst of green palms and vineyards and walls of yellow brick.

They stopped there, with the city in sight, while some of the soldiers drove their carts off toward the city. They returned a few hours later with two larger carts that were completely enclosed by wood and rough cloth canopies.

One of the soldiers untied Jala and shouted at her to get in. She did as she was told, but then they had some of the sailors get in with her. "Wait!" she shouted. "I want Marjani with me. Marjani." She pointed at her friend, but the soldier just shouted back at her and banged on the wood with the flat of his sword.

The cart creaked and shuddered as it made its way over the city's brick streets, and seemed to hit every bump in the road, but it was still a relief not to have to walk. If only Marjani was there with her. She wished she'd never brought her here. She wished she'd never brought any of them.

The smells of the city wafted into the cart, and she heard people all around them. The wood of the cart was old and warped, leaving gaps in the slats. Once her eyes adjusted to the bright light the gaps let in, she was able to peer out at the city. Mostly she just saw the same yellow brick broken up by the occasional stone or rows of thatch.

The people they passed looked like the Hashon, though some had darker skin and curlier hair than their captors or wore clothes from far-off places that still reminded her of home. It seemed to her that more than a few of the Hashon had burns on their faces, bright pink and red welts around the nose and eyes and forehead. Jala saw flames painted on the side of buildings or crudely carved into the stone. They seemed to be everywhere, and she wondered what it meant.

People shouted at them as they passed. At first Jala thought they must know about her, that they were angry about the book. But then she realized they were shouting at the Hashon soldiers, not at her people.

A rock thudded against the side of the cart, and then another. One of the soldiers swore, and then Jala heard swords being drawn. Jala heard a scream, then the drivers cracked the horse's reins, and the carts bounced on again. Jala craned her neck and only just caught sight of a group of soldiers fighting to control a quickly growing mob.

Soon after that, the light dimmed as they entered some kind of tunnel. The cart's doors were thrown aside and Jala was dragged out. They were somewhere underground, dank and dark. They led her down one corridor and then another before leaving her in a small cell. Marjani and the rest of the soldiers were taken away, and Jala heard more cell doors clanging shut farther down the passageway.

She waited, hoping they would remember to return. Hoping she wouldn't die here, alone in the dark, in a rank dungeon an ocean away from home. Somewhere nearby she could hear water flowing. An hour passed in silence. Maybe two. She hummed softly to herself just to hear her own voice.

And then they finally came. A few soldiers entered the cell first, one holding a grimy lamp and two others pushing Boka the Trader in to stand beside her. Seven robed figures followed the soldiers inside, each wearing an elaborate mask.

Each mask was different: there was a mask covered in eyes; a mask with a wide, grinning mouth; a mask covered in hands. One had nothing, no mouth and no eyes—not even eyeholes for the wearer. There was a mask of suns, a mask of moons, and a mask of mountaintops.

It was the mask with the grinning mouth that spoke, while nearby a short, round-faced woman wearing only a plain white robe translated for Boka using the trade speech of the Constant City, a mix of speech and hand signs.

"She says you will tell her where the book is," Boka said. "If you don't return the book, we will be tortured and killed in front of you."

With the only light in the room coming from the one lamp, the brightly colored masks seemed to float in front of her, eerie and alien. The people wearing the masks wore loose, dark-colored robes that hid their bodies. In the dark it was sometimes hard to tell who was speaking. Or maybe that was just her hunger or exhaustion.

She was frightened, and all she wanted to do was curl up on the floor and close her eyes, yet somehow she was speaking. "I want my clothes," she said. "I want to wash and eat. My friends will want to eat too. Then I'll talk with you in the halls where you greet honored guests."

Boka hesitated. Jala snapped her fingers at him without looking away from the seven Hashon lords. He translated. Some of the masks turned to look at their own translator as she relayed Jala's message. Some of the masks whispered to each other, then an order was given. One of the soldiers left.

A minute later the soldier returned with Askel in tow. The grinning mouth mask spoke, pointing at Askel.

"This one will die first," Boka translated.

"Without him the Anka is lost forever," she said. There were murmurs when she said their word for the book. She spoke over them. "The Anka is buried under the sand, and only his magic can lead me back to it. If he dies, the magic dies." She wasn't even sure if this was true, but she didn't want to try to find the book herself using magic she didn't understand. *If the magic dies, we all die*, she thought. Standing in the dark, cramped cell, surrounded by people who wanted to kill her, the whole plan seemed like a really stupid idea. "You have two days, maybe, if my hand still bleeds. You will treat us as guests, and then we'll leave as guests before the guestrite is over. And I want my clothes."

"I'm not saying that," Boka hissed. "They'll kill us both."

"They'll kill us if you don't. I'm not giving them the book for nothing in return."

"Maybe you're willing to sacrifice us, but I'm not." He glared at Askel. "Take them to the book, and maybe they'll let us go. We don't mean anything to them. Let them keep her if they want." Askel laughed softly, an ugly sound from deep in his throat. Boka clenched his teeth. "You'll just tell them anyway. They'll torture you, and then you'll do anything to make them stop."

"What can they know of pain that I don't?" Askel asked. "I've drunk the blood of the fire mountain, felt it burning away the years of my life. Let them try. Better to die here than choking to death over the mountain's bowels."

Jala stepped closer to Boka and took his hand. "I know, my friend," she whispered. "I'm scared too. But the wind's blowing too hard for us to turn away. We can only see where it takes us."

Boka's hands shook as he repeated Jala's words. She could see the translator's eyes following Boka's hands with ease, but then the woman asked Boka to repeat himself. When she turned back to translate to the masked lords, she acted confused. Jala thought she could almost guess what the woman was saying. *I can't understand this islander, this one must have been hit on the head too many times. I'll ask again, but it's like talking to a fish.*

Well, maybe he wouldn't have said fish. She hadn't actually seen a lot of fishing along the riverbanks. Too many boats.

She shook her head, forcing herself to pay attention again. The translator was signing and talking to Boka, but in the midst of asking him to repeat and explain she flashed a new sign, one Jala didn't recognize.

"What's going on?" Jala asked. "Can you make her understand or not?"

Unlike the translator, Boka seemed to be genuinely confused. "No, she seems to understand, but she made the sign that means she has a better offer for us. I think she's working for someone else, not just these Hashon lords. Someone else who wants the book."

Jala glanced at the translator, and the woman met her eyes for a moment. Then she turned back to the masked lords, made some more apologies, and signed at Boka again.

So the woman was only pretending not to understand. "Boka, what the hell is going on? What sort of better offer?"

"She says that if you remain here, it will be easier for her master to meet with you. She says they'll help us escape."

Jala stared at the translator again. Her head ached. She couldn't remember the last time she'd been given any water. Before they were stuffed into those carts, probably. She wanted to feel clean, to eat, to make sure Marjani and the rest of her people were safe. "This is some kind of trick. Tell her to repeat exactly what I said before."

Boka did as she asked. The translator shot her a hard look, as if to tell her that this second, secret conversation wasn't over yet. A moment later the masked lords left, taking Boka with them. She was alone again, wondering if the translator had passed on her message. Would they come back with one of the sailors? With Marjani? She wished Azi were with her, which was such a selfish wish.

But when the soldiers returned, none of her people were with them. They motioned for her to get up, without yelling at her or hitting her, and led her out of the dungeon and up into the palace itself.

CHAPTER 24

$\mathcal{J}$ ala was taken to a room in the palace with a shuttered window facing the river. Looking through the slats in the shutter, she saw ships being built on the riverbank. They were slow, heavy barges not unlike the ones that had landed on the islands. She counted twenty. There were probably more. Were they preparing for another attack?

She pulled on the shutters half-heartedly, but they'd been nailed shut, and the wood was strong. And where would she go, with no ships and nothing to trade? She couldn't even speak the language.

Someone knocked on the door. The door only locked from the outside, so they could have just entered. *I guess they're being polite, for now.* But when she opened the door, it wasn't one of the Hashon servants. It was Marjani.

"You're all right!" Jala said just as Marjani cried out, "Jala!" They hugged each other tightly.

"When they took you away, I—"

"I didn't know where they took everyone, and I was afraid—"

They stopped and laughed nervously. Jala straightened her dress. "How do I look? Like someone you'd want to make peace with?"

Marjani's smile faded. "So there's no peace yet? When they took us up to these rooms, I thought maybe things had gone well."

Jala shook her head. "Not yet. We're their guests for now, that's all. I think we'll be safe for a few days. But they'll have to come for me soon if they want their book, right?" Jala smiled for Marjani's sake. "I don't think we'll be stuck here for too long."

Marjani squeezed Jala's good hand. "You look lovely," she said. "Especially when you lie."

"It's not a lie. I just . . . I'm scared. Not just for myself, but for everyone. For you, for Captain Natari, for poor Boka, for all those sailors. I keep thinking, did I really need thirty sailors? Couldn't I have taken twenty? Fifteen?" She sat down on the soft bed. "Are they all here?"

Marjani shook her head. "I don't know. They took us up into the palace, then brought me here."

The door opened again. It was Boka. Behind him stood the translator and two Hashon servants, all dressed in the same plain white robes.

"They're taking you to dinner," Boka said. "That's what she said, at least."

"Where is everyone? Are they treating you well?" Jala asked.

Boka shrugged. "They took everyone to different rooms all over the palace and put guards on the doors. As far as they're concerned 'guest' just means we get beds and maybe some food now and then."

"All right," Jala said. "That's something, anyway. Just give me a moment." She hugged Marjani one more time, then touched her earring for luck. It was heavy and annoying sometimes, but it helped her feel like a queen, and it was her last connection to Azi. It was hard to feel queenly when your kingdom was a world away.

The palace itself was unimaginably huge. Though she tried, Jala couldn't keep track of the passages they took, the identical halls lined with smooth green stone, the many gates and doors, the tapestries and lamps and paintings. Even here she could hear the sound of the river flowing through the walls and under her feet.

Finally they reached a large hall, magnificent in its height and decorated with precious stones. Daylight streamed through the tall windows set in the walls and ceiling, and the entire hall sparkled with reflected light. But more precious than stones was the food laid out on one end of a long table. Jala's stomach growled at the sight.

The masked Hashon sat waiting for her at the other end of the table. They didn't look so frightening in the light. She could see which of them was short or tall, which one had a large gut, which were women and which were men. All of it reminded her that beneath those masks they were still people, and people were willing to make trades for what they needed.

"Thank you for your hospitality," Jala said.

Standing nearby, Boka spoke with the translator, then said, "You are welcome, island queen, as a guest of the Hashon. We invite you to sit at our table, eat our food, and drink of our river."

"You're sure they said guest?" Jala said.

"As sure as I can be."

"In that case, have you eaten, my friend? Tell them you'll sit and eat by my side while we talk."

Jala sat and ate with Boka while the masked figures watched. They seemed to have no interest in eating. Only their translator seemed restless, standing beside the table and shifting from foot to foot. To fill the silence, and to show how unconcerned she was, Jala asked about the food. There was horse meat in a sauce made from oranges and dried grapes served with rice. There was also beer that she was expected to drink with a reed, so thick it was as much a meal as a drink.

When she was finished, Jala waited for the table to be cleared, then addressed the masked Hashon. "You already know my name. Perhaps you would honor me with your own names before we begin."

The translator pointed to each of the masks and spoke their names. "Lord Mouth," Boka said. "Lord Eyes. Lord Hands. Lord Empty Face. I think she means mute and blind. Lords Far and Near. Lord Stone." Boka hesitated. "She also says that Lord Stone can't be trusted. At least that's what I think that sign means."

Jala stared. "Is that supposed to be a joke?"

"It's what she said. How can I tell whether they're mocking you when I can only get it second-hand and they always wear those masks? Maybe the masks are a joke, too."

"All right." Jala cleared her throat and spoke to the Hashon. "It's a pleasure to meet you, my lords. I'm truly glad you have accepted us as guests, and I hope that in your wisdom you will also accept my proposal." She spoke slowly and clearly, with a forced smile on her lips.

Boka translated. The masks listened, and Lord Mouth spoke. Their translator made a single gesture, one fist slapped twice into her outstretched palm. "Make your offer," Boka said.

"This is my offer: the book, the Anka, was taken by mistake, and the Gana, the family that took it, has paid in blood." This was a lie, but Jala figured they wouldn't really know the difference between one island's family and another. "They are no more. We'll return the Anka to you and pledge peace with the Hashon. Our ships will leave your caravans and your villages alone. We'll trade with you. We bring many things from the far corners of the coasts to the Constant City, and of these you'll have the first choice as long as I am queen." Jala waited for Boka to translate, then went on. "In exchange, you will pledge peace with us. You will stop the invasion and return our ships to us. You will give us supplies and allow me and my people to leave unharmed, as guests and friends."

Jala wished she could see the faces behind those masks. They spoke in whispers among themselves, but she couldn't tell anything from their flat, even voices.

"How can you guarantee such a deal?" Boka translated.

"By marriage," Jala said. "One man or woman from each family of the Five-and-One will travel here to marry the noble sons and daughters of the Hashon, and people of the Hashon will travel to the islands to marry into each noble family. Through marriage and trade, our two peoples will be joined and ties of peace will replace bloodshed."

She listened, her heart pounding, as Boka passed on her message, as the white-robed translator spoke to the masked lords, and as the lords conferred. They spoke in a dull monotone. Jala wondered if they cared at all.

They're just trying to unnerve me. They want their book back. They'll bargain for a while, but sooner or later they'll have to say yes. She just wished they would hurry, before her heart exploded or she passed out or started screaming. What was taking so long?

The voices stopped. Jala held her breath.

Lord Mouth spoke a single word. *"Osh."*

Jala stared at their translator. The woman seemed surprised by their response, but when she spoke to the masked lords, Lord Mouth simply repeated himself. The translator punched her palm once, then slashed her hand sharply through the air. The answer was clear even without Boka's help. "No. They refuse."

"Mountain's piss," Jala whispered to herself, feeling suddenly faint. *What have I done?* She opened her mouth to speak, but she had no words left. She had nothing.

Lord Mouth was speaking again, but Boka wasn't looking. Jala grabbed his shoulder and shook him, pointing at the translator.

"You and your people will be treated as guests until the guestrite passes. Then you will be displayed, tortured, and killed. Blood . . . I think it's blood, it's hard to understand," Boka stammered.

"Tell me. You know what she's saying," Jala said, trying to keep her voice firm.

Boka nodded and took a deep breath. "Blood pays for blood. I think that's what she said. She could be lying to make us sorry we didn't take her offer earlier. Who knows what they're really saying? For all we know *osh* means yes."

Jala stared into the masked faces. She tried to keep her voice from shaking. "I don't think she's lying about their answer. Ask them what they want. Ask them how we can make peace. There must be something."

"I'll try." His speech and hand signaling was hesitant still, and he spoke with the translator for several minutes, clarifying what Jala wanted to say. When the translator was satisfied, she spoke in her own language to the masked lords.

As they did, Jala stepped closer to Boka. "Do you need to sit down?"

"No, my queen. I'll finish."

Jala put a hand on Boka's shoulder. "I'm sorry I brought you here, my friend. I truly am."

Boka shrugged off her hand. "You'll be my queen until I'm dead, which shouldn't be long now. But you're not my friend."

This time it was Lord Stone who spoke, not Lord Mouth.

"For ten days the river flowed red with blood," Boka translated. "Many died to feed the magic, but you and your king still live. Your ships still sail the endless waters. The guilty must pay."

Then Lord Mouth spoke again. Jala didn't bother listening to him. The meaning would filter through eventually. Why would they sacrifice so many to reclaim this book, this Anka, only to give it up again? Maybe it wasn't what they wanted all along. Maybe revenge was all they cared about.

"Give us the book," Boka translated. "Then maybe we'll show mercy. Perhaps the girl you brought doesn't have to die. Perhaps we'll let some of your people return home."

At least that would be something. The book'll be lost in a few days anyway, and worthless. I could save Marjani. But for what? So that she could die in the next invasion? Well, if Lord Stone couldn't be trusted, what about the translator? If that was a trick, it would have to be a pretty bad one to make their situation any worse.

"Tell the translator I want to meet with her master. If they have a better offer, I'll hear it." She waved a hand at the masked lords. "Tell them I need time to think about their offer."

Boka started to sign, then stopped. He stood straighter. "No. I won't say it. Just give them back their damned book. There's still a chance they'll let us go home that way, and that's better than nothing."

"Haven't you seen their ships?" Jala said. "Do you close your eyes every time you visit the Constant City? We're fish trying to make peace with a killer whale. All of the Five-and-One are at stake. Your family, my family . . . do you want to live just to see them all die? Are you that much of a coward? Tell them."

Boka's hands stayed at his sides. "What if this new offer never comes? Then what?"

Jala shut her eyes. "Then I'll give them the book. I swear it."

"Thank you, my queen," Boka said, and he told them. "They say you have two hours to make your choice. And she says her master will meet with you soon."

CHAPTER 25

Hashon soldiers led Jala back to her room. Marjani looked up from the bed, and her face fell as soon as she saw Jala. "They refused, didn't they?"

Jala nodded, not trusting herself to speak. She walked over to the bed and sat down beside her friend.

Marjani took her hands. "You're shaking."

"There's still hope," Jala said. "I think there is, anyway. The translator said someone else wanted the book, someone who might be willing to trade for it instead of the Hashon. There's a chance that whoever she's working for can get us out of here. It's not much. I don't know what I was thinking. I'm sorry I ever brought you here. It was so stupid of me. So stupid and selfish. Whatever happens, I promise I'll try to keep you safe."

"Don't be silly, I had to go. I didn't know if you were ever coming back. But, seeing as we might be dead soon . . ." Marjani leaned forward and kissed Jala on the lips. She pulled away before Jala had a chance to react. "Sorry. I wanted to do that, just one more time, before you went away to live on the First Isle. Before you got married. I wanted to the night we snuck out to go swimming, but I was scared."

"You don't have anything to be sorry for," Jala said. She poked Marjani's arm. "Though I hope the thought of our impending death is a *little* scarier than the thought of kissing me."

"I'm still sorry," Marjani said, and her smile was sad. "Azi should have been the last person to kiss you."

"Then I'll do my best to make sure he is."

"I know," Marjani said. She hugged Jala, not like someone who wanted to kiss her, but like someone who needed a friend. She wasn't the only one. Jala hugged her back.

"Did you hear that?" Marjani said, pulling away suddenly. "It sounds like . . . someone shouting. There it is again."

Jala listened. Marjani was right, someone *was* shouting. *Are they coming to kill us after all?* But the sound was coming from outside. Jala rose and walked over to the window. She peered out through the shutters, and for a long moment she wasn't sure what she was seeing. There were flames, people running this way and that. One of the barges was on fire.

"What's happening?" Marjani asked.

Before Jala could reply, a whistle cut through the shouts. A moment later, the nearest barge exploded, sending a ball of flame high into the air. The heat blasted Jala's face, and she turned away, shielding her eyes.

Marjani rushed to Jala's side. "Are you all right?"

Jala coughed and rubbed the tears out of her eyes. "I'm fine. Something is happening down on the streets. Some kind of riot, I think. There's fighting, and some of their barges are on fire."

There was a scream somewhere outside their door, but it was cut off. "We have to block the door with something," Jala said. "Help me push the bed."

But it was too late. The door swung open, and three figures entered the room, all of them wearing the white robes of the Hashon. All but one were stained with blood. Each of them held a long, curved knife, and Jala stared at the bloody steel for a moment before she could force her eyes up to their faces.

She didn't recognize the two men, but she knew the woman who stepped forward. It was the translator. She stuck the knife into her belt, then held up a mask decorated with blue waves.

"Who are they?" Marjani asked, her voice so quiet it was almost inaudible.

"Hope, I think," Jala whispered. She craned her neck to see past the men. "Where's Boka? Didn't you bring him?" The two men in blood-stained robes just stared at her. *Damn it, I should have had Boka teach me some of the trade language on the way. Why didn't I think of that?* She made exaggerated signing motions with her hands. "Boka! Why didn't you bring Boka?"

The translator slipped the mask on over her face. Suddenly she seemed to fill the room with her presence, and when she spoke her voice sounded stronger, deeper than the translator's ever had. "I am Lord Water," the woman said in the language of the Five-and-One Islands. "You will take us to the place where you hid the Anka, island queen."

"In exchange for what?" Jala asked.

"For your lives," Lord Water said. Who or what was Lord Water? Had the mask transformed the translator into something else through some kind of sorcery? Maybe the Hashon were so fixated on masks because they had power and magic. She didn't know, but she knew the woman behind this mask wanted to make a deal. She'd asked for this meeting.

The men behind Lord Water shifted, and Jala couldn't help glancing at the knives they carried. "What about my people? Free them and I'll give you the Anka."

"Some have already been freed. They will distract the misled while we make our escape. The rest will be released once I have taken the deceiver's place. If you had remained in the lower palace, all might now be free. The lives lost today are on your hands, island queen. Do not delay and waste yet more."

"How do you know she's telling the truth?" Marjani said, coming up behind Jala.

"You can hear the chaos outside," Lord Water said. "Lord Fire runs wild. This is the only chance you'll have, island queen."

"And if I take you to the book, what then? What promise could you offer me that you'll keep your word?"

"None but that Lord Stone is my enemy, and once I have the book, he will fall. The city will be mine. It was Lord Stone who sent ships to kill your people. And it was your people that gave me this chance. I have no need, no desire, to make war on you. What other promise could I give?"

Jala took a deep breath. This strange masked lord would help her because they had a shared enemy. That she could understand. "All right. You'll have the book in exchange for my people's safety and freedom. And we need the sorcerer, Askel. We can't find the Anka without him."

"He will be waiting for us," Lord Water said. She said something in the Hashon tongue to one of the men, then turned back to Jala. "There are few safe places in the city tonight. Your friend will stay behind with Sadiki. He will protect her until we return with the Anka."

"But I'm coming with you," Marjani said.

Jala reached for her friend's hand and nodded. "I'm not leaving her behind."

Lord Water shrugged. "Then we don't go. You have something of mine. I will keep something of yours until our deal is complete. A guarantee of good intentions."

"How can you ask me to leave my closest friend behind, alone, in a strange city, with a stranger?"

"I'm not asking," Lord Water said. "She will not be harmed so long as I return with the Anka."

Marjani squeezed Jala's hand. "It's okay. You'll be back soon and we'll all go home. The sooner you leave, the sooner we can get out of this place."

"Are you sure?"

"No. But it doesn't sound like we have a choice."

Jala closed her eyes. Marjani was the only thing she had left. Marjani could get her through anything. Lord Water knew that. And she had something Lord Water needed. "If I don't make it back, will you still honor our deal?"

"As long as I have the Anka, our deal will stand. Now come. There is much to do, and the fire spreads quickly."

"Then let's go." She gave Marjani a quick hug.

"You'll be back," Marjani said quietly. "And I'll be fine. We both will."

Jala nodded, not trusting herself to say anything else. She couldn't cry, not now. There would be time for crying tomorrow, when they were on their way home.

Sadiki bowed and led Marjani away.

Then Lord Water removed the mask, and the person standing before Jala seemed to shrink into herself. Jala couldn't say how she sensed it, but she knew the woman was no longer Lord Water, no longer full of strange power and intensity. The translator drew her knife and waved for Jala to follow. Jala followed, with the bloodstained man close behind her. As they walked, quickly and silently, Jala heard more shouts, screams, and the screech and clang of steel. At one point a Hashon man half-dressed in armor stumbled into them, and the translator cut his throat. Watching him choke to death on his own blood, Jala gagged, but the bloodstained man pushed her onward.

They went down a set of stairs, into the dungeon, then through a gate that had been left unlocked. The sound of running water was almost deafening. The river had to be nearby somewhere. The translator pressed her hand against the stone wall and felt around for a moment, then wedged her knife into one of the cracks. One of the stones came loose. She pulled it out and set it on the floor, then reached into the hole and pulled out a small tin lamp.

The translator lit the oil, and the lamp gave off a small, weak light. The river flowed through a wide channel only a few feet away. The water churned against the stone walls, foaming as if in anger. Then the woman covered the lamp with her robes for a moment and flashed a signal. At the other end of the tunnel another light flashed.

Along the walls on each side of the canal was a narrow walkway, barely wide enough for a single person to stand on, worn smooth by the river and covered in slime. They walked along it, hugging the walls, the small lamp lighting the way. Jala's foot slipped and she almost fell in, but the man behind her caught her arm and yanked her back. The sound of rushing water swallowed her cry. She moved with extra care after that, but her heart was in her throat the entire time.

Not long after that, the lamp went out. Jala felt a brief moment of panic, and then she saw the night sky ahead of her, full of moonlight and stars. Over the roaring water she thought she heard the neighing of horses.

They were waiting outside the tunnel, six horses held by a man wearing robes so dark he blended into the night. He nodded once at the translator and disappeared into the shadows like he'd never been there at all. Askel sat, shivering, on a stone nearby. When he saw her, he smiled an ugly smile. "Hello, oh queen. Have you made your deal?"

"Something like that," Jala whispered, sitting down beside him and trying to catch her breath. The sorcerer looked thin and skeletal in the moonlight. She started to tell him what was going on, but then the bloodstained man said something to her and pointed at the horse.

"I think they expect us to ride," Askel said. "I tried to explain, but that one just kept threatening me with his knife."

Jala shook her head. "I can't. I'm sorry, I don't know how."

The translator was already on one of the horses. The woman motioned Jala over to her own horse, indicating she should sit behind her. One of men knelt in front of Jala and laced his hands together for her to use as a step.

"I've never ridden one of these before," Jala said nervously. The horse was looking sideways at her in what she was sure was a threatening way.

The Hashon were growing impatient with her stalling.

Jala glanced at the horse, then down at her dress. That wasn't going to work. Before the kneeling man could stop her, she took his knife and cut her skirt down the center. Then she dropped the knife in the sand and put one foot in the man's hands. The translator took her hand, and Jala felt herself lifted up. She swung one of her legs around the horse, tearing the dress further, and wrapped her arms around the other woman.

The woman spoke again, and Jala thought she was trying to be reassuring. *Why doesn't she just tell me? She could speak our language well enough before.* Then the translator kicked the horse and they were off, like a gray-ship with sails full of wind over storm-mad waters. Jala could only squeeze her eyes shut and hold on tight. *I won't fall*, she told herself as they rode out into the desert. *I won't fall. I won't fall and smash my head open on a rock.*

They rode for a long time. When carrying two people became hard on the horses, they switched to the other three. When all the horses had been ridden, they walked them for a while. At these times Jala was able to open her eyes. Stars filled the sky overhead, and the moon was bright. In the distance, she could hear the river. They rode out of sight from it, among the dunes, but she could tell they still followed its path.

Askel sat on another horse, holding on to one of the soldiers. He had no qualms about the horse. He seemed to have no fear at all.

The sun rose, and in the heat of midday they rested. Jala watched the Hashon. They spoke softly to each other. One of the men was taller than the other, with a long face and a short, neat beard that gave him a serious look. The other was clean-shaven and had a rounder, kinder face, and when the Hashon quietly prayed before their meal, his eyes glistened with tears. Jala wondered if he had lost people to Lord Stone's crusade to retrieve the Anka. Maybe that's why he was helping her now.

"I thought the whole point of these horrible beasts was to make travel easier," Jala muttered as she hobbled over to the kindly-looking man to get her meager meal. "I feel like I walked a thousand miles. I won't be able to walk at all if I have to sit on that creature much longer."

Watching her, the bearded man said something and laughed. He had a rich laugh, and it made his eyes crinkle in a way that changed his face completely. She wondered if he understood her meaning even if he didn't understand her words.

Dinner the night before had been water and strips of dried horse-meat. Today's lunch was water and a handful of wrinkled, sugary fruit. The kind-faced man tried to teach her the words for them as he handed them to her. *Fig. Date. Grape.* She repeated the words but quickly forgot which was which.

The translator took no more food than the rest of them but fed half to her horse. She seemed very alone, in spite of the two men traveling with them. She commanded, and the two men obeyed, but they never had real conversations with her. She carried the mask with her always, and sometimes Jala caught her reaching for it only to stop herself and press her hands down to her lap.

They rode again, into the afternoon heat, while the city of the Hashon grew small and distant behind them. Soon Jala saw they had circled back around to the river, and the two men took the horses down to the water.

Jala was growing increasingly uneasy around the kind-faced man. Sometimes, when everyone grew silent waiting for sleep to take them or for the sun to lessen its hold on the world, the kindliness would slip from his face. His eyes would dart back and forth, as if he was watching an insect flit about in front of his face. He often stared at Askel.

When she asked the sorcerer if he knew why the man watched him, Askel held up his arms, indicating the patches of burns that covered him. "Maybe our friend just can't tear his eyes away from my beauty, oh queen."

"So you don't know anything?"

"I know he draws flames in the sand for me, when the other two aren't looking," Askel said. "Perhaps he knows of the fire mountain."

"Perhaps," Jala said. But she began to think of him as the haunted man instead of the kindly one, and she avoided his gaze.

They followed the river closely now, and occasionally the translator would look back at Jala and ask something in the Hashon tongue.

"*Osh*," Jala said, shaking her head. "Not here. Farther."

The translator frowned. She was growing impatient. But then, as night fell, Jala's finger stump began to itch worse than it had in days. "Can you feel it?" Askel asked. "The closer you get the stronger the sensation will be."

Jala only nodded in reply. She closed her eyes and held out her hand, moving it back and forth in front of her. She could almost feel it . . .

"Stop," she called. "We're going to miss it."

The translator called to the others, and they slowed their horses. She reached into her robe, pulled out the mask, and put it on. "It's here?" she asked, again speaking Jala's language with ease, her voice once again strong and commanding.

"I think it's close," Jala said. "Let me off, I can't concentrate sitting on this thing."

With another word from the translator they stopped and dismounted. The horses were almost spent anyway. The two that had been carrying Jala and Askel were panting loudly, their mouths covered in foam.

"They breathe too loud. Take them away," Jala said. Then she closed her eyes again and let the strange, unpleasant sensation lead her away from the river and into the desert. The itching became stronger, and her finger began to throb. The blood had slowed to a mere trickle before, but now it soaked into the bandages, the way it had when it had first been cut off.

"It's here," she said.

The two men began to dig. Jala edged away from the horse as the monstrous thing huffed and stamped sideways, nervous without its rider's hands on the reins.

Jala looked at Askel. "You said the finger still lives. Can you . . . reattach it somehow?"

"There would be a high price," he whispered back. "And I'm hungry, and tired."

Jala didn't ask what that price would be. It was only the smallest finger.

The digging was hard. The wind blew sand back into the hole as they dug. Jala could feel Lord Water's impatience.

Then both of the men jumped back from the hole. "Anka!" the bearded man said, while the kind-faced man whispered a prayer under his breath and touched a hand to his heart.

Jala bent down and grabbed the book before it was covered again. Her little finger was still tied to it, oozing blood. She snapped the reeds and let the flesh fall to the ground, where it shriveled and dried. The throbbing in her finger subsided, and the bleeding stopped.

As Lord Water watched, she picked up a handful of sand and rubbed it gently on the front cover, scouring off the blood.

When she was done, she held it out to Lord Water. "I've kept my promise. Now, if this book is truly holy to you, keep yours."

Lord Water took a deep breath and touched the book. A shudder ran through her. Then she grasped it with both hands. "The Hashana will remember you, island queen." She raised the book over her head and shouted in triumph. The two men fell to their knees before her, touching their heads to the sand. The bearded man was crying joyfully.

They're only stories, Jala wanted to say. *Stories that don't change.*

On the ground, the kind-faced man reached into his robe, to the place where he'd held his hand over his heart, and fished out a piece of paper.

"Good-bye, island queen," Lord Water said as she lowered the book and reverently placed it into a satchel at her side. The two men rose, and the bearded man led the three horses to Lord Water.

"You're going to leave me here?" Jala asked. "What about Marjani? You said she'd be safe."

"I will keep my promise," Lord Water said. "Your friend will be sent to you, along with any of your people that still live."

Jala saw something move out of the corner of her eye. It was the kind-faced man. He had a creased paper mask in his hands, and his eyes darted wildly as he lifted it to his face. It was a mask of flames. Somehow, in that instant, his eyes seemed to dance.

His knife was out of his belt, and Jala cried out, but it was too late. He screamed Hashon words as he leapt at Lord Water. The steel slid into Lord Water's gut. The man jerked his hand to the side, and Lord Water fell back, clutching her entrails as they slithered, dark and bloody, out onto her lap.

The kind-faced man took another step and struck Lord Water in the face, sending the water mask flying. The woman tried to scream, but her voice was weak. He reached for the satchel holding the Anka. He never made it. The bearded man grabbed him by the hair and opened his throat with his own knife.

The translator whispered something, but Jala couldn't understand the words. The woman's lips were bloody with foam. Then she smiled and fell back onto the sand, eyes open but unseeing.

Jala stared, frozen in place. It had all happened so fast. The bearded man fell to his knees. His knife fell from his hands. He mumbled a prayer under his breath but did not move. The horses neighed and stamped the sand, their eyes wide and their nostrils flaring.

The animals are going to run, Jala thought. *They're going to run, and then we're going to die.*

"Do something," she said to the bearded man. "Take your book, your Anka." She reached into the translator's satchel, heedless of the blood, and pulled the book free. The man backed away from her, averting his eyes. "*Osh*," he said, followed by words she couldn't understand. He wouldn't listen to her. And why should he? What was she to him? Only the little island queen. Not anyone important. Not Lord Water.

The water mask lay only a few feet away. Such a simple thing, just wood and paint and a leather strap. She tucked the book under her arm and then, with trembling hands, she picked up the mask. She wondered, briefly, what good it would do. She couldn't speak the language. The man might even kill her for touching it. *Like that really matters now.*

She placed the mask over her face. It smelled of sweat, and the narrow eyeholes made it hard to see. *Such a simple thing.* She clutched the Anka tightly.

"Listen to me," she said, trying to make her voice deeper, more confident, more like the translator when she was Lord Water.

The man looked up sharply, and his eyes grew wide. "My lord," he whispered. He touched his forehead to the ground once more. Askel stared at her, wide-eyed.

"I have the Anka," she said, and there was something strange about her words, something strange about her voice. "You will take me and this sorcerer back to the city."

"At once, great one," the man said.

He had understood her. Jala had understood him. She realized what had sounded strange. When she spoke to him, she had spoken in the tongue of the Hashon.

A cold wind blew across the sand. The paper mask fluttered away from the dead man's face. Beneath it, his skin was blistered and burned. The mask tumbled in the air, then curled in on itself in red and orange flames.

CHAPTER 26

Azi sat on the beach and watched the waves come in one after another. The sky was bright and blue, with only the occasional wisp of luminous white cloud. No storms gathered in the distance. No ships appeared on the horizon. He held the King's Earring in his hands and toyed with it mindlessly while he waited and watched.

Someone was walking down the beach behind him. He could hear them breathing heavily as they approached. It was a long walk to this empty stretch of beach, but from here he could look out toward the mainland. Here he was usually left alone.

If her ship came, if it ever came, this was where he'd see it first.

"Leave me, Uncle," Azi said softly. "I've heard it before."

But his uncle said it anyway. "The storm season is over, and there's no sign of her. She's gone. You have to accept that."

"Why must I accept that?" Azi asked, not bothering to turn around.

"Because I expect you to act like a king, not some sulking child," his uncle said. He grabbed Azi by the shoulders and spun him around. Azi opened his mouth to order him away but stopped. He wasn't alone. Kona was there, a determined look on her face. She met his eyes.

"What's going on?" Azi asked, looking from Kona to his uncle.

"You have to remarry," his uncle said. "Rebuild our alliance with the Rafa, father sons to take your place. Do your duty, to the Five-and-One and to your family."

"Your uncle says we can be together," Kona said. "All you have to do is let Jala go." Her voice was neutral, almost hard. He couldn't read her expression.

"I've made a deal with the Rafa," his uncle said, his voice softer than it had been for a long while. "You won't have to choose a girl you don't know again. As soon as you're done officially mourning for that lost Bardo girl, we'll hold another wedding."

"But she's not Rafa. I don't understand how this would help the alliance," Azi said.

217

"My father was Rafa," Kona said. "He took my mother's name to be with her."

"She will be adopted as a long-lost daughter of the Rafa, and you will marry her and make her a Rafa queen. No one will dare question it. Jala's left the Bardo without a leader, and whoever they send to the next Sectioning will still be struggling to convince the captains they should listen to him. We'll give him a few scraps of land to make him look stronger than he is, and then he's under our control.

"The Gana are no more, and without allies the Nongo are little threat. We'll return Two Bones to the Rafa along with the other cities taken from them. So long as the girl does what I say, and carries the Rafa name, they'll stay loyal to us. And with only four families, things become simpler, don't they? By the time your son is ready to be king, he might marry a Kayet queen."

"You sound just like Jala's father," Azi said.

"Except unlike the former Lord Mosi, I'm not the one who caused all this in the first place," his uncle said stiffly. "But I'll do what it takes to make sure the Kayet remain strong. This is the course the winds have laid for us, Azi. We'd be fools to try to steer into them instead."

Azi met Kona's eyes. "What about your family?"

A smile tugged at the corners of Kona's mouth. "They'll get used to my Rafa name a lot faster than they'll get used to having me as their queen."

"And you? Can you be happy as my queen? Can you still love me knowing that I chose her instead of you?"

"Of course she can," his uncle said. "The Bardo girl made things hard on herself. It's easy enough to do what we tell her and take care of your children when you have them. She won't even have to leave her family."

"Is that all you think a queen should be, Uncle? What about the king? Should the king simply do as you say, too?"

"I may not be your father, but I'm doing everything I can to teach you to be a good king," his uncle said. "I won't be around forever. Listen to me now, and you'll know what to do once I'm gone. There's no reason to deny it now. That Bardo girl twisted your head around until you couldn't steer straight. But it's not too late."

Azi turned away from his uncle. The man was more of a father to him than the old king had been, but at that moment he couldn't stand the sight of him.

"Is that what you believe?" he asked Kona. "That I was tricked by her? That I never really loved her?"

"You're still here, aren't you?" she asked.

Azi started. "What?"

"You wanted to know if I'd be happy as your queen. I don't know. I never wanted to be queen. Your uncle says you need me, and maybe you do. Maybe I can help. Everything that's happened is so much bigger than either of us. Will I love you? How can I answer that? I don't know this king I see in front of me where Azi used to be. You will not rule, but resent your uncle ruling for you. You say you love her, but do nothing to help her."

Azi tensed. "I do love her. More than anything. But what can I do?"

"You can sail into the wind," she said softly. "If that's what it takes to get her back."

"What are you doing?" Lord Inas spat. "You're only confusing the boy more."

She turned her hard stare on Lord Inas, and her expression made him fall silent. "The Kayet don't need a boy, and I don't want one." She turned back to Azi. "If you were seduced by her, then you were a fool. Maybe I could love a fool. But if you do love her and choose instead to stay here, with me . . ." She hesitated only for a moment, just long enough to close her eyes and breathe before meeting his eyes again. "I could be your queen, but I could never love you."

"I love her," Azi whispered. "I'm sorry."

"No. You're not," she said. Her eyes glistened with tears, but she blinked them away. "You're sorry you hurt me, or you're sorry you had to see me hurt. It's not the same thing at all."

Azi felt his own eyes burn, but he wasn't about to let her see him cry. He didn't have the right, not after what he'd done to her. After what his uncle had done, using her like nothing more than a token in a game.

"You could have stayed with me if you really wanted," Kona went on. "But you chose her. That was easy. So choose her again now, when it's hard."

"What am I supposed to do? Get a ship and sail off to the mainland alone?" The thought had in fact crossed his mind more than once, but it was impossible. Wasn't it?

"You were a sailor once. And you're the king."

"Are you mad, girl?" his uncle sputtered. "Do you wish him killed?"

Kona ignored his uncle, as if he wasn't even there. "A part of me still wishes you won't go, even now," she told Azi. "I don't want to say good-bye. But if—when—we see each other again, it'll all be different. So this is still good-bye, in a way."

She leaned forward and kissed him, lightly, on the cheek. She smiled at him, and Azi knew it was the last time she would ever look at him like that again. Then she turned and walked away down the beach without a second glance.

Azi's uncle was still trying to find the right curses to throw at her back, the right threats.

"Uncle?" Azi said. "Shut up. Your king commands it."

Lord Inas spun back around to face him. "Or what? You'll exile me like that wretched Bardo girl exiled her father? Go ahead. If this is what it takes to get through to you, to make you act like a king, I'll gladly go. Forget her, take any girl you want to be your queen, but let the Bardo girl go."

"Her name is Jala," Azi said. "Jala. Your queen. The woman I love."

"She's a corpse, and you're throwing away your family, your throne, your *life*—"

Azi grabbed his uncle by his shirt with both hands and pulled him close, ready to shake him. He was surprised how light the man was.

"You know it's true," his uncle said. "You're just too weak to admit it. A sentimental weakling. Jin would never have been so foolish. I don't even know whose son you are."

He was holding him up off the ground, Azi realized. Since when had his uncle been shorter than him? Underneath his buttoned shirt the great Lord Inas was thin, wasted away with grief and wine and worry in place of food and life.

Azi set him down gently. "You've been like a father to me, and you know it," he said. "I can't exile you, Uncle. I'm not as strong as Jala. But it's easier to let someone you love go when you don't know what it's like to lose them."

His uncle clenched his fist, and for a moment Azi though the man would hit him. But instead Lord Inas just seemed to deflate. "So you would have me lose you because you can't bear to admit she's gone?" He sounded old. He was old, Azi realized.

"If you don't want anything to do with me when I return, that's your choice, not mine," Azi said. "I won't just let her go. If there's even a chance, if there's something I can do . . ."

Lord Inas spat in the sand at Azi's feet, and then he, too, walked away.

His uncle was right. He was throwing it all away. Only his love for Jala would be left.

CHAPTER 27

J ala, Askel, and the remaining Hashon man rode slowly back to the city. They each rode a horse of their own now. The Hashon man was in the lead. Jala's reins were tied to his saddle and Askel's tied to hers, and the remaining horses trailed behind them in a crooked line.

The desert wind blew at their backs as they rode, scouring them with sand and tugging at their clothes. Jala thought it would tear the mask off her face, but the mask didn't move.

"What will you do when you get there?" Askel whispered behind her.

"Find Natari, get Marjani, and get out of here," Jala said. "We'll burn the grayships if we can find them." It was what she should say, but the words sounded hollow to her, like the things she cared about mattered less than they had only hours before.

Escape, her people, even the vast expanse of desert felt small compared to that other thing slowly flooding her mind.

There is a price for this, island queen, the voice whispered, as soft as sand, as old as the river. *Lord Stone the deceiver, my old enemy, still holds the palace, but with the Anka the people will rally to us. This is why I brought you here.*

"What did you say?" Askel said. He was looking at her strangely.

"Nothing," Jala muttered, though she wasn't sure. Her voice sounded so very far away.

Who are you? she asked.

Who are you? the voice of the river asked her in return.

She was the voice of the river. The true leader of the Hashon, the river-people. On her banks the people lived, and on her banks they died. When the people came down from the far-off mountains, fleeing from the cold, cruel stone, the river had taken them in and nurtured them. But the stone was jealous and stole the heart of the people. The Anka. All their stories, all that made them who they were, the stone kept as a hostage. For a while, the river was silent.

But now the Anka had returned to the river, and on the river it would stay. Lord Stone would fall, and Jala would once again take her place among the people.

Jala shook her head. *I'm not Lord Water*, she told herself. But the thought had come so easily, so naturally, just like the tongue of the Hashon had come to her when she needed it. Was this sorcery, then? Or something else? She touched the mask but dared not take it off. She needed Lord Water's voice if she was going to free her people.

There is a price . . .

There was always a price for sorcery, Askel had warned her. He'd tried to make others pay the price for him. Someone else could wear the mask. But who could she trust to free her people and burn the ships? Who was she willing to sacrifice in her place if the price for this sorcery was her life? There was no one else. She had to be the one. If she stopped now, this would all be for nothing.

"You have to remember for me," she said to Askel. "In case I forget. We have to free everyone. We have to burn any ships we can't take. Then we have to flee this place."

"My queen? What are you talking about?"

"If I forget myself, you have to remind me. Promise me."

"Is it the mask, my queen? Is that what worries you? Let me wear it for you." He sounded hungry. "I am a sorcerer, my queen. Let me use my skills to help you."

"Promise me!" Jala said, and the power of the river was in her voice again.

Askel reared back, his eyes wide. "I promise," he said. Then, after a long while, he spoke again. "Who are you?"

Jala faced Askel. "I am Lord Water."

CHAPTER 28

Wearing the mask, Jala walked through the city's streets with the Anka held high. Her followers—Lord Water's followers—surrounded her to protect her from those wearing the paper masks. "Stone feels nothing for you," her followers called to people they passed. "The river brings us life. The river brings us the Anka."

It was like living a dream. She walked and talked, but it was like she watched herself from some small part of her mind. Thoughts and feelings washed over her, engulfed her, and even though a part of her knew they were not her own, she felt and thought them all the same.

A dream, but a dream that was more real than anything she'd felt before. She could lose herself in this. She could become this.

People filled the streets. A man ran past wearing one of the fire masks, a broken chair in his hands. He threw it into the nearest window, shattering the glass. A woman ran up behind him and flung a flaming bottle of oil through the broken window panes. Within moments, flames had begun to engulf the building.

Jala kept walking. The glass from bottles and broken windows crunched under her feet.

More fires lit the sky, and the graffiti flames that marred the city's walls seemed to shimmer in the orange glow, as if they, too, might burn at any moment. Lord Stone had caused this, she knew. He'd sacrificed too many people in his drive for revenge, left too many broken families and grieving friends. Hurt, anger, and desperation had always been the kindling Lord Fire used to twist the people to his madness. He whispered to them until they put on the fire masks and let the fire carry them.

Lord Fire had been an unknowing ally to her, for a while, but now she needed the people to return to her. "You have been deceived," she called out. Her voice echoed off mud brick walls and limestone, her voice was carried on the wind and the angry waters of the Hashana. "It was Lord Stone who stole the Anka from you, Lord Stone who sacrificed your brothers and sisters, your sons and daughters. Lord Fire would have you

0s

'S MASK

burn the city in your grief, but the water can quench even the strongest flames. Follow me, and let your madness wash away."

Her words brought hope, and people looked at her with eyes clear of madness, and they saw the Anka. They believed in her, and with their belief her power grew. This was her city. These were her people. Soon even Lord Fire began to lose his hold on them, and those who were not completely lost pulled off their masks. They cried out as they began to feel the burns on their faces and ran to the river, seeking solace from their pain in its cool water.

Some rose again to follow her. Some remained on the bank, crying fitfully. Some drowned rather than feel the burns again, and their sacrifice gave her strength. For an hour, for two hours she walked through the city, collecting the people who were not yet too burned to follow her.

"Lord Stone has done this to you. Lord Stone will break," she cried, and the people cheered for her. A madness filled them still, Jala thought from the small place in her mind, but not the kind that burned.

Palace guards stood to block her path, but when they saw her and saw the Anka, they lowered their weapons and stepped aside.

Jala heard the voices of the other masked lords as she walked through the palace, carried on the waters of the Hashana that flowed through the walls and beneath their feet.

"He is here," said Lord Near, the Close Seer. "He carries the Anka."

She was remembering things she'd never known. The names of the masked Hashon lords, their voices and their domains. She tried to tell herself it was Lord Water's knowledge filling her head, but she felt as if she had always known these lords and this place.

"He wears down the mountain," said Lord Far, the Distant Seer. "He puts out the flame."

She'd known they would see her. But it didn't matter. Let Lord Stone see her coming now that it was too late.

"The red poison spreads far and wide, and the living ships no longer hear their heartsong," said Lord Empty-Face, the Never Seer, who only saw things that had not happened yet and might not happen ever. "The great fire stirs in its sleep, awakened by the silence, and the islands burn. The leviathan lifts his bulk, and the god-waves break on stone and shore. The king takes a new queen, and the old burns in the desert."

Lord Never Seer's words were about the islands, about her home. What if something terrible was going to happen? What if it had already happened? What did he mean about the king and a new queen? But the islands were far away, and small. She didn't need them now that she had the Anka. Jala held it out before her, and though she had brought only a few of her followers with her, the palace guards let her pass. She was Lord Water. They saw her and they believed. Only the fire and Lord Stone would dare touch her now. But water had put out the fire, and water would wear down the stone.

When she reached the secret room where the seven Hashon lords met, she waved a hand, motioning her people to wait. She went in alone.

The room was lit only by a single lamp, with seven shadowed alcoves where the masks were sometimes kept when their vessels succumbed to the weaknesses of living flesh. Lord Stone stood behind the lamp, waiting for her. The three Seers stood on either side of him, Near and Far on his left, Empty-Face on his right.

"You choose a strange vessel," Lord Stone said softly.

Jala laughed. "The river does not always run straight. The fire almost took me and the Anka, but the fates are, as always, on my side."

"This isn't fate," Lord Stone said. "Your puppets stole the Anka. You woke the fire. You almost destroyed the Anka, the people, and yourself."

"That's not the story the people will tell," she said softly. "I didn't steal the Anka but brought it back to its rightful place. I will bring healing where you brought only death and flames. Your people have abandoned you."

She reached over the lamp and grabbed Lord Stone's mask with both hands. She pulled. It was like trying to break a boulder with her bare hand. Like trying to pull up the root of the mountain. But even the largest boulder can be moved by flowing water, even the deepest mountain roots eaten away by hidden lakes and streams. Cracks formed on the mask's surface. Lord Stone grasped her wrists, but there was no holding on to water. The man behind the mask screamed.

Slowly, slowly the mask came free. The man fell to the floor, sobbing and gasping for breath. The air around the mask hummed.

"Go back to your mountain," she whispered. "Flee back to your holy city. I will tend to the heart of the people."

Jala took the mask in both hands and broke it with a resounding *crack!* Splinters rained down on the stone floor at her feet. The broken man touched what was left of his mask, of his god, and sobbed.

Jala reached out and drew a knife from the belt of a nearby soldier. She knelt beside the man and held the knife out to him. "You may follow him, if you think he'll have you."

Tears streamed down the man's face, and he shut his eyes. With a trembling hand he took the knife and cut his own throat.

CHAPTER 29

I t started as a single shout when a Kayet sailor found the guards in the cellar bleeding and unconscious, and from there the commotion spread through the entire manor and out into the nearby villages.

Lord Mosi had escaped.

From his window, Azi could see lamps and torches bobbing in the distance as they searched the beach, the forest, and the villages for signs of Jala's father.

Azi belted on his sword and knife, then reached up and pulled the King's Earring out of his ear. He set it down on the table and walked out without looking back. He'd had everything ready for a few days now. All he'd needed was the right time to slip away, and this distraction was too good an opportunity to pass up. By the time his uncle realized he was gone, they'd be too far away for any other ship to catch them.

Nobody paid much attention to him as he made his way through the manor and out onto the beach. The grayships were lined up along the shore. The ship he meant to take was at the far end, as far away from the bonfires and merriment that accompanied a new raiding season as possible.

Azi looked around and spotted Captain Darri. He touched the woman's shoulder then leaned in to whisper. "We're going. Gather your sailors."

It wouldn't take long. They were only taking ten sailors, just enough to get Azi to the Constant City. The trade fleets would be there. He'd borrow one of the traders to translate for him. Surely there was some news of Jala. Any news. He had to know for sure. After that . . . well, after that he'd figure out what to do.

For her, Uncle, I'd throw away not just a throne but my life. It's no less than she's done for me.

Azi reached Darri's ship and climbed aboard, landing on the deck with a dull thud. He knew everything was ready, but he couldn't help checking anyway, just to have something to do. He was too anxious to just sit.

Something moved on the deck. He squinted, trying to make his eyes readjust to the darkness, when the sharp point of a knife dug into his back and an arm snaked around his neck. "Make a noise and you die," someone whispered in his ear.

Four men rose from the shadows. "Dry hells. What do we do with him?" one of them hissed.

"Just give him a tap on the head and dump him in the brush," another said.

"It's too risky. We need to push off before someone realizes what's going on."

"Greetings, my king," the fourth one said, coming closer. He was a thin man, his hair unkempt and his eyes wild in the moonlight. But Azi recognized the voice. It was Lord Mosi. "You know, when my friends here freed me, I'd wanted to find you and your uncle. They convinced me it wouldn't be wise. I let myself be content simply to take this ship, so conveniently placed away from all those lights. But it looks like I'll be able to kill you after all. How nice for me."

The other men glanced at each other. "My lord, we don't want any killing. And this is the king. Freeing you is one thing, but killing a king is war."

"Don't think of it as killing a king," Lord Mosi said. "Think of it as killing the man who stole my daughter from me. Who made her betray her own father, her own family, and then threw her away to die on the mainland." He reached out and took the knife, then held it against Azi's throat.

"Wait," Azi tried to say, but the moment he opened his mouth he felt the blade bite into his skin.

"Quietly, my king," Lord Mosi whispered. "Speak your last words quietly, so I don't have to interrupt them."

"As if I could make Jala do anything," Azi said. "She gave you the choice to back down, and you spat in her face. You made her choose between being herself and being nothing but your mouthpiece. What was she supposed to do?"

"She was supposed to choose to be my daughter," Lord Mosi growled. "She was supposed to choose her family."

"You could have chosen your family," Azi said softly. "And you made the same choice she did."

Lord Mosi glared at him, then shrugged. "Maybe you're right. She turned out stronger than I thought. You, on the other hand . . ."

Azi's heart raced. Where was Darri? He had to buy some time. "Fight me," he said. "Kill me honorably, in the wind-dance, like a man instead of a murderer."

Lord Mosi stared at him. At any moment Azi expected to feel the knife cut out his throat. But Mosi smiled. "I accept, my king. But know that if you make a single sound, my men will kill you."

Azi nodded slowly. Lord Mosi pulled the knife away from his throat, and the man behind Azi stepped back into the shadows.

"Give us a beat, my friends."

The men glanced at each other. Then one of them began to slap the bulwark lightly with the palm of his hands. The rest did likewise.

"It's been a long time since I danced the wind-dance to the death," Lord Mosi said as he took off his robe and jumped over the side of the ship, landing lightly and immediately moving to the soft beat.

Azi took off his sword and knife and held it out for the man behind him to take, then stripped down as well. In the days before steel from the mainland became a man's weapon, nobles settled their scores inside a ring of chalk or sand. But that was a long time ago. When could Mosi have possibly fought to the death?

As he climbed down, he wondered if he could make it if he ran. The man with the knife jumped down after him and stood tensely, tossing the knife from one hand to the other. How well could he throw that knife? *Just stall him until Darri gets here. It's the only way you'll be able to find Jala again.*

He dropped his center down and began to let the rhythm move his arms and legs. They circled one another. He could only see Lord Mosi as a moonlit outline, arms moving back and forth, feet sliding across the sand.

Then Lord Mosi jumped and kicked. Azi flung himself back, then spun into a kick, but Mosi had already moved aside. Another kick, another dodge. The man was too fast. His hard, wiry muscles were taut, and his face was lit up with bloodlust. He looked ten years younger, and far more dangerous. When they'd danced together the night he met Jala, it had been performance, but this was something else entirely. Lord Mosi danced closer to him, almost seeming to mock him. Then Azi saw an opening. He spun and kicked, expecting his foot to connect with the side of Mosi's head. Instead, his foot swished through empty air, and Mosi's foot caught him in his calf.

He fell onto his back, the wind knocked out of him. The stars came into focus, and he rolled, just managing to avoid Lord Mosi's heel as it came down hard in the place his head had occupied only a moment before. As Azi rolled to face the sky again, sand hit him in the face, blinding him. He scrambled up again, spitting sand, spinning round and round trying to find Lord Mosi.

It was no use. He couldn't win this fight. He stopped and forced air into his lungs. "I didn't throw her away," he said, his voice barely a whisper. "She wanted to go. I'm going to find her. She has to be somewhere out there."

Lord Mosi danced in front of him but didn't attack. "You're king. You can't just leave your throne. Your uncle would never allow it."

"My uncle can rule if he wants," Azi whispered. "I'm going to find Jala."

Lord Mosi stared at him, then turned his head sharply as though he'd heard something. "Tell your friends to stop where they are."

Azi held up a hand. "Wait," he cried as loud as he could manage. He risked a glance back. "My crew. Just enough to get me to the Constant City. If you love her, if you ever loved her, let me go and try to bring her home."

Lord Mosi stopped, then. He laughed. "Mountain's piss, I never thought she'd have that kind of fire in her. I thought . . . well, I thought a lot of things that don't matter anymore. Lord Mosi is dead now. But he did love her once, even before he imagined that she might be queen." He gestured at the men up on the ship. Azi heard soft thuds as they jumped down. "Board your ship, Azi of the Kayet. Bring her back if you can." Then Lord Mosi turned and ran lightly across the sand, vanishing into the night.

"What was that about?" Darri asked.

Azi shook his head. "It doesn't matter. Let's hurry and push off before anyone wonders what we're doing."

CHAPTER 30

"My queen. You said you would take us home. Do you remember? You made me promise to remind you."

Jala stirred from the dream of Lord Water. It was Askel's voice that woke her. Slowly, like the tide pulling back from the shore, Lord Water receded from her mind. Like the tide, she felt herself changed, felt parts of him still lingering, but she was in control of herself again.

It took her a moment to remember how to speak on her own. "I remember," she said, her voice raspy in her throat.

She regarded Askel through the eyes of the mask but didn't take it off. She wasn't done with it yet. She had let Lord Water use her to take back the Hashon people. Now she was going to use him to get the rest of her people back home.

Askel's brow furrowed, and he seemed to be trying to peer through the eyeholes in her mask, as if he wasn't sure what was behind it.

"I'm all right," she whispered. "I remember now. Thank you."

She looked around. The other masked lords watched her. The same men and women who had refused her offer of peace now waited for her commands. Or was it the masks that waited for her? Were these men and women nothing more than messenger birds, repeating the words of gods?

The few men and women who'd come with her waited outside. Their voices were carried to her on the river as it flowed beneath the floor.

"I can't believe it's over. It's like waking from a nightmare, only you're not sure what was real and what wasn't."

"Lord Stone was real. See? That's part of his mask. A little souvenir, something for my last daughter's children to remember me by."

"Get that away from me, it's probably cursed. You should throw it in the river."

There was a long silence. "What happens now?" one of the speakers asked softly. "It's going to be better than before, won't it?"

"It will be better," Jala said, stepping out to meet them. They looked up and held their breaths. They were afraid of her, and they would die for her. "The Hashana will wash away the blood, and soon life will return, just as it always has."

Lord Water was speaking again. It was so easy to let his words overwhelm her. She had to remember why she made this bargain in the first place. She had to stay awake.

"Listen to me," she said. "Lord Stone blamed the islanders for stealing the Anka, and maybe some of you do as well. But they're not to blame. Lord Stone is broken. You've had your justice, more than any mortal has a right to. You've had your revenge. The islanders played the part that was set out for them, and now they'll be allowed to leave, with the river's blessing to speed them home."

The Hashon glanced at each other but said nothing. She knew they would obey her as long as she was Lord Water.

"Bring the islanders to me. Bring their ships, find their clothes and their weapons. Give them coins and clothes and trinkets to trade when they reach the Constant City. Set them on the Hashana and think of them no more."

They moved quickly to obey, scattering toward different doors. She had to speak quickly before they all disappeared.

"One more thing. There was a girl here. An islander girl, left here in the palace when we rode into the desert. Take me to her. The rest of you can go. Askel, go with them, make sure the islanders understand they're being freed and don't need to fight their way out."

Askel nodded, and then they left, all except for a woman who wouldn't meet Jala's gaze. "I know where they took the girl," she whispered. She led Jala out of the palace and down through the streets. She stopped in a narrow alley in front of a short wooden door hidden in the shadows. It might have been a shop once, but the sign painted on the door had faded and cracked until it was illegible, and the wood was splintered and rotten. The rusted hinges groaned as the woman pulled the door open.

"I've brought the great lord," the woman whispered into the darkness.

Jala pushed past her and stepped inside. She had nothing to fear from these people. "Where is the islander girl? Bring her to me." Then, in a voice that was all her own, in a language that she knew, she called out, "Marjani, where are you?"

"Jala?" Marjani called out from the darkness. Jala heard the sound of feet running on the wooden floor and of people shouting. Marjani appeared, her face lit up with relief, her arms outstretched. But then she saw Jala, and she stopped, uncertain. A man and a woman caught up with Marjani, ready to grab her, but they, too, stopped and stared at Jala.

It was good to see Marjani again. It made it easier for Jala to remember who she was and what she had to do. Jala took a step forward. The rest of them shrank back, but Marjani stayed, though she still eyed Jala suspiciously.

"Are you all right? Did they hurt you?" Jala whispered.

"I'm fine," Marjani said. She hesitated. "And you?"

"I'm taking us home." Jala glanced at the woman who had brought her here. She only needed to be Lord Water for a little while longer. "Have the grayships brought to the water outside the palace. I will wait for the islanders there."

Then she walked away, down the alleys, without having to be led. She may not have known where Marjani was, but this was her city so long as she wore the mask. Her blood flowed through the sand and the bricks and the people here.

No, this wasn't her city. She had to remember that, had to remember where she ended and Lord Water began. It was hard, and she took Marjani's hand and held it tight in hers. She thought of home, of Azi, of being queen. That was who she was.

"What was that?" Marjani hissed. "You sounded just like them when you spoke."

"It's the mask," Jala said. "I can't explain it. Not now. Maybe when we're on our way home I can tell you what it's like."

"If it's sorcery . . . what if you turn out like Askel? All shriveled up like a date left out in the sun?"

"Then I'll be shriveled up," Jala said with a laugh. Marjani gave her a disbelieving look, but it just didn't seem important right now. Lord Water didn't see individual lives as any great things. He had seen a thousand thousand such lives flourish and die, like reeds on the riverbank. Jala had to keep reminding herself that getting her people home was what mattered.

Soon I'll be able to take this damn thing off, Jala thought, touching the edge of the mask. It would be such a relief to have her mind and body to herself again. But the thought scared her, too, even if she didn't know why.

The two grayships stolen from the Gana had been placed on the river flowing out from under the palace, and her people waited by them, just as she'd commanded. Captain Natari, Boka the Trader, Askel, and the sailors. They whispered among themselves, glancing around nervously and eyeing the Hashon who had brought them here with suspicion. A few of them surreptitiously picked up stones or bits of sharp wood. One sailor had managed to acquire a knife. But it didn't look like anyone had been killed, at least not here, and the bloodstains she saw looked hours dry.

They looked up at her as she approached, confused by what they saw. Only Boka sputtered at seeing her wearing one of the masks. The rest had no idea what it meant.

"We will not return the way we came," Jala said. "We'll sail the ships down the Hashana River, until its tributaries lead us back to the Great Ocean. From there we'll return to the Constant City, then home."

The islanders cheered, and Marjani squeezed Jala's hand quickly. The Hashon whispered among themselves but made no move to stop them as Captain Natari divided up the remaining sailors between the two ships and assigned an eager-looking younger woman as captain of the second ship.

"My queen, what about the mask?" Askel asked. "They may simply kill us as soon as you take it off. Keep it with us. Who knows when we might need it again?"

"They'll do as I tell them," Jala said.

"They'll do as Lord Water tells them," Askel said. "Keep the mask. Who knows what power it might have?"

She wanted to. She'd be naked without the mask, weak and powerless. Some part of her thought without the mask she would die.

I'm going home, she thought, and looked at Marjani again. It wasn't any easier. But it was possible.

"No," Jala said. "The mask stays here. Lord Water stays here."

Askel looked like he wanted to argue, but then he shrugged and followed Boka onto one of the ships. Supplies were brought for them, and the sailors loaded each of the ships in turn. There were clothes, dyes, fruits and wines, coins. All the things they would have taken if they'd raided the city instead of saving it. Not that she was entirely sure they had saved it, whatever Lord Water said.

"Is it good, what I did?" Jala asked Marjani. "Leaving them to Lord Water?" He cared for the Hashon, but only as a whole. He cared no more for any one life than Lord Stone had. Perhaps that was the way of it with gods.

"Well, it's good for us," Marjani said. "We're going home. How could that be wrong?"

"My queen, we're ready to leave now," Captain Natari said. "The farther we go while the night still hides us, the better, I think, no matter what power you have over these people."

Jala looked at Captain Natari, then at Marjani. She lifted her hands to the mask. It had looked like such a bulky thing, but even now it was hard to imagine being without it. Like taking off your own arm.

What do you have to go back to? whispered Lord Water's voice. *You've lost your family. You've lost your love.*

Then she heard Azi's voice, whispering, full of passion. "I do love her," he said, and she could almost feel the man behind the words. She could almost touch him, the words felt so real. Somewhere, Azi was saying these words. "Can you be happy as my queen?"

Was he talking to her? Could he feel her too? She couldn't breathe. The mask felt stifling, and she lifted her hands up again to pull it off.

Then she heard Lord Inas's voice, echoing in her head. "There's no reason to deny it now. That Bardo girl twisted your head around until you couldn't steer straight. But it's not too late."

Her hands froze on the mask. *Stop it*, she thought. *I don't want to hear this.*

But it was too late. Kona's voice floated into her mind, as inevitable as the tide. "Your uncle says we can be together." A soft whisper, almost uncertain, so quiet it seemed to fade at the end. "You wanted to know if I'd be happy as your queen . . ."

The king takes a new queen, and the old burns in the desert.

Her head spun. This couldn't be. She wouldn't—couldn't—let herself believe it of him. Azi loved her. He wouldn't run back to Kona while she risked everything for the islands. It was Lord Inas scheming against her, that was all.

It had to be. Or everything between them had been a lie. She'd never seen the real Azi. He'd lied to her. She'd lied to herself.

But I have only ever told you what is true, Lord Water whispered in her mind.

She felt the truth of his words settle on her. Jala let her hands fall back to her sides. The mask no longer felt stifling. As long as she had it on, no one could see the tears. Behind the mask, she didn't have to feel what she felt, didn't have to be what she was. The queen had hidden the girl, and now the mask could, too.

She shut her eyes. The tears were gone, nothing but dried salt and stillness. She was the beach after the tide, the ruin after the storm. She let his voice fill her mind. She let him speak through her.

It was easier this way. It was better.

She was Lord Water.

"I'm not going with you," she heard herself say. Captain Natari started to say something, but she wanted them gone. She had no need of the islanders now, when she had a city and a faith to restore to former glories.

"Go," she commanded, her voice like a great wave washing over them. Captain Natari and Askel stumbled back. Natari looked at her in fear, uncertain if he should argue. Askel only looked at her with hunger.

"My queen," Captain Natari said uncertainly. "I can't just leave you here. You must come with us. What would the king say?"

He might thank you, Jala thought. She'd caused nothing but trouble for him, for her family, for everyone. And he wouldn't be alone. She was growing small again inside her head. It was easier that way. Like falling asleep.

Marjani was shouting at her. "Jala, what are you saying? You can't stay here, you have to come home. What about me? What about Azi?"

Jala pulled the Queen's Earring out of her ear and held it out to Marjani. "Tell him I'm dead," she said softly.

Marjani stared at the earring, then back at Jala. "No. No, I can't. I won't let you."

"There is sorcery here beyond your understanding," Askel hissed. "Beyond mine, too."

"I could take the mask from her," Captain Natari said, though he made no move to do so.

Askel shook his head. "If she didn't kill you, the rest of them would."

"We can't leave her here," Marjani said. When the two men did nothing, she growled and threw herself at Jala, clawing at the mask. Immediately the Hashon were on her, pulling her off. She fought them the whole time, but there were too many of them. They held her back.

"Go," Lord Water commanded. "Forget Jala."

"Don't listen to her," Marjani said. "It's the mask, it's not her."

Captain Natari bowed to Jala. "All of the Five-and-One will know what you did for them, I promise you. And I thank you. But my crew wants to go home, my queen, as do I. They've had enough of this strange city with their strange masked lords, enough of sorcery."

Enough of their queen's madness. He didn't say it, but she could hear it in his voice, see it in the way he looked at her. She scared them.

"Then go home," she said. She held the earring out again. Captain Natari took it. Jala waved a hand at Marjani, not daring to look at her. "Put her on the ship."

Marjani shook her head. "They can't keep an eye on me forever. Sooner or later they'll look away, and I'll jump off and find my way back. I won't leave you here."

The sailors weren't waiting. They pushed off the shore with long sticks the Hashon had brought and turned the grayships toward home.

"Let me stay with you," Marjani whispered. "You'll always be Jala to me. Always. You're my oldest friend, and I won't abandon you." Her voice grew small and scared. "Please. Don't make me leave you alone here. I couldn't bear it."

"You'll be alone here," Jala said.

"I'll still have you. Whatever's left of you," Marjani said.

Jala made herself speak in spite of Lord Water's words filling her mouth and mind. "It doesn't matter. Let her stay if she wants," she said.

"Find her a room. Bring her food, water, whatever she needs." The gray-ships began to move. Jala returned to the palace without looking back.

Behind her, she could just make out Marjani's whisper. "I'll find a way to save you. I will. And if I don't, at least you won't be alone."

What is time to a river? The storm season comes, and the river swells with rainwater. Is this a heartbeat? A breath? A whispered word? Then the rains are gone, and the river ebbs again. The lives of fish are seconds, the lives of men and women days.

To a river, time is the rocks on the shore made smooth. Time is the slow erosion of a bank.

Yet there are times when the river notices the minute as keenly as a human or a fish. When the land shifts and the river bends. When the riverbank breaks and the river cuts a new path to its destination. When the water running beneath the mountain finally breaks free, and a tiny spring burbles as it begins to reach out across the land as if in search of something.

So the time passed for Jala. While she wore the mask, she was Lord Water, and the words she spoke and the things she did seemed like a dream. She floated on the surface of her thoughts and feelings and memories, and felt them only distantly.

But though her mind was free, her body wasn't, and after many years—or was it merely hours?—she was forced to take off the mask.

Without it, the world seemed gray and empty. The seconds dragged across her mind like stone scraping against stone. She ate without tasting. She slept, if the fitful tossing and the nightmarish visions could be called sleep.

"You're getting that faraway look again," Marjani said. "And you've stopped eating. You promised me you'd eat today."

Jala started. She'd forgotten Marjani was there. She looked around. They were in a small, round chamber deep in the palace. There were no windows, only candles on the walls and a small table with two stools. There was food laid out in front of them.

Nearby, the sound of rushing water filled her ears, and she wondered how long before she could wear the mask again.

CHAPTER 31

Azi stood at the bow of the ship and watched the Constant City draw near. He'd been raiding many times but had never been to the Constant City itself. In the past, some kings had made sure their sons went trading in the Constant City instead of raiding, but his father hadn't been that way. He imagined Jala standing on her ship watching the city just as he was now.

Where are you? Azi wondered, just as he had every day since he'd left. He'd been impatient to reach the mainland then. Now, a part of him didn't want to know. What if she was dead? What if it had all been for nothing?

But what if she wasn't? What if he could help her? His mother would tell him he was being a fool, that like all men he thought the winds only blew if he was there to help them. Well, maybe he was a fool, but he'd rather be a fool than live the rest of his life wondering if he could have made a difference.

"Captain! There are grayships in the harbor," called one of the sailors.

Azi's heart rose as he squinted in the direction the spotter pointed. "Can you tell whose ships they are? Is one of them a Bardo ship?"

"One of them looks like the Bardo grew it," the sailor said. "The others look like Gana ships to me."

Azi sighed and sank down to his knees. He laughed. It *had* all been for nothing. She hadn't needed rescuing after all. He was a fool, just like his mother said, and he didn't care.

"Go to them. Call out to them," Azi said. "I have to see her."

The sailor glanced at the captain. She nodded, and the sailor called directions to the navigator. Slowly, far too slowly for Azi, the ship turned. They were spotted long before they were close enough to be heard. Azi could see the sailors on the deck pointing.

"Peace and good wind," one of the sailors on the Gana ship called when they'd drawn close.

Azi didn't wait for the *Whaleshark*'s crew to shout back a greeting of their own. "Where's Jala?" he shouted across the shrinking gap between the ships. "Where's the queen?"

The sailors glanced at each other, but none of them spoke. Azi's chest felt hollow. "What happened to her?" he demanded, trying to keep the fear out of his voice.

By now the *Whaleshark* had drawn up beside the Bardo grayship. On each ship, four sailors pulled out oars and held them out for someone on the opposing ship to grab, as much to keep them from colliding as to keep them together. The ship lurched from the sudden shift in momentum, but Azi was ready for it after years aboard ships. That wasn't what made his legs unsteady.

"What happened to Jala?"

"They left her behind, my king," said an old man sitting on one of the benches nailed into the shipwood for rowing. "Not that she gave them any choice."

"Left her? Where? Why?" Azi didn't wait for them to answer. He placed one foot on the bulwark and jumped. He cleared the gap and landed heavily on the Bardo ship's deck. The ship rocked from the impact.

"She wasn't herself anymore," one of the sailors said.

"She put the mask on and it's like she was gone," said another.

"They would have killed us all."

The sailors were all talking at once now. They fell quiet as he met their gaze, but they didn't look away. It wasn't guilt on their faces but exhaustion and defiance. Whatever had happened, they weren't happy about it—but they would do it again.

"She was Bardo," one of the sailors said, as if she could hear his thoughts. "We don't leave family behind easily."

"But she's still alive?" Azi demanded. "Somewhere?"

"She's alive," the old man said. "But it's a long way to the city of the river people, my king. I can help you find her, though."

Azi focused on the old man. "Who are you? You're no sailor."

"Askel, my king. A sorcerer from the fire island, though I hope to make my home on a more hospitable isle after this. She promised me, my king."

"If you can help me find her, I'll make sure my uncle knows what you've done." *Though I don't know if he'll thank you for it*, Azi thought.

"Thank you, my king. I ask only that and one other thing . . . a small thing."

"First I have to find her," Azi said pointedly.

The sorcerer smiled and reached into his dirty robe. He pulled out a bound rag, then carefully unrolled it. Inside was a shriveled lump of black and red.

Blood. Fingernail. It was a finger—Jala's finger, Azi realized, recognizing it somehow in spite of its hideous state. Before he'd thought anything else, he found himself grabbing hold of the sorcerer's robes and throwing him over the side of the ship. Azi didn't let go of the man but let him hang, bare feet skimming the top of the water, his skin sliced open as he bounced against the sharp sides of the ship.

"What did you do to her?" Azi hissed.

But the sorcerer just laughed. "She did it to herself. She did it all to herself. If you'll set me down, I'll explain it all, and then I'll tell you how you can use this same magic to find your queen again."

Azi felt a hand on his shoulder. "My king, he's telling the truth," one of the sailors said. "She cut her own finger off, though it was for this one's magic. Captain Natari was there. He'll tell you."

One of the other grayships was already pulling up beside the one he stood on, and the sailors greeted their captain across the water.

Azi forced himself to breathe. Carefully, he pulled the sorcerer back into the ship and set him back on the bench.

"I'm sorry," he said, mostly meaning it. "It's not really you I want to hit. I don't know *who* to hit, in fact. If you can help me find her. . . . I think you and Captain Natari need to tell me everything. Then show me how the magic works."

He reached out his hand, palm up, and the sorcerer placed Jala's finger on it. Blood oozed, slow as mud, from the dried stump.

Azi closed his fingers around it carefully and listened. The sorcerer, with unasked-for help from the sailors, told Azi what had happened in the city of the Hashon. He told Azi about the masks, about the war between the followers of stone and the followers of water, about the

Hashana River that flowed through the lands and the people. He told Azi what Jala had done.

"There might not be anything left of her by now," Askel whispered. "Only the mask. Only Lord Water. Do you still want to go?" Azi nodded. "The magic works in reverse. Hook your finger around hers, the way two children might when making a promise. Close your eyes and still your mind. Feel the weak pulse in the dying flesh? Feel the way it pulls you in her direction? Just like one of your grayships pulling toward the reef that grew it."

"I feel it," Azi whispered, his voice hoarse.

"Then your queen's body still lives, and the magic has not yet faded. As for her mind and spirit, I make no promises."

When the sorcerer was done, Captain Natari offered Azi the Queen's Earring. "She might need this," he said. "I hope she does."

Azi shook his head. "I hope she does as well, but I can't take it with me. I may never come back. Take it to my uncle when you're back on the Five-and-One. If we ever make it back home . . . then we'll see."

Captain Natari nodded. "Then I hope a strong wind fills your sail, Azi of the Kayet."

Azi returned to the *Whaleshark*, Jala's missing finger clutched in one hand. "I'll take whatever supplies you can spare and trade for more in the city. I want to leave tomorrow as soon as there's light to walk by." He glanced around at the sailors who had fought by his side on the Fifth Isle, at Captain Darri, who'd taken Paka's command when the man had died. He'd gotten used to giving orders, he realized.

"You don't have to come with me," he added. "I'm not your captain, and I don't know if I'll still be king when I return. If I return. I can't command you to go with me. And after what we all saw, what we survived, you deserve better than to have me ask you to risk your lives again when there's only two lives on the line and not an entire island. But I'm asking you anyway. Come with me. Help me bring Jala home."

"Three lives," a woman said. "Her friend who went with her, Marjani. She stayed behind too. I heard the Bardo talking about it. So that's three lives."

"I heard what the queen did," a man said. "And I see the way you look at her. I'll go."

"We saw what you did, too," Captain Darri said. "Even if we could only help one villager, you went with us on the Fifth Isle. Three lives isn't so little. I'll stay by your side, king or no."

"I get a feeling, sometimes," an older sailor said. "Like this is the last storm season I'll see aboard a ship. I think I'd like to look at the mainland one more time, just in case I'm right."

In the end, four sailors stayed behind to watch the ship and sail it back to the First Isle if they didn't return. The rest set out for the mainland for supplies. There were Kayet traders there, just as Azi had expected, and they managed to get enough to start them on their way, though it was less than he'd have liked. They even managed to get hired out as guards on a merchant's caravan. Here Azi's scars seemed to impress them almost as much as their swords.

"Who are we supposed to be protecting them from?" Azi asked.

"Islanders," the old sailor said, with a laugh.

They left the next morning, just as Azi had wanted. The journey was a long one, strange and boring at the same time. They ate what they were given as payment, sparing their own limited supplies. When they talked among themselves, the merchants and other guards gave them strange looks, so they talked little.

For a while, the caravan drove them closer to their goal. But eventually they turned down a road that led away from Jala. Then Azi and the other sailors left in the middle of the night, taking some of the better food with them. No caravans wanted anything to do with a group of armed, road-spattered men and women, and none of the sailors knew enough of any common language to convince the caravans otherwise. They walked alone, the food supply slowly dwindling.

One night, they were attacked by bandits, men that looked even hungrier than they did. They fought in the night by the light of a dying fire, both sides shouting curses their enemy couldn't understand. Two sailors died and three bandits. The rest fled into the night.

"There's no water here, and we can't take them with us," Azi said, looking down at the bodies of those who had died for him. "What do the mainlanders do with their dead?"

"Bury them in the ground," the old sailor said. For all his talk of being old, he'd managed to escape the fight with only a shallow cut across his arm.

They didn't bury them. It didn't seem right for a sailor to be trapped in the earth. Overhead, birds were already circling, so they left the bodies there to be eaten. There was nothing else to do. The next morning, they pressed on.

Finally, Jala's severed finger led them to the great wide river the Bardo sailors had spoken of. They had no one who could speak the language here, but these people were sailors too, of a sort. Once they had made themselves understood, they managed to get work rowing on a barge heading up river.

They worked and ate and slept and stayed silent.

Sometimes as he rowed or laid on the deck watching the stars and waiting for sleep, Azi listened to the foreign language whispered around them. Most of it was meaningless, but a few words he thought he recognized. One of the words for water was close to the island word for fresh water. The word for palm was practically the same. Their word for rain was nearly the island word for a clear sky. Maybe the speaker had only meant to be sarcastic.

Azi had been to the mainland many times, but he'd never listened to the people there. Of course, mostly they yelled or screamed or cried.

Now, they talked and argued and laughed. The next time the river-sailors played one of their gambling games, he watched. The next night, they offered to let him play. He did, and laughing they won his dinner, his shirt, and his sword. The next night he won them all back, along with a few battered coins. They laughed at this, too, and shared their wine with him.

When they asked where he was from, he told them he was from the Constant City. He knew enough sailors' stories of the place to pass off as his own, but his attempts to tell them mostly led to mockery. His accent was thick, and he didn't know the words for simple things. But he told the stories anyway, gesturing and laughing with them, and whenever they understood what he was speaking of they taught him the Hashon word for it.

By the time they saw the city in the distance he was able to speak well enough to trade with some of the fishermen, and he turned his winnings into some rope and a hook, and then he paid the man to shave their hair with a clean, sharp knife so that they wouldn't stand out so much among the straight-haired Hashon.

They were close to her now. Azi could feel her nearness when he held the withered finger hooked around his own.

They entered the city among the fishermen and farmers and traders and travelers. In an alley behind a tavern, an old man drunk on wine Azi bought for him told stories about the palace. He'd been a rat-catcher, a kitchen boy, servant, now a gardener—or at least that's what Azi thought he said. His speech was slurred and it made him even harder to understand.

"Tell us—where—" Azi waved his hand in front of his face, trying to act out the word for mask. "Tell us where. A map."

But the old man hardly seemed to be paying attention to them. "My favorite garden. Little, hiding in the corner. Why even build it? Lords never go there. But the island queen does. Her favorite goes there too, sits and looks up at the stars."

"Island queen?" Azi asked, his heart suddenly beating so fast he could hardly breathe. "Where is the garden? Show me. Map." Then Azi took the man's hand and pressed one of the last silver coins they had into it.

The old gardener stared at it for a moment as if not understanding, then he laughed and spoke words Azi didn't know and began to draw in the dirt.

They waited for a moonless night, when the streets were dark and the stars clear, then gathered in an alley across the street from the palace walls. Captain Darri was with him, and the old sailor, dressed in rags like a beggar so he could go unnoticed and act as lookout.

Every few minutes a pair of guards passed by the wall. Both wore tall helms with eyes painted on. They had long knives at their sides and clubs in their hands. One of them carried a torch. Azi had to turn away and shut his eyes to keep from being blinded and losing his night vision.

Azi waited for the guards to pass several times, counting the seconds between rounds, letting them settle into the night's routine and hoping Jala hadn't come and gone already. Finally, as the torchlight disappeared around a corner, Azi and Darri ran to the wall. Azi threw the hook up. It scraped against the top of the palace walls, then fell back down with a crack. They stood still, breathless, but no one came running.

Darri counted softly under her breath. "Forty-five. Fifty. Fifty-five." Azi threw again. It held for just a moment, but when he tried to pull himself up it slipped.

"Back!" Darri hissed.

Azi gathered up the rope as quickly as he could, then together they ran back to the alley and waited for the guards to pass once more. This time when Azi threw the hook it caught the first time and held his weight. There were iron spikes at the top of the wall, but they seemed to be more decorative than anything else. Azi ducked and waited for Darri to climb up after him. Then he pulled up the rope and tossed it to the ground on the other side. It landed with a soft thump just as the light from the guards' torch appeared again.

Azi quickly slid down off the wall, catching himself with his fingertips for just a moment before letting go entirely. His hands and feet slid over the stone, and then he hit the ground and rolled. The ground was soft here, but the fall still winded him.

When he could breathe again, his nose filled with an overpoweringly sweet scent. A flower garden, just like the old man had said. He was in the right place. It was a small nook, half the length of a grayship and just as wide. At one end was a plain wooden door. Flickering yellow light seeped out from between the door and the frame.

Darri was already by the door, listening, a knife in her hand just in case. Of course, if she had to use it, the whole thing was almost certainly lost. Even if they managed to kill a guard without him shouting, they had no way to hide a body. But no guards came. In the thin light Azi managed to make out the shape of a tree. It was shorter than the palm trees of the island but was covered in thick leaves.

Azi climbed up into the tree, high enough that it would be hard to see him from the doorway. Captain Darri followed after him and found her own branch.

They waited, perched awkwardly, trying not to cause too much rustling.

Azi held the severed finger in his hand. The pull was strong here, but he couldn't tell if it was coming any closer or not. He hoped she hadn't picked this day to skip visiting the garden, that she hadn't felt ill or gone to sleep early. He'd go looking for her if she didn't come, though he had no idea how he'd avoid being found out then. But it had always been a fool's plan.

He was halfway to falling asleep when the door opened and light spilled out into the garden. He blinked at the two shapes—a woman in a guard's helm, holding a lantern and armed with the same long knife as the guards outside. And beside her . . . was a girl that wasn't Jala. His fingers dug into the bark of the tree. He felt like screaming. So close!

"I will wait here for you, little queen," the guard said, bowing her head slightly.

"I'm not a queen," the girl said in Azi's tongue. "And it's stupid to guard me like a prisoner when Jala could send me home any time I want."

Then Azi remembered. Of course it had to be Marjani, Jala's friend, the one who'd stayed behind with Jala. He'd met her, spoken to her a little. He remembered the way Jala's face had lit up, like a beam of light after a storm, when she was with her friend. He felt stupid for not recognizing her sooner, selfish for being angry that it had been her and not Jala walking through the door.

The guard looked at Marjani patiently and clearly had no idea what Marjani had said.

Marjani sighed loudly. "Thank you," she said in very broken Hashon, then shut the door in the guard's face. She stood for a moment, staring at the door and breathing slowly. Then she turned around and walked over to the bench. She sat down and looked up at the sky.

"I see you up there," she said. "So either the king of the Five-and-One Islands suddenly fell from the sky . . . or I've lost my mind. I suppose you could also be some kind of demon, but you're not wearing a mask, and that seems to be how they do things around here."

It took Azi a moment to find his voice again. "I'm real," he whispered. "I'm here for Jala. And you, of course. I'd come down and prove I'm real but . . ." He pointed toward the door.

"Don't worry about the guard," Marjani said. "She's used to me talking to myself out here. I tell myself Bardo stories so I don't forget them. Anyway, she leaves me alone when I'm out here or in my room, so it's safe for you to come down." She looked away again and up at the stars burning bright above them. "But I understand if you don't. It's not even like I mind so much that I'm seeing things, because at least it feels like there's someone here to talk to."

Captain Darri shifted slightly on her branch. "You're starting to make me wonder if he's real," she said softly. Marjani started at the new voice, then found the source and laughed. "Beautiful women are falling from the sky too? Now I know this is a dream. I must have fallen asleep outside. I hope I don't wake up too soon."

Darri's mouth twitched as though she might smile. "My king, I think you better prove to her that you're real, and that she's finally going home," she said lightly. But she looked at Azi, and he heard the words Darri wasn't saying. Marjani was barely holding it together.

Azi dropped down as quietly as he could next to the bench. He froze and stared at the door. When he turned to look, Marjani was staring at him, her hands holding tight to the bench.

Azi held out his arm, and slowly, tentatively she reached out and touched him. Her finger was cool against his skin. She stared at the point where it pressed into his arm.

"You are real," she said calmly.

"I'm sorry I couldn't be here sooner," Azi said. "Where's Jala?"

Marjani pulled her hand away, and then she threw her arms around him and held him tightly. "You came for her," she said. "I didn't think anyone would ever come. I thought we were alone."

Azi wrapped his arms around Marjani and hugged her back. "And you stayed for her. Thank you. I won't forget you did this."

Marjani sighed and pulled away. "Thanks, but I don't know if it helped. She's gotten so . . . quiet. She hardly ever takes the mask off now, and when she does, it's like she's not even there. Like she's getting smaller and smaller to make space for Lord Water. She thought that you'd abandoned her."

Captain Darri had climbed down from the tree to stand beside them.

"You will see her again, yes? Tell her he's come, bring her here, and leave the guards. We have rope. We'll leave the same way we came in."

Marjani shook her head. "I don't think she'll believe me. She hears things. Or at least, Lord Water lets her hear things. She heard you talking to that other girl, telling her you love her and you'll make her queen."

"What? I never said that," Azi hissed.

"It's what she heard, and it's what she believes. She needs to see you when she isn't wearing the mask." Marjani tapped her fingers against her temple. "When Lord Water isn't navigating."

"She must take it off when she sleeps," Azi said. "Maybe . . . maybe we can sneak through the palace and get to her now."

But Marjani was shaking her head. "She's surrounded by guards most of the time. And . . . I don't think she sleeps much anymore. Or maybe she sleeps all the time, while she's wearing the mask. It's like she's sleepwalking." Marjani shook her head again. It was like she was trying to drive out weeks of fear, of watching her friend slip away from her. A moment ago Azi hadn't imagined there was anything worse than his slow, plodding trip across the mainland, not knowing what he'd find at the end . . . but now he thought maybe he'd been lucky. He'd had the finger. He'd had some hope.

"I'll fight through every guard in the palace if I have to," Azi said. He smiled grimly. "But I don't think I'd make it very far."

"My king, I won't risk my life or my crew unless there's at least some chance," Captain Darri said softly. "There must be some way to get you into the queen's presence. Some chance, however slim."

Marjani closed her eyes and nodded. "We still eat together, whenever she remembers to eat. The guards wait outside. She hardly eats nowadays, but when I urge her . . . she has to take off her mask to eat. All we have to do is get you in there. All we have to do is make everyone think you're me."

"And how do we do that?" Azi asked.

"We need a disguise," Marjani said. "So it's a good thing we're in a city of masks." Then she told them what she wanted to do. When they'd agreed on a plan, she glanced at the door. "We need to get you inside, where no one will notice when we change places. You could hide in my room. No one bothers me there. Could you follow us without being seen? I think I can trick the guard into taking us the long way around, where there's hardly anyone in the halls."

"I can try," Azi said. He looked at the captain. "We'll need a boat to take us down the river. Something fast if you can get it, but any fishing boat will do, so long as it doesn't sink."

Marjani nodded. "I'll throw two stones over the wall if everything's ready to go. Three if something's gone wrong."

"We'll watch for it," Darri said, "and if we see three stones we'll have the rope and hook ready to get you back out."

"Thank you," Azi said to the captain. "For everything you've done."

Darri took his arm and held it tightly. "I'll see you soon, my king. And then we can go home." But she wasn't speaking to him as if he was a king. More like a captain to a young sailor, trying to instill confidence he didn't have. It helped.

"Thank you," Azi said again.

Then Captain Darri waited for the guards along the wall to pass and threw the rope again, while Azi pressed himself against the wall beside the door. Darri reached the top of the wall, and then she was over. Azi heard only the slightest scuffle as she landed, and then there was nothing. They waited just a moment longer, Azi and Marjani both holding their breath, straining to hear a shout from a guard—but there was nothing. She'd gotten away.

Now it was their turn.

Marjani opened the door and made it clear to the guard she wanted to be taken back to her room. Then when the guard turned around, Azi slipped past and Marjani closed the door. That was the worst moment, wondering if the guard would turn around before Azi had found any kind of nook or shadowy corner to hide in. But the guard didn't turn around, and Azi pressed himself against a wall and waited for them to move ahead so he could follow away from the light spilling from the guard's lamp.

Just as she'd said, Marjani insisted on taking detours as they walked. The guard didn't argue. She seemed resigned to her charge's strange, incomprehensible ways. Marjani led them through parts of the palace that had clearly seen fire and bloodshed, and now were dark and mostly empty. It made it that much easier to spot anyone else carrying a lamp, and gave Azi time to avoid them.

It seemed to take forever, but in the end they reached Marjani's room without incident. Once the guard was gone and the way clear, Azi ran over and knocked softly. Marjani let him inside and quickly shut the door. Then they both leaned against the wall and tried to catch their breath.

Azi slept on the floor that night, the sound of the river underneath them filling his dreams. The next day he spent hiding under her bed while she was gone, just in case someone came in to clean. For company he had only his own fears, sailing in circles in his mind, and the occasional sound of footsteps or voices in the halls beyond the door to make his stomach drop and his heart skip.

CHAPTER 32

$\mathcal{J}$ ala ate alone except for Marjani. She would have preferred a feast so she could be surrounded by voices, so she didn't have to feel so alone. But she didn't like having others see her without her mask. She didn't like how naked she felt, didn't like the way they looked at her.

It wasn't until halfway through the meal that she finally noticed Marjani's clothes, a flowing robe of dark silk that shimmered in the firelight.

"Where did you get that?" Jala asked.

Marjani smiled at this. Jala knew she often went through whole meals without speaking, and she often forgot to even ask how Marjani was doing. It was hard to remember things like that.

"Do you like it?" Marjani asked. "I asked my guards for something a Hashon noble might wear, and they let me pick this out."

"I liked your other clothes better. They reminded me of the islands," Jala said. Her voice sounded dull, even to her. Her tongue felt thick and slow.

"All they reminded me of was how long it's been since I'd had them washed," Marjani said, laughing. Jala didn't often laugh anymore, but Marjani made up for it. She was grateful for that.

"But I was wondering," Marjani went on. "I saw some of the nobles wearing masks, too. And even some of the servants. Are they the same as your mask? Do they also talk?"

"Every mask talks. Every mask is a purpose and a reason. Every mask lets you hide yourself behind an idea. Some ideas are just louder than others."

"Could I have a mask then?" Marjani asked, only half-looking in Jala's direction.

Jala started, and for the first time in the entire conversation her voice took on some of her old self. "Why would you want something like that? I want to be able to see you."

"I'd take it off when we're alone together," Marjani said. "But the guards and servants all look at me like I'm some kind of exotic fruit they've never seen before. It makes me trip over my own feet. It wouldn't be a Hashon mask, of course. Something from home. Not a mountain. I don't think your Lord Water would like that. A reef? A killer whale? I've seen painters here, I could try to describe home to them."

"You don't speak their language," Jala said, dodging the question.

"I'm getting better at it," Marjani said. "Listen." She repeated some of the words she knew.

"Oh," Jala said.

"You don't know what they mean, do you? You don't remember any of it when you take off the mask?"

Jala shook her head. "I can feel the words on the tip of my tongue, but when I start to speak, they're gone."

"We'll leave soon. I promise," Marjani said. "I'll get us home, somehow, once I know more words."

"There's nothing for me at home," Jala whispered. "If you wish to go, just say the word and I'll send you to the Constant City."

"No. Not until you say you'll come. Until then, can I have my mask?"

Jala sighed, and nodded. The emotion she'd felt a few moments before was gone. That's how it was so often now. If she felt anything at all, it was only for a brief moment. Even her guilt at letting Marjani stay was weaker every day.

Then she noticed she had finished her food, and without a word she left the room through another door disguised as stone.

Lord Water was waiting for her.

CHAPTER 33

The next morning, Marjani had her mask, and Azi began to think their plan might have a chance. She wore the mask with the same flowing robe she'd asked for the day before. From what she'd told Azi, it sounded similar to what the Hashon lords wore, meant to obscure the person wearing it. Marjani spent most of the day walking around the palace and letting herself be seen.

When she finally returned, she tore the mask off her face and stuffed it in a chest beneath her clothes. She shuddered. "They've started calling me Lord Far-From-Home, the Lost Lord. They think I can't understand them, but I can."

"They actually think you're some kind of god?" Azi asked, incredulous. "Just because you're wearing a mask?"

"They don't mean it," she said. "They think I'm crazy and they're making fun of me. But what if wearing it really does invite some kind of demon into my head? What if I lose myself just like Jala did? What if you do, and I'm here all alone again?"

"If that happens, you'll think of some other way to get yourself and Jala out," Azi said. "Darri and her crew will still be out there waiting for a signal. But it's just a mask. Nothing's going to climb into our heads."

It was an hour before Jala usually sent for Marjani. Time to change. Marjani passed the mask and robe to Azi and helped him with the straps. Smooth, dark lacquered wood pressed against his face, the thin eye-slits blocking out the light. His heart beat faster and he tried not to think of demons or gods. *It's just a mask*, he told himself.

"How are you supposed to see out of this thing?" Azi asked.

"You get used to it," Marjani said. "Just try not to fall over, or the guard will try to help you up, and then she'll figure out you're you instead of me. Remember to keep your head down and your shoulders hunched so they don't notice that you're bigger than me."

"I know," Azi said. "All I have to do is stay quiet and follow the guard to Jala and they'll leave me alone with her."

"Try not to stomp too much when you walk, either," Marjani said. "You're a scared, skinny girl, all right?"

"You don't look very scared to me," Azi said.

"I'm terrified."

"That makes two of us, then. You're sure she won't have the mask on?"

"Never at dinner. She can't eat with it on. Once you have her, which way do you go?"

Azi shut his eyes. "Second hallway on the left, then another left, down the stairs, straight through the gallery." He'd spend the day memorizing the way out of the palace, and Marjani had even included alternate paths if any of the guards were in the wrong place. Once he had Jala, they were going to meet up and take the sewers out of the palace, just as Jala had when she'd first fled with Lord Water. Hopefully Darri and a crew and a fast riverboat would be waiting for them.

"Hey!" Marjani snapped her fingers in front of Azi's face. "This is going to work. It has to, right? What do they care if three islanders get away? They probably won't even look for us. Oh, one more thing." She opened a small pouch and pulled out a necklace made of pearl, then another made of silver and hung them around Azi's neck. "In case something happens, you should be able to sell these somewhere. I've been asking for all sorts of jewelry just in case a chance like this came along."

When the guard arrived to escort Marjani to dinner, Azi followed the woman into the hall. He stared at his feet through the slits in the mask as she led him through a dizzying array of hallways until they reached the room where Jala took her meals.

The stone door opened in front of them, and the guard nudged him to go in.

Wait for him to leave before saying anything, Azi told himself over and over. He was going to see Jala again. He was going to take her home.

"I thought you promised you wouldn't wear it all the time," he heard Jala say. "Not with me."

It was the first time he'd heard her voice in months. Her words were heavy with regret and exhaustion, like she'd been drained of life. From everything Marjani had said, even her talking like this was rare.

She was so close to him. All he wanted to do was to reach out to her, tell her everything he'd thought as he waited for her on the First Isle, as he traveled the Great Ocean and the ocean of sand just so he could be with her again. *Fill your sails with hope and see where that gets you*, the more cynical sailors liked to say. Well, it had gotten him here. To her.

"You're quiet today," Jala said. "Come and sit down." Azi was frozen in place. If he moved, he'd run to her and ruin everything. The guard was leaving, but so slowly. Far too slowly. In another moment he'd tear off this damned mask.

"Marjani? What's wrong?"

The door closed behind him with a heavy thud, and finally Azi allowed himself to look up at her.

She looked thinner, as if she hadn't been eating well. Her face was drawn, and there was a grayness to her complexion. She looked drained, yet her eyes were bright as if with fever. His brother's eyes had looked like that before he died. This wasn't the same Jala who had sailed away.

But it was still her. His heart beat quickly, blood rushed in his ears, but it was all something happening far away. In his head this moment had taken place a thousand times, and each time he'd known what to say.

In each of them, he'd assumed that he'd be able to speak.

He was still looking into her eyes when lips—lips he still wanted so much to kiss—parted in a quiet *oh*.

"Azi?" she said, her voice quivering, so quiet he almost hadn't heard.

Fill your sails with hope and see where that gets you.

"I love you," he said. And he took off the mask.

CHAPTER 34

Jala looked at the figure standing before her and knew that it wasn't Marjani behind the mask. The shape wasn't quite right, the way the figure stood, everything was off. She felt something different. Something familiar, something she hadn't dared to hope for.

It had to be a spy, or an assassin. One of Lord Stone's devoted still fighting for a lost cause, or one of Lord Fire's fanatics. Had he hurt Marjani? Lord Water's mask hung on a belt around her waist. She would make him tell her, and then she would make him pay. She reached for the mask . . . and then she saw the eyes behind the mask.

She knew those eyes. Not even Lord Water could drive the memory of them out completely.

Her voice was barely a whisper. "Azi?"

"I love you," he said. His voice, his words, his breath. He took off the mask, and it was him, it was Azi. He loved her. He'd come for her.

"I love you too," she said. "But you can't be here. You're just a dream."

Since she'd put on Lord Water's mask, her dreams were filled with beautiful, horrible things she could never remember when she woke. Dreams that seemed to last for years, dreams of water and stone and changing seasons. Nothing like this. Nothing so human.

If this was a dream, it was all her own.

There were tears in his eyes. "Jala, I'm real. I'm here. I crossed the Great Ocean not even knowing if you were alive, and you are, and we're going home."

She had to shut her eyes to hold back her own tears. She couldn't cry, not now. If she let herself go, she wasn't sure she'd be able to stop. Then Lord Water's dreams would fill her mind again. Or maybe this time it would be the other one. The Hashon called him Lord Fire, but his true fire was the fire of the mind, the fires of madness.

How long had she been sleepwalking through her days? Weeks? Months? How long had her mind been adrift on the thoughts of Lord

Water? Even if Azi was a dream, a figment, she felt the bright, sharp ache of hope inside her. For the first time she felt awake. She felt alive. Painfully, wonderfully alive.

A small ember of her old strength stirred within her. If she could still dream her own dreams, if she could still hope for things like this, maybe she wasn't completely gone.

Azi reached for her, but she held up her hands, palms out. He stopped.

"Wait," she said. Her voice quivered, but it sounded stronger to her than it had for a long time. At least, when she wasn't wearing the mask. "I have to say this first. If it turns out you aren't real . . . I'm still leaving. Not just for you. For Marjani, because I can't let her stay here with me. For my mother, who I want to see again even if she hates me. For—" Her voice caught in her throat for a moment, but she hadn't let fear stop her yet, and she wouldn't now. "For Mosi-No-Name, who still lives somewhere on the islands. For my cousins and my captains and what's left of the Gana. For the Bardo and Kayet and Nongo and even the Rafa, because I'm still their queen, and maybe I can still do good."

Azi started to speak but then shook his head. He took her hands and held them tightly in his own. Real hands. *His* hands. "If I turn out to just be a dream, you should go," he said, and his breath was warm on her cheek as he leaned closer. "Find your way back to the First Isle and break my nose for leaving you here."

She laughed at this, and some of the tears did come. But there were no dreams, and there was no fire.

"If you're not a dream, kiss me," Jala said. And then, not bothering to wait anymore, she turned her head slightly and pressed her lips to his.

The lips, and the man attached them, turned out to be completely real.

For a long, still moment there was no need for words. She lost herself in the kiss, in the heat of his body, in the touch of his hands holding her tight and in the feel of his skin and his muscles under her touch in turn.

Finally they pulled away, breathless and teary-eyed and trying not to laugh or cry and alert the palace—maybe all of the city, all of the Hashon—that they were here.

"There really are friends waiting for us," Azi said. "So we should go now, while we're still supposed to be eating dinner. How long do you usually take to eat?"

"Not that long. Not really long at all."

"Then we have to leave. Do you think the guards will try to stop us?"

"I don't know," Jala said truthfully. "I hardly went anywhere without the mask. I hardly wanted to."

"If you put the mask back on, they'd let us through?"

"No. I can't. Not ever again." He nodded, though it looked as though he wanted to argue. "Azi, if I put that mask on again . . . if I let Lord Water back in . . . I think I'll lose myself forever. I'd rather take my chances with the guards. And before you suggest it, you're not putting it on either. You'd be just as lost, and I'm not letting that happen."

"All right. Then we have to leave as is. I'll at least keep wearing Marjani's mask." He knelt and picked the reef-and-sand mask off the ground. He lifted it to his face, but a pang made Jala reach and put a hand on his arm. She kissed him again, quickly, once on the lips and once on the cheek.

"I'm glad you turned out to be real," she whispered. Then she let go of his arm and let him put the mask back on his face. "Try not to kill anyone if you can help it. This isn't their fault."

"Not until they try to stop us and there's nowhere to run," Azi said, his voice muffled slightly by the mask. "I didn't come here for a fight. There's more of them than there are of us, and I don't even have a proper sword, just one of their knives."

Jala nodded, and in spite of her request she grabbed one of the knives off the table and slid it up the sleeve of her dress. It was better than nothing, probably, though she wasn't sure she could actually kill any of the Hashon. Not just because she couldn't shake the feeling that these were her people still, even if they'd become the enemy. That was part of it. But those were Lord Water's thoughts, and Lord Water wouldn't hesitate to kill any one of them. Hundreds had died as part of his plan. Individual lives meant little to the Hashon lords.

But she didn't want to be Lord Water anymore. She was tired of blood and fire.

There was one last thing she had to do. She steeled herself and pulled Lord Water's mask off her belt. She held it for just a moment, repeating to herself all the same reasons she'd given Azi why she couldn't wear it. Then she tossed it onto the dinner table and sighed.

"Now I can leave," she said.

They stepped through the door into a circular room with walls covered in elaborate etchings. More stories, this time cut into marble instead of written down in a book. The part of the wall that told Lord Stone's story had been removed.

"Where are the guards?" Azi whispered.

"Nearby somewhere, waiting to be called. Throwing bones in some side room, probably. We're not exactly prisoners, you know. Marjani has nowhere to go, and I'm . . . their job was to take me where I wanted to go."

"Would they take you to Marjani, then?" Azi asked.

Jala shrugged. "I never asked. I'm not even sure *how* to ask. Their words get all jumbled in my head without the mask. Ordering them around might work, but it might only work once. I don't suppose you know how to get to Marjani?" Jala asked.

"She had me memorize the way," Azi said. He didn't seem surprised that she didn't know, though it was hard to tell when he was wearing the mask. "I think I can do it."

"Then let's go," she said.

Jala closed the door behind her. It blended into the design etched into the wall, so that it was impossible to tell a door was even there if you didn't know already. The palace was filled with nooks like this, and she'd only seen a few.

Azi started walking.

"Don't walk so fast. I shouldn't look like I'm following you," Jala said. "We need to look like we belong. Not too fast, and not too quiet, either. I'll keep talking, as if we're having an important conversation. They can't understand our language anyway."

Azi counted off turns under his breath. They turned once, passed several corridors, turned again.

"As if? Our lives are important, aren't they?"

"I talk. You stay quiet," Jala said. "You don't sound anything like Marjani." Though he did kiss like Marjani. Like he loved her. "It seems so long ago that we stood on the beach on the Second Isle." Years. Decades. Did he feel the same way, or was that Lord Water's influence on her? He stayed quiet this time. "All the things that kept us apart, they don't really seem important anymore. I can barely remember what they are."

He touched her hand briefly, squeezed it, then hid his large hands from sight again.

"Maybe when we get back we can—"

But Jala didn't get to finish her thought. From behind them they heard shouts and the pounding of many running feet. Azi swore under his breath and drew his knife, and Jala did the same. They ran.

Jala focused on the feeling of her feet hitting the marble floor as she ran. What would they do when they found her? Kill her? Or put the mask back on her face? A part of her still felt like it wouldn't be so bad. She ignored it. That wasn't what she wanted; it was what Lord Water told her to want.

"There," Azi hissed, pointing toward an open door. "Marjani. Come on, we have to go."

As they reached the door, a guard stepped out, dragging Marjani by the arm.

"What are you still doing here?" the guard was saying. "You were summoned."

"Let me go," Marjani said in his language, though she sounded more scared than commanding. "I wasn't feeling well and she sent me back. Let go."

"Marjani," Jala shouted.

Marjani and the guard both stopped and looked at them. At Jala without her mask, at Azi still wearing his. She could see the confusion on the guard's face as he tried to figure out who was in Marjani's mask if Marjani had been in her room the whole time.

Then everything happened quickly. The guard's hand had loosened on Marjani's arm for just a moment, and she yanked her arm away and ran toward them. The guard sprang after her. Jala tried to stop him, but Azi was faster. He barreled into the guard from the side and slammed him into the wall. Azi tried to pull away, but in the struggle his mask had come loose, sliding down so he couldn't see.

The guard hit Azi once in the gut. Azi's knife clattered to the marble floor. With one motion the guard ripped the mask off Azi's face and drew his own knife, pressing the steel against Azi's throat.

CHAPTER 35

"Stop!" Jala commanded.

The guard looked up at her and hesitated. "He's an intruder. He was trying to kidnap you. The little queen must have been working with him. I will kill them both for you."

Jala grasped at the Hashon tongue. It had been so easy when Lord Water was with her, but now she had to struggle for the simplest commands. "No. Leave him to me. He is mine." *Mine. My love. My friend. My king.*

The guard glanced from Jala to Marjani and back. "I will give him to Lord Water, not his wearer," he said at last.

There were footsteps down the hallway. No more shouting now, just terse orders.

"Here," the guard called out, loosening his grip.

Jala felt her own hand, tight and clammy, on her knife. She moved her weight to her back leg, ready to attack. Azi met her eyes. He looked scared. His shoulders tensed, ready for her attack.

But Jala hesitated. She'd never killed anyone before. She wasn't sure now was the time to start trying. Azi had said it himself. People got hurt when knives came out, and you couldn't depend on it not being you. Or in this case, Azi.

She heard the thudding of footsteps. They were out of time. Either they were going to surrender and be captured, or she had to try to kill this man. There was no other choice. If she had the mask, she could make this right. If she could speak with Lord Water's voice, if she could just remember the words, the way it felt.

It was so close, a word on the tip of her tongue, a memory she could almost grasp.

Jala's throat burned, and her nose tingled with the half-remembered smell of sorcery. Her mind roiled, and she clung to the thoughts she knew were her own: her love for her friends, her family, her home.

She shut her eyes, breathed in deep, and spoke.

"KNEEL."

The sound burned her throat and tongue and lips as it left her mouth. She tasted sand and mud and river-water. Her vision blurred, and she barely saw the guard kneel down, his head pressed to the floor. What happened? Where had that voice come from? Azi was kneeling too, but she couldn't remember why it mattered. The room spun about her and she wondered if she should kneel as well.

"Jala!" Someone grabbed her, shook her. Marjani. A sudden sharp pain across her cheek like a splash of cold water.

Jala shook her head, and her vision cleared. "What?"

But Marjani was already pulling Azi up off the floor. "Come on, we have to go."

"Right, of course," Azi said. He glanced at Jala. "What was that?"

"You sounded just like Lord Water again," Marjani said. "How is that possible if you're not wearing the mask?"

"I don't know," Jala said. "Probably just the last of his power leaving me." Her throat was sore. It hurt to talk. "Does it matter now? I want to go home."

Azi started to speak, but Jala didn't wait for him. She ran, and Azi and Marjani had to follow. She wanted to run from all of it, from the guards and Lord Water and the sound of the river lingering in her ears. But she couldn't. There was only one way out, the same way she'd left before. Down through the river-ways beneath the palace.

"Jala, wait!" Azi said. "Do you know where you're going?"

Jala nodded. Everything about that night when Lord Water's people came for her was a haze of blood and fire. But she didn't need to remember the way. She knew. She could hear it, feel it, even from here.

She led them quickly through the palace, through unmarked doors and winding stairways.

The river's whisper grew louder as they descended, until finally they were back in the tunnels beneath the palace. The river had become a roar, an almost physical thing pressing against Jala's ears. Or was it only in her own ears that the sound was so overwhelming? Jala didn't want to know. The effect of being surrounded by the river was made that much worse because they hadn't brought any light with them.

"Which way?" Azi's voice echoed for just a moment before the river swallowed it.

"Turn right," Jala said. "We just have to follow the river."

They waited for a little while, hoping their eyes might adjust to the darkness. Water sprayed up in a thin mist on Jala's face. She shivered.

"Are you all right?" Marjani asked her. Jala thought she could just make out the silhouette of her face now, a shadow in the shadows.

"I think I should have eaten before letting him try to rescue me," she said, and Marjani laughed. She'd wanted Marjani to laugh, because that meant she knew Jala really was all right.

Even if she wasn't. Even if she didn't know what was happening to her.

I just have to leave this place and then I'll be fine. I'll feel normal again, she told herself.

"I think I can see a little now," Azi said.

"Be careful," Jala said. "The stone's worn smooth. It's slippery."

She saw him nod. He splayed his arms out, pressing himself back into the wall. She did the same, giving his hand a quick squeeze. He shuffled forward carefully, and she shuffled after. The walls and floor were as slimy and slippery as she remembered. The river churned beneath them, fast and angry. It made it hard to think. It made it hard to make herself move.

Jala slid her right foot forward, shifted her weight, then slid her left foot up. Again and again.

Water sprayed in her face and lapped her feet. She could feel the current tugging at her, trying to pull her in. It called to her.

The tunnel and the darkness spun around her.

"Jala?" Marjani yelled into her ear. "What's wrong? We have to keep moving."

Marjani was right. Jala knew she was right. But the strength seemed to have left her muscles. She felt cold and weak, and the water was still rising. It couldn't be high tide.

The water sloshed against her legs, her waist, and her chest. Waves where there was no wind. It was no use running. The river meant to have them all.

She tried to slide her foot along the walkway but instead found only water. Then she was falling, the river pulling at her dress, pulling her down into the cold dark.

The water closed over her face, and it felt just like putting on a mask.

CHAPTER 36

*W*ake up. Wake up, little queen.

Jala hadn't thought she was asleep. The last thing she remembered was falling into the river. She tried to breathe but couldn't. She panicked and kicked her arms and legs, trying to swim, but there was no water. No air. Nothing.

Jala. My little queen. Open your eyes.

It was her father's voice. But that didn't make any sense; he was back on the Five-and-One. He'd called her "my little queen," the way he used to. Maybe he'd forgiven her for what she'd done . . . but that seemed impossible. This was a dream, and if she opened her eyes, he would be gone.

You don't need to breathe here. You don't need to be afraid. This is a quiet place, a place outside.

"Outside of what?" she asked. She spoke without drawing breath, but her voice still echoed around her.

Outside, her father repeated.

It was just as he said. There was no pressure on her lungs or pain in her chest. She didn't need to breathe. Even in her dreams she'd always needed to breathe.

Jala opened her eyes and looked around. There were stars above her, the same stars she'd seen all her life. Palm trees grew around her, leaves swaying gently in a breeze she couldn't feel. She was on the Second Isle again, lying on the shore of the bay where she and Marjani had gone swimming the night before her wedding.

Jala looked down at her hand. Her finger was still missing. In her dreams, her hand was still whole. But though the wound was still a bright, ugly red, it didn't bleed.

"This isn't a dream," Jala said. "But this isn't real, either. I'm still drowning in the river. Or am I already dead?"

Her father stood behind her, dressed in clean white robes, a half-smile curling one corner of his mouth. "Not yet, my little queen. Time will pass slowly here, and we have so much to talk about."

"And when we finish talking, am I going to drown?" Jala asked.

"You may," her father said. "You may not."

Jala looked away from him. Far out over the water, where the bay flowed into the Great Ocean, a storm was brewing. "I know you're Lord Water," she said. "Pretending to be my father won't help you trick me."

"You have no father," he said.

Jala winced. "I know what I said, but he's still my father, even if he can't be Bardo. I can't just forget him and everything he's done for me, good and bad." She ran her fingers through the sand, let it fall through her fingers. It felt real, but the way it glinted in the moonlight was too beautiful, too perfect.

"I could be a father to you. My adopted daughter. My adopted people."

Jala tossed the sand away. "No. I'm done with you. I'm done with the Hashon. You have to leave the Five-and-One alone, that was our deal."

"Yet you chose to stay."

"Because you tricked me," Jala said. "Azi still loved me. He came for me."

"You didn't believe in him," her father said. "You wanted to be tricked. It was easier than going home and facing what you did to me, facing an uncertain future with your boy king."

"Maybe at first," Jala said softly. "But I'm ready to face it now, without you."

"Yet you called on my power, used my voice. You want me to leave your people alone, yet you reach for me constantly."

"I'm done," Jala said again.

"It's too late," her father whispered close to her ear. "You've worn Lord Water's mask too long, spoken with his voice too often. It's changed you. If you go back to your islands now, you will take me with you, and your people will be changed. I promised I would leave them alone, but you will unmake our deal if you return to them."

"That's not fair," Jala said.

"Isn't it? When you call on my power for the greater good once more, will it seem unfair that I answer?"

"Then I won't use the voice again. Ever."

"You will," her father whispered. "There will always be some reason. And your people will hear me, and I will be a part of them."

"Why wear my father's face?" Jala demanded. "I've already rejected him once, just as I rejected you. Do you want me to say no? To drown in the river?"

"I'm offering you a choice," her father said. He reached up and put his hand on his face. When he pulled his hand away, his face came off with it. A moment ago, Jala couldn't have told her real father's face from this one, but now it looked like a plain wooden mask. Where her father had been a moment before stood her mother. Lady Zuri dropped the mask of Lord Mosi on the sand.

"Perhaps a mother, then, instead of a father?" Jala's mother asked. "The water that nourishes and feeds. That washes away the wound, that listens to you in the middle of the night. I would be a better mother than your uncaring fire mountain, don't you think?"

It hurt so much to see her mother again. It felt like it had been years, and maybe it had. They'd fought so often. But while her father wanted to be great through Jala, her mother had always just wanted Jala to be great.

"Why are you doing this to me?" Jala asked, her voice hoarse. This place, whatever it was, might have been outside breath and time, but it wasn't outside tears. They stung her face and she had to blink them back.

"Because you have a choice to make, Jala," her mother said softly. She'd never called Jala "my little queen" the way her father had. "You think I am Lord Water, and so you think you know me. But Lord Water is a mask and a name. He is not all of me. I am the rivers and the streams, the springs and the creeks, the seas and the lakes. All the children of the Great Ocean. The Hashon think of me as one great river, but I have other names, other faces. There are other stories told about me. Stories must change to fit those who tell them. Isn't that what your people say? So choose what our story will be. Choose what my mask will look like when you wear it."

"Mother of Water," Jala said, as if she was tasting the words. And they did have a taste, warm and comforting, familiar and old. But . . . "No. You're not my mother, or my people's mother. You would drown us." In some ways, her mother's expectations for her had been as smothering and controlling as her father's ambitions.

"Only a child thinks they can ever be free of someone else's influence," her mother said with a laugh. Then she reached up and took off Lady Zuri's face, dropping that mask on the sand as well. Now it was Askel who stood before her, eyes burning with fever in his gaunt, gnarled face.

"There are other kinds of sorcery in the world, my queen," he said in his scratchy voice. "The power of your fire mountain burns away your life. But you could use the magic of water to heal. You could live beyond your years as a great sorcerer-queen. You could rule the islands with wisdom and sorcery and fear, and they would all bow to you and your daughters."

"I won't make anyone bow through sorcery," Jala said, though she knew she'd done just that only a short while before. "And to live longer, someone else would have to live shorter. There's always a cost for these things, no matter where the magic comes from. I've learned that much at least."

Askel smiled his toothless, hungry smile. "Small lives are often cut short in service of greater ones. You risked many such lives to get here, and your king risked more to bring you back."

"I don't want any of this," Jala said. "Any mask you give me would swallow me up again. There'd be nothing left of me."

The sorcerer took off his mask. Marjani looked back at her, her mouth turned down in worry. "And who are you?" her friend asked. "Queen Jala of the Bardo? Another mask. Jala, daughter of Mosi? Another mask, and one you've broken. Jala, love of Azi? Love is a mask, too, and it can swallow you up as certainly as any power or sorcery. You humans die a thousand times across your little lifetimes, and what's left of the people you once were?" She reached down and scooped up the glittering white and yellow sand, let it run through her fingers just as Jala had. "A scattering of memories. A lesson learned, perhaps, though not as often you'd have yourselves believe. Is this so different?"

"Stop it," Jala said. She forced herself to stand. "This is just another trick. You twist everything around, just like you twisted Azi's words to make me think he wouldn't come for me. You have no right to use her face or her voice."

"But these are your masks," Marjani said. "Every title, every loved one, every duty, every hope, and every dream is another mask. You can't be free of them."

Jala hesitated, looking back at the distant storm. It didn't look like a storm at all, now. Just a great roiling darkness swallowing up the moonlight and giving nothing back. "I could let myself drown."

"Even the dead sometimes wear masks," Marjani whispered. "And they can't ever take them off."

Jala shuddered. For a moment she could almost feel the weight of cold river-water pressing in around her, feel the tightness in her lungs. "Let me go," she said. She felt so small, so lost. "Let Azi and Marjani go. We don't matter to you."

Marjani took a step toward her, reached out, and took Jala's hand in hers. Jala flinched at the touch, but didn't pull away. Marjani bent forward and kissed Jala on the forehead. "You know so little of what does and doesn't matter. Can't you tell how much I love you?"

"What could you possibly know of love?" Jala demanded.

"I've loved since the beginning of time. I've loved stone and sky, animals and humans, gods and demons. I'm more full of love than you could ever know Love is all there is—and it, too, wears many masks."

Then Marjani's mask fell to the sand. Jala didn't look up. She knew who would speak next, and she didn't want to see him like this. She stared at the mask on the sand, Marjani's face carved and painted on the dark wood.

Azi whispered in her ear. "I love you. My queen, my Jala. That's why you get to choose. Choose my name, choose the mask you'll wear to be my lover. Choose what form your goddess will take. You can't be free of me any more than you can be free of any of the other masks you wear—those you love, those you hate, all the years you've lived and the memories you've made. But those masks were made slowly over time. My mask, the mask you'll wear to hear my voice, the mask that will shape my thoughts and my power, that mask you can make now. Choose the way your people will know me. Choose the way you'll love me."

She thought about Azi, about the way she'd been afraid he had forgotten her as soon as she was gone. Would he still love her if she became . . . whatever it was that wearing a god's mask made you? But to her surprise, she found that she wasn't afraid to find out. Either he would love her no matter what she became, or he wouldn't. Just as she might love him or not. They still knew too little of each other, and they'd both changed so much already.

She looked at the other Azi standing before her, wearing his *I'm really just a simple sailor* smile, warm and secretive and just a little humble. She looked at his eyes and his lips, at the ugly scar on his forehead and the slightly weathered lines the ocean and the wind had left on his face. The Five-and-One were scarred now too. All of them had changed and would have to keep changing, and she had no idea where they would end up in the end.

"I don't know what kind of goddess we'll need, or want," Jala said. "So I choose the not knowing. I choose all the possibilities at once. I choose the newly broken spring, the creek that hasn't yet cut its path, the river that suddenly changes its course. I choose to wear an unpainted mask, and I'll draw on it with chalk and erase it and draw on it again. The Hashon chose a book that can never change, but I choose the story that's told in a hundred different ways, the story that can change from day to day depending on what the listener and the teller need it to be."

She smiled, and she was full of fear and sadness and hope. She felt free. "Who knows what kind of goddess the people of the islands will want? We'll find out together."

For just a moment, Jala looked into her own face, and the other Jala smiled at her, and her eyes were filled with stars. "It's done, my queen," the other Jala said, and kissed Jala once on each cheek and her forehead.

Then Jala was alone, and all the masks were gone but one. The other masks had been polished, lacquered, and painted. This mask was unpainted and roughly carved. The masks of the Hashon lords all had small slits for eyes and no opening for the mouth at all. This mask had large slits for both. Wearing Lord Water's mask had felt like she was being swallowed up, but this was a mask she was meant to see clearly out of. A mask she could wear and still speak with her own voice.

She reached down and lifted the mask up to her face. Though it had looked rough, the inside felt smooth and warm, and it tickled her skin like hot springwater.

Something tugged on her. Something far away. She hesitated, because it was easier to stay still than to move, but the pull was strong, dragging her toward the water, into the water. Into the cold dark. Into that place of pain and fear again.

Only this time the cold and pain didn't go away.

She was dragged through it and out of it. She tried to cry out, but instead she choked and sputtered, heaving up river-water.

Jala opened her eyes to see the stars. For a moment she thought she was still in that other place, the place between . . . but then she tried to breathe and ended up on her side, coughing into muddy ground. Someone else was doing the same nearby. She forced herself to look.

She saw Marjani first, then Azi, lying in the mud only an arm's reach away. They were on the bank of the Hashana River. Five Hashon dressed in white robes stood away from them, watching her. Behind them the city loomed like a shadow against the star-filled sky.

The river had carried them out of the palace and the city. It seemed impossible that they hadn't drowned. But then she remembered the choice she'd been given, and the choice she'd made, and it seemed less impossible to her. She glanced back at the Hashon and realized one of them wore Lord Water's mask.

Well, if these five wanted to kill them, they could have by now. She tried to stand, then thought better of it and crawled over to Azi and Marjani.

"Are you all right?" she asked.

"Are you?" Azi asked as he sat back and met her gaze. He and Marjani wore identical expressions of worry.

"You mean am I myself," Jala said.

Azi nodded.

"One of the Hashon over there is wearing that cursed mask," Marjani said hopefully. "Does that mean they'll let us go? That you're free of it?"

"I . . ." Jala hesitated. Would they understand? Everything she'd said in that other place had felt right, but now that Azi was in front of her it was a lot harder to think about him rejecting her. "I'm free of Lord Water and his mask. And I'm definitely myself. For good this time."

Azi breathed a sigh of relief. "We just need to find my friends who helped me here and then we can go home together." He touched her cheek with his hand and leaned in to kiss her.

Jala put her hand on his but pulled back from the kiss. He stopped. "But I'm not the same Jala I was before I left."

"What do you mean?" Marjani asked.

What could she tell them? That there was a water-god in her head that wasn't Lord Water anymore, but something new, and that she had to help choose what kind of god it would be? That she had to choose what she would be? That all the Five-and-One would be affected by the choices she made?

Well, maybe that last one wasn't so new. She was still the queen, after all.

"I'll try to explain," Jala said. "Later. When we're on our way home. But I'm still me. I'll always be me, even if I change."

"Are you sure?" Marjani asked softly.

"I'm sure," Jala said, and she hugged her friend tightly.

She turned to face Azi. "More sorcery?" he asked.

"Something like that," she whispered. "Just not the same as before. It'll be all right, I promise." Then she added, "I hope."

He sighed, and for a moment she was afraid of what he'd say next. But he just smiled at her. "Then let's go home."

CHAPTER 37

As the First Isle came into view, Jala wished she could fling herself onto the sparkling white sand of the beach and lie there for hours. Or for weeks. Small sprays of saltwater touched Jala's face as the ship rocked over the waves, and somehow even the water felt like home.

"We're finally home," Azi said.

"Are you afraid of what we'll find when we get there?" She touched his ear, where the King's Earring usually hung.

Azi shook his head. "No. This is home. Even if we're not king and queen anymore, there will be a place for us. And if there isn't, we'll just become mad sorcerers on the Lone Isle. That wouldn't be so bad, would it? But you'll have to promise not to cut off any more of your fingers. I like your fingers. And you can't start talking to the fire mountain. One god inside your head is plenty."

"I'll try," Jala laughed. The laugh turned into a burbling cough. She gripped the bulwark and leaned out over the side to spit up a mouthful of brackish river-water. Azi rubbed her back with concern while she spat, then stood to find her something to drink. The water seemed to build up in her lungs like a small spring, and for a while on their journey back to the ocean she'd wake in the night thinking she was drowning.

She'd gotten used to it now, mostly. It was a reminder of the bargain she'd made, of the power she carried within her. Not that she thought it was at all necessary, but the water god didn't respond to her complaints. And the water was better than the whispers she heard in the quiet hours of the night when she closed her eyes, better than the strange, disjointed dreams she could never quite remember. Whatever the future held, it wouldn't be easy.

Azi returned a minute later, followed by Marjani. He had a mug of honeyed tea that he gave to Jala. He'd bought it for her in the markets of the Constant City, and she sipped it gratefully. It soothed her throat, raw from the water and still burning from speaking with Lord Water's voice back in the palace.

"Will you stay with us on the First Isle?" Azi asked Marjani. "Assuming Jala and I still have a place there."

"I think so," Marjani said, looking out over the water at their destination. "At least for a while, when I'm not visiting the other islands. They seem so small now, don't they? I know it's only because they're far, and yet . . ."

"They probably shrunk," Jala said as she leaned into Azi and let him wrap his arms around her. "That happens sometimes. It's a good thing you came with me, or you'd have shrunk too."

They laughed. It felt good to laugh, even if it hurt her throat and almost made her spill her tea. Azi held her closer. She could feel his worry, but he said nothing. She'd told him everything already, and there was nothing left to say for now. So he joked sometimes, and watched her with concern at other times, and he held her and brought her tea, and when they could sneak time alone together they kissed and touched and forgot everything else.

There wasn't much kissing to be had aboard the grayship, unfortunately. Another reason she couldn't wait to get home, and another reason she hoped they still had rooms of their own on the First Isle.

She tried not to think of what would be happening outside those rooms. About whether she'd still be queen. She told Azi it was all right either way, but there was still so much she wanted to do. She wanted to help the Gana rebuild their razed island, if she could. Azi had told her about the clay wine, and she could only hope the reefs hadn't been poisoned yet. She wanted to travel to the Lone Isle and talk to the people. Maybe it was time for the Five-and-One to become the Six? Askel had told her there was power in the fire mountain. Could she speak to it, the way she'd spoken to the water god? Did she dare?

And whether they had sorcery or not, the islands couldn't keep raiding the mainland to survive. Not anymore. She and Azi had talked it over in hushed whispers late into the night as they sailed. It might take a lifetime to change things, but they had to change.

"Look, there's your uncle." Jala pointed at the beach, where a group of Kayet were gathered, waiting for them.

"I can't see his face," Azi said. "Can you tell if he looks like he wants to kill me?"

Jala squinted, shading her eyes with her hand. "No, but I bet I can guess the answer."

Behind her, the sailors were preparing to land.

"Lower the sails and row ashore," Captain Darri yelled.

"That means me," Azi said. Captain Darri had treated Azi the same as any other sailor on the way back. After all, who knew if he was even king anymore?

As they rowed closer, Jala could see Lord Inas looking stiff and somber. But then, he always looked like that when he wasn't drunk.

They hit the sand with a soft shush. The sailors jumped over the side and pulled the ship ashore. Then Jala and Marjani climbed down.

Jala held Azi's hand as they approached Lord Inas.

"Hello, Uncle," Azi said. "We've come back."

Lord Inas stared for a moment, and then a smile slowly appeared on his face. He bowed. "Welcome home, my king." Then he came forward, grasped Azi's hand, and pulled him into a tight embrace. "I'm glad you're back," he whispered. Then he pulled away and coughed, embarrassed. He opened his palm and held out two earrings made from the heart of a shipwood reef. He let Azi take the King's Earring. Then he turned to Jala.

"You brought the Queen's Earring too," she said. "After you tried to convince Azi that I was beyond lost."

"I thought you were," Lord Inas said. "And him, too. I knew he wouldn't come back without you."

"For Azi's sake, I wish there could be peace between us," Jala said. "Everything's going to change. More than you can imagine. My father's gone, and both of us will need advice. Though I don't promise to follow it."

Lord Inas glanced at Azi. "I suppose my nephew told you everything?"

"About Kona and about the clay wine."

"And you still think there can be peace between us?" Lord Inas asked. "You'll never trust me. I wouldn't expect you to."

"You've made mistakes. So have I. But I'm not the same girl who arrived on the First Isle months ago. I've risked everything for the Five-and-One. I've lost my father and my finger and . . ." She let the thought trail off. She wasn't sure yet what else she had lost, or what she'd gained. "All I'm asking you to give up is your pride."

Lord Inas's brow furrowed, and then, suddenly, he laughed. It was the first time she'd heard his laugh when it wasn't full of bitterness and anger. "You're right, everything has changed. How else could it be that Mosi No-Name's daughter is lecturing me about pride? How could it be that she's right?" He sighed and held the earring out to Jala. "You don't need my permission to be queen, and you could take the earring from me. But for as much as it means, I want you to have it. Azi put his trust in you, and he was right. I will . . . try to serve you both as best I can, my queen."

"Good enough for now," Jala said. She took the earring out of his hand and slid it into her ear, then took Azi's hand.

"Do you think we'll ever do anything that mad ever again?" Azi whispered.

"I hope not," she said. But she could still remember putting on the uncarved mask, could still taste river-water at the back of her throat. She still saw the fire masks when she closed her eyes. No, things couldn't stay the same as they had. Not anymore. "But I don't think we'll have much of a choice."

"The wind blows where it blows," Azi said. "We'll hang on for our lives together."

Holding hands, they walked back up the beach.

ACKNOWLEDGMENTS

This book has been in the works a long time, and for much of that time it wasn't very good. Without the heroic support of our family and friends it probably wouldn't exist. We want to thank Dave Ross for reading the very first drafts and being the first to point out major character issues; Jenn Kastroll for reading every draft since and being the best friend and cheerleader any writer could ask for (but if they DO ask, you're ours, and they can't have you!); Joe Monti for sticking with the book and pushing us to actually write a real ending to it; Barry Goldblatt for stepping in after Joe fell through the looking glass; and superassistant Tricia Ready for doing all the things. Thanks to Marc Simonetti for the amazing cover illustration. Finally, thanks to our editor Lou Anders, our copyeditor Julia DeGraf, and the rest of the Pyr team for their awesome work getting the book across the finish line. You all brought this book to life.

ABOUT THE AUTHORS

Rachel and Mike Grinti are a husband-and-wife writing team. They met at a writing workshop and have been writing together ever since. They live in Pittsburgh, PA, with their Boston terrier, Miles, who interferes with their writing at every opportunity.

Photo by Jenn Kastroll